Praise for Dominic Smith's lyrical debut

The Mercury Visions of Louis Daguerre

"[A] vibrant first novel . . . Smith has an artist's eye and he gives Daguerre an artist's heart."

—Detroit Free Press

"Accomplished and impressive . . . Smith's gifts as a storyteller and writer are obvious, sometimes overwhelming."

—Baltimore Sun

"A striking meditation on memories and photography . . . You can read it and reread it . . . and still be struck, on every page, by an indelible detail or turn of phrase."

—Austin American Statesman

"Beautifully written . . . A compelling psychological study, a thoughtful tracing of the birth of a new art form, and an atmospheric portrait of nineteenth-century France: impressive on all three counts."

—Kirkus Reviews (starred)

"A splendid novel. You don't often see such a graceful command of historical detail in a first book. Or such striking and elegant prose. Dazzling and wondrous."

—John Dalton,
author of *Heaven Lake*

"What starts out as a feverish, dreamlike novel of lost love, apocalyptic visions, and the social upheaval of Napoleonic France turns into a quiet, remarkably moving study of how the human heart endures."

—The Portsmouth Herald

"A lyrical journey into the world of a man lost to nostalgia and undone by beauty. Smith has generously rendered an artist in desperate pursuit of the sublime."

—Paul Jaskunas,
author of *Hidden*

"Dominic Smith writes with an authority very few first-time novelists possess. He wonderfully evokes nineteenth-century Paris through a chemically addled consciousness—a formidable achievement that he manages with humor and grace. A remarkable debut."

—Mark Jude Poirier,
author of *Modern Ranch Living* and *Goats*

"By the time it reaches its final pages, *The Mercury Visions* has become a genuinely moving experience."

—Anthony Giardina,
author of *Recent History*

"Smith renders a clear-eyed portrait of Daguerre and his thinking, against a backdrop of tumultuous times."

—*Publishers Weekly*

THE MERCURY
VISIONS OF
LOUIS DAGUERRE

A NOVEL

DOMINIC SMITH

WASHINGTON SQUARE PRESS
New York London Toronto Sydney

Washington Square Press
1230 Avenue of the Americas
New York, NY 10020

ISBN-13: 978-0-7432-7114-1
ISBN-10:   0-7432-7114-9
ISBN-13: 978-0-7432-7124-0 (Pbk)
ISBN-10:   0-7432-7124-6 (Pbk)

First Washington Square Press trade paperback edition January 2007

1   3   5   7   9   10   8   6   4   2

For information regarding special discounts for bulk purchases,
please contact Simon & Schuster Special Sales at 1-800-456-6798
or business@simonandschuster.com.

For Mikaila and Gemma

AUTHOR'S NOTE

Although this is a work of fiction and the characters are inventions, I have borrowed details from the biographies of Charles Baudelaire, the poet, and Louis Daguerre, an early inventor of photography. Wherever possible (and expedient to the story) I have tried to capture the flavor of the real Daguerre's life and the historical context in which he achieved his fame. There were several books that were invaluable for aiding this process: *L.J.M. Daguerre: The History of the Diorama and the Daguerreotype* (1968), by Helmut and Alison Gernsheim; *An Historical and Descriptive Account of the Various Processes of the Daguerreotype and the Diorama* (1839), by Louis-Jacques-Mandé Daguerre; *Dickens's Dictionary of Paris* (1890), by Charles Dickens; *The Poem of Hashish* (1895), by Charles Baudelaire; and *The Hashish Club* (1971), by Théophile Gautier. I also found many of the articles and resources on the Daguerreian Society's website (www.daguerre.org) to be useful.

Mercury vapors were used extensively by Louis Daguerre during his photographic career. His basic process was to expose a sensitized plate inside a camera obscura, take the plate into a darkened room, then pass it back and forth above a heated mercury bath. Millions of tiny mercury drops settled over the image, fixing it permanently. The presence of mercury gives metal-plate daguerreotypes their luster and minute level of detail, but it can also lend them a ghostly, holographic appearance. The image can appear to change based on the eye-level and perspective of the viewer. In later years, as Daguerre tried to minimize exposure times in an attempt to capture faster-paced movement (such as galloping horses and birds in flight) he experimented with increasingly deadly substances — cyanide of mercury, nitric acid, and gold chloride. Daguerre, who suffered from various physical complaints until he died of a heart attack in 1851, was probably unaware of how harmful such substances were.

THE MERCURY
VISIONS OF
LOUIS DAGUERRE

PROLOGUE

hen the vision came, he was in the bathtub. After a decade of using mercury vapors to cure his photographic images, Louis Daguerre's mind had faltered—a pewter plate left too long in the sun. But during his final lucid minutes on this cold evening of 1846, he felt a strange calm. Outside, a light snow was falling and a vaporous blue dusk seemed to be rising out of the Seine. The squatters had set fire to the barrens behind the Left Bank and the air was full of smoke. Louis reclined in warm water perfumed with lemon skins, a tonic he believed to be good for his skin and nerves. The wind gusted under the eaves. He placed a hand against the adjacent window and from the bath, perched high in his rooftop belvedere, he felt the night pressing in against him. His head was partially submerged and he heard the metallic click of the tenant's pipes below. It was a message; he was sure of it. The world was full of messages.

He sat up, wiped the steam off the window, and looked out. There was something ghostly about the boulevard in the wintry pall. The bare-limbed almond trees were flecked with snow. A nut vendor pushed his cart through the smoky twilight. A man stood before a storefront, staring at a pyramid of startling white eggs. Was he counting them? A man was counting eggs on a street at dusk while the peasants were trying to burn the city down. This pleased Louis, though he couldn't think why. He leaned back in the bathtub again and heard, as if anew, the ticking of the pipes. He lay there, letting his mind go still, and became aware of his own heartbeat, the sound of a tin drum through water. This was the time of day he grew speculative or nostalgic, and he set to thinking that the pipes and his heart were talking to each other, exchanging notes in a secret, mechanical language. Then, as Louis watched the increments of darkness grow at the window, he heard his heart skip a beat. His chest tightened and he felt a dull, cold pain in his fingertips. This had happened before, a stutter in his pulse on account of the mercury in his blood. But he had never listened to it, and now his heart stopped for a full second. It was like a small death.

He felt something shift in the room. Holding on to the rim of the tub, he pulled himself to a standing position. He reached for a robe and put it around his shoulders but was unable to move farther. Looking around the washroom, he felt himself alien to his own life. Poison-blue bottles of iodine lined out the medicine shelf like Prussian soldiers; his straight razor stood agleam on the washstand; a flask of mercury shuddered on the sink. Everything seemed directed at *him.* He looked out the window and saw the moon rising behind a cloth of weather. An enormous albatross perched amid the stone gargoyles of Notre Dame. The peasants had looted the zoo, and all kinds of exotic animals had escaped. A Bengal tiger was said to be prowling the Latin Quarter. Louis saw that the barrens continued to burn, but now there was a barge loaded with firewood drifting down the river in flames. Night was everywhere. People had quit the streets except for the man counting the eggs. The man stood with his hands in his pockets, fingering his change. *The little life one leads.*

Louis threw open the window and felt an inrush of cold on his face. There was a moment of tremendous clarity, as if a scrim had lifted. The vision, now that it came, was really a series of insights and hallucinations, a feeling of things coming into focus. The egg-man looked up at him, startled, and Louis understood that he was returning from a funeral, perhaps his father's, and that he'd stopped to observe the precariousness of life in the pyramid of white eggs. Louis looked down to the river and saw that the burning barge was not carrying firewood at all but the bones of the dead. At the street corner, the hands on the neighborhood clock had slowed to half time. *Everything is a portent.* A low, rushing noise rose from the heath—men's voices on the edge of panic. They were going to burn the city down. Not now, not tonight, but eventually. The lootings and the fires, Louis understood now, were acts of fear, not rebellion. Men could sense oblivion coming, feel it in their knuckles and teeth. Then Louis saw that it was not an albatross on the rooftop of Notre Dame but a young girl in a white dress, her hands laced behind her back. She had felt wings pinned to her dress and she was going to jump from the ledge. She didn't jump; she leaned into the air in front of her and shot straight down. All the way down, she refused to unlace her hands from behind her back. A burgundy ribbon streamed out from her long dark hair, and Louis watched it until she disappeared into the smoke. The egg-man looked on with his hands in his pockets. *The end of the world is contained in a man's pockets.*

Louis closed the window, stepped onto the rug, and dried himself thoroughly with a towel. There was a kind of relief in knowing about the end, a kind of symmetry and beauty. For years he had felt a strange sense of foreboding in the smallest detail—a tarnished coin, a glossed pear—and now, he saw, these had been a thousand small proofs. He looked at himself in the mirror and noticed beads of spilt mercury on the medicine shelf. They resembled tiny planets of glass. He stood there staring at them, his head cocked as if listening to a distant voice. Each bead captured his reflection and the light from the window.

ONE

he following spring, in April 1847, Louis Daguerre stopped by the brasserie where he knew Charles Baudelaire took his meals. It was a single long room inset like a cave, wedged between a tobacconist and a haberdasher. The poet sat in the corner, brooding behind a bottle of absinthe and a demitasse of coffee. His hair had been shaved off several weeks earlier in celebration of his new prose poem—"The Fool and the Venus"— and his ponderous head seemed to gather the room's light to a focal point. On the table in front of him smoldered a wooden pipe with an amber mouthpiece. Baudelaire looked up as Louis approached and saluted. "Mind your manners, gentlemen, here comes a member of the Legion of Honor." A few of the drunken poets nearby raised their glasses to Louis, then returned to their brandied rants.

Louis sat opposite Baudelaire and took a kerchief from his pocket to wipe his forehead.

"How's the end of the world coming?" asked Baudelaire, eyes scanning his twin drinks.

Louis examined the kerchief—a bloom of sweat. "Fine.

Good of you to ask." So far he'd mentioned his prophecy only to Baudelaire. He needed to be careful; *The End* was a delicate matter and he didn't want to find himself in a straight waistcoat at one of the meetings of the Institute.

Baudelaire looked up. "I was about to order food. Will you join me?"

"I'd be delighted," said Louis.

"I was thinking about some bouillon and bread for me. But that's hardly your pleasure. We must keep our national dignitaries well fed. The true artists, on the other hand, produce better when they're emaciated."

"I'd be glad of some herring and eggs," said Louis.

Baudelaire picked up his pipe and went to the counter to order. He was dressed in his customary English black, from lacquered shoes to satin cravat.

Louis looked around the brasserie. It was the kind of smoky venue where painters, philosophers, and poets huddled in a din of verbiage, where the dandies and the rag-cloth romantics argued about the sheen of a winter apple, the role of virtue, the beauty of the comma. Men with pipes and chapbooks sat around the scuffed oak tables or reclined on the threadbare rose-print divans. A grave-looking man in a woolen jacket, a fez, and Cossack boots nodded repeatedly and said, "Yes, we all knew him. He was a ladies' poet—moonlight and taffeta and all the rest of it." Whenever Louis had come in here before, he couldn't help feeling hated. Now he found himself avoiding eye contact with the fieriest of the fellows—the particularly rabid poets, the sullen painters in Basque berets—who might attack his bourgeois attitudes, the national pension he'd been awarded for his daguerreotype invention.

Louis watched Baudelaire return from the counter with another demitasse of coffee.

"Voltaire drank seventy-two cups of coffee a day," Baudelaire said. "He must have had to shit between paragraphs. Where would the Enlightenment be without the brown goddess?"

"Indeed."

Baudelaire plunked down and said, "And what's Armageddon without a good cup of Costa Rican?"

"I have serious business to transact." Louis took out a piece of paper and placed it on the table. It was a list of all the things he wanted to daguerreotype before the end of the world.

Baudelaire picked it up and scrutinized it as if it were an insurance contract waiting to be signed.

1. a beautiful woman (naked)
2. the sun
3. the moon
4. the perfect Paris boulevard
5. a pastoral scene
6. galloping horses
7. a perfect apple
8. a flower (type to be determined)
9. the king of France
10. Isobel Le Fournier

Baudelaire moved his lips as he read the list several times, then placed it back on the table, facedown. He looked appalled. "The end amounts to *this*?" he said, his nose at the rim of his porcelain cup.

"I'd like to find a woman to pose naked for a daguerreotype. Can you help me find one?" It was not easy to find nude models, though Louis had heard that artists in the studios around the Luxembourg Gardens were convincing street waifs to pose for a bowl of soup and a pinch of snuff. But he needed something more than the bared frame of a rag-and-match seller; he needed a high-blown frailty, something worthy of oblivion.

Baudelaire relit his pipe and puffed on it meditatively. It was this posture and his ethereal poetry that had earned him the nickname the Prince of Clouds. He removed a speck of tobacco from his tongue and prepared to speak with some gravity. He believed in Louis Daguerre's apocalypse as an invention of the artistic mind, no different than a belief in God or Beauty or Piety. He enjoyed watching Louis, the pensioned scientist and artist, hatch and unfold inside this epic delusion, seeing his mind clamor at the fidget wheels of madness.

Baudelaire said, "You know how I feel about this photography. Let the tourists use it to ogle the pyramids or the Louvre, let the geologists capture fossils, the excrement of the ancients; but don't touch art. Leave that to the painters."

Louis said, "I won't have this argument again. I'm willing to pay you a finder's fee. A hundred francs if you find me the right woman."

Baudelaire looked down at the list, then chased a sip of coffee with a swig of absinthe. He said, "Have you established some criteria? The world's last naked woman captured with a camera—that's quite momentous."

"Yes, I'm aware." Louis ran his hands along the edge of the table.

The young counter-girl arrived with a plate of hard-boiled eggs and herring, and a bowl of bouillon. They watched her as she laid out cutlery, a wisp of tawny hair hanging down from her bonnet.

"What is it you want in a nude?" Baudelaire said loudly. The counter-girl smiled, then blushed and wiped her hands down her apron. She fled to a nearby table. "She's new here," Baudelaire added.

Louis cracked an egg on the side of the plate and began to unpeel it. "She must have grace and youth."

"Yes."

"The curvature of the neck must be gentle, perhaps a slight sway in her back."

"I concur."

"A vitality in her cheeks."

"You've done some work in this area," Baudelaire said, suddenly delighted.

"Neither too noble nor too common-looking. She must carry herself between airs and humility."

"A shopgirl with fiery green eyes."

"Full and crimson lips."

"I don't think I can eat." Baudelaire clasped his hands together and rested his chin for a moment on his fingertips. He looked out the window into the street, where a group of mourners was walking home from a funeral. "I would reconsider the apple on your list," he said.

"How so?"

"The apple is not exotic enough. Apple is plain, like the English. The Frenchman wants something darker and juicier. The end of the world, it seems to me, is a peculiarly French idea."

Louis looked down at the list and tapped his lip with his index finger. "What would you think of a pear?"

"You know I am a poet," Baudelaire said, "and having said that, I should say that my sensibility is one of integration. I seek coherence in the cockerel cries and the street dung. I would choose your fruit the same way you choose your woman. Clearly, the queen of the fruit empire is the greengage plum — strange, juicy, sinister."

"But the apple represents the original sin, the fall from grace."

"Yes, and the plum represents seduction and lust," said Baudelaire.

"I knew you were the right person to consult."

"I have opinions about flowers, too."

"Tell me."

"'Aroused flowers burn with the desire to outdo the sky's azure by the energy of their colors, and the heat, turning scents visible, seems to make them rise to the stars like smoke.'"

"Very nice."

"My point is, there needs to be some symmetry among your flower, your woman, and your fruit. I suggest wild roses. There it is, the divine trinity: wild roses, greengage plums, and green-eyed shopgirls."

A brief silence settled over the table.

"The sun and moon were not my ideas," Louis said. "François Arago, a friend at the observatory, has asked me to make some plates of them." The fact that an esteemed man of science such as Arago wanted the sun and moon to be cataloged further suggested to Louis that human enterprise was winding down.

"Seems fine. Everyone likes the sun and the moon." Baudelaire took several mouthfuls of his bouillon. "And who is this Isobel Le Fournier?"

"A woman from the past."

"Lost love and all that—how tiresome."

Louis took a bite of his egg and refused Baudelaire the eye contact he wanted. Isobel Le Fournier was his first and only substantial love; she had occupied his thoughts and longings for forty-four years, six months, and eleven days—ever since that day she had kissed him in a wine cave outside of Orléans.

Baudelaire said, "Don't look so glum. After we eat, we'll go walking in the Latin Quarter in search of our Madonna. We'll trawl the streets. And I'll think of some names as well. I must know some nudes."

People stared at Baudelaire as he tapped out with a Malacca cane, his bald head tilted, shouldering into a headwind. Wooden barrels belched tar smoke, men shoveled horse manure into pot-holes, flanks of meat hung marbled and sinister in the darkened doorways of butcher shops. But what Louis noticed was a cabaret festooned in yellow paper lanterns and bunting, an out-door bookstall towering with hundreds of green and vermilion clothbound volumes. The mercury poisoning was beginning to filter out the unsightly. He was growing blind to the squalor of the dying days of King Louis-Philippe's reign. He didn't see the plank-board alleys in the Carousel District, the dark rows of bird-seller shacks, the mud-daub shanties of the tooth pullers and the dog clippers. He saw only the markets full of honey and tulle, ladies in poplin sitting for open-air concerts under a Nile-blue sky. The world, it seemed to Louis Daguerre, was drowning in plenty.

As they walked through the serpentine streets of Mont-martre, Louis mentally auditioned the women as nudes — maid-ens in two-wheeled charabancs, ladies in bonnets and cashmere shawls, wives and daughters displaying the subtle inflections of the body beneath calico and merino.

Baudelaire said, "See anything you like? How about that Botticelli in the blue brougham?"

Louis reeled and looked at the compact carriage. Sitting high was a woman with pinned raven hair and the raised chin of no-bility. She looked as if she were being borne aloft, floating above the hubbub of the street.

"A little haughty," said Louis.

Baudelaire stopped beside a fruit and vegetable cart. "Do you have any plums?" he asked the vendor.

"No plums yet this year," replied the man. "But I have some oranges from Spain."

Baudelaire's face filled with infinite regret. Louis looked down the street and noticed a woman stepping across the flag-stone pavement in front of a restaurant. She was wearing a merino dress and carrying an apple-green parasol at her side. She sat on a wooden bench in front of a fountain, impatiently waiting for her driver to fetch her.

"Why are there so many queens in the Latin Quarter today?" Louis asked.

"The charm of the uncivilized," said Baudelaire. He took Louis's arm and led him towards the bench. "Good day, mademoiselle, may we impinge upon you for a moment? You see, my friend and I—surely you know him—the esteemed inventor of photography, Monsieur Louis Daguerre, well, he has been commissioned by the king to find a lady of refinement to pose for a new series of daguerreotypes."

"How splendid," the lady said, her eyes darting over the approaching traffic for her man and carriage.

"May we sit awhile?" Baudelaire asked.

Louis bowed and said, "Madame, you must forgive my colleague's conduct, he is a little brash in these matters. I'm sorry if we've troubled you." The woman smiled curtly, then stood and walked down the street. Her green parasol flashed open and shielded the back of her neck. Louis watched her disappear into the throng of people, her parasol floating through the multitudes like an apple bobbing downstream.

"Friendly," said Baudelaire.

"You lack all manners."

They sat on the bench and Baudelaire took out his pipe and lit it. He stared into the bowl of the pipe, at the pulsing orange eye of the tobacco plug. "Did you smell our mademoiselle?"

"I certainly did not."

"A woodland herbage, I assure you."

"God help our country," said Louis. He dusted his sleeves. "Come, we're going to execute the science of this. We'll walk the grid, down to Palais Bourbon and east to the Pont Neuf."

"Yes," said Baudelaire, raising his malacca cane like a sword, "we will map the city in the name of nudity."

Louis stood and clicked his heels together in a sudden display of officiousness. There was something regimental about him—the groomed mustache, the pomade-heavy wedge of gray hair, the Napoleonic jacket with epaulets. At fifty-nine he looked and dressed like a retired admiral. But he had a painter's eyes: Antwerp blue and prone to fits of moisture and reflection.

They walked up a small hill, Baudelaire now in front, his amber-tipped pipe clenched between his teeth. He waved at a passerby and called, "We are on a mission of the apocalypse."

Louis caught his reflection in a bakery shopwindow and noticed that his mouth was ajar, as if in profound thirst. He pursed his lips, then settled his mouth as his figure floated across the aqueous frontage of glass. But the seizure was already coming. The sun flared and whitened. Rivulets of sweat formed along his spine. His cravat and neck cloth restricted his breathing, and the mercury cough ascended from his groin, producing silver flashes in his peripheral vision. The taste of green copper in his mouth. He leaned against the brickwork of a building and was aware of Baudelaire standing beside him. Then the noise of the street bounded towards him, the clop and clatter of the wagons, the shriek of the vendors' cart horses. He doubled over, hands in spasm, and fell to the street. He felt the dankness of the macadam against his cheek. A small crowd ringed him in and he could see their glaucous faces, their eyes narrowed. In the midst of the seizure, a woman stood preening her gloves. He was aware of everything—his own pulse, his blood breaking its banks, the kettledrum of the street, this lady's chamois gloves. He could feel his head banging against the pavement, then Baudelaire's hand and then the slowing, the release of pressure in his jaw and rib cage, his teeth coming apart, air being drawn back into his lungs. He lay there for some time, panting. The crowd dispersed.

"Are you all right?" asked Baudelaire.

"Yes," said Louis, sitting up.

A deep calm always followed the seizures. He felt hollowed out, capable of great insight. He took in the street again, became aware of the light. It was now dusk and the objects of the afternoon were slipping away; one would position the camera obscura from a loft window to catch the diffusion of day. Nearby, a woman's face floated inside a window. Her skin a smoky pearl, jade-green eyes, lips that curved with the grace of violin hips. Louis stood in front of the deserted wineshop and looked within — a cavernous interior of empty shelves. A dusty crate stood in the middle of a floor covered with editions of *La Gazette de France.*

"I saw her," Louis said.

"Where? In here?"

Louis nodded. He placed a hand against the windowpane and became aware of his own reflection looking back at him. The entire shopfront was a photographic plate, and here was his own specter trapped inside the waterfilm of glass.

"I don't feel very well," Louis said.

"Let's get a cab. I'll take you home."

"She's out there somewhere," Louis said. "The woman I once loved."

"Every woman we once loved is out there alongside the women we are yet to love. They exchange tips about how to ruin us." Baudelaire stepped into the street and flagged down a cab. As he did so, he composed the first line of a new poem: "Twilight agitates madmen."

As they rode through the Paris dusk, Louis leaned his head against the leather seat back. Baudelaire was talking to the driver about socialist causes and the rumblings of insurrection in the garrets. The air was cut with the smell of paraffin and rotting oysters. Several times Louis had to cough and spit in the road, and he prayed that nobody would recognize him. When the cab pulled up in front of Louis's apartment, Baudelaire told the driver to wait, and he helped his friend down from the carriage. Together they climbed the long flight of stairs that led to Louis's rooftop studio. Louis gripped the railing, careful not to stumble. At the landing, he handed Baudelaire the key from his waistcoat and they went inside.

"Let's put you to bed," Baudelaire said as they moved through the darkened interior. The main room was cluttered — tripods, zinc cameras, copper plates, tall glass jars filled with briny-looking solutions, salts heaped into earthenware bowls. Baudelaire found the air decidedly pickled. He helped Louis into the bedroom, where the walls were covered in daguerreotypes, portraits and landscapes framed under glass. Baudelaire set Louis back on the cotton mattress and removed his shoes. "We're having a party at my house in a few weeks. It's going to be very elaborate," Baudelaire said. "There will be schools of minnow."

"What does that mean?" asked Louis, his eyes closed.

"Women fluttering by the curtains. I've thought of some nudes for your project."

"Excellent."

Baudelaire patted Louis on the shoulder. "Should I pour you some brandy?"

"No, thank you. I'll be asleep by the time you get to the bottom of the stairs."

"The nervous attacks are getting worse," Baudelaire said. "You should see a doctor."

"With their invoice pads and leeches — no, thank you."

"Take care of yourself," said Baudelaire, turning to leave.

Louis heard the door close at the bottom of the stairs. His chest was on fire, a tightness that made him pinch-eyed. He reached for the brandy decanter and drank a small swig straight from the glass lip, spilling some on his bedsheet. It loosened his breathing enough that he could relax and wait for sleep to settle over him. The bedroom window was open and he heard the noises of the street below—the submerged sounds of Paris descending into night, the shrill bell that announced showtime to the actors at a nearby theater, the street mongers calling their wares out against the brickwork alleys. Louis felt more of the deep calm. He took off his clothes and got under the swansdown quilt. He looked up at his daguerreotypes and saw that they were more eerie than beautiful. Portraits of bankers with waxed mustaches, their faces grim, old brasserie maids with henna cheeks, a sea merchant with sad tea-brown eyes, a riverside picnic where a wooden boat rippled in a wave of amber and the sun appeared as a pale ball of wax. The portraits appeared to him now as images of the dead—the shipwrecked, the drowned, the hangdog.

TWO

ouis Daguerre fell in love with women and light on the same day. This was in 1800, when he was twelve and living outside of Orléans. His father was head clerk on an estate that belonged to a distant cousin of the now executed Louis XVI; the estate had somehow been spared from the purging of the Reign of Terror. The hundred hectares seemed immune to change, a protectorate of the old aristocracy. The père ruled with a benevolent hand; he gave out cloth bags of sugared almonds at Christmas and lent money to those in his employ when they were sick. And while Paris abolished, for a time, the use of *monsieur* and *madame* in place of *citoyen* and *citoyenne;* while it gave up the Christian calendar—making March *Wind,* May *Flowers,* July *Heat,* etc.—all in the name of Liberty, Fraternity, and Equality, the estate brimmed with antiquity and servitude. For the most part, the peasants and clerks here regarded the revolution as an excess of the city. They had never seen a bread riot or a barricade. They served the royal bloodline the same way their forebears had done for six generations—with that odd mixture of pride and complaint that is the hallmark of a career servant. Only they kept it secret from the revolution.

Louis Daguerre's family lived, at this time, in a cottage that stood at the edge of a glade, surrounded on three sides by fields and with a view to the château. Louis had a bedroom in the attic, and from his window he spent hours watching teams of horses plow the fields back to russet, or the gardeners prune the apricot trees, or the maids go out with their woven baskets to pick gillyflowers and foxgloves. From this vantage point he imagined he was the duke of this estate, and when he was sick, which was often as a child, he stood in his bedclothes and quietly directed the bucolic scene: *Now, plowman, turn your gig to the west; maiden, pick those flowers at the end of the rhododendron tunnel.* If the gardeners came into the orchard to remove a dead apricot tree with handsaws and axes, as they sometimes did, Louis closed his curtains and refused to watch.

One day in August, after being sick for a week with a fever, Louis was convalescing in his rooftop bedroom. A maid who had a way with herbs had been sent over from the main house as a goodwill gesture on the part of the old aristocrat. The girl was all of fifteen, though her servant's papers declared her two years older. Louis thought her pretty in a defiant sort of way. Her caramel hair spilled loosely from a bow, and her eyes—a vivid green—seemed to suggest scrutiny, even scorn. She came into Louis's room with head presses and broth, and each time she closed the window and drew the curtains. As she did so, she spoke to Louis about her belief in the healing properties of camphor baths, valerian teas, brown sugar dissolved in warm water. Then she paused at the end of his bed and said, with complete authority, that those with fevers should not endure sunlight.

"Best keep the window and curtains closed," she added gravely. Her voice was nasal, from the South, an accent Louis already knew to be several stations beneath him.

Louis waited for her to leave the room, then crossed to the window and opened the curtains. They continued this shuttle-cock match of wills until his fever broke and Louis demanded that she leave the curtains open. "I'm better now. Stop closing the curtains or I'll tell my father that you've disobeyed my instructions."

She cinched her hands behind her back, crossed to the window, and pulled the curtains shut in one swift movement. The room dimmed and Louis noticed a small tear in the middle of one of the calico curtains. A cone of August light came through the tear and cast a series of shapes onto the ceiling. Louis felt he was at the bottom of a pond looking up at the brocaded surface. The maid walked slowly through the half-light and sat down beside Louis. She took up a piece of torn fabric and dipped it into a metal bowl filled with lavender-scented water. Louis closed his eyes, trying to indicate that he wanted to be rid of her, that he no longer needed a nurse, but she simply placed the head press over his eyelids. The water dripped down into his ears, his mouth, and the blossomy smell was drawn into his lungs. He was rendered complaintless.

"What if I don't want you to get well?" she said. "When the fever goes, I'll be back in the laundry room and at table."

Her voice floated through the lavender darkness.

"Nobody can be sick forever," Louis said.

"A little longer. Wednesday is bed linens."

"Fine, Isobel. I will get better on Thursday."

Louis felt her cheek against his forehead as she checked his temperature. For a moment the sound of her breathing was indistinguishable from his own; he could feel a strand of her hair grazing his neck. After a while, she quickly kissed him on the forehead, mumbled a *merci bien,* and was gone. Louis took off the head press and sat up in bed. The light was still dancing on the ceiling. He lay back down to watch it. Then, slowly, he took the soaked cloth and put it beneath his eiderdown, under his nightclothes. He wanted to cool his blood, an effect he knew from swimming in springtime brooks when the chilled water would banish his testicles like mussels to their shells. But the blossomed water energized his skin, and soon he was recalling Isobel at the window, the sunlight silhouetting her thighs, her breasts through the gossamer of her tunic . . . or her face in the blue aura of the spirit lamp when she came to tend him in the middle of the night. Louis looked up at the ceiling, at the flickering of dusk, and let out a truncated sigh. He felt the fever come back in a burst and shot a hand under the bedsheet. His hand emerged drenched and salty to the smell. He began a prayer to Saint Ouen, the patron of his father's dinnertime toasts, guardian of hallowed vineyards, in hopes of a celestial blessing. *Bless the soil with your goodwill. Give me the patience of a grape ripening on the vine.* But it was soon interrupted by Isobel coming back into the room.

"I heard you cry out," she said. She looked down at the soiled cloth.

Louis had tears in his eyes. She sat beside him on the mattress. Five seconds of silence passed between them. Isobel blushed, then collected herself.

"Poor boy, don't be humiliated. You have just become a little monsieur." She took the cloth from him with the simplicity of passing vinegar at the table. She handed him a clean piece of cloth. "Do you need to bathe?"

"Should I?" Louis asked.

"No hurry."

She looked away while Louis cleaned himself beneath the eiderdown.

"Don't tell my father," he said.

"This is our secret," Isobel said. She smiled and gathered the used cloths. On her way out, she said, "You might be better after all."

When she was gone, Louis closed then opened his eyes. The light from the torn curtain dappled on the ceiling and the amorphous outline of a tree appeared. He got up from his bed feeling lightened and cool. He took a piece of white linen from the bedside table and carried it to the window. Holding his eye to the hole in the curtain, he looked out at the late afternoon. The sun was going down behind the grain fields, and as it descended, it shot an orange glow from behind the hedgerows and poplars. Louis held the piece of white linen in front of the small curtain hole and saw, projected on it, the shimmering image of the lone walnut tree that stood by the stone fence. At the time he thought it merely a trick of nature or the convalescing mind, but years later, he would realize the importance of this discovery. The compression of light through the small hole had borne along the image of the walnut tree, projecting it onto the ceiling. Nature could sketch herself. He was growing into a man inside a dark chamber, a camera obscura fashioned by worn curtain fabric and August light. He went back to his bed and wrote in his journal: *I plan to be ill for some time.*

THREE

t the end of his fifth decade, Louis Daguerre had surrendered to the vice of scheduled pleasure. He rose each day at dawn, drew a scented bath, and lay in it for precisely thirty minutes before dressing in a pressed linen shirt and a woolen suit. He believed in the inviolability of bathing and perfuming the skin. Dressing in front of a silver-backed mirror, he gave himself a thorough inspection, from teeth to fingernails.

The physical symptoms of his poisoning were, by now, plainly apparent: his gums bled upon waking, a metallic taste lingered in his mouth, a cough rattled in his chest. He understood that his body was faltering, a by-product of working with chemicals for more than a decade, but he had never made an association between his physical symptoms and his erratic mind. On the days when his mind felt overexposed, he often felt physically robust. There was light in his eyes, color in his cheeks. And even when his mind was the foggiest, there was always a submerged layer of clarity, something glimpsed, as through the wave of insobriety between a second and third glass of burgundy. He walked through the streets and felt that everything was in its place; Paris hung gathered and calibrated by the great balance wheel of life.

At eight o'clock, amid the commotion of masons and tanners and soap boilers going to work, he strode out with top hat and cane, high-backed, nodding fraternal good mornings to passersby. He stopped at a canopied café where he read the newspapers. He followed with great interest the advancements of science and commerce, read about chloroform as anesthesia, the discovery of ancient human bones in Africa, the gold rush in California. After the café, he returned to his studio workshop and spent several hours in pursuit of a new daguerreotype. At exactly three o'clock each afternoon, he took a nap with a black silk scarf wrapped around his eyes. Upon waking, he drank a cup of strong coffee and ventured out for his afternoon walk.

The first Monday of each month, Louis went to Corbin's barbershop for a shave and trim. A week after the seizure on the Montmartre street, he sat in the pedestal leather chair, surrounded by the smell of brilliantine and the old barber's cheroot, and had the sensation that he and the barber shared a secret understanding. Buried in the barber's monologue about iron stocks and the pleasure of mohair in winter, there was something clandestine. The barber's face was whey-colored and pocked with age; it suggested ravaged wisdom. He looked at Louis in the mirror and there was a pause, as if here he would name the unknown shadow. Their eyes met briefly, then Corbin puzzled over a rogue whisker. He opened his straight razor, and for a moment Louis saw it as a silver glaive flashing beside his neck.

He emerged from the barbershop replenished, a slight sting of cologne on his cheeks. The air felt brazen, sharp as pine needles. He walked down the street carefully, light on his arches, like some provincial mayor rehearsing a stage walk. He wanted to savor everything, the clack of his shoes on the macadam, the press and tuck of his waistcoat. He had made further inquiries about Isobel Le Fournier. This was not just to prove her continued existence and take her portrait. It was, in a way, to close his accounts with life before *The End*, to balance the ledger where her name appeared mostly on the left and in red. He had removed a page from the Paris directory where the addresses of the city's two Le Fourniers were listed — one in Faubourg St. Victor and the other in Montmartre. He climbed up into his carriage and rode towards the first address.

Many years before, Isobel had been living under this surname, and it stood to reason that the name had persisted. Of course it was quite likely that Isobel did not live in Paris; after all, he knew her last to be living in Lyons, married to a banker. But Louis believed he had seen flashes of her around Paris — a woman with fine-boned hands one October day at the Sorbonne. He was late to deliver a lecture on his daguerreotype process when he saw her from a distance of fifty feet. Her hair was pinned under a brocaded scarf, and she was collecting autumn leaves and pressing them into a heavy book. It was not a physical recognition but the resonance of behavior. If Louis extrapolated from what he remembered of her during their last meeting in 1807, when she was twenty-two and he was nineteen, and added forty years of weather, revolution, illness, childbearing, she was more or less what he imagined: a woman aged with grace, a certain defiance in the way she gathered gold- and wine-colored leaves from the Sorbonne lawn while law students clopped across the pavestone in their gowns. Another time, he saw this same woman driving her own carriage, hurrying along Rue St. Honoré, this time with her hair down. Louis had emerged from the haze of a tobacconist and squinted into the glare of the street. The woman's silken hair ribboned in the wind and there was a moment, an interstice, of hapless eye contact between them. Again, it was not so much recognition as pause. The past asserting itself in the present. It was that slightly dazed ex-

pression between strangers which suggests anything from day-
dreams to bemusements at a hat or gown, to that subtle infatuation with the mystery of another person's existence. The carriage
drove on. Louis watched it disappear, the bolt of the woman's
hair diminishing into the crowded street. Then there was last
week's sighting of Isobel—but that was altogether different. The
sight of her youthful aspect in a deserted wineshop window was
surely a delusion, something that came in the twilight of a
seizure.

The first address was buried inside an enclave of widows.
Austere mansions gave way to crumbling homesteads on acre
plots, verandas worn to driftwood. These were the houses of the
old guard, indigo and coffee barons whose fortunes had been
winnowed by the revolution. These merchants, it seemed to
Louis, had died all at once, leaving an army of widows to live like
squatters. Three undertakers and a carpenter's casket shop occupied the head of the road. Widows, dressed in black day
dresses and woolen shawls, were out buying bread and glancing
at the coffins that faced the street. Some of them traveled in pairs
and made gestures to coffins of pine and walnut and beech, and
Louis found himself wondering what interest these dovetailed
boxes held after the loved one had departed. Were they discussing innovations in the field of coffinry? Had prices gone up
with decades of revolution and restoration? Was inflation such
that a man already in the ground was a man dispatched with
some thrift?

Dotted among the black-shawled widows—flanked and dispersed like a murder of crows—were shopgirls and maids on
their days off, carrying apples and boxed cakes, dressed in scarlet and burgundy. One girl wore a bright purple hat under which
she ate a wedge of Brie from a bakery stoop. These were the
women who no doubt worked for the wealthier widows, tending
their soup and death vigil. *Who is better prepared for the end?* Louis

wondered. The widows who had found a kind of integrity in their grief, donning black for a year or more, distilling life down to its essentials—prayer and bread and vigilantly run households; or the young girls who were oblivious to calamity and death, whose awareness of life's inclination towards decay was based on scrubbing creosote from fireplaces and wringing the necks of chickens each Sunday for a widow's after-church meal. *Who will die more righteously? The woman in black or the woman eating Brie in a doorway?*

Louis stopped his carriage in front of the last house on a dead-end street. The roadside ditches were full of mown thistle and briar, and the air was redolent of dead flowers. He descended from his carriage. The house was fronted by a high-walled courtyard and a hem of brushwood. He walked towards the wall of small Roman brick and placed his hands against the wrought-iron gate. The house was in a state of ill repair. The eaves sagged. A bloom of ground-rot had inched beneath a windowsill. These could be symptoms of grief and regret, he thought, the hallmarks of a woman plagued by her past. It had once been an elegant house—there was a patina of wealth beneath the rot. It had been built as a provincial château, twenty minutes from the Champs-Élysées. There were garden beds, parterres of roses, flowerpots that made Louis think of Isobel's country upbringing and earthy ways. Then he noticed a figure kneeling and weeding at the edge of a flower bed. It was an elderly woman, tossing tentacled weeds into a pile. She wore a white scarf and a blue housedress instead of a widow's smock and shawl. If Isobel had lived to be over sixty and was now widowed, then surely she would have defied the custom of somber dress in some measure. Louis watched the woman for several minutes, the way her gloved hands picked at the base of flower stems, the economy of her hand at a trowel, the suggestion of prayer in the way she knelt beside her camellias. He realized he was gripping the iron gate, and suddenly the ancient hinges let out a rusty moan. The woman looked up from her gardening. When she stood, she wiped her cheek with the back of her wrist and Louis felt his shoulders turn for the carriage. He would say that he'd lost his way, an errand man on a cul-de-sac. She walked towards the gate, removing her gloves.

"Monsieur?" she said. It was less of a question than a statement—*a man is standing outside my gate.* This may not have happened for some time.

"Madame, I am sorry to intrude." He studied her face for memorable traits. "I seem to have lost my way."

"I see," she said.

"I am delivering flowers to a Madame Le Fournier."

She looked at his fine-weave trousers, then at the empty carriage. "But you have no flowers?"

"Yes," said Louis. "You see, I have been robbed. And I must find Madame Isobel Le Fournier to explain the theft of her flowers. There were road bandits."

"You poor man. I am Madame Le Fournier, but I haven't received flowers in many years. Are you sure of the address?" The woman cocked her head to one side.

Her eyes, he could see now, were blue instead of green. Could eye color change in the old and widowed as it did in infants? Could grief turn a woman's gaze from jade to cornflower blue?

"Quite certain," he said.

"Who was the sender?"

"Do you know a Monsieur Louis Daguerre?"

There was a slight quiver in her voice. "Of course," she said. She loosened her scarf and retied the bow under her chin. "Half the country knows that braggart's name because of that abomination of his. If you ask me, it's not God's intention to suspend our images in such a manner. It's idolatry."

He knew now it was a different woman; he was simultaneously thankful and dashed.

The old woman, a different Le Fournier whose stories of romance and widowhood were entirely unrelated to Louis Daguerre, placed her two varicose hands against the iron gate and began a tirade. "The saints and apostles do not wish us to harbor vanity. No. For when the Day of Judgment arrives, we shall be appraised according to measure. The seraphs will ripple over the fields. A great sweeping storm and a cleansing of the likes we've never seen. The vain and the proud will be among the first to perish. My monsieur died in the battle of Waterloo with his face in the mud, martyred by the emperor, and he, my husband, cared nothing for his own image. Never looked at mirrors. You will not find mirrors in my house to this day." She let out an asthmatic but satisfied breath. She glanced back at the garden beds. Her bottom lip gave a tremulous pout. "My flowers are being eaten by worms."

"I'm sorry to have troubled you, good madame."

"Tell Monsieur Daguerre that giving widows flowers will not make them buy his daguerreotype. Not while an angel is called Gabriel."

Louis began a retreat from the gate. "Good day, madame."

She swatted at something in the air and lowered her face. Louis climbed up into his carriage and drove back through the neighborhood of sackcloth.

FOUR

ouis lived inside his rooftop camera near Orléans, making that awkward passage from boy to young man. In many ways his boyhood mirrored the revolution—born in 1787, two years before the Bastille fell; showed signs of rebellion against his father as Parisians raided the royal tombs of the Abbey of Saint-Denis; clambered towards puberty during a coup d'état; departed for Paris in 1804, aged sixteen, to find his place in the world as Napoleon crowned himself emperor.

But at fourteen—two years after he'd watched sunlight etch a walnut tree onto his ceiling—he was a sensitive boy lost to love and distraction. He spoke about sunsets and the lustrous effect of high noon on bird plumage; he quoted Voltaire; he walked alone through thickets of orrisroot with a set of magnifying glasses, in pursuit of miniature kingdoms. With the bone-handled glasses and a leather notebook to record his observations, he would sit before a dynasty of granulated quartz and clover and study it for hours through the various lenses. He discovered colonies of ants, parades of aphids, gangs of pollinating honeybees. He studied the way the light intensified when he used a higher magnification. He set dried leaves or dead butter-fly wings aflame with narrow bands of condensed sunlight. He felt a part of things. Sometimes he hid in the rhododendron tunnel and flashed secret, glassine messages to Isobel as she worked in the upstairs of the château.

Isobel cared nothing for the vagaries of light. She washed bed linens and sometimes served at table inside the mansion. She knew about arnica and nettle teas, about the day in the spring when rapeseed sprouted from sandy soils. She made poultices with cheesecloth and mustard leaves. As she walked around the estate—smelling of herbs and camphor—she sang pastoral melodies, shepherds' laments. When Louis was sick, or when he pretended to be sick, she wore a white apothecary apron and carried a mortar and pestle in a small basket. They struck up an arrangement out of mutual need: Louis needed a woman to study, to fall in love with, and Isobel needed distraction from her household chores. She loved him, but there was nothing carnal in her affection—he was the unformed kernel growing inside the husk of a man. He wrote her love letters, made her crowns of tuberoses, painted watercolors of her transformed into a nymph on a bed of heather. He was in love with her, and she was in love with the man he might become.

She was, of course, three years older than he. This age gap—a stone dashed across the pond of his longing—kept their love-friendship within certain bounds. Regardless, there was something wild about her love for him. Sometimes when he appeared in a pair of ill-fitting pantaloons and a broad-rimmed beaver hat, off to see his Latin tutor, she wanted to strip him bare and roll with him in a paddock of oat grass. But this was not lust. No, this was the boisterous love that swells inside a woman who wants to marry a man who is still a boy at heart. This was the vision a girl-maid has of marrying her sister in the male guise—someone to wash her hair with rainwater and rose hips, to read her sonnets, to lie with her in a field of wheat and renounce the follies of the age. But this person, this boy-man she imagined spending a life with, would never possess her body or mind.

As Louis grew into a young man who wandered through the walnut grove with a set of watercolors instead of sitting at his desk with a set of calipers, his father became irksome. Although the clerk served the remains of an aristocracy, he found the laziness and ethereal concerns of the upper class intolerable. Monsieur Daguerre was a clerk with an impeccable sense of timing and order; he believed in an honest day's work, sacrifice for king and country, marriage before the age of twenty. The house at the end of the glade — remodeled as a tribute to his services to the crown — was run with regimental precision. Each dawn Madame Daguerre served hearty breakfasts of soup and bread and eggs; she darned her husband's black stockings the last Sunday of the month. To ensure his punctuality, Monsieur Daguerre synchronized the cottage clocks with those inside the château. The machinery of a household, he believed, needed to be as simple and reliable as a winepress. Nothing faddish, nothing wanton. God had designed man to calibrate with nature: to sleep with the stars, wake with the sun, hunger in proportion to his yields.

He tried to rein Louis in, at first with offhand comments: "Here, little man, come sit beside me and we will go through this pile of bills together. Ordered accounts and no debts, these are the hallmarks of any gentleman's household." In response Louis would sit on a high stool, take up his father's daybook and inkwell. But soon he was sketching fir trees and ferny hollows in the ruled margins, and his father would dismiss him with the wave of a hand. Sometimes Monsieur Daguerre in-

sisted that Louis accompany him to his office in the main building, and he would wait for the tardy boy to come downstairs.
On one occasion Louis appeared in a topaz cravat and plaid
trousers. The head clerk, appalled, said, "If my employer sees
you in that yellow cravat, he'll fire me. Where did you get such
a thing?"

Isobel had made the cravat for Louis as a kind of dress-up,
for when he was a duke out in the briar. Louis had spent the
morning tying and untying the cravat. He found its style and
color impossibly elegant. Louis stared at his father boldly and
said, "Either that or he'll give me your job."

His father was riled by this comment. Rising from an ottoman, flushed with anger, Monsieur Daguerre said, "I will see
you both this evening." He pecked his prim wife—a woman of
devout churchgoing and sunbonnets—and walked off through
the glade. Louis ran up to his bedroom, ripped off the cravat,
and watched his father from the window as he pinch-walked towards the mansion. *Hope you step in cow shit.*

There was also an attempt to rein in Louis's artistic sensibility with catechism classes. This was not because his parents were
called to God—his mother prayed with the same domestic vigi-
lance she employed when baking bread, and his father held the
matter of God to be a meddlesome affair—rather, it was because
Catholicism was seen as a bridge back to a time of superior dis-
cipline and manners. Before the revolution had topsy-turvied the
nation's mind and soul, young men and women knew the sacra-
ments, and church was a forum for vetting another family's re-
spectability. How much could be determined by the polish and
gleam of a man's Sunday shoes or the hem of a lady's skirt! Now
the country was awash in eclecticism and revolutionary zeal, and
boys like Louis were becoming indolent and doe-eyed. So Louis
began a weekly routine of catechism classes under the supervi-
sion of a seminary student from Orléans. Together they studied

the lives of the saints, the stations of the cross, the cardinal sins, the infallibility of the pope, the nature of purgatory and limbo. But what Louis absorbed from the scriptures and the asides of the hair-collared seminarian only intensified his fascination with art. Louis remembered the Bible stories as panoramas—the exodus from Egypt a stretch of pumice-colored sand under a high-blue sky; the parting of the Red Sea like two walls of fire; the saints in the desert with their forlorn faces upturned, their eyes made luminous by faith. Catechism only convinced Louis that the world existed to be rendered.

Summer afternoons, whenever they could escape their respective households, Isobel and Louis played out their pantomime of love. Isobel, rose-crowned, pale against the heather, sat motionless for Louis as he sketched her with charcoal. She sat, a chain of poppies about her splayed skirt, and looked off at hills blued by distance. He studied the slope of her neck, the triangulation of chin, elbow, and ankle. When he felt bold, he put the flowers in her hair himself, tucking blossoms into the crossweave of brown and blond. They discovered new backdrops for his sketches—limestone ruins, the shell of an old carbine—each giving occasion for new intimacy in the portrait. Louis was riveted by the gentle line of her bared shoulders, by the sight of her thin-boned feet swaddled in rye grass.

Louis also served as a kind of model for Isobel. He was her patient. Under a hollowed-out den of willow boughs, Isobel kept her apothecary. She lined a rock shelf with tinctures and herbal remedies and sat Louis down on a tree stump to inquire of his health. He was instructed to invent various maladies for which Isobel would concoct medicinal blends. "Night sweats, followed by vomiting in the mornings," he might say. Or "I have itchy eyes and feet." Or "I dream about horses in the grove." She would administer an examination that was based on various modalities she had studied: she'd learned how to take a pulse according to Vedic tradition; she ran her hand over his spine and felt for engorged glands; she asked homeopathic questions about whether his throat itched when he sneezed and if his morning urine burned on the way out. Louis lay on the ground, his shirt open to her organ probes, and lied with all the seriousness of art. "A little burning, but not too much. The most dreadful headache whenever Father enters a room." She did not laugh, but sometimes her hands gave in to nondiagnostic touch. At first Louis thought he was imagining it—that slow, undulating finger at his spine, or the light caress following a circumnavigation of his stomach. He saw his own body, the sallow skin, the bony chest, in the broadness of daylight. He became self-conscious and she seemed to sense it, moving to the remedy shelf to take down a jar of pressed pomegranates or silica powder.

They swam together in the cold spring behind the fields. She wore a petticoat and he a pair of cotton trousers. Isobel eased herself in among the lilies and floated on her back, her hair fanning out across the light-grained surface. She stared up through the branchwork of willow and elm, listening to her breath and taking her pulse from within. Louis dived for thrown coins and collected rocks. There were long stretches of silence. Isobel sloughed her skin with river sand and washed her hair with lilac. Louis came upon a monarch butterfly on a leaf platform and studied the geometry of its wings. Then something would quicken one to the other, a particularly fragile plant or insect, and they would find themselves squatting on the bank entranced by one of nature's curios. Louis looked at her body when she wasn't watching—the summered hairs on her arms, the whites of her fingernails, the wet-cloth rise of her chest. And Isobel looked at Louis when he dashed off in pursuit of a glistening pebble or when he shimmied up a tree trunk for wild apples. She looked at the mystery of a boy's sinewy back and shoulders, at his knuckles and wrists, at the flats of his stomach. Then they returned to their dark houses and Louis wrote her love letters in which he compared her to a swan. She pretended she never read them and he never asked. She lay in her bed in the servant quarters and drank minted tea and laughed to herself that she had fallen for a fourteen-year-old boy when she needed to be finding a husband.

One day Louis took his father's horse—an old gelding that came with an off-kilter trot and a hunting saddle—and he rode out into the countryside with Isobel snug behind him. Louis had been given a new set of watercolors from a bourgeois uncle and he wanted to make a portrait of Isobel in a new setting. It was mid-autumn; the sky was oyster, the fields straw. The leaves were turning from claret to gold. The gris meunier grapes had been harvested and the stems pruned, leaving long varicose lines of stem and stock. Louis knew from his father that the technique of pruning the miller's gray vine had been discovered by the monks of Marmoutier centuries ago. It happened one season when their donkeys ate a harvest down to the ground. The next year the grapes rebounded to produce the best wine to date. Louis told this story as they rode, calling back to Isobel over his shoulder.

"So we owe the delicacy of our wine to an ass?" she said, laughing.

He could feel her laughter on his neck. He nudged the gelding into a loping trot. Isobel had no choice but to hold him tighter.

"Where are we going?" she asked.

"To find the perfect place for a portrait."

They trotted on. Louis had imagined they could ride out to

one of the medieval castles or to an old abbey. He pictured Isobel on a rampart, her prone figure beside the mossy capstones. But they kept riding and it was getting late. They had to stop and water the horse where a vineyard led down to the Loire. There were cliffs adjacent to the river. They stood and waited for the horse to finish drinking. Isobel looked down at the river. They were abruptly at a loss for conversation. Louis noticed an opening in the chalk bluffs and realized that the vineyard kept a cellar in the cliff face.

"Look," he said. "That's where they mature the wine."

"Let's go see," Isobel said.

"I don't care to be shot by some drunken vintner."

"Don't be such a coward. Let's go see," she said.

Louis quietly tied his father's horse to a fence paling and walked in front of her, leading the way. He began repeating wine lore he'd heard from his father — that if the weather was still hot in September, they had to harvest the grapes at night, that there were winepresses powered by windmills that could crush a man, that the Germans had discovered ice wine one year when the grapes froze. Isobel found this folk litany tiresome. She caught up to him just shy of the cellar entrance and said, "And tell me, Monsieur Vin, was this year a good vintage?"

"The grapes this year are too sweet. They're calling it a year for the ladies."

"Well, not all ladies like their grapes sweet. I prefer mine bitter, wild, and still on the vine." She pushed in front of him and went inside the cellar. Louis followed.

Inside was more a system of quarries and galleries than a cellar. There were skylights chiseled into the facade, and these gave enough illumination to make out the winemaking apparatus. They walked between several winepresses and into a racking area. Against one chalk wall were open barrels of residue, the excess pressings destined for pickling vinegar or the Loire. The smell was bitter and tannic; the vague scent of oak softened it as they walked into the fermenting area. Hundreds of green bottles were inserted into the augered wall.

"Let's drink a bottle," Isobel said.

The light was fading and Louis couldn't make out her face. "If we get caught, we'll be done for."

"So cautious," she said. There was the hint of a test in her voice.

"Fine. Pick a bottle."

"Oh, no," she said. "The gentleman chooses the wine."

"And what does the lady do? Get planked?"

Isobel walked up and down the aisle of wine bottles. Louis came behind her and pulled a bottle from above his head. He dusted it off and held it in front of a narrow band of light coming from above. It was from 1785, from before the revolution.

"Oh my Lord," said Isobel, taking it in her hands.

"We can't," said Louis.

"I'll kiss you if you open it," she said.

He wanted to see her face, but all he could make out were the whites of her eyes. He felt his blood pushing into his temples and his mouth becoming briny. Clearing his throat, he reached into his back pocket and retrieved a cheese knife he carried for the purpose of sharpening his sketching charcoal. He dug around the cork and, after almost cutting his finger, managed to push it down into the bottle.

"Hardly the Right Bank," said Isobel. She took the bottle from him and took a long drink. Louis did the same. The world had been reduced to the threat and promise of a tannic kiss—he imagined their mouths brimming and heavy with wine. They passed the bottle back and forth until it was half gone. Then Isobel said, "If you're going to kiss me, then go ahead."

An elaborate silence.

"I want to see you if I do," he said.

"No," she said. "Here or nowhere."

"But we're hiding in—"

She took his face, a face that was smaller than her own, and brought her mouth to his in the darkness. Here was the winey cup of his mouth, the feel of his jawbone set against her fingertips. She would regret this later, but only in the brassy aura of a twilight hangover. For now she took her fill of him, drank him down like spring water, and pictured, in the darkness, an older and stouter version of Louis. She pictured him with a mustache and brass buttons. She was kissing the man he would become and yet here were his hands all about her—pressing into her bodice, spanning the small of her back. Roused, Louis clamored for her in the dark. And Isobel felt her body undulate almost uncontrollably towards him; she was a virgin and this was a rehearsal for the wifely arts. This was practice, she told herself, a preparation for a future husband. She stopped kissing him when she inadvertently placed her hand behind his head and realized she was still several inches taller than he was. She took his hand and led him, stunned and silent, outside. It was now dusk; the river held a trace of daylight. Louis watched Isobel move towards the horse and thought abstractly about the portrait he'd wanted to paint of her. She stood waiting to hoist herself onto the saddle—her mouth slightly scalded by the kiss, her eyes darkened, her hair caught up in a halo of river light. Louis knew these to be effects of water and twilight, but he couldn't help feeling he'd found a moment of perfection—Isobel captured in her sulky bloom.

They rode home in silence. Something was different now in Louis. An insistence flared up in his chest. He spotted, through the woods, the yellowed windows of hunting lodges and the candle lamp from a bridge keep. He heard the low, jovial chiding of Parisian horsemen paying a river toll. Men were out in the night, making their way amid the cry of night fowl. Today he'd kissed a woman. He wanted to yell that as he passed the men on the bridge. He was a part of them now.

Fourteen, beardless, acting on the basis of one inebriate kiss, Louis proposed marriage to Isobel not long after. He planned it down to the last detail, choosing an hour by the brook when the day-lilies turned west. He dressed in the topaz cravat and his church-suit herringbone and donned his beaver-skin hat for good measure, because several times Isobel had said the hat made him look like a shepherd of the Pyrénées. Louis mistook this for flattery. So there he stood, an hour before Isobel's appointed time of arrival, rearranging the decorative aspects of their little den. He treated it like a drawing room, aligning willow branches as if they were drapes, laying out polished stones like Venetian chocolates, combing the sandy bank with a broom of sticks to ensure she would have a soft place to receive his proposal. He floated linden blossoms on the water and coaxed a turtle to stay on a particular rock by spreading out slices of apple. By the time Isobel arrived, the little alcove had a monastic fragrance and serenity.

Isobel took in the arranged scene and her face grew white. She was immediately aware of the turn things had taken. The countless leaves of paper on which Louis compared her to doves and dahlias, swans and river idols, the hapless drunken kiss inside the wine quarry—these were so many articles of evidence in support of this terrifying and humiliating moment. She looked around for him in the ferny shadows. He stood, hands on hips, looking down from an island of granite in the brook with a glazed and maniacal love in his eyes.

"Isobel," he said loudly, "I have something to ask you."

"Please don't, Louis." She took off her shoes and came towards him, her bare feet pale in the chill water.

Louis hitched up his pants and ran his sweating hands down his rump. "I have made it known to you that I have every intention of fulfilling our destiny together. I don't think I need to list my assets and talents. I come from an honest, clerkship family who will no doubt become property owners within the next generation. I am smart. I am also a good swimmer, which you know to be true." He looked down at his hands. "Someday I will be a famous artist. I'd like you to be my wife. We'll marry when I'm sixteen. If you say yes, I will write to your father."

Isobel had moved out into deeper water, standing in front of his igneous pulpit drenched up to her thighs. Her maid's skirt floated about her, raised and darkened by the water. The linden blossoms spun in small, tight circles and occasionally ran into her legs. Louis could see that she was crying, her face down, her fingertips gliding across the surface of the brook.

"You're supposed to be sitting on the little beach," he said.

She ignored him and came closer and wrapped her arms around his legs. She kept her face down but squeezed with a ferocity he would not forget. She thought of him as a doe she'd found out in the woods, an animal brought into her custody. She loved him fiercely and there was no denying that. But she wanted to lease the boy from the world as a friend and then buy him when he became a man. The kiss had confirmed that. Some time ago she had decided on the one unspoken rule of their ambiguous love—*do not ask me to decide what you are to me, for that will ruin everything*—and now he had violated it. Now he was a child in love with a woman, a boy trying to learn the anthems of men.

"Why did you have to do this to our friendship?" she said.

He looked at her with a dark and pure anger. "I do not wish to be friends," he said.

"And I do not wish to be the wife of a child."

The plainness of it struck him. He'd wanted to believe that those had been tears of surrender and that her embrace was an act of compliance. He looked over at the turtle sunning itself on the mossy rocks, idling its head from side to side. A long silence unfolded. The river weeds bent with the pull of the brook.

"Say something, Louis, or we will both suffocate."

Louis stood up from the rock and looked down at her. The rage pulled at his mouth, making it thin and tight. "I seem to have made a mistake," he said. "I thought you could see it. But look at you, you're just a maid standing in her uniform, drenched up to her cheap underwear."

He turned and leaped off the rock and began wading through the stream. He dashed up the small bank and ran out into the open. Isobel watched him disappear across the glade.

The marriage proposal lived in the air between them; they kept the hurt rubbed and silent as polished brass. The weeks dragged on and the silence plagued them both. They lived, half dazed and preoccupied, in each other's troubled thoughts. She dropped vases and dinner plates. He stubbed his toe on the stairs that led to his bedroom and misplaced his magnifying glasses every other day. Louis would retreat whenever he saw Isobel out on the grounds. He replayed those moments in the ferny den and saw himself as a fool, a circus dog groveling in the dirt. The images of that afternoon paralyzed him with bitterness; every detail was a humiliation. As for Isobel, the guilt and sorrow lingered in the months that followed—she felt it at the edges of everything she did. An accidental reminder could come in the form of a flower arrangement with linden blossoms or a glass of water resting on a table. All at once she would see that scalded look in his eyes and feel tears brimming.

FIVE

ouis was going to the Paris Observatory to take twin portraits of the sun and the moon. He dressed before the mirror in a silk waistcoat and woolen coat. He wanted to look serious and hoped the weave and cut of his clothes would lend something formidable to his appearance. Around his neck he hung the Legion of Honor cross on a chain and buttoned his shirt to conceal it. With its five silver points and enameled laurel wreath, it was both ornate and stately. It had been designed for official ceremonies, but Louis had taken to wearing it as a daily talisman, as proof of his own ascent. As he stood in front of the silver-backed mirror, he wondered if man's reflection was the precedent for photography. Daguerreotypes were, after all, mirrors with a memory. Before his invention, men had stared into stilled ponds, plates of glass, and mirrors with simple fascination at their own aspect. Now they imagined themselves in the stop-time of a photograph, their flaws etched, their lucent eyes alighting on some future viewer, a grandchild in an attic, a bereft widow, and they were taken, if only for a moment, with their own mortality and the residue of a human life. They felt a fond-

ness for their future dead selves, the specter laid down in the mercurous grain.

Louis had a stable hand bring his carriage around and carried his daguerreotype equipment downstairs. He emerged onto the street and noticed the perfection of the day. The pavestone had been glossed by an overnight rain, and from his stoop the entire boulevard stretched away like an expanse of oiled slate. He could smell the bakery ovens firing and the chalky odor of wet sandstone. As he loaded his equipment into the carriage, old men passed with their dogs, traveling in twos and threes behind leashed spaniels and hounds, complaining about their wives and the price of tobacco. *Fraternity is not dead. We will die as brothers.* Louis ran a hand over a horse flank and climbed up onto the box seat. He filled with the pleasure of the day ripening, with the wild luck of being alive in the middle of the nineteenth century. An artist, a scientist; he was on his way to chronicle the heavens.

The Paris Observatory stood on its namesake avenue, a stone rectangle with two wings attached, each facade facing a cardinal point of the compass. Louis admired the building's symmetry before entering. The building marked zero latitude — it was literally the center of the world.

Louis knew from François Arago that the foundations and basement of the observatory were as deep as the building was high — about fourteen meters. The subterranean rooms were guarded with some secrecy. On one occasion, a colleague had mentioned that beneath the observatory was an underground portal into the catacombs. These tunnels serviced rock quarries of the Roman era and the mass graves of the revolution, when the cemeteries were abandoned for below-street tombs. In the high and final days of Charles X, before the July Revolution of

1830, the king had thrown wild parties in the catacombs as an affront to revolutionary blood: he held underground orgies, strange feasts of shaved ice and marinated eel. This had always struck Louis as wretched; even though he sometimes favored the monarchy over the revolution, the image of the monarch ravaging courtesans beside entombed remains saddened him on behalf of the people. But it pleased him to think that above this debauchery, science went on unabated. Astronomers continued their night watch at the height of state corruption; they tracked and measured, gave names to the flash of comets and the pinwheel of stars.

As Louis entered the building, it occurred to him that the catacombs were the perfect place to store his doomsday portraits. Sealed off, far below the city, they stood a chance of surviving whatever storm of terror came with the final days. He would ask Arago on some other pretext for access to the catacombs. François Arago was not the sort of man to share an apocalyptic prophecy with—he was, among other things, a professor of analytical geometry. He believed in form and coherence, that a set of parallel lines extended to infinity.

Louis was led up a long spiral staircase and into a waiting area outside Arago's office. From out in the street he heard the sound of attendants unloading the photographic equipment from his carriage. There came a loud clatter, and he crossed swiftly to the window. A man in overalls was carrying the tripod over one shoulder as if it were a side of beef.

"Mind the equipment, you oaf!" Louis yelled from the sill.

He was surprised by the volume of his voice. The man looked up, swore under his breath, and plodded into the observatory. Louis felt oddly proud of having yelled out the window. A stand had been made. Most of his life he'd observed decorum and custom, but now he felt an urge to bellow. He looked around, a little annoyed to be kept waiting. He had no faith in daguerreotypes of the sun and moon. In 1845, Hippolyte Fizeau and Léon Foucault had made an image of the sun. To Louis it appeared as a ball of pale wax giving off smoke. It was not the method of the men that was in question. Both were sound methodologists — Hippolyte had several other images of limited acclaim, and Foucault's pendulum was already under development, inching nearer to proving the rotation of the earth. No, Louis was not here to remedy the image. He was here to repay a debt to Arago. As the director of the observatory and secretary of the Academie des Sciences, Arago had rallied for Louis Daguerre's national pension of ten thousand francs. It had been Arago who believed in the importance of Daguerre's invention when others called it lunacy, an affront to painterly art and tradition.

A clerk ushered Louis into Arago's office. It was a bare stone chamber with a single brass telescope poised at the window. Arago sat behind a large desk stacked with dossiers bundled in twine. He rose to greet Louis. "Monsieur, how can it be all these years and only now you've come to fetch me the heavens? Very good to see you."

They embraced. Arago was an elegant, precise man with a square jaw and a Roman nose. He dressed like a Burgundy vintner, despite being an ardent Republican — an heirloom cravat pin, cuff links, moleskin trousers.

"You look good, François."

"I'm balding and I don't sleep well, but I appreciate the lie. It's quite touching. Please make yourself comfortable," said Arago, sitting back down.

Louis sat in a high-backed chair.

Arago said, "Where have you been? You dropped off the face of the earth."

"I've been very busy with the process — making improvements and such."

Arago leaned forward, his hands together. "Are you eating enough? You look ill."

"You were always known for your tact. I'm too busy to eat these days."

"Have a cigar," Arago said. "Health is for the idle." He reached into a top drawer, produced two cigars, and cut off the ends with a bone-handled knife. He handed one to Louis. "I hear," he said, "that the Americans are quite taken with your invention. There are hundreds of portrait studios in New York. Even Samuel Morse has one."

"I hear that also," said Louis. He lit his cigar, being careful not to ignite his cough.

Arago leaned back in his chair, lit his cigar, and blew smoke up at the ceiling. "You must be pleased."

Louis settled in his own chair. "I owe much of it to you. I'm always indebted for your sponsorship."

"So indebted that you don't answer my letters for five years?"

Louis felt himself about to stammer, then relaxed his mouth. "I don't always read my mail."

Arago's mouth puckered with a sarcastic smile. "Ah, the vagaries of fame."

A smoky silence filled the room.

"Some men might be bitter, Louis. I went before the Academie for your invention, recommended a national pension. Meanwhile, I measure the speed of sound and chart the stars and planets, and your average Frenchman doesn't know who I am. They're not going to name a street after me when I'm dead."

Louis looked down at his feet and spoke quietly. "I wonder if the dead are vainer than the living."

"What's that?" Arago gripped the arms of his chair.

Louis watched the red eye of Arago's cigar flash, then recede. "François, I have had trouble with my eyes, and that's why I didn't read your letters. My vision fails me at certain times of the day. The doctors say it's a reaction to the nitric acid I use in my process."

Arago cocked his head to the side, a little unwilling to yield his irritation. "I'm sorry to hear about your eyes."

"It won't matter before long."

Arago did not react to this comment. He rose, put his hands in his pockets, and poised an eye behind the telescope. He rested there for several moments, cigar in his mouth, squinting through the eyepiece.

"How are the stars these days?" Louis asked.

"Still there. You wouldn't believe the idiocy we endure. Paris is full of madmen, I tell you. When we announced that Neptune had been proved, a man came to us declaring that the world was still flat and showed us a map of Atlantis. Off the coast of China, it was."

"If Atlantis were real, Napoleon would have tried to colonize it."

"The emperor may have been a little hotheaded, but he got things done."

"Beheadings, mostly," Louis said.

Arago took his eye from the telescope and they looked at each other, leaned into this old disagreement.

Arago took a notebook and pencil from his desk, looked at his watch, and wrote something down.

"What are you doing?" Louis asked.

"Take a look for yourself."

Louis crossed to the telescope while Arago held it in place. He positioned his eye and looked out onto a rooftop where a very old Muslim man stood in a tunic on the edge of a prayer rug. The man bowed slowly, his head down, before moving into a kneeling position. There was something otherworldly about this feeble man suspended above Paris, facing Mecca, and moving with a halting reverie. Everywhere people were preparing.

"He prays five times a day, and I have been writing down the exact time of three of those prayers for years. Midday, late afternoon, and just after sunset. I have no faith of my own, but it gives me a great deal of comfort to watch this man. We keep time for all of Paris, and in some strange way, I keep time from this man's prayers. I have a precise record of his devoutness."

Louis straightened and took the notebook from Arago. It was meticulously ruled, and each prayer time had its own column. He returned to the eyepiece and watched as the man pressed his nose and mouth to the rug.

Arago said, "One day he'll die and I'll be very sad not to see him out on his rooftop."

Louis felt he was witnessing something deeply personal. He pictured Arago watching from this spot, measuring time by another man's prayers, and understood that his friend was full of regret. Arago had waited his whole life for greatness to arrive; he dressed like a man who expected to discover a planet. Louis felt impossibly sad that Arago's hopes and ambitions would come to naught, that darkness would descend from the very sky he'd spent his life studying. Louis backed away from the telescope, keeping his face down.

"François, before I take the daguerreotypes of the sun and moon, there is a favor I'd like to ask. There isn't much time."

"Please, sit."

Louis returned to his seat. "I am looking for a storage area for my portraits, and I was wondering if I might get access to the catacombs via the observatory basement."

Arago returned to his chair and thinned his lips in speculation. He was a man who counted right angles and noticed a wall out of plumb upon entering a room. "But surely it's too dusty and filthy down there. Our revolutionary brothers are buried below."

"Yes, I'm aware. But I need somewhere protected. The daguerreotypes will all be under glass, so the dust won't damage them."

"I see." Arago tapped his fingers gently on the edge of his desk. "You realize that access to the catacombs is controlled by the crown. They are off limits to citizens."

"I didn't realize."

"Of course, we have a key to the gate because—and this is not widely known—one of our founders is buried down there. Cassini, the man who mapped the moon. The key is in this very drawer. But this is madness. Your images belong in museums, not catacombs full of bones."

"The circumstances are special."

"The truth is special."

Louis looked into Arago's face. A perfect meridian ran vertically down his forehead; he was a scientist kept awake by the great questions of his time. Louis wanted to confess and warn. *François, take your family to an abbey and pray with the monks, leave your scientific post and go to Venice, learn how to paint and rise each morning while the stars are still white-lit against the dawn. Be a boy again. Play cork-penny in the lane and set paper boats afloat on the Seine. The time is upon us.*

Instead, Louis Daguerre said this: "The truth is, I fear they will be stolen from me. As you know, there has been jealousy on all sides, claims that independent inventions were made earlier. I need them in a safe place."

"You imagine that someone will rob you?" Arago asked.

"I am sure of it. In fact, there has been one attempt already." The lie was effortless, and it filled Louis with a salesman's confidence; he was sure Arago would acquiesce. For good measure, he added, "I could lose my entire collection, my whole life's work, if I don't find a safe place to store them."

Arago folded his arms. "Well, these *are* special circumstances.

But we must keep this a secret. You tell me when you want access, and I will arrange it."

"Many thanks. I owe you much kindness."

"Yes, so you keep saying. Next time I want to reach you, I'll hire a town crier to come and stand outside your door." Arago laughed at this, dabbed a scuffed patch on his calfskin boot, and said, "Now, shall we go look at the sun?"

Louis followed Arago out into the hall. They climbed to a rooftop observation platform above the eastern tower where various telescopes were set up. Louis saw that his equipment had been piled by a railing. He placed the camera obscura on the tripod and prepared a copper plate with carded cotton and powdered pumice. The day was growing hot and Louis loosened his collar.

"Are you still using quicksilver to fix your images?" Arago asked.

"The marriage of mercury and silvered copper is a lasting one."

"Few marriages last forever," Arago said absently, peering off at the Paris rooftops. "I thought perhaps you'd found something less abrasive."

"It's destined to stay in the process. It's a noble metal, neighbor to gold." There was a high pitch of vitriol in Louis's voice. "Hardly an accident that it plays a role. And Priestley never would have discovered oxygen without burning mercury oxide. Where would the observatory weather station be without mercury in your thermometers?" He looked back at the plate and rubbed it with carded cotton. The threat of a cough made him regret the cigar.

"I was merely asking." Arago leaned against the railing and looked high overhead at the sun. "Did you know the king has granted my eleven o'clock curfew on the new moon? People in this neighborhood are not permitted to burn candles or lamps after that hour."

"Excellent news," said Louis. In truth it sounded trivial, a royal concession to the trifle of stargazing. Louis aimed the camera obscura skyward. His face was flushed and he could feel sweat on his back. "Do you have any specific instructions? I'm using a filter to diminish some of the glare."

"For both the sun and moon I require only one thing — some indication of their surfaces."

"And do you mind if I make two plates and keep one for myself?"

"Not at all. I didn't realize you were interested in the heavenly bodies."

"I find of late I am more and more interested in what goes on up there."

Louis positioned himself behind the camera. The sun floated almost directly overhead and appeared more white than yellow. He would use a very brief exposure on account of the sheer brightness. He opened the diaphragm and started to count, staring into the sun. The solar flare triggered something. He felt a prickle at the back of his neck, a raked sensation in his fingers. His eyes began to smart, but he couldn't look away from the tin-hued glare. He thought he could see thermal waves, whorls of hydrogen. Then a burn, a scalding in the back of his throat. He looked down at the ground and closed the diaphragm just as the seizure nabbed him by the neck. He knelt, shuddered, fell to the floor. His head hit the wooden planks. Arago was at his side, calling his name as if through a tunnel. The seizure passed quickly and left Louis staring up at the angry white sun. There were spectral colors in his vision, spirals of red and yellow. He made no sound. A bright and throbbing pain swelled up in his mouth.

"My God, Daguerre, are you all right?" called Arago, bending down. "Did you faint?"

"No, no, I'm fine. The sun blinded me for an instant." There was a slight sputter in his voice. He smoothed his tongue against his teeth to investigate. Arago squatted beside him. Louis tasted the sulfur of blood in his mouth, a warmth pooling behind one cheek. At the same instant the two men looked a few feet away and saw one of Louis Daguerre's teeth on the observatory platform. It was a front incisor, yellowed by age and diet, and with a delicate recess of blood in its crown. Arago looked at it with a mixture of disgust and disbelief. Louis fought a desire to grab it and put it back in his mouth.

After a long pause, Arago said, "Is that your tooth?"

Louis took out his kerchief and wadded a portion of it into his mouth. He saw himself as Arago might: the blood on his waistcoat, the maw of some wild animal crouched on the timber boards of the Paris Observatory. Louis gave in to a series of nods designed to control his own astonishment and repulsion at the sight of his tooth.

"A serious artist must give of himself for the work," he said. But neither of them laughed, and Louis had no choice but to acknowledge the moment by picking up his tooth with his kerchief.

"You must see a doctor. I insist," said Arago.

"That tooth has been loose for some time," Louis found himself saying. "The sun saved me a few francs at the tooth puller's."

Arago helped Louis to his feet and called for a clerk, who came hurrying with a chair. Louis recognized him as the reckless man who had unloaded his equipment from the carriage. He felt a burst of anger in his chest. "Get this man away from me. Don't let him touch me!"

"He's trying to help," Arago said.

Louis looked squarely at the man. "I remember you. We know each other, you and I." The man shrugged and Arago gestured for him to leave the chair. Louis reluctantly sat and watched the man withdraw a few paces. Louis mumbled, "No man is safe from the fury of the end."

Arago loosened Louis's neck cloth and unbuttoned his shirt, revealing the large emblem of the Legion of Honor. Arago and the clerk looked on as a single drop of blood spilled from Louis's mouth onto the nation's crowning symbol. He looked down at his chest. "On my way to get it resilvered."

Arago paused, his eyes locked on his friend's chest. Louis thought he could see, in that instant, an immense contempt wash over Arago's face. Was the sight of the cross on his bloody chest an act of desecration? Did he think Louis was an embarrassment to a noble tradition?

Arago recovered and said to the clerk, "Fetch him some water and a clean shirt from my study."

Louis said, "No, nothing from him."

The man hauled off. Arago put his hand on Louis's shoulder. "You're acting very strangely. You must have really smashed your head."

Louis shrugged with elaborate indifference. He put the kerchief to his mouth. "I got the sun. If you'll leave my equipment set up, I'll return tonight for the moon."

"There will be other full moons," said Arago.

"I insist. I feel perfectly fine. That tooth must have been a little rotten. I'm too much with the black-currant brandy these days."

The clerk returned with water and the shirt. Louis took the water, imagining it an act of contrition. He made a few tentative swallows. The blood seemed to be slowing.

"You can dress in the library. Nobody is in there," said Arago. "You'll come to it at the base of the stairs."

Louis moved uneasily across the platform. The sight of his own blood brought the smell of ether into his nostrils. He followed the stairs down to the library and closed the door behind him. Arago's shirt was made from broadloom cotton, the kind of shirt one wore sailing. Louis removed his bloody neck cloth, cravat, waistcoat, and shirt. He wiped the tooth with his kerchief and placed it on one of the shelves, next to a clothbound volume on celestial orbits. An odd sensation of satisfaction, of shedding bone, settled over him. He put his tongue into the newly created socket. It was on the bottom right and probably wouldn't show during a smile. Arago's shirt felt cool and smelled of lime starch. He tucked it into his breeches and walked back towards the observatory platform, holding the bundle of his clothes to his chest. Arago was pacing the rampart, occasionally looking up at the sun. He walked with his hands behind his back, shifting between the cardinal directions.

"Thank you for the shirt. I will return it this evening when I come," said Louis.

"I'll leave instructions with the guard to let you in. Are you certain that you are in good enough health?"

"As I said, an old rotten tooth."

"Well, I must get back to my dossiers. Very good of you to come, Daguerre," Arago said, patting him on the shoulder. Something had changed. Could you see a man spit out a tooth and take him seriously? Louis took out the exposed copper plate, wrapped it in hessian, and went downstairs to his carriage. He threw the bloody clothes next to him on the box seat and took off at a pace.

He didn't know which was worse, the humiliation of losing a tooth before one of France's fathers of science, or the scalding embarrassment of Arago seeing the Legion of Honor cross around his neck. He was a boy playing dress-up. He remembered with further humiliation that he'd left the tooth inside the observatory library—a bloody morsel of himself at zero latitude. Louis had almost brought himself to laugh at this when he saw a

flash of brown disappear beneath the carriage wheels. He heard
a high-pitched yelp and drew the carriage to a halt. He stepped
down and looked beneath the gig. He'd run over a small dog that
now lay, broken-limbed, panting in the dirt. The day could get
no worse. The animal was a motley hound, a reddish-brown cur
of the type found slinking behind wine barrels and feeding on
alley scraps. Its eyes were a dazzled yellow and it looked at
Louis while attempting to scoot forward on its two front legs. As
a boy, Louis had cared for lame sparrows and frogs rescued from
the jaws of cats and now he found himself fetching a felt blanket
for the injured dog from the wagon. When he crouched beside
the animal, it halfheartedly snapped at him before allowing itself
to be bundled in the blanket and placed in the carriage. One of
the hind legs appeared to be broken and rested at a strange
angle. Louis covered the dog with the blanket and rode back to
his studio slowly, trying not to pain it further. He carried it up
the long flight of stairs and placed it on his divan. Then he went
back for the hessian-covered plate. An hour had almost passed
and he would have to fix the sun's image rapidly. The thought of
ruining the plate after his degenerate display at the observatory
was gruesome. He heard Arago's voice at parties—the patri-
arch's baritone—as he lamented the passing of another great
man into obscurity. *Daguerre, yes, he was where it all started. Pity he
lost his mind. Mad as a hatter. Lost all his teeth.* Louis went into his
darkroom and lit the lamp beneath the mercury bath.

SIX

arly in the winter of 1803, a theater performance of *The Enchanted Forest* toured Orléans
and Isobel invited Louis to go along. After so
many months of silence, she could stand it no
longer. And if she dropped any more vases or
plates, her employer would surely dismiss her. She knew that neither of them had been to a play before and that, on some level,
Louis could not resist. He lived, after all, in a natural state of
drama, riveted by the three acts of dawn, noon, and dusk. For
Isobel it was a chance to be someone she was not — to take her
place among the theater ladies in their pelerine capelets and laced
bodices. She thought it a lark to be a pagan healer in disguise, an
alchemist in a borrowed petticoat — the only woman seated in
that shadowland who knew the medicinal power of wolfsbane.

On the arranged night, they stole out from their respective
households and met out on the glade after dark. Louis was
dressed in the topaz cravat and a worsted suit that made his
crotch sweat and itch. When Isobel came from the main house,
she saw him under the walnut tree, hands in his pockets. She
walked slowly towards him. She was expecting anger and si-

lence. Instead, Louis turned on his heels and said, "Hurry, my good wife. We'll be late for the theater, and I do so like opening night." For tonight he'd let the resentment go. Louis looked surreptitiously at Isobel's outfit. She wore a pale rose gown with scooped shoulders. Her hair was pinned up to reveal her slender neck. He couldn't bear it and looked down at the gravel.

They walked towards the road where Gustav, the coachman, had been persuaded to wait. The monsieur of the estate was away on business, and accordingly, all manner of infractions were being committed throughout the estate—stolen hams, illicit naps in the guest bedrooms. By comparison, Head Clerk Daguerre had redoubled his efficiency, showing up to work an hour early each day in an attempt to set the tenor of his employer's absence. Isobel and Louis passed through the rhododendron tunnel. They came to the carriage where Gustav was sitting on the driver's box, smoking a stout cigar obviously stolen from the château's library. He looked at the two of them—Isobel half a head taller than Louis—and jumped down from his seat.

"Allow me, my lordship and lady," he said, bending at the waist. He took Isobel's hand and helped her up into the carriage.

Isobel said, "Very good, Gustav. It's too bad the royalty seem to end up with their heads cut off, because you're very good at this."

Gustav looked at Louis. "Your father will tan my arse if he finds out."

"He's in bed by nine."

Gustav gave Louis a gentle shove and ruffled the boy's hair. Isobel let out a gasp of laughter.

"Stupid oaf," Louis said, climbing into the carriage. He recomposed his hair and put his hat on to prevent further spoilage.

They rode into Orléans, passing the stone canals that drained the Loire and the cloven pathways that led to darkened monasteries. Louis looked out at the crops of saffron; the crocuslike flowers gleaned silver in the moonlight. In the last days of autumn, farmers and their children harvested the flowers, bundling them into thatched carryalls. When Louis imagined these families at their kitchen tables, working to remove the delicate threads of spice and color from the flowers, he was overwhelmed by a sense of their happiness. The Daguerres were not known for passing peaceful hours in one another's company. Mother cooked and read the Bible, Father kept books and made commentary about the machinery that held the world and good commerce together, and Louis meandered the woods reading books and watching butterflies. Outside of household affairs — fetching water, chopping wood, minor repairs to the piebald walls — they had little to speak about.

A quarter hour before the performance, they pulled up at the theater and again Gustav acted as footman. He helped Isobel and Louis out of the carriage while the gathering theatergoers looked on. A low, scandalous murmur went through the crowd — doctors, lawyers, society wives, dress-uniformed officers in Napoleon's army. Isobel and Louis were dressed in the right style. Despite the revolution and the call for an egalitarian society, gentlemen still favored three or four waistcoats, a lineage of gold buttons, Polish trousers; the women continued to wear barege and merino gowns, gold fringed velvets, their hair up in chignons. So it wasn't the clothes of the two failed lovers that were amiss. It was their manner that faltered and, on closer inspection, their ages. Isobel walked as sure-footed as a dairymaid, and Louis, the supposed gentleman of the duo, trailed behind like a boy at his mother's skirts. Inadvertently, he'd given the woolen crotch of his pants an insistent tug as he stood up from the carriage seat. Sensing the scrutiny of the crowd, Isobel took his arm once again and told him to retrieve the tickets she'd given him. Louis rifled through his pockets, his fingers lingering over his good-luck charms: a magnifying glass, several butterfly carcasses, an acorn, and a piece of quartz.

"Here they are," he said, thrusting the tickets into the air.

They stepped up to the brass doors of the baroque theater, and Louis handed the doorman the tickets. The doorman's face, stern as a magistrate's, brightened when Isobel asked, "Are we permitted to sit together?" They'd imagined a section for the ladies and a section for the gentlemen. The doorman ripped their tickets in half, then let out a patronizing chuckle and told them not to heckle during the performance. Isobel's cheeks fumed red, and Louis began fidgeting in his woolen pockets for a favored piece of twine.

The theater was cast in a low light from candelabras and oil lanterns. The proscenium stage stood covered by a tasseled burgundy curtain. Louis craned up at the gilded ceiling and the cantilevered balconies that jutted above the house seats like great warrior prows. Isobel rustled a little in her gown.

"Thank goodness it's dark in here," she said. "I was about to challenge one of those awful staring ladies to a duel."

Louis leaned back in his seat. "They think we're married."

"I hope not."

Isobel knew from the silence that she'd said the wrong thing. "Poor boy," she said. "One day you'll see this as the hopeless thing that it is."

"One day when you marry some gouty old farmer, you'll remember how elegant I look tonight."

"You do look dashing. Perhaps the ladies were staring at you."

Louis raised a finger to his lips; he could hear the orchestra coming to the pit. The house lights dimmed and the curtain lifted to reveal a backdrop of canvas. A painted landscape of mountains, forests, and lakes. Pales of soft bluish light threw themselves against the set, giving the appearance of night. Louis looked for the source of the light. Long metal tubes with gas lanterns and glass lenses were suspended from a series of iron railings on the side of the stage. Colored pieces of glass had been placed in front of the light apertures. Now a yellow ball of light rose from the mountain range. As the sun swam into the sky, it banished the pale blue of night, and the sound of birds could be heard. Louis could see a man holding a cage of chirping sparrows at the edge of the orchestra pit. Louis leaned forward, lost to a new devotion.

The husky sound of a cello opened the score. Actors and dancers came out onto the stage. Violins, mimicking the birds, rose steadily; flutes and the timpani coaxed a brighter day onto the set. The light changes were gradual and each new effect, it seemed to Louis, was tied to some emotional shift. The damask and melancholy morning, the first blues of dawn and the yellowing of tree crowns; a noon of lustrous lakes and white haze; then an afternoon of verdure—the greens darkening, shadows becoming visible in the groves. An entire day spanned, cradled in the palm of the ethereal music. Isobel's hand found his in the darkness. She held his fingers lightly. He closed his eyes. He could smell her—camphor and rain, a perfume distilled from clouds. He knew she loved him.

After an hour of hand-holding and shimmering displays of light, the dramatic climax of the piece emerged. Isobel took her hand back and Louis lost himself to the drama. He had not been expecting such a dramatic ending. Although he read novels and knew something of how a tale unfolded, he had half expected the spectacle to simply wither and die without a crescendo. So, as a pale moon turned to oxblood, as a mountain stream was transformed by light and trumpets into a raging torrent, and as stage trees opened to reveal dryads and demons, Louis reflexively stood up from his seat. The man next to him tapped him with the butt of a rolled newspaper, and Isobel grabbed his hand and pulled him back down. A gale—the timpani unleashed—caused the trees to fall down, and a fiery red glow erupted across the stage. The demons and the dryads wheeled. As night fell, the dance-combat slowed between the guardians of the underworld and the wood nymphs, and the keepers of the safe ferny places had won out. The stage darkened and the final note of the cello floated up from the orchestra pit. Louis was unable to move. He closed his eyes for fear of seeing something as ordinary as a man dusting dandruff from his shoulder. He was sixteen, in love with a woman he could not have, moved by a desire to trap loveliness. Isobel took his elbow—she knew his moods and passions—and they remained in their seats until the theater had cleared. Finally, Louis opened his eyes, stood, and walked towards the front of the theater. Isobel watched him as he climbed the stairs to the stage. He leaned into the gold-tasseled curtain, trying to find the opening. Then, in an instant, he disappeared, swallowed by the proscenium arch. He was gone for several minutes and Isobel fought the desire to go after him; surely the ushers would come through the house any minute. When he came out, he was holding a green paper leaf. He looked at Isobel, his eyes on the verge of something. He opened and closed his mouth several times in consideration of speech. At last he said, "Nothing else matters."

She guided him out of the theater, through the lobby, and out into the alley where Gustav was waiting. They rode home, Louis with his head against Isobel's shoulder. He was entranced; there was no other word for it. As they neared the estate, Louis noticed the smell of wood smoke in the air. A caravan of peasants was spilling out of the estate's main gates—old farm nags hauling box carriages loaded with armoires and high-backed chairs, sides of meat, carpets; the village blacksmith, hunched, was carrying a Venetian mirror on his back; a rag-and-bone merchant looked up from his wagon of spoils and pointed to their carriage, to what he thought was the approaching aristocracy. Some cries came from the front of the caravan. Several people scrambled on the side of the road for rocks to hurl. Gustav turned the gig and galloped towards the graveled pathway leading behind the mansion. They could hear the sound of breaking glass and the crack and hiss of a fire as they rounded the fields and came upon the château. Gustav pulled the horses to a standstill and they watched the furious black smoke pour from the windows and doorways. The flames were more blue than orange, as if the trunks of jewelry, the lacquered walnut desks, the pelted chairs, the ivory trinkets hauled across the deep from Africa burned hot and pure on account of their value. Gustav ran to find the rest of the servants, to hear the story of peasant looting. Isobel and Louis watched the mansion burn to the ground, unable to speak. The revolution had found them.

SEVEN

he night after Louis Daguerre lost his tooth at the observatory, he dreamed of his own death. He was a boy again, running along a beach. It was nighttime and the salt air pressed into his lungs as he ran. The sand was coarse against his bare feet. Something moved swiftly behind him, gaining. The beach tapered to a narrow sandy spit, and soon he sprinted across the shallows. A boat strung with yellow lights sailed for the horizon and he knew that he must swim towards it. It was safety. He plunged into the cold sea, into a great rushing darkness. He tumbled and raked in the blackness. Then everything slowed and shapes emerged; amorphous shadows loomed from the green depths. He struggled, called out, the salt water filling his lungs. Right at the moment when he felt his chest would burst, there came a release, an emptying. He felt himself rise. As he did so, the shapes receded and he could see the luminous stars magnified and blinking through the ocean's surface, as if through a sheet of ice.

He woke coughing to find blood on his pillow—a chain of

small red islands. Sitting up in bed, he looked across the room and thought, *I'm dying*. The injured dog was asleep at his feet, its breath slow and rasping. Daguerre took a sip of water. He looked around the room, disoriented. A flask of mercury stood on top of his dresser, though he could not remember putting it there. He reclined against his pillow and stared at it—five pounds of the liquid metal, glossed by the yellow of the gas streetlights. This had been his boon, the addition to two millennia of experimentation with fixing a permanent image using sunlight. And he had discovered it quite by accident. It was Divine Providence, the hand of God. He had been chosen to bring this invention to his era.

Once he had discovered the power of this metal as his fixing agent, he delved into its history and lore. He became a devotee, a reader of the epic poem of quicksilver. It was a monarch in the ordained *tria prima* of alchemy, brother to sulfur and sister to salt. It had been the secret furnace of tantric recipes in India, had been poured into the kernels of Italian hazelnuts to form amulets against bewitching. It was the gleaming polish rubbed onto the point of a Prussian plow to prevent the growth of thistles in a turned field. It was the deathly unguent infused into loaves of hard bread to locate drowned and trapped bodies in the British fens, the loaves sinking to dead men like their souls in reverse. This metal that would not yield to form, that resisted the clutch of the human hand and yet was absorbed by the skin upon touching. A gift from the cinnabar mines of Spain. A metallic sonnet, a love letter written by God and veined through the earth for millennia, fissured through slate and sandstone, waiting for its highest calling.

He looked at the flask and suspected that mercury played some role in the end of the world. Objects and liquids had secret lives. A bent flower or a shiny brass button was part of a larger conspiracy. Everything conferred, leaned in. The signs and portents were coming faster now. Birds were singing on his balcony in the middle of the night. He needed to find Isobel Le Fournier before the world expired.

EIGHT

ouis left the glade for Paris. On the day of his departure, his parents came out to the carriage and his father pressed an envelope into his hands, saying, "Fifty francs towards your future. Found a household without debts and you'll always be your own man." There was a pause. Daguerre senior looked down at his fob watch—a clerk's old habit—before adding, "Don't marry a dancer. That's all I ask." Louis's mother handed him a basket of hard-boiled eggs and told him to go to church and bathe every Sunday. Louis climbed up into the carriage and it began to pull away. He knew that Isobel had already left in search of work, but he half expected to see her standing barefoot in the brook, a branch of rosemary in her hands.

In Paris, Louis found an apprenticeship as a scenic painter. He arrived in the city between an execution and a coronation. Midsummer, the duke of d'Enghien stood before a firing squad while a silk hot-air balloon rose from a hillside of heather. Then in December of that same year—1804—Napoleon, cloaked in embroidered honeybees and stars, crowned himself emperor while the pope looked on in the stony light of Notre Dame. The

Paris streets were full of bravado—the Municipal Guard lined the squares in their dress uniforms, the chestnut trees were draped with bunting. There was talk of invading England. Spies had been sent into Persia, India, and Australia. Louis had expected awe in the Parisian attitude towards Napoleon, but people spoke of him as a freak flood or a torrential storm. When he shot Josephine's pet swans one night after a tiff, or when he kicked his economic minister in the genitals after doubting the man's statistics, his deeds were recounted as episodes of weather, rants of nature.

That winter the sky hung pale and close; the river became tin. Louis took long solitary walks and tried to banish his love for Isobel. He knew that she'd gone south, to the vineyards. Despite this, he saw her everywhere in Paris that first winter—as a nut vendor's daughter sitting on a barrel near the Pont Neuf, as a young maid lighting a tallow candle in a mansion window, her eyes cutting through the dusk. He became aware of women breathing under corsets, of hair pinned by whale-bone barrettes. A young woman came in from a downpour and stood shivering on a grocer's stoop, Louis beside her. She smelled of rain and tea, and he found himself turning away, forcing himself out into the weather.

Each afternoon Louis walked a brisk circuit, a loop through Montmartre and out into the barrens behind the Left Bank, before returning to the theater. He walked past the public works that Napoleon had sponsored as part of the new empire—the granaries and wine cellars, the quays along the Seine. He waved at the old men who stood neck-deep at the river baths, bantering in their red stocking caps, their breath smoking up from the water. Everywhere men deliberated and conferred. Quarrymen trudged home from the gypsum pits, their faces dusted white with plaster of Paris. He would try to greet them, but they were lost to each other, to a flurry of advice about someone's destitute niece or anguished brother. Louis wanted to be recognized out in the street, to share the camaraderie of a people who now owned the streets and the markets. But nobody waved back or returned his civic greetings. He went to the same bakery every day for three months before the shopgirl said hello back to him.

For the first time in his life, he was frequently cold and hungry. His apprenticeship allowed him porridge, soup, mutton stew on Sundays. His wool coat was wearing in the front, and one of his boots was split at the seam. When Isobel rose into his mind — the camphor flame of her presence — Louis counted his steps and felt his hunger. It was a bone-deep hollow, an ache that carried into his spine. He found himself staring into restaurant windows, stupefied by families of cheerful diners. The taverns spilled a festive light out into the street. One night, in front of a patisserie, he was transfixed by a tiered wedding cake. It was a perfect landscape of snowcapped terraces, an artifact of happiness waiting to be delivered out into the world. He stood there, O-mouthed, his shoulders up from the cold, and understood that he was waiting for life to begin again.

Louis had earned his apprenticeship with Ignace Degotti, the master scenic painter at Theatre Clementine, on the strength of two watercolors — *The Glade at Dusk* and *Isobel on the Riverbank*, the light perfectly inflected in both. He also had to pay an entry fee — the *bienvenue* — of twenty-five francs for the privilege of joining the theater. As the latest apprentice, he was known as the *rapin,* which, he came to realize, was shorthand for brush washer, floor waxer, outhouse cleaner, canvas stretcher, paint mixer.

Louis slept alongside the other apprentices in an old storage room behind the stage. A number of iron cots had been dragged into the room to make a dormitory so that the boys — future prop

masters, carpenters, scenic designers, lighting and effects masters—retired beneath Gothic portals, Roman architraves, jagged
sections of Parthenon, painted shop facades, carriage wheels,
papier-mâché busts and statues. Louis slept under a small mullioned window that overlooked a back alley. Marius, the head
apprentice, had a bed at the end of the room inside a gold-
painted gondola that was suspended from the ceiling by metal
ties. He'd cut his mattress to fit the shape of the boat, and there,
in his suspended cocoon each bedtime, he enumerated the chores
for the next day. He was a big-nosed prop-master-in-training
and treated his apprentices like ship hands—calling them by last
name only and refusing to eat at the same table. The scenic design apprentices looked down on him, on his sausage fingers and
his nails bitten to the quick. He was a tradesman and they were
becoming artists; he was from Marseille, the son of a shipbuilder,
and they, for the most part, were part of the petit bourgeoisie, a
class on the ascent. Louis and the other scenic boys nodded to
his commands and called him Pork Chop behind his back.

One night, at the end of Louis's first month at the theater,
Marius woke the apprentices in the middle of the night and told
them it was time for the *rapin*'s initiation. Louis had been told by
the others to expect this, that Marius was particularly ingenious
at scheming up ways to induct the new boys. They all dressed in
silence. Louis, in what he thought was a flash of resourcefulness,
slipped a pocketknife and some coins into his back pocket. He
could imagine having to cut himself free from ropes or having to
pay for a carriage from the other side of Paris.

Out in the street, the apprentices fell in behind Marius and
he led them through the damp and gloom of Rue du Tourniquet, where the passageway was so narrow that two men could
not walk abreast. They walked single file, Louis in the middle,
through a district of brothels and underground gaming houses.
Near the dog markets they fanned out and Louis felt a sudden

urge to yell or run, to break the stupor of the dozen boys marching him to some unknown humiliation. The smell of canine squalor, something like wet fur and urine, was everywhere. Louis noticed a row of wooden cages that held that day's unsold inventory — Russian wolfhounds and Great Danes leering from the shadows; herding dogs from the Alps, their ribs worn into relief. The dogs were too tired or hungry to bark. For a moment Louis thought he was being brought here to fight a dog and wondered if his pocketknife could bring down a wolfhound, but Marius kept marching them in the direction of the Seine.

They finally stopped at the Quai du Marché, where the city morgue rose from the riverbank. Louis had not yet visited the morgue, though he knew it was a popular destination; the curious and the morbid came on Sunday afternoons to move among the dead. There was an exhibition hall where the corpses were arranged in naturalistic poses and the murdered reclined in armchairs. In another room, the new arrivals were laid out on marble slabs with their clothes hung at their side, waiting for identification.

Marius stopped a hundred yards from the morgue and turned to face the bedraggled boys. As if on cue, the boys pushed Louis forward. He felt their hands at his back.

"Apparently you can paint, but can you sketch?" Marius said.

"Of course," said Louis.

Marius reached into his coat pocket and produced some crumpled paper and a piece of charcoal.

"You want me to sketch the morgue?" Louis asked. "From the riverbank?" He looked over at the building: a rectangle of stone and mortar, fronted by a low wall.

The boys laughed at this. Marius took his time answering — the delight was in this particular moment.

"No, *rapin*," said Marius. "You have a special model waiting for you inside."

The boys had formed a half-circle around Louis and Marius. They leaned in, waiting.

Marius said, "You must sketch a particular corpse and stay in there for an hour. When you see the night watchman, ask for Frederic, a friend of mine. We will wait for you here."

Louis felt an insistent shove at his back and began walking, paper and charcoal in hand, in the direction of the morgue. He heard Marius say from behind, "And no fucking any dead old ladies, *rapin*."

The boys snickered at this and Louis heard them walk down towards the riverbank. His hands were numb from the cold and he put them in his pockets. He knew they would be watching him, so when he reached the front stoop of the morgue, he bounded up the stairs and knocked loudly on the wrought-iron doors. The night watchman appeared after several moments — a disheveled man in his sixties, a reek of whiskey on his breath.

The man peered through the heavy doors and said, "We're closed unless you're dead."

"I am here to see Frederic," Louis said.

"Is that true?"

"How would I know his name otherwise?" Louis said, shuffling from one foot to the other.

"Come in and be quick about it."

The door opened and Louis entered. He was immediately overcome with the smells of damp clothing and formaldehyde. They stood in the entrance to a long hallway, with dimly lit rooms leading off on both sides. The man settled into an armchair stationed by the front door and arranged a blanket over his lap.

"Frederic is all the way at the back. Follow your nose," he said.

Louis started down the hallway, his feet echoing across the slate floor. He passed the exhibition room where divans and armchairs stood arranged by the windows, where leather-bound books were splayed open on side tables. It resembled a sunroom in a country manor, a room where houseguests might retire to read after a meal. Further on was a series of closed doors, each marked private, then a flight of stairs. A wall sconce lit a small area beside the stairs and Louis could see a human silhouette through an open doorway. He came closer and heard a low murmuring—a man talking to himself.

"Hello?" Louis called.

The low-set voice stopped abruptly. A boy, not much older than Louis, appeared in the doorway, wiping his hands down his shirtfront. "Are you the *rapin*?" he said cheerily.

"I'm supposed to sketch a model."

"Excellent timing. I've put everyone away for the night except your special lady. My name is Frederic," the boy said. He extended his hand and Louis shook it. Frederic's hand was effeminate and cold.

"My special lady?" Louis said.

"Some of the others like to give the dead girls names, but I don't like that practice. I do like to call them ladies and give them proper treatment and all. They found this one in the river, black and blue like someone had taken a mallet to her." Frederic clasped his hands together and shrugged. "A whore, most probably, not that I've looked, but the ones they haul out of the river are usually whores. Sometimes they're suicides, with notes and rocks in their pockets."

The high, caustic smell of death became overwhelming. Louis put his nose and mouth into the crook of his arm and inhaled through the tweed of his jacket.

"Come on, friend, smells like a bed of roses in here," Frederic said. "Follow me and we'll get you set up."

Frederic led Louis back down the hallway and into the exhibition room. They walked towards the large windows that overlooked the river. An amorphous figure lay covered by a sheet on a divan.

"You get comfortable, and I'll get some more candles so you can see better. But first you need to meet each other so we can all start off on the right foot. I covered her up to keep her fresh. Dear, I'd like you to meet the *rapin*."

"My name is Louis."

Frederic said, "Louis, this is Lady."

Louis feigned a smile.

"She's not fussy, don't worry, your name could be Dog Balls for all she cares. Have yourself a seat."

Louis sat on a footstool at the end of the divan and Frederic lifted the sheet. At first Louis could not make out the naked girl's features, but then Frederic brought a number of candles and, by degrees, her mutilated form came into focus. She was a blond girl, no more than sixteen. On the side of her face was a bluish gash that ran from temple to chin. Her throat was swollen and purple, her lips gray. A series of diagonal welts covered her breasts and stomach. Louis could feel his throat tighten. Her body smelled strongly of vinegar and damp earth.

Frederic said, "Somebody had some fun with this one. They say drowning is the worst way to go, but I reckon in her case that drowning was the best part of her whole day."

Louis had never seen a dead body before, and what struck him was the vulnerability of the human frame: it was little more than a constellation of fracture points, a net of skin over some bones. Every woman—his own mother, even Isobel—carried the possibility of this kind of death, the threat of a secret and brutal end wrapped inside her delicate flesh. Frederic continued to bring candles, and soon Louis and the dead girl were encircled by a ring of half-light.

"No more candles," Louis said. "I can see her as well as I need to."

"As you wish."

Louis took out his paper and charcoal. He sat on the floor and spread the paper out on the footstool. He looked over at the windows where he and the dead girl swam in a reflection of candlelight. Outside, the river flowed dark and wide, and he wondered how many dead bodies were lying at the bottom of the Seine.

He put his first line on the paper, a curve that would become her hip and leg. He would leave her face until last and transpose the gash to the shadowy side of her face. The feeling in the pit of his stomach began to recede, and soon he lost himself to the problem of composition, to the trade-off between suggestion and clarity. Her hands were curled and he found the courage to touch her and straighten her fingers. There was a stiffness in her joints, but he managed to flatten the palms of her hands and lay them across her thighs. Her fingernails held river silt. Louis saw a flash of her in the murky Seine, an image of her climbing and raking through the brackish cold water.

By the time he was ready to sketch her face, two hours had gone by and Frederic had come in several times to inform him that he was free to leave whenever he wanted.

"I get the five francs from Marius after you've been here an hour," Frederic said.

"I'm almost done," Louis said absently. Without looking up, he reached into his pocket and held out a few coins.

Frederic took them and said, "Well, I've got to put her back in the cool room before long. I can't have her sitting out here all night."

Louis handed him the rest of the coins in his pocket. "Leave me alone and I'll be done shortly."

Frederic left the room. Louis reached up and moved a strand of hair from her cheek. She'd bitten her lip badly, and there was a speck of dried, russet-colored blood in the corner of her mouth. Louis would omit this detail from the portrait. The proof of her murder would not be in her gashes and bruises, but in the startled aspect of her face, in the martyred angle of her chin as it tilted towards heaven. Louis took his time with her eyes, sharpening his charcoal with his knife to ensure a good edge. Her features did not possess a deathly peace; her eyes suggested a lapse into troubled dreams, and her mouth was poised as if she might call out. Her lips were parted a fraction, just enough so that Louis could make out an edge of white tooth. That millimeter of space was the only suggestion that she had been alive, that her mouth had once moved—laughed, pouted, sung—because now it was a thing unhinged, a door that stood ajar between the living and the dead. Frederic came back a while later and stood insistently beside Louis.

"Outside it's morning," Frederic said. "I'm going home to sleep, and you have to leave."

Louis looked down at the portrait. The lines and shadings depicted as much as they concealed. The girl was both solid and ethereal, both beautiful and terrible.

"Very well," Louis said, standing.

Frederic looked down at the portrait. "That's not her," he said.

"She seems to be the only dead girl in the room." Louis folded the drawing and placed it in his coat packet. He turned for the hallway. From behind he heard the sound of Frederic wheeling a cart into the exhibition room. He kept walking, eyes down, because he did not want to see Frederic heft the girl's body like an animal haunch. The night watchman was smoking out on the front stoop when Louis opened the main doors. They stood there for a moment, neither of them speaking. The sun was coming up behind the tenements. They watched a wine barge pull slowly up the river.

Louis went down the stairs and made his way along the bank. The apprentices were nowhere to be found. He took the picture out one more time to look at it. Something in the defiant face and the upturned chin reminded him of Isobel. She was lost to him after all, as good as dead. He allowed her image to settle over him. He remembered her thin-boned feet and pictured them crushing grapes in some far-off vineyard. Her hands, her feet, these were objects in the world, no different than hinges on a door, but they seemed to him out of reach and utterly mysterious. He walked through the bustle of a Paris morning, imagining her feet stained muscatel. He watched the faces of passersby, looking for a smile to brim or a whistle to purse a set of lips, something to rally him back to the living.

When Louis arrived back at the theater, the boys were lined up in front of the main stage. The venerable Ignace Degotti, who kept a small apartment above the apprentice dormitory, was pacing before them in a silk bathrobe, his hands butterflying behind his back. As Louis entered, Degotti and the boys turned to face him.

"Ah, our illustrious *rapin* has returned for breakfast," Degotti said. He continued to pad across the floor in his leather slippers, head down, his shock of white hair ablaze under the houselights. "Please line up with the rest of the boys, Monsieur Daguerre."

"Yes, sir," Louis said, falling into line.

Marius scowled down the row of boys, but Louis refused to make eye contact.

Degotti folded his arms, addressing Louis but looking at the floor. "Our head apprentice has told me that you went out last night without permission and that the entire class of apprentices went out in search of you. Is that correct?"

Louis hesitated. Marius and the other boys stared straight out at the balcony.

"I had an appointment to take a portrait, and this was the only time it could be done."

"I see," said Degotti. "You do realize, my country friend, that Paris is a city with millions of people and that half of those are pickpockets and murderers and the other half are whores and common thugs. Did it occur to you that going out in the small hours of the night might have been, what, a little unwise?"

Louis shrugged.

Degotti nodded slowly, his fingers forming a church steeple in front of his lips. "I'd like you boys to start your chores immediately. There will be no returning to bed, and if I catch any of you napping, you'll scrub the pigeon shit off the rooftop."

The boys began to file out of the theater, Louis among them.

"Monsieur Daguerre, you can come to my study," Degotti said.

Louis stopped. A few of the boys patted him on the back as they walked by. Whatever the test had been, Louis had passed it. Degotti went out into the hallway and Louis followed.

Degotti's study was a rummage of books and canvas at the top of a flight of stairs. It was filled with artifacts from a life of artistic pilgrimage—lapis lazuli and gold-leaf etchings from Spain, jade figurines from the Pacific, African tribal masks—but all these objects teetered against the walls or rose amid a pile of ink drawings splayed across his desk. Degotti sat in an ancient leather chair and gestured for Louis to sit down. The only other place to sit was an ottoman that was half concealed by scrolls of tracing paper. Louis perched on the edge of it.

"I'd like to see the portrait so special that it brought all of our apprentices out into the Paris night," Degotti said.

Louis felt for the portrait in his coat pocket and slowly brought it out. He felt an odd and brief moment of betrayal, as if some secret he and the drowned girl had shared was about to be violated. He handed it to Degotti. The master painter took out his half-rim spectacles and held the portrait by the window. The sun had risen above the rooftops, and Louis could see the outline of the girl through the back of the paper. Degotti held the picture at different angles — flattened, then broadside — before resting it on his desk.

"Who is this girl?" he asked, still looking at the drawing.

"Dead, sir. A drowned girl at the morgue. She was quite beaten, but I didn't want to show so many of the bruises. She had one gash, for example, on the side of her head."

Degotti squinted. "The place where the neck meets the shoulders is wrong. When a head is tilted back like that, the neck is broadened. Also, the feet look too small in proportion to the hands."

"I tried to draw what was before me."

"No, you drew what you wanted to see," said Degotti. "You tried to make a dead girl appear beautiful." He looked at his fingernails.

"I thought she deserved to look beautiful," Louis said.

"Are you sure the dead want our flattery? Look at this." Degotti picked up the portrait and pointed at it. "The cheeks, the eyes, the way her mouth is poised, the way you allowed a shadow across her stomach and breasts to give her some modesty . . . the angles and the light, although flattering, are not possible."

"I took some license," Louis said.

"However, I have to admit it's fairly remarkable. You managed to find something that was still alive in her."

"Thank you, sir."

"Who said that was a compliment?" Degotti put his hands

into the pockets of his bathrobe. "Do you know what a scenic painter does?"

"Paints the sets for dramas," Louis said.

"Sometimes what we paint is the last thing Paris sees before she goes to sleep for the night, before people go to their dreams. But we don't paint just for the sake of an arresting image — we must serve the drama. We must be able to paint the sea exactly as it appears during a storm or as somebody who is dying might remember it. We follow a vision larger than our own. I was asked once to paint a portrait of the pope in the Vatican. My instruction was to capture only that which was godly and stern. The portrait looked nothing like the man, but the Vatican paid me twice what I asked for."

"I see." But Louis had no idea what the point of the story was.

"Every artist must have the technique to first capture what he sees, then the vision to capture what he doesn't see. And you seem to want to skip the first stage."

"I'm sorry," said Louis.

"No, you're not. There's arrogance in this kind of technique, a hunger." Degotti cut his pale eyes across the desk at Louis. The old Italian had a habit of avoiding eye contact; he spoke to an undefined and shifting space before him. "Now," he continued, "as to your punishment. It's clear you need to be reined in, or soon you'll be painting angels and wood nymphs when we ask for villagers and peasants. Each morning you'll get up at four and start your day in the mixing room. You'll be our master paint mixer and brush washer. When you can mix anything that I ask for and its hue is perfect, then we'll consider that part of your apprenticeship to be over. You won't paint a single inch of a set until you can provide the most distinguished palette in all of Paris."

"I didn't join the theater to mix paint," Louis said, holding back the note of anger he felt gathering in his voice.

Degotti shifted his hands in his lap. "Take your portrait and go join the other boys."

Louis stood and picked the portrait off the table. When he went out into the hallway, the apprentices were gathered at the foot of the stairs—all of them but Marius. Louis was holding the portrait in front of him, and one of the boys called for him to show it to them. Halfway down the stairs, Louis turned the picture to face them and they all looked at it in silence. When he reached the bottom, he delivered the portrait for closer inspection. The apprentices—teenagers from Provence and Burgundy, boys waiting to cross the threshold into manhood—stared at the delicately wrought flesh and bone of a drowned whore, and not one of them could think of anything funny or crude to say.

Light was different in Paris. Around Orléans it was green-tinged and full of lucerne haze, or it was saffron-hued from the flower and spice harvests, and these had the effect of softening the edges of things. The hills near Orléans were washed out by crop shimmer and distance; they stood perennially out of focus. Farmers thought they had myopia. But here, in the city, the light was hard-edged; it refracted off a million windows, sharpened by glazier's sand—a yellowy-white powder from the riverbanks of the North. It was absorbed by masonry and alleys of brickwork. Paris light was complex and variable; it traveled in vectors, condensing here, refracting there, whitened by the aqueous mirror of the Seine, taking on greens and blues and reds in summer. As Louis took his walks in the spring, he tried to memorize the light and the effect it had on color.

At midday he saw the sunny splendor of the Tuileries Gardens, where men sat in lawn chairs, reading newspapers and magazines rented from a kiosk. He saw the diamond white of the glasshouses, where a three-hundred-year-old orange tree still hung with fruit. The shopwindows in this district were full of delftware—a cross between pewter and bone in broad day-light—and slabs of Belgian chocolate that stood as solid and brown as the earth itself.

He learned how to mix all these colors in the cold and damp of the theater basement. In the hours before dawn, he worked the vats of oils and tints, re-creating the strange metallic blue of the Seine in winter, or the umber of the tenements after rain. He learned to mix test swabs on the back of his hands, to spit in a batch of paint that was too clumpy, how to keep Degotti's camel-hair brushes in spirits for just the right amount of time. He did this for more than a year. When he took his walks after break-fast, his hands were calloused and there were specks of cobalt and sienna under his fingernails. He watched the day form in the shopfronts, in the avenues of glass and stone. Each day, between his paint-mixing duties and his house chores, he had several hours of leisure. He concealed this fact from the other boys and complained of his aching shoulders at breakfast. Marius—smelling of wood glue and tobacco—would nod smugly at these complaints and devise new chores for the *rapin*. Once a month Marius told the boys to line up their shoes around Louis's bed and instructed Louis to clean them. Louis could imagine hurling the shoes out the window, but instead, he cleaned them each in turn, smearing a rag in shoeblack and buffing them to a shine. He wouldn't let Marius unhinge him.

Degotti allowed this to happen, partly out of a belief that one should conceal talent from the young. Although he knew that Louis could make a startling vermilion from mercuric sulfide, that he could probably make the finest Moroccan turquoise in all of Paris, he was waiting for the moment when the arrogance he'd seen in the portrait of the dead girl would bring Louis storming out of the basement. He would not allow the boy to paint a set until Louis demanded it.

In his hours of leisure, Louis began preparing for life as a gentleman. He took dance lessons in a studio in Montmartre. He sat alone in the bohemian cafés where actors and poets gathered. He made lists of writers and philosophers as he followed the thread of an argument. On a hilltop behind the barrens, he read the letters of Saint Augustine, the allegories of Plato. On the last Sunday of each month, he wrote to his parents. These letters were full of long passages about the cafés and the river spilling light. He trained his handwriting to be beautiful—a convent nun's hand, the hooped and fluid cursive of feminine devoutness. Louis's father wrote back with an economy of style and ink, chronicling the weather in Orléans and speculating that Louis had fallen in with gypsies and vagabonds. *No,* Louis wrote back, *I am preparing for a great and serious life in the theater.*

And he felt that life gathering in small gestures and moments. In the smile that rushed across a woman's face as he bade her good morning, in the streets brimming with exotic fruits and flowers. One autumn evening, he spoke to a table of serious-minded poets at his regular café. They stared at him. He was seventeen, tall and lean, with a dozen specks of paint on his hands and clothes, and they took him for a seasoned artist from the neighborhood. They had been discussing the idea of absolute truth. Louis said, "There are infinite shades of blue, but there is only one that is the primary blue. Surely truth is no different." At first several of the men scoffed and glowered at their mugs of beer, but later, Louis was brought a glass of wine compliments of the poets. He drank it and felt something light in his chest. He thanked them on the way out and they called him *little brother.* The rest of the day he dreamed of his future self—a young man in a vest, a painter and philosopher, someone who could dance a waltz and a jig, who could tell a joke and recommend a restaurant. But each time this excitement for a vibrant future ended with an ache for Isobel. He saw an image of Isobel on a daybed, curtains aflutter in a sun-dappled room. He saw a wooden house in the country, children playing in an orchard. And he wondered who had fathered these phantom children.

More than anything, he wanted to be rid of the penance of these images. Midway through his apprenticeship, still mixing paint in the basement before dawn, Louis decided to seek out the company of women. He did not want love; he wanted distraction. Initially, he frequented venues where he was bound to find young women with lamentable scruples. He went to provincial hall gatherings and market soirees on the fringes of Paris, to cabarets in the Carousel District. He did not approach the most beautiful of the young women he encountered—that rare class of beauty which had found its way into a shopkeeper's family like an embezzled diamond. Instead, he circumnavigated the venue and looked for a flaw that drew him in: a narrow gap between the teeth, a widow's peak pointing down like an index finger, excessively thin lips, distended elbows, pigeon toes. These traits aroused his curiosity; he thought they might be signposts, as if a woman with gapped teeth might be prone to self-doubt and pity, as if thin lips might betray a poverty of the spirit. He wanted to solve the riddle of imperfection.

He kissed a girl named Matilde—a sea merchant's daughter with a mealy mouth—in the halo of a gas lamp outside the Institute for Deaf-Mutes in the second arrondissement. In the cheery lantern light of a dance hall, he held hands with Claire, a nut vendor's daughter. The girl would not kiss him and talked incessantly about the wood pigeons she fed slivered almonds each morning. Then came Rose and Audrey, two English cousins visiting their spinster great-aunt on the Right Bank.

Degotti, in an attempt to jump-start Louis's ascent, had arranged for him to give drawing lessons to the girls. Louis was delighted to augment his apprenticeship with a few extra francs. He borrowed better clothes and showed up at the spinster's mansion with his camelhair brushes and inks and charcoals, a purple cravat ablaze around his neck like some tropical bird. He was shown into the large drawing room, where a white spitz slept on a large divan. The walls were mounted with bear heads and oil paintings of British admiralty. Madame Treadwell, the spinster aunt, came into the room a short time later.

"I imagine you are the art tutor," she said in superb French. She was tall for a woman and still rather young to live under the weight of the title *spinster.* She sat opposite Louis, petting the white dog on the divan. She spoke with her eyes down, as if to the cur. "There will be no drawing of nudes, do you hear me? I am rather interested in perspective and should like my nieces to learn the structural aspects of drawing. I assume you are versed in all the foundations?" She looked over at Louis as if in afterthought.

"Yes," said Louis, "all the basic principles." The truth was he drew and painted mostly on instinct.

Madame Treadwell allowed herself a smile. She took out a cigarette and smoked it while divulging stories of her childhood days in Africa, mentioning three times that her father hunted leopards and bushmen in the same afternoon. Louis realized, after an hour, that he was being held captive in the room. Several times she got up and took a drink of brandy at the side cabinet. She stood at the window, waving smoke from her hand as she gestured. There was something sibylline in her carriage and bearing, a glazed and diaphanous look to her eyes, as if she might be plagued by communiqués from the dead. After some time she leaned close to Louis and said, "You may go and conduct your first lesson, monsieur."

The butler—undoubtedly British, to judge from his jowls and melancholic eyes—reappeared and showed Louis out into a courtyard where two girls sat before easels like repairing aristocrats in a Swiss valley.

"We'd all but given up on you," said the shorter one. Her French was atrocious; she sounded nauseated.

"I was being interviewed," said Louis.

"Seduced, more like it, if I know anything about my aunt," said the taller girl. She placed her accents on the wrong vowels.

They introduced themselves. The taller one—a seventeen-year-old girl with a mole on the side of her neck—was Audrey. The shorter girl was Rose, a pale-faced delight, the skin around her neck and shoulders so white it was luminous. She sat beneath an epic sunhat.

"What are you going to teach us?" asked Audrey.

"Perspective," said Louis.

"I should think the French know very little about that subject," said Rose. Audrey offered a well-timed giggle.

Louis wanted the fifteen francs he'd been promised and refused to be baited. "Well, ladies, let us draw the confines of this courtyard, using all the rules of proportion. First we will draw a grid on our blank paper," he said flatly. The young ladies reluctantly turned to their easels.

This appointment continued for the better part of six months and led to a three-part addition to Louis's romantic experience. Audrey told him to kiss her one day when Rose had taken ill with a cough. Audrey said she was going to kiss a Frenchman before she went back to England, and it might as well be him. Louis complied. It was a dry-mouthed, brief affair that sent Audrey into the house chuffed. Two weeks later, Rose said she knew of the illicit kiss and threatened to tell the aunt if he did not repeat the favor with her. Louis obliged with a kiss, and he would have gladly unfolded many more across the veiny riverbed of her neck. But she stopped him, walked towards the house, then returned and put her hand inside his trousers to the count of ten.

"If you move or touch me, I will scream," she said. "My aunt is taking her nap and she so hates to be disturbed."

Louis stood with one elbow on an easel while Rose's hand gripped him. He felt faint and slightly sick to his stomach. He walked home that evening, his desire groaning like an ale press, and for a day he failed to think of Isobel and was thankful. He pictured Rose in a thousand different ways. When he returned to the mansion, he was told that Madame Treadwell had summoned him. Louis went upstairs and found the woman reclined on her bed, a cigarette wafting from a limp hand.

"From now on the girls are going to be studying mathematics instead of art," she said.

"I see," said Louis. "Have you been unhappy with my services?"

"Come in here, Louis, and close the door."

Louis obeyed. He could smell brandy beneath the tobacco.

"I'm going to do something for you that should have been done some time ago. I thought they treated this kind of thing in a civilized city like Paris. My God, there's a mademoiselle of the night everywhere you look." She sat up on her bed and placed her hands on his shoulders. "How old are you, Louis, and don't lie."

"Almost eighteen," Louis said.

She began unfastening his pants and removing the plumage of his cravat. She moved without hesitation or lust, the look of a simple chore on her face, as if she might be portioning a teacake for guests at a party. Louis found it hard to breathe. He was standing naked, a foot from the bed. He became aware of his knees.

"Now, don't be anxious. Lie down and get under the sheets. We'll take a little nap together."

Louis found himself obeying. The faint smell of down came from the pillows. Then came the surprise of her hand beneath the white bedsheet. He felt as if his chest were going to explode.

"In general, a gentleman who looks intently up at the ceiling or at the weave of a rug might find a way to delay climax. This will prolong the pleasure, if you receive my meaning." Her speech and her hand were mismatched—her languorous voice defied the steady stroke of her fingers. After several minutes she guided Louis on top of her. Louis felt the odd moment of perfection as she gave way beneath him. Something in the room crystallized and he looked her dead in the eyes, startled, for the first time. The fear was gone; whatever power she'd held on account of her wealth, age, and parentage evaporated in this one cleansing moment. They were both surprised by his vigor. He did not study the fleur-de-lis in the ceiling or the faint roses of the rug; he studied the lines in her face, the blemishes that came with a decade of resignation to a childless middle life, and it was pity that kept him on top of her for two hours. They made love until they were sweaty and exhausted and sore about the joints.

Afterward, Louis walked home, jaunty and light on his feet. He returned to the theater to find an assemblage of scuffed footwear around his bed. A note from Marius read *Clean enough to eat off.* Louis looked down at the shoes—boots with lopsided heels, shoes with ragged leather tongues, the footwear of provincial chumps who fancied they could paint. He kicked the shoes under his bed and went to find Degotti. The Italian was sitting in his study, door open, slippered feet up on the desk, nursing a cup of coffee.

"I've come to tell you that I wish to leave the theater," Louis said. He was surprised by the forceful tone of his voice.

"And why is that?" Degotti said, a half-smile on his lips.

"Because I didn't come to Paris to clean shoes and mix paint for boys who have half the talent that I have."

Degotti said nothing for a moment. He pointed at the empty chair with his chin. Louis, his hands curled and his shoulders tense, took a moment to uncoil and sit.

"There's a mountain village outside of Sienna where the women go to bed with volcanic mud on their faces. They say they dream of Vesuvius and wake without wrinkles. I spent a summer there hauling buckets of pigment out of caves, just so I could capture the color of the clay on their faces. I didn't paint a single picture all summer. I hauled the clay back to Rome. Then, months later, I woke at three in the morning and began a painting of the women, and it became my most celebrated work. A painter needs to know when not to paint."

Louis said, "I can't stand it any longer. I have to paint. I can create the most delicate shade of blue, but then some halfwit from Dijon slaps it on the canvas like it's wallpaper glue."

Degotti smiled. "I've been waiting over a year for you to come bursting in here."

Louis felt a flush of anger in his cheeks; everything in this theater seemed orchestrated for his belittlement. "I want to leave and join another theater."

Degotti folded his arms. "Without my letter of recommendation, that would be very difficult. I will be happy to let you go, but first you have to paint me a set. It's only fair, after I've invested in your education."

Louis looked down at the floor.

Degotti added, "As you paint the set, you will answer only to me."

"And I won't clean another shoe the rest of the time I'm here?"

"Agreed."

Louis allowed himself a smile; the spectacle of a whitewashed canvas fifty feet across came to him. He stood and left the room before the image evaporated.

❧   ❧   ❧

Louis's first stage design was for a drama set in Tuscany. There was a village surrounded by a wall, olive groves hemmed in by cypress. He worked twelve hours at a stretch, until his eyes ached from the close work of foliage. Degotti was true to his word, and nobody tried to instruct Louis except the master himself. He spoke to Louis in a vague, personal shorthand, asking him to silver the clouds or shimmer the treetops. Louis understood the effects Degotti had in mind, the way movement and shifting light could be implied by brushwork. For a year he'd walked the Paris streets with his eyes squinted so as to reduce the world to swaths of color and light.

On his days off, Louis returned from his dance lessons or his evening walks to stand alone in the theater. While the apprentices slept above him, he brought up the houselights. Sitting in the front row, knees drawn to his chest, he stared out at the Tuscan panorama. Everything was in balance; the eye moved from one delight to another. He wanted to enter the panorama, to stand among the gilded trees. One night, as he engaged in this secret act of indulgence, Degotti shuffled into the theater. Louis anticipated anger at the misuse of the gaslights, but Degotti looked pensively up at the set. He nodded, cocked his head, then finally spoke. "A boy who paints this well is either in love with a woman or in love with the world. I hope for your sake it's the latter."

They stood there a moment, dazed by the Tuscan hillside, before Degotti slipped quietly from the room.

Louis could not sleep. He went back out into the overcast Paris night and found himself walking in the direction of Madame Treadwell's mansion. Several afternoons a week, for months now, he had made love to the spinster in a mahogany bed that had been hauled across two oceans from Mozambique. While Rose and Audrey strained their minds around trigonometry in the courtyard with their new tutor, Louis and their great-aunt bedded each other with the pluck and technique of gymnasts. They never kissed. It was bed sport, an exchange of wills and pleasures. They spoke little, except to instruct the other. Tonight, when Louis showed up unannounced, Madame Treadwell looked both pleased and appalled. She led him quietly upstairs to the bedroom. She drew the curtains with a sense of ceremony, as if closing a country house for the summer. Louis took off his clothes, lay on the bed, and looked up at the ceiling.

Madame Treadwell lit a candle, undressed methodically, and began kissing Louis's stomach. It was not so much tender as businesslike—a profusion of meager kisses, a bread-crumb trail that led to his groin. When she straddled him, Louis felt his mind go blank. It was this captive moment that he craved. He watched her above him, her eyes closed, a stray hand clutching at her own breast. He watched the sway and bob of their shadows on the ceiling. It made him think of the drowned girl from the morgue, of something rising through water. Suddenly, he wondered what that girl's name had been.

A few moments later, Madame Treadwell stopped moving. He looked up at her. She unstraddled him and took his limp penis between her fingers. She held it the way a scullery maid might hold a kitchen mouse. "I can't do much with this," she said.

Louis felt himself redden with shame. "Sorry. I was daydreaming."

Madame Treadwell stood and began dressing. "Do us both a favor and don't ever come back to this house."

Louis sat up in bed and reached for his clothes. He was surprised to feel a tremendous sense of relief. He stood for a moment in the doorway, watching her dress. Neither of them said goodbye. He descended the stairs and went outside. The streets were dark and empty. He moved among the neglected Right

Bank mansions. For the length of several blocks, he had the sensation of being the only person alive in Paris.

At the end of his apprenticeship to Degotti, Louis, eager to try his talents on a larger canvas, accepted a job with the renowned panoramic painter Pierre Prévost. As a farewell present, Degotti allowed Louis to work on the scenic painting for Cherubini's opera *Medea*, which was being staged at the National Opera House in the spring of 1807. Louis spent months painting sections of canvas — endless Greek statues and architraves — but was never permitted to see the completed set. Degotti had made Louis paint eight different versions of ancient Corinth, each time changing only the most minuscule detail — the width of a temple facade, the color of the rooftops.

On opening night, master and apprentice went to the opera together. From the exterior, the opera house resembled an elaborate train station — Waterloo Station with baroque swirls and turrets. But as they merged with the crowd of haircloth collars and chignons, Louis saw the rather drab lobby open into a cavernous temple. They had seats in the balcony, and from this vantage point Louis could take in the whole opera house — the musicians in the orchestra pit, their violins and oboes captured in small nets of light, the cantilevered balconies with their hooded archways suggesting grottoes.

Louis sat in his borrowed cape and watched the old aristocrats move to their seats, the paper-faced women in their burgundy gowns and jewels, the timber barons in their stovepipe hats. They chatted with vivid hand gestures and elaborate nods; money, it seemed to Louis, allowed one's personality to expand. He watched them until the lights dimmed. The conductor raised his baton and the curtain lifted. As the proscenium opened, Degotti nudged Louis and showed him the program where *Louis-*

Jacques-Mandé Daguerre was listed as assistant designer. Louis whispered a thank-you to Degotti and turned to look at the stage. *I am part of this now.*

What amazed Louis was the way the set had been married to the action. His own scenic rendering of Corinth—cypress trees diminishing into a red-sky horizon, flagstoned streets the color of tarnished bronze—looked like a bygone city. Degotti had told Louis to make it resemble "the museum of a city that once knew wealth and happiness," and Louis had created suggestions of opulence from a previous era: corniced public houses, stone-cut steps, well-constructed battlements, but all of them strewn with ragweed and dulled by age. It was as if the city's destiny had been poisoned by the murderous spells of Medea. The busts of Greek gods had been arranged in a semicircle, and as Medea threatened Jason and her children with murder, they were lit in such a way as to suggest ghosts floating through an ether. When Medea's servant, Neris, delivered the poisoned diadem and cloak to the new bride, there came the sound of ringing bells, and Jason's screams lifted from offstage. Then Jason's tenor aria, a lament for his dead bride, surged as the Greek gods disappeared one by one and the stage was swallowed in shadow. The temple burned to the ground as Jason realized Medea had also killed his children. Midstage, an oxblood bolt of silk flowed across the steps. Columns toppled. The scenic depiction of Corinth— Louis's montage of Greek masonry—was set to flame. Louis leaned forward, startled, then looked at Degotti. The Italian moved closer and said, "If I told you I was going to burn your work every night, you never would have painted the set." Louis looked back at the stage and watched his canvas go up with the slow flames of paraffin. The audience was aghast; the sound of Jason's voice mirrored the glimmering of the town, a long and undulant death wail. It was perfect and terrifying.

When it was over, Louis heard the sound of three thousand

people standing to applaud. He watched the stagehands douse the set with water and blankets. Finally, he and Degotti stood in silence and went downstairs to the lobby. Louis walked in a half-trance, reliving key moments, gliding his hand against the banister, when he saw a striking woman standing with a man by the main entrance. It was Isobel, now in her early twenties. He felt his blood jump. Louis made his way to the bottom of the stairs, unable to take his eyes off her. She stood in profile and hadn't seen him yet. The man she was with looked old enough to be her father. He noticed Louis staring and sidled towards the door, a proprietary hand at Isobel's elbow. But something in the man's gait made Isobel turn and look towards Louis. At first she did not recognize him, due to his additional height and heft, but then she must have seen him smiling. Louis pushed off the railing and began to walk towards her. He heard his heels on the marble floor and knew that tonight he'd been at the source of something great. He was smitten with his role in this grand conspiracy. Isobel was holding a program. *She saw my name, yes, and insisted on waiting for me.*

He was a few feet away from Isobel when Degotti came shuffling across the marble in his Turkish slippers. Louis felt a flush of pride that three years after the night of watching the old mansion burn to the ground, he was now beside one of the most esteemed artists in the nation, emerging from an opera he had helped to design. Then the sheer weight of seeing her again. Her beauty was etched in; it no longer had the transient quality of a girl buoyed to loveliness by adolescence. She was still a middle-risen peasant girl, but there was now a veneer of gentility, and Louis realized in an instant that she had undergone her own apprenticeship these last few years. Someone with money, undoubtedly the gentleman at her side, had taken her under his wing. She was, after all, a maid at the opera.

"Isobel," Louis said. That was all he could manage.

"I can't believe it," she said.

Louis turned to Degotti and introduced him, then Isobel introduced the man—Gerard Le Fournier, a banker from Lyons. Degotti, in a sudden display of loyalty to his apprentice, engaged Gerard in a serious conversation about commerce and art and led the stiff-backed banker outside. Louis and Isobel passed ten seconds of silence.

"There's only so many times I can look at your shoes," Louis said.

Isobel laughed and folded her arms across her gown. "When I saw you at the stairs, I wanted to run and kiss you."

"I'd like to talk to you," Louis said. "Are you living in Paris?"

"No, we just came in from Lyons for the opera. We're staying at a hotel and returning in the morning." She glanced out through the glass doors.

"Gerard is your—"

"Fiancé."

Louis pitched his hands into his pockets. "There—I am looking at your shoes again," he said.

There was more silence. Louis heard the echo of the ushers' footsteps. Isobel adjusted her pearl necklace and shawl.

"Do you still carry dead butterflies in your pockets?" she asked.

Louis lifted out a coin and a piece of lapis lazuli. They both stared into his palm.

"I can find a way for us to speak. Can you meet me at a café at midnight?"

Louis nodded. "Café Senegal, near Pont Neuf."

"I'll wait for you there," she said. She turned abruptly for the glass doors.

Louis walked slowly into the men's washroom and splashed some cold water on his face. A man in a white linen vest appeared out of nowhere and commenced doing the same beside him, splashing the Seine up into his flushed face. Louis realized after a moment that it was the conductor, a Czech man with counter-sunk eyes. He stood before the silver-backed mirror and, without looking at Louis, said, "Did you enjoy the opera?"

Louis straightened his cape and said, "I painted the set."

The man smiled and headed for the door, saying, "That's funny, you don't look like a seventy-year-old Italian." The door closed and Louis stood before the mirror. He was growing a mustache and realized it looked terrible. He waited several minutes to avoid the spectacle of the banker from Lyons.

They met at the café. Isobel, still in her opera clothes, arrived flushed and a little breathless. Louis sat at a table outside, rolling the piece of lapis lazuli in his hand. He watched her approach. She still had a flat-footed walk, and she held one arm at a slight angle, as if it might be injured.

"Is your arm broken?" Louis said.

She sat, shook her head. "When I saw you at the opera, I thought you were a gendarme. You've broadened."

"Good, we've exchanged our first insults. Now we can talk. And I don't think I can bear to sit here. Shall we walk?" he said.

"Yes," Isobel said, standing. She took his arm and they headed towards the Pont Neuf. The streets were still busy with theatergoers and cabaret crowds siphoning out towards the river. Louis composed routes in his mind. By now he knew the city as only a daily pedestrian could—the secret courtyards where widows grew their antique roses, the view of Notre Dame from the barrens, its Gothic silhouette against the skyline—and he wanted to show her passageways and shortcuts, evidence of his time here. Paris was a city of warrens, of escape routes. He could feel her gloved hand at his elbow, the hand pressure one reserves for dancing.

"I'm tremendously proud of you," Isobel said. "You still seem like a boy to me but you're not. Look at you."

"I'm nineteen," Louis said. He felt a moment of condescension approaching. He warded it off by taking her hand and helping her across a loosened plank. "There's so much to catch up on," he said.

"Tell me everything first. You must be outrageously talented. I saw the set. My God, Louis, people were mesmerized by the temples."

Louis found her speech affected. "People are easily mesmerized," he said.

"If you're going to be falsely modest, I'll leave right now. You must be very happy."

"Thrilled," he admitted.

They stood on the apex of the Pont Neuf and looked down at the Seine. It was dark with field runoff, and at the base of the bridge there were eddies of flotsam—twigs of straw and wine corks in a brownish foam. He would kiss her. That thought hummed at the base of his spine. These three years had led to this, to kissing Isobel by the Pont Neuf after midnight. She leaned against the railing of the bridge.

"I've thought a great deal about you these last few years," she said.

"Me as well. I tried not to, but you've cursed my mind."

"That estate near Orléans was enchanted, even if he was enslaving us. Sometimes I think liberty is a waste of time."

"Is that why you're getting married?"

His question lived in the air for a long time. She pulled her shawl around her and turned her back on the river. "I met Gerard after working in a vineyard. They were horrible people, I can't tell you. Mean-spirited. They made me scrub the vats until my hands bled. I went to Lyons penniless and tried to get employment as a governess. Gerard is a widower and his wife had died from consumption. He placed an advertisement looking for a maid to cook and clean."

Louis could not look at her. "And now you're betrothed and attending the opera together. I suppose you found exactly what you always wanted. A man with more money than talent. Someone to let you dabble in plants and herbs. Voltaire said people do not change."

"Voltaire also said weakness on both sides is the motto of all quarrels."

"Good. We've both read Voltaire." Louis began to walk towards Notre Dame and Isobel followed. He walked fast enough that she had to stride out to keep up.

"Are you jealous?" she called from half a pace behind.

Louis stopped dead and turned to her. "I have loved you since I was twelve." He waited for a man with a cane to pass by. "These last three years you've walked the stage of my mind every night. Do we choose these things? Or do they choose us?"

"Voltaire again?"

"No, that was me."

She was softened now. Was she glad he was jealous? He walked on, holding this moment of power like a ball of wax in his pocket. A single kiss and then adieu to this boyhood fantasy; the kiss would be the bridge to his new life. They walked more or less side by side and found themselves in the forecourt of the grand cathedral.

"Where were you the day Napoleon was crowned?" Louis asked.

"I don't know. Cleaning grape stains from my feet."

"I was right here, watching. On that very stone wall over there."

They walked towards the building. Louis looked directly up at the gallery and said, "Does the bell ringer live inside?"

"Surely he must," said Isobel.

"Ringing the bell four times an hour—that must be quite a life. But in its own way, it has beauty. His tones are heard all over the city. He wakes a million men for work every morning. Yet none of us knows his name or what he looks like."

"You're still prone to philosophy and grand ideas," she said.

"And you're still prone to pragmatism and a lack of feeling."

She shrugged as if this had been expected. They stood in front of the main portal, where Louis had watched Napoleon linger in his honeybee-and-silver-starred cape. He had gone in a general and come out an emperor. In the precalculated seconds leading up to the kiss, Louis did nothing exceptional. There was no sweetness of words, because in fact this kiss would be a protest, a lament for everything past. He simply stared at her lips. He could see the porcelain edge of her teeth, the tumescent tremor in her lips that indicated either imminent tears or the contemplation of a new topic of conversation. Louis closed his eyes, thought of Napoleon crowning himself, and moved his mouth to hers. There was soft on softness. There was the slight wetness of her mouth and then the surprise of her hand on his neck cloth. They stood kissing in the mouth of the cathedral, inside a Gothic dragon's open jaw. It was not one kiss but a multitude. A dozen repetitions, each slightly different. The corner of her mouth, the piece of flesh beneath her nose, the bottom lip in isolation. To Louis she tasted exactly the way he had sewn into fantasy—orange rinds and the saline of tears. Louis was the one to stop first, and he would remember this as one of his proudest moments, that he had the dignity to cease kissing a betrothed woman. He was entitled to this kiss. They looked at each other.

He said, "That first kiss in the wine cellar didn't count. We were drunk."

"You've looked at me funny ever since I used to bathe you and put cold presses on your head. You were a sickly boy."

"You used to poison me so that you could be my sickmaid."

She laughed. She held her arm at that strange angle again. This time Louis thought of an injured bird.

"We won't talk about this kiss anymore," she said.

"No."

"We'll walk some more, and then you'll take me back to my hotel."

"And then you'll get married to that old banker and have children and find excuses to come to my operas. I'll leave signals in the sets for you. If you see a red lamp, that will mean I haven't stopped loving you."

"Louis."

"I can't help it."

"But look at us."

"I will never ask you if you love me, because somewhere you decided that you didn't. I suggest somebody inform your mouth of that decision."

"You stole that kiss from me."

"Like you stole the first one. And if I did, the vault was wide open."

"Life is more complicated than you know."

"Life is more mysterious than you know."

She tightened her shawl and walked across the forecourt. A light rain had begun to fall and Isobel held her face up to it. Louis came beside her.

"The pagan peasant girl is still in there," Louis said.

"I suppose you realize our country no longer believes in those divisions."

"Yes, and that's why we see the beggars wearing purple capes."

"I suppose you believe in the monarchy," she said.

"I believe in the system that gets in the way the least. I want to paint and apply my art and be left alone."

"You will never be left alone."

"Why do you say that?"

"Because you're going to be famous."

Louis knew this to be true; he saw it sometimes in the shop-windows when his reflection passed, the glimmer of who he was becoming.

"So you could marry me and I'll have enough money to keep you. I'll build you a hothouse for your herbs."

"Is that a proposal?"

"More of a prophecy."

"I could never marry you, Louis."

"And why is that?"

"Because I am carrying Gerard's child."

Louis stopped walking. He looked at her stomach. He found himself squinting. Isobel put a thumb to his cheek and wiped away a tear. He felt a burning in his stomach. He looked down at the ground, then back at her stomach. There was no bulge yet, but he imagined a child burrowed within, perhaps no bigger or more elaborate than a walnut. He could not stand here any longer. His life was a lie.

"I'm sorry," he said, "but I have to leave. Can you— A carriage. Over there, they will take you."

She tried to grab his wrist, though this would come to him later, along with the kiss and the walk and the drizzle. What he wondered was how fast he could run. He took off running, thudding across the humpbacked bridges and bounding up the alleyways, striking his fists out at the air and allowing his breath to get loud, taking the steps between garrets two at a time. His chest heaved and a foot began to come through one of his shoes. He leaned against a railing and threw his shoes into the river and ran on barefoot, a part of his mind contemplating his shoes as two sloops making their way to the Mediterranean, another part feeling the macadam and gravel on his feet. He sprinted towards the theater and arrived in the dormitory to a pile of shoes on his bed — a farewell present from Marius.

He walked, calmly now, to Marius's suspended golden gondola. The head apprentice sat up, somehow waiting for what had been coming. Louis positioned himself beneath the gondola, a hand on each side, and lifted it free of the metal hooks. The other boys were awake now, sitting up in their beds, as Louis carried Marius in his boat around the room. The boys cheered, drowning out Marius's demands and threats. They came alive, boys who were too young to fight and bear arms at the Bastille or in the battlements now had their moment; the revolution was here; it was everywhere; it arrived one morning at breakfast, it slipped into your room at night and asked you to pummel those in charge, to defy your station, to assert your will. Louis dropped the gondola. It splintered and buckled on the hard floor. Marius fell out and covered his head out of reflex. The boys descended, fists flying. Somebody covered Marius's mouth to stop him from yelling. Louis punched through the darkness like the rest of them.

NINE

t Louis's insistence, Baudelaire sent a party invitation to a Le Fournier at 72 Rue de l'École. Louis had dispatched a messenger to the address in question, and the boy returned with two facts that seemed hopeful: the mailbox read *Madame Le Fournier,* and in the window of said dwelling sat all manner of strange-looking plants. Louis imagined valerian, pulsatilla, arnica. He added a single line at the end of the printed invitation: *An old friend looks forward to your company.* He wrote it in his monastic cursive, included several rose petals inside the envelope, and finished it with sealing wax. If this Le Fournier turned out to be a different person, there was still the possibility of finding his nude model in the party crowd. He had, by now, captured the relatively easy items on his doomsday list — a boulevard, a flower, the sun and moon — and was ready for the more challenging images. It was possible that the bohemian gathering would yield both an apocalyptic nude and Isobel Le Fournier.

That the bohemians knew how to throw a party was widely known, and word of a night of excess had spread to the outer

stands of the city, passing on the lips of cabdrivers and costu-
miers and tobacconists, all of whom stood to gain from the pomp
of the dandies. A thousand people turned out this Saturday night
in May 1847. For the previous three years, since his parents had
cut him off from his capital, Baudelaire had lived in an abandoned mansion with a dozen other artists on the Boulevard de
Budé. They had divided the house according to bohemian
schools: Poet's Corner on the top floor, complete with rooftop
terrace; the Painters and Philosophers on the floor below, each
with separate washrooms; and the Aesthetes on the ground
floor, men who spent their last francs on musk perfume and
Neapolitan shoes.

The mansion stood at the end of a street built too close to the
cabaret district. As the century wore on, the boulevard's inhab-
itants—coffee importers, ship owners, the thin-boned relations
of nobility—had sold their mansions on the cheap or abandoned
them for their provincial châteaux. Baudelaire and his friends
called this district the "graveyard of the ancien régime." The
houses were built in a high-Gothic style, hewn from stone, tre-
foils over the lead-framed windows. A procession of gargoyles
lined out the pointed gables and the ramparts. To Louis, the
mansions looked like mausoleums, the mortuary houses of a people who worshipped conceited and spiteful gods—sinister half-
men, crazed chimeras, griffins with one claw dipped over the
roof ledges like cats drinking from an abyss.

Louis walked through the urine stench and the gas-lit aura of
the cabaret streets, then emerged into corridors of warehouses,
and finally passed into the long row of squatter-mansions. He
was thrust along by the sheer momentum of the crowd. There
were so many people in front of Baudelaire's mansion that Louis
thought briefly about returning home. In his greatcoat and Louis
XIII hat, he felt like an aging diplomat come to call on a man of
the people. He looked into people's faces, categorized them ac-

cording to age and gender. When he entered the front gates, he felt a moment of pity. *Here are the masses shuffling through one last hurrah.* He looked at their feet and spotted a woman's exquisite leather shoes, boneblack and glossed under a sconce. He felt a tear brim. Lately, he was easily brought to tears — a by-product of slow mercury poisoning. A country glee or a well-made shoe could set him off. It was a kind of nostalgia for everyday objects and sentiments.

He collected himself. First thing was to find Isobel. She was in her early sixties, perhaps long-haired, grace-figured, and there would be a note of discord in her appearance, a subtle sign of rebellion. Perhaps a startling set of gloves, a mismatched stole. Since the passageways of the mansion were congested, and because Louis feared an eruption of his cough in close quarters, he set off through the side gardens. An old orangery had been plundered with rocks, and thistle crested through the shattered glass. Stone cherubs were poised to urinate into dry fountain beds. Some of them had been decapitated, perhaps a gesture of the 1793 revolutionaries when they had barricaded and looted these streets. Louis tried to appear friendly to passersby while scanning for an elderly woman. He walked towards a strange and lilting music. A band of mysterious figures went by: a man in a red Basque beret was walking a lobster with a piece of twine; a tall fellow dressed in a polar-bear costume carried his bear head by his side, its great maw agape at his armpit. They were talking about the animals of Asia, about birds with curved beaks and tigers that could outrun a steam locomotive. *The strange ether of other people's lives.*

Behind the mansion, under trees on the verge of blossom, was a makeshift carnival. Musclemen lifted stone garden angels above their heads. Acrobats climbed ropes tethered to tree branches. Stunt-makers in tights juggled fire sticks. Rockets exploded from an unknown source. People cheered and hooted from the balconies of the decaying house. Louis looked through the crowd. He felt old and dull. He was sure the crowd saw him as a costumeless old sod, somebody's father or flatulent uncle, a man who wandered into other people's parties for the brandy and the company, with scraps of paper in his pockets. A skinny man on wooden stilts towered over him. Louis moved close to a stone pillar for safety. He watched a blind man dressed as a clown play a street organ, its hurdy-gurdy drone like some heretical witch call. *Are we already dead and these are hell's prefects?*

He wanted to go home, take a glass of rum and seltzer before bed, and dream of that day in 1802 when he kissed Isobel amid the tannic air of the wine quarry. Perhaps the memory was better than meeting the woman transposed four decades. Just as he thought this, he saw Baudelaire, dressed in a silk frock coat, running across the lawn towards him. The poet was holding a ball of nougat in his outstretched hand as if the fate of the Christian world lay in its circumference. *Here comes hell's warden with the latchkeys.*

"The thief of light himself," said Baudelaire, bending into a regency bow.

"Hello."

"What do you think of the party?"

"You've outdone yourselves," said Louis, attempting levity.

"Our function is to tickle the boundaries of taste. I have a surprise for you." Baudelaire nibbled at the nougat.

"Dare I ask?" asked Louis.

"I think I may have found her."

"Madame Le Fournier?"

"No. Your nude. She claims to be a cabaret dancer, but I have a feeling she's a lioness, if you receive my implication."

"What? Is she a prostitute?" Louis could feel his head perspiring under his hat.

"Don't be so vulgar. She's an aspiring consort."

Louis heard the high whistle of a launched rocket and instinctively ducked. He raised his voice. "I didn't bring my camera, and nighttime is not so suitable, so we best leave it for now."

"I don't imagine she'll undress for you in my garden. But I can introduce you. She's at the back, in the garden pavilion. We agreed on a hundred francs, correct?"

"If she's the one," said Louis. He fought a very real desire to flee. He couldn't focus on the idea of the nude portrait with the possibility of Isobel at the party. "But I need to find my friend," he said, gesturing towards the teeming crowd.

"Come meet the nude and have a drink. I'll send word around with the Aesthetes to find Le Fournier. You must press on with your portrait list. France needs you, Louis." Baudelaire looked at his friend and smiled. He took a strange pride in knowing that he was the only one privy to Daguerre the national hero *and* Daguerre the doomsday oracle.

Baudelaire took Louis by the coat sleeve and led him out towards the darkened corners of the garden. The garden pavilion was an apparition of glass and sandstone. Two jasper columns guarded the entranceway. Above the half-walls were sheets of glass fitted between sections of welded iron, and these sheets formed a transparent peaked roof. As Louis entered behind Baudelaire, he smelled something earthy and fungal. It reminded him of when he was a boy on the estate and he had sometimes watched the farmhands rooting for truffles with sack-bellied sows, the pink and bristling necks of the pigs bulging from short catches of rope. That smell, something like dead leaves, was enough to make the pigs bite and shriek. Louis followed Baudelaire down a passageway containing espaliers of miniature fruit trees, and up ahead there came murmuring voices, lost and speculative in a meandering conversation. A series of candles was alight in various positions around the open area. Two women and a gentleman sat in armchairs, watching a small fire pit. A noxious ribbon of smoke spiraled up towards an open glass ceiling panel.

"Friends, this is Monsieur Louis Daguerre, father of the daguerreotype," Baudelaire said as they came close.

"Good evening," Daguerre said.

They introduced themselves: Monsieur Girou, an astronomer; Eggshell, a barmaid; and Pigeon, the alleged cabaret dancer. Eggshell and Pigeon appeared to be in their thirties, and neither of them wore a wedding ring. Louis attempted to exchange a few pleasantries about the balmy evening and the large crowd, but they would have none of it. They were intent on the fire. Louis thought he could make out the object on fire: it appeared to be an old coat of arms, crossed heraldry swords and full-plumaged birds stuck to a shield. The coat of arms was damp and full of mildew — hence the smell.

"What is it we are burning?" Louis asked after several minutes of silence.

Baudelaire said, "It used to hang in the drawing room inside. It belonged to the previous owners — a general and his family. We're sending out their ghosts."

"Yes, of course," said Daguerre. He sat down beside Pigeon and stretched his hands towards the fire pit. Pigeon and Eggshell found this very amusing.

"Are you cold, Monsieur?" asked Pigeon over her wine goblet.

"I have a cold."

Some nodding. Some silence.

Baudelaire was over by the other man. "Monsier Girou is what we might call an avant-garde astronomer," he said.

"How so?" asked Louis.

"He doesn't believe in the existence of the sun. But after popular pressure, he has conceded the existence of the moon." Baudelaire smiled at the women, who were in giggles. Arago was right; Paris was full of madmen. Louis looked at the astronomer. He was a man of perpetual lip-licking and hand readjustments; something hemming and bucolic about him—a nervous country vicar on the brink of a sermon. The man nodded, fondled his hairy knuckles, and raised his eyebrows, braced for mockery.

"I would have thought Copernicus had put the issue to bed some time ago," said Louis.

"Sir, just because we see perhaps something orange in the sky doesn't mean it exists. We see dreams at night, does that make them real?" Girou said.

"My dreams are real," said Louis.

The astronomer said, "No, no, here is the thing: the sun is, how should we say, an invention of the calendar . . . a convenience of the state."

Louis stared at him, waiting for the linchpin item in his behavior that would allow him to hate the man without remorse.

"Mystical astronomy. I have to say, it's quite a notion," said Baudelaire. "What do you think, ladies?"

Eggshell, pretty in a childish manner, fresh-skinned and bright-eyed, rubbed a hand down her dress pleats and said, "I knew a man, a regular at the tavern, who believed the sun had set inside his own head."

"Sunset cranium!" cried Baudelaire.

"This is madness," said Louis, scanning the faces for a rational ally. "I make photographs from sunlight. I have spent my life studying its movements, the way it travels between two fixed points. If there is no sun, then none of this is real."

"Perhaps that's true," said the idiot astronomer.

Louis felt a cough rattling in his lungs like a rat in a sewer. Suddenly, he looked over at Pigeon and his chest expanded. She sat peeling an orange with her long bone-white fingers, laying the crescents in her skirt. "Would anyone care for a piece of orange?" she asked. "It's a little bit like the sun." Her face was delicate, a fine nose, high-blown cheeks, but her mouth was solid, wrought by some heavier flesh and perpetually a little open. Her mouth reminded Louis of a basalt cave. Her hair was the color of cinnamon bark, a color Louis knew would register well in a daguerreotype. She painstakingly pulled the pith off each piece of orange so it was smooth and flawless. This attention to detail seemed natural in her. As he selected a piece of orange from her ruffled skirt, Louis grazed a wave in the gown with a finger. He put the orange in his mouth. It was extraordinary—a quince bite followed by an explosion of sweet citrus. Baudelaire, Girou, and Eggshell each took an orange portion and ate in silence, dumbstruck by flavor. Mercifully, the argument about the existence of the sun abated.

Eggshell, in a burst of jocularity, said, "Know what they call this color taffeta I'm wearing?"

"Do tell us, my gooseberry," said Baudelaire.

"*Spider meditating a crime.*"

They all laughed at this, even the astronomer.

"Oh, that's very good," said Baudelaire. "Tell me some more of the colors at the department stores."

"Light green is *lovesick toad* and pale gray velvet is *frightened mouse.*"

"Poets of the gown." Baudelaire nodded, grinned, then stood abruptly and began twirling around. "These are the times, friends, the crucible of the heavens. In America, Poe is scaring a nation, and here we are naming the spectrum of ladies' garments after startled mice and jilted toads. Splendid, splendid. Any more of that wondrous orange, Pigeon?"

"One more piece," said Pigeon.

Baudelaire tiptoed over to her lap and lifted the piece with extreme delicacy. "I think our friend the lonely astronomer should have it." He turned and marched towards Girou, who looked admiringly at the piece of orange. "If I give you this last piece of orange," said Baudelaire, "you have to promise you'll stop this miserable mule shit about the nonexistence of the sun."

Girou looked at the orange, then swallowed. "Esteemed sir, I cannot make such a promise."

"Fine," said Baudelaire. He threw the orange piece into a small parabola above his head before opening his mouth to receive it on his tongue. The fruit poised there a moment, an orange star at the entrance to a grotto.

"Bravo," said Louis. He hadn't wanted the astronomer to get the last piece. In a wave of confidence, he leaned over to Pigeon and was about to mention his need of a model when a man in a Venetian mask came into the garden pavilion. The man came to Baudelaire and whispered something. Baudelaire's face brightened. He said, "It's time. Come with me, friends."

Eggshell clapped and jumped up, grabbing Pigeon by the hand and running outside. Girou, still miffed about the orange, stood slowly and looked one last time at the fire pit before plodding across the slate floor. Louis came close to Baudelaire. "What's going on?" he asked.

"What do you think of Pigeon? What a find," Baudelaire said, taking Louis by the arm.

"She may do fine."

"Don't you think it fitting that the final portrait of a woman should be of a whore? The Madonna of our age charges by the hour."

"I really must go find Madame Le Fournier. Could you ask Pigeon if she's interested in modeling for me?"

"There's plenty of time for Le Fournier. As we speak, my minions are stopping any woman over forty. We will find her, Daguerre. I'm not sure who this woman is, but if she is here, I will find her for you. Now," Baudelaire put his arm about Louis's shoulders, "I'm having a secret gathering up in Poet's Corner, and you're invited. We're doing a scientific experiment. Pigeon will be there."

Pigeon stood in the entranceway by one of the espaliered trees, touching the spindled branches with her long fingers. Louis found himself caught between the past and the future, between wanting to balance the cosmic ledger and wanting to sit for an hour beside a beautiful woman who smelled of oranges. He looked at his watch: ten o'clock. There was still time.

"Come," said Baudelaire. He turned and dashed out of the pavilion. Louis followed him outside but soon got caught up in the crowd. The poet, the astronomer, and the two ladies disappeared ahead of him.

Inside the mansion, people spilled from all directions, out of the ruined drawing rooms and anterooms, hoisting carafes of wine, eating yellow custard from plates. Ladies in pleated dickeys were being shown a line of oil paintings that hung in a long hallway, illuminated behind candles in sconces. Men in sugarloaf hats held court with Moroccan pipes in one hand. Louis took the wooden stairs two and two. On the second floor, he waited a moment while his chest convulsed. Down the hallway, an argument was under way between two groups of men who were loading small boys into a laundry chute. "Yes, yes, petit Jerome, five francs if he makes it all the way to basement." Jerome, his sooty face peeking over the metal chute hatch, looked terrified. There was some money exchanged, and then the chute closed and the boy's voice echoed as he shot between floors.

"Where is Poet's Corner?" Louis yelled to the men.

"Top floor," somebody yelled back.

Louis turned and took another flight of stairs. The walls were cracked and bloated with moisture. Copies of Italian masterpieces, caked in grime and dust, hung in the final stairwell. One depicted the torture of a saint, his rippled white back being flayed by dragonets and archangels. Louis felt his throat grow dry as he looked at it. He took the last steps, calling out for Baudelaire. The top floor was quiet, and the rest of the house and the partygoers seemed distant, as if he were listening to a banquet from the end of a tunnel. There were bedrooms off the main hallway, and as he walked, he caught glimpses of the poet lairs, like monk cells, where antiques lay stripped and mottled by age. Louis XIV chairs with splintered legs and frayed seat cushions now seemed ascetic and grim. The feather mattresses—the conjugal bed of a French general, the bedding of his virgin daughters who'd fled the revolution in the night—were now piss-stained and tawdry. Louis leaned against a door frame and found to his disgust that he was weeping. He took out his kerchief and dabbed at his eyes. It wasn't the stained mattress or the chairs that looked like objects dredged from the Seine; it was something else. He tried to retrace the tears. First the tortured saints on the stairwell, then the general's daughters escaping their mansion in the night . . . given enough time, the poet and the general sleep in the same bed . . . Was that it? No, it was a memory of the older revolutions, of coming to Paris the year Napoleon became emperor and noticing the jasmine in bloom and peasant children playing cork-penny in the alleys. There had been a feeling of change in the open-air markets, of salt before a sea storm. Those days, he thought, everybody was building utopias, like castles in Spain. That was when he'd begun crying. A box of matches, the beds of generals where poets now slept— the end of the world was being sung to him in its details. *Who will eat the last orange on earth?*

He put away his kerchief and walked towards the end of the hallway. He opened a heavy door covered in crushed Utrecht velvet. Inside, his companions were seated around a large round table under a domed ceiling. A gentleman whom Louis did not know bent over a side table, tending a range of dishes.

"Come on, Grandfather, we're waiting on you." Baudelaire

gestured for Louis to sit in the empty seat between him and Pigeon.

As Louis came towards the table, he looked up and noticed a painted allegory faded beyond comprehension. Some shadowy greens, perhaps some foothills in Italy, and an expanse of bleached blue that may have been a lake. He looked over to the man at the side table.

"The doctor is almost ready," said Baudelaire.

"Doctor?" repeated Louis, sitting down.

"I'm terribly excited," said Pigeon.

Louis nodded and, out of pride, gave her to understand that he was abreast of the evening's agenda. The doctor, a man in his sixties wearing a black smock, turned and carried to the table a wooden tray filled with Japanese porcelain saucers. He placed the tray on the table beside Baudelaire and smiled magnanimously. Louis stared at a crystal dish out of which rose a dark mound.

"Greetings, good friends, and thank you for coming to our first dinner," the doctor said. Louis looked over at the grim-faced astronomer.

"As you may know, Charles and I share a common interest. We are currently collaborating on a series of experiments involving cannabis indica, which is a member of the nettle family. We are privileged tonight to sample and experiment with some very rare Bengalese plants that just came ashore. We have mixed the cannabis with butter and opium, forming a potent green paste. I recommend you swallow it, then drink a cup of coffee. Throughout the evening I will be noting your reactions to the paste, and I may, with your acquiescence, ask you some questions."

Louis, unable to contain himself any longer, said to Baudelaire, "What is this?"

But Baudelaire ignored him and addressed the other guests.

"Herodotus describes how the Scythians gathered piles of hemp seeds on which they threw stones heated in a fire. It was a steam bath of sorts, with far-reaching medicinal and meditative effects. This plant, which is scorned by most of our countrymen, is being accepted in some quarters of the medical establishment. Our esteemed Dr. Aultisse is conducting research that may prove, once and for all, the benefits of this plant for the insane, for those with chronic maladies, and so on."

At the conclusion of Baudelaire's comments, the doctor handed each of the participants a saucer with a smear of the green paste and a vermeil spoon. Louis formulated a plan in which he would spoon the paste into his kerchief when nobody was looking. But when the Turkish coffee — black and with the grounds left in — was dispensed by the doctor, it was clear that he intended to inspect the mode of ingestion. Monsieur Girou ate the green paste and swilled his coffee with the expression of a man tasting an uncertain vintage. To Louis's horror, the others began applauding, and the doctor, his arm crooked as that of a Right Bank waiter, said, "Very nice indeed." Eggshell went next. Her mouth bittered at the hashish, then she swallowed her coffee with her eyes pinched shut. She waved a hand in front of her mouth and gestured to the water jar. She drank some water and recomposed herself. Baudelaire spooned his hashish into his coffee and downed the concoction with a swift throwback of the head. The doctor sidled around to Pigeon, his face demure, lost in a kind of ministerial efficiency, and watched her drink the coffee.

"Will I see things?" she asked.

The doctor remained silent and gestured to the Japanese saucer. Pigeon filled the vermeil spoon and brought it to her mouth. When she swallowed, she placed a hand to her throat. The doctor returned briefly to the side table, then came and stood next to Louis, who saw the small wooden spatula the doctor carried in one hand. Everyone was watching him—passengers pulling away from a train station. He thought about outright refusal, but he didn't want to seem antiquated, especially to Pigeon, whom he regarded as more suitable to his photographic task as the hours passed. He tried to formulate some scientific interest in the plant, draw some allegiance with the Greeks and their hemp baths, but in truth he found the whole enterprise childish. The world was slipping away while men sought their salvation in the solace of wine and the balm of crazed nettles.

"We're leaving without you," said Baudelaire.

"Sir," the doctor said in a genteel, professional way.

Pigeon gave Louis a brief, encouraging smile.

"In the name of science," said Louis. He picked up his coffee in one hand and his spoonful of paste in the other and in two movements consumed both substances. He felt a slight convulsion in his stomach.

In a short while, the doctor served a meal. Louis had a brief coughing spell that left his fingers tingling and a cold sweat on his back. No one seemed to notice. He looked down at the table. The silverware was agleam, laid out as if for surgery. Nobody spoke as the doctor came around with slim-necked flasks encased in raffia, German steins, Flemish water jugs, earthenware plates arranged with sausage and buttered asparagus. Louis was relieved to find that he had an appetite. He noticed that his companions had been transformed in the candlelight—their pupils dilated and ominous as owls', their mouths like mail slits in old wooden doors. They ate in a silent reverie, the silver arc of their utensils cutting through the half-light.

Louis watched Pigeon cut her sausages into little logs and swim them through her butter sauce. He wondered whether now might not be the time to ask her to be his model. He wanted to go downstairs and begin his search for Isobel. Suddenly, he became aware of Girou and Baudelaire engaged in conversation.

Baudelaire smiled over his plate of food, cutlery poised, and said with some delicacy, "I suppose you realize, Monsieur Girou, that you have a very large head?"

A long silence. Louis heard the Utrecht velvet sway on the double doors.

"I beg your pardon?" said the astronomer, spittle in the corners of his mouth.

Pigeon and Eggshell erupted into laughter.

"I am merely commenting on the size of your cranium. It's a behemoth. I suppose you are accustomed to people commenting on it."

Louis looked at Girou's head and noted its size; Baudelaire seemed riveted by its sheer volume. Louis held back a colossal urge to snicker.

The astronomer scratched a wrist and cocked his head to one side, a planet shifting on its axis. Louis laughed despite himself.

"My head is the normal size for my body," said Girou plaintively.

"Balderdash, it's a good three sizes too large. You must have your own hatter. I don't mean it as an insult, because surely it indicates a very large brain. But I wonder," Baudelaire said, glancing at the near-hysterical Eggshell, "if you find that you've developed certain eccentricities on account of your head. I have a good friend who has a very large nose, a proboscis of sorts, and he's modified his personality accordingly. He wears very colorful waistcoats and cravats—you see my point? A kind of camouflage."

The doctor, poised at the sideboard, scribbled something in a leather-bound book. The scratch of the nib on the paper filled the room, a knife blade on whetstone.

Girou said, "I don't wish to continue this conversation. I was under the impression that I was a guest here, not a source of ridicule." He took a swallow of brandy and left the table, shuffling over to a divan against one wall.

Louis could feel the man's humiliation; for a moment he *was* Girou, sitting on the divan, flummoxed and sour. "Leave the man alone," he said.

Baudelaire set down his cutlery. "He's a fraud. The sun could be rising and setting inside his own anus and he wouldn't know it."

"Charles, the ladies," said Louis in a curt tone.

Baudelaire looked up from the table, his eyes softened, and said, "I am sorry."

"You should apologize to your guest," said Louis.

Baudelaire nodded gravely and stood. He walked and sat next to the sulking astronomer on the divan. Eggshell rubbed a drop of wine into the side of her neck.

Pigeon leaned close to Louis and said, "His head is not so terribly large. I've seen bigger. Poor man." He looked at her. The drug had flushed her cheeks and brought dimples into her smile, added conspiracy to her tone. She said, "Perhaps Baudelaire's point is merely an aesthetic one."

"You don't sound like a cabaret dancer," Louis said, regretting it instantly.

"Because I have opinions and speak proper French?"

"I meant no offense."

Pigeon cut another sliver of sausage and put it in her mouth. Louis looked briefly at his fob watch: it was past eleven. Pigeon stood and crossed to a window in the rear of the room. He followed her. They came to a double window that overlooked the rooftop terrace and the Paris night. Great blue clouds plodded slowly over a silhouette of weather-vaned rooftops and church steeples. The stars and the gas lamps of theaterland pinholed the grayness.

"Those clouds are like the great thoughts of the century,

waiting to be had," said Louis. He heard his own voice from a distance.

Pigeon said, "My hands are humming." She loosened the latches and opened the window. A light breeze, cut with almond blossom, came in. "It makes me want the countryside," she said.

"I grew up in the country," said Louis.

"Lovely, isn't it?" It was a question that wanted no response. She closed her eyes as the light wind blew in over the terrace. There were a number of poets out there, sitting in Gothic armchairs, drinking from goblets. Louis could hear a sporadic conversation about Shelley and Keats. He looked out at the cindery darkness, at the array of chimney cowls and ivy-laden turrets. The scene was maritime, the mastheads and riggings of a flotilla. He was about to offer this insight to Pigeon—whose eyes were still closed—when he heard someone approach. He turned and saw the doctor walking towards them with his leather book.

Louis said, "Madame, I have some rather delicate business to discuss with you."

Her head now swaying slightly from side to side, Pigeon said, "I'll do it. Baudelaire told me. A hundred francs for an afternoon."

Louis didn't know what to say. Finally, he said, "I will be in communication." Isobel was downstairs; he was certain of it.

"Baudelaire knows how to find me," Pigeon said matter-of-factly. "I've done it before. Modeling, that is."

The doctor was upon them, leafing through pages, dipping the nib of his pen into a little ink bottle he carried in one hand. "How are things progressing over here?" he asked.

"I feel quite wonderful," said Pigeon.

"And you, sir?"

Louis turned on one heel. "Doctor, I have to take my leave. I hate to mention this, should it invalidate your research, but the dosage seems to have had little effect on me. Perhaps there is a question of potency." He liked the way *potency* sounded; it was the conferring tone of a fellow of science. Surely the doctor and he fished in the same waters, believed in the secret destinies of certain chemicals, in the ability of nature to provide poison, antidote, and cure. Louis pulled curtly at his waistcoat.

The doctor said plainly, "Sir, you have a soup spoon in your lapel."

Louis looked down at the spoon, impeached. The doctor returned to his side cabinet.

"Good evening, Pigeon," said Louis.

"Oh, yes, a delight," she said, roused from the armada of rooftops. "By the way, my real name is Chloe. Chloe Le Fournier."

Coincidence increases as the day grows near, the web tightening.

Then,

Isobel is not in this city. Perhaps she is dead.

Pigeon pushed off the sill and stood erect. "Do you take such offense at my real name? Chloe isn't so bad, is it?"

"No, no. I'm sorry." He would simply abandon the search. Foolishness had led him to imagine he still occupied a place in Isobel's mind. There might be a hundred Le Fourniers in France and another thousand in heaven and hell. Reunions could wait until the afterlife.

Then she said, "I'm from Lyons."

A silence uncoiled through the domed room.

Louis fiddled with the brim of his hat. "And your parents are —" The tremor in his voice was absurd.

"My father died about five years ago. And I don't speak to my mother. She is dead to me."

"How so?"

"That is a long and complicated story, monsieur."

"I see."

There was no way of asking for the mother's first name without prying. Daguerre put his hat on his head, then, a second later, removed it. "What profession did your father engage in? I am merely curious. As you know, I am somewhat of an artist, and family histories take their place in my portraits."

"Suddenly you're all questions."

"Yes, I apologize."

"He was a banker." She turned towards the window. Louis thought of how he would find another model, how this moment existed only for him and that no one could ever pinpoint the intersection of their lives if he turned and went out into the night. Louis stood still, aware of his tight-fitting shoes and the seam of his pants, the neck cloth pressing against his artery. He saw himself the way God might, from above and with affection; here was a man prone to pride and vanity, but with a profound belief in good works and progress. *Surely I will be shown compassion.*

"Is your mother happy?" he blurted.

"What?" She wheeled around.

"I'm sorry. I don't know what's come over me."

Pigeon blinked slowly, another wave of cannabis on its way out. "I haven't spoken to my mother in five years. But no, I don't think she is happy. How could she be?"

"Good night, Chloe," Louis said.

"Don't forget to arrange my portrait. Truth be told, I need the money."

Louis turned and left her by the window. He walked towards the crushed-velvet doors. Baudelaire and the astronomer were staring up at the domed allegory. Baudelaire had his hand cradled around his amber-tipped pipe as he spoke. "This is my favorite part. You are seated and you are smoking and you think that you are sitting in your pipe and it is you that your pipe is smoking; it is yourself you exhale in the form of blue clouds." The astronomer had a hand extended towards the ceiling, a finger pointing lithely at some shadowy nuance. Eggshell was lying on the Persian carpet beside them, tracing her fingers across the arabesque of worn thread. Louis did not say goodbye. As he opened the velvet doors, he heard Baudelaire say, ". . . the world loosens and everything sings. You feel a part of other men." He walked out into the long hallway and descended the stairs to the second floor. The two teams of men were still hurling young boys between the floors of the mansion.

TEN

he kiss on the stoop of Notre Dame unburdened
Louis, at least for a time. The certainty of Isobel
with another man's child sealed things off, divided his life into eras. And this was the era of
finding fame. His painting took a turn. The
memory of life on the glade, of Isobel, had given his cloud work
and trees an impressionistic shimmer; now, with her banished,
there was a kind of indignation, a sharp-edged realism.

A dozen years after his apprenticeship, Louis was the head
designer for the second-largest theater in Paris. He lived behind
the flower markets, in a terrace apartment. At work in his
rooftop garden, he stretched bolts of canvas from post to wall,
preferring the noonday sun to the perennial twilight of the theater. Deliverymen took his rolled canvases back to the stage.
From his rooftop, he watched flower women carrying baskets of
dahlias on their heads, barges hauling Montreuil peaches up the
Seine. He watched gentlemen play backgammon in shaded
courtyards. The city inspired him—the bustle of the boulevards,
the way a winter dusk seemed to rise up out of the river and settle all at once over the shopfronts.

At the end of each day, he brought his canvases inside. His apartment was well lit but disheveled. It smelled of whitewash and turpentine. Rustic furniture rose out of a sea of tracing paper and canvas. The copper pans in the kitchen ruminated with purple and orange paint. He rarely cooked. But sometimes, especially at the end of a performance run at the theater, he invited his colleagues to his rooftop for a late supper.

One night in the summer of 1821, a crowd of actors, poets, philosophers, and painters arrived at his apartment well after midnight. They had all come from the final performance of a play that featured Louis's most accomplished set — a panorama of Paris as a Roman outpost, from hilltop to river. In the spirit of the play, Louis was hosting a Roman feast.

He had transformed his terrace with a perimeter of lit sconces and garlands of cut flowers. There was a large canvas concealed against the half-wall that faced the markets and the street. Reclining chairs and divans were scattered around a long wooden table piled with food: wild figs, whole fish in garum, perfect rosettes of field greens. He didn't cook so much as assemble food based on symmetry, color, and texture. He moved among his guests in a white toga and a head wreath, pouring wine. All night they called him Senator. Everyone had come from the theater via the taverns, and the talk was animated and speculative. The men spoke of politics, of Napoleon, who had died the previous month on the island of Saint Helena. "The British murdered him," a poet declared, "I'm sure of it." A clutch of women stood in the kitchen, debating whether actors or directors made better lovers. Louis came towards them, a smile brimming.

"Ladies, I feel a little slighted by this conversation. What about the painters of this world? Don't we even figure a mention?"

"A man in a toga can't be taken seriously," one of them said.

A young actress from Amsterdam took him by the hand.

"Painters fall in with philosophers and poets—you are all too much within yourselves."

"Nonsense," said Louis, clenching her wrist. He turned to the others. "I'm sorry, but this woman will have to leave unless she agrees to take me as her lover . . . just to prove my point."

The women laughed at this, their cheeks pink from the wine. The Dutch woman—a pale-eyed blonde in her twenties—said, "I don't think it's that easy, but if you'd like to paint me sometime, I'd be honored. Your talent is wasted on those beautiful scenes of Italian seacoast and crumbling Greek ruins." Her eyes floated slowly above her wineglass. Louis thought of two tropical blue fish.

He brought her hand up to his face. "You would like me to paint you?"

"Yes," she said.

Louis wheeled around, took a camelhair brush from a copper pan of orange paint, and dashed a heart on the back of her hand. The women applauded and the Dutch actress, her cheeks ablaze, looked down at her hand.

"That was terrible of me," Louis said. "But I couldn't resist seeing you in bright orange."

The woman, trying to recompose herself, held up her hand and said, "You can wash this off now."

"That would require some turpentine, which, unfortunately, is in my studio at the back of the apartment."

"That sounds like a ploy," she said.

Louis took her by the hand, and they walked down the hallway. She looked back at the other women and called, "I'm being conquered by Rome." The women raised their glasses and went out onto the terrace. Louis opened the door to his studio and brought her inside. They stood against his drafting table, kissing. She knocked over a bottle of India ink with her painted hand. These kinds of exchanges were the extent of Louis's romantic life. In the years since Madame Treadwell, whose stone-walled mansion he still passed, he'd never taken a lover for more than a month. These were typically women in transition or jaded about love—actresses from Prague and Budapest, girls from the garrets who'd been left behind. This woman from Amsterdam was certainly not auditioning for a husband: she took his hand now and placed it inside her dress. Louis kissed her neck and felt her body rise towards him; he was sure that they were about to make love on his drafting table. Then, as a volley of drunken laughter lifted from the terrace, Louis remembered that she was a terrible actress—an affected speaking style and a mannered set of gestures plagued her performances. He took his hand from her breast. "I fear they're going to ask me to make one of my toasts out on the terrace. I should probably get back to my guests."

She waited a moment before speaking. "What they say about painters is true, then."

"I'm afraid so. We're terrible at love."

"Who said anything about love?" she said, adjusting her dress. "Incidentally, the front of your toga is covered in orange paint."

He smiled, looking down. "I'm a disgrace to my profession." He took her hand and wiped it gently with a cloth dipped in spirits. "Shall we see what debauchery is going on out there?"

"We were promised an orgy," she said indignantly. "A Roman feast has to have an orgy."

"Your night has been ruined," he said, laughing. He took her arm and led her out into the hallway.

Out on the terrace, the guests were slumped on divans and reclining chairs, eating with their hands. A cloud of cigar smoke hovered above their heads. The talk was wild and studded with moments of song and raucous laughter. The crowd turned to look at Louis, and his toga received fresh mockery and delight.

Louis sat with the poets, and the Dutch woman went to find her fellow actresses. A veteran actor, a decade beyond his prime, stood in a dinner jacket with a glass of champagne and delivered a monologue to nobody in particular. The speech was full of wild flourish and rising pitch. Louis watched him, wondering if there was still a voice inside the man's head, however faintly, that said, *Nobody is listening to me.* Louis feared becoming irrelevant, discovering that he was a boorish man standing at a party with war stories and specks of paint on his cheap shoes.

When the sun rose behind the river, the mood at the party shifted. The diatribes petered out; the veteran actor fell asleep on an ottoman. Louis tapped a spoon on a wineglass and stood before his guests. Someone called, "Quiet, the senator is making his toast."

Louis walked in front of his covered canvas. "First," he said, removing his head wreath, "I want to thank you all for coming. And I also want to thank you for eight wonderful years. I think we have changed the way Paris views theater. I've never worked with such dedicated artists. Here's to the theater!"

They all raised their glasses and drank.

"What's this?" a scenic painter called. "A farewell speech?"

"Actually," Louis said, his eyes on the wreath of laurel, "it is. I've decided to leave the company."

There was silence for a moment. "What will you do?" asked the woman from Amsterdam, still a little miffed.

Louis looked up. "These last few years I have been experimenting with a new kind of painting. I plan to open a gallery."

The guests murmured. Louis turned and removed the cover from the canvas. It was a replica of the street and market scene in front of his terrace. The shadows and pools of light had been painted to match this exact time of a summer's day. Every color — the cobalt of the river, the dun brown of the marketplace in the dawn — seemed to match perfectly. The crowd moved towards the painting, then stood comparing it to what they saw on the other side of the wall.

"It's quite marvelous," a theater patroness said. "How did you do it?"

"The canvas is transparent calico, and I paint the shadow and the light on two different sides. The light shining behind it gives the effect."

A man's voice rose above the crowd. "The angles are all wrong," he joked.

It was Degotti, padding along in his leather slippers, a cane at his side. Louis hadn't seen him in several years and was amazed by how old he looked. The two men embraced. Louis stared at him, unable to speak.

"Aren't you going to introduce me to your friends?" Degotti said.

Louis turned back to the crowd. "Friends, this is Ignace Degotti, the father of scenic painting. I apprenticed with him when I first came to Paris."

The guests smiled and nodded; they knew the name.

Degotti, now in his eighties and a little stooped, said, "Old men get up at this hour, and you people haven't gone to bed yet."

The crowd laughed.

Degotti turned and looked at the painting behind him. He touched it gently with his hand. "I don't think anyone has painted like this before. I think we can expect great things from Louis Daguerre."

"To Daguerre!" a man called.

Everyone raised their glasses and drank.

Louis looked at the painting and felt, for the first time, an almost painful sense of pride. It had taken him a full year to paint. He had mixed the colors to match a June dawn, preserving the exact tints of the cornices and the facades and the sky on the backs of envelopes. Using a camera obscura, he had painstakingly copied the shadow lines and the trapezoids of sunshine. There were a hundred shades of yellow and blue trapped inside the painting, a thousand inflections of daylight and shadow. Without knowing it, Louis Daguerre had tried to paint a photograph.

People drained their glasses of wine and champagne. The sun was high enough to make them squint and, taking this as their cue, the guests readied to leave. Louis saw them out, shaking hands, kissing cheeks. He stood with Degotti on the front stoop. The Italian wore his age like a stylish but outmoded hat; there was something formidable and sad about it. "Let me know when your gallery opens and I'll be sure to attend," Degotti said. "I don't get out much these days but will make exceptions."

"I'd be honored. Thank you for coming."

"I've been meaning to drop in for years, and when I heard you were retiring from the theater, I couldn't resist."

"You mean people already knew?"

"Of course everyone knew. They say that a man cannot change his undershirt in the Latin Quarter without all of Paris knowing."

Louis looked down at his feet.

"Good luck, Louis. Your painting has matured a great deal. You now paint exactly what you see instead of what you wish to see."

"Goodbye," said Louis, shaking Degotti's hand.

Degotti walked out into the street towards a waiting carriage. The markets were coming to life; the flower stalls were being stocked with daylilies and pansies. Louis watched his old master move among the flower women, suddenly certain that he would not see him again. The man would be dead within a few months. He carried the certainty of it in his halting walk and mannerisms, a calm awareness that nothing else was expected of him. Degotti had come to say goodbye, to pass along the torch.

Saddened and touched by this gesture, Louis stood in his door-way and watched the markets flood with daylight.

Louis called his gallery the Diorama. With a bank loan, he had financed a custom-made building with a rotating gallery. It housed scenic paintings of enormous proportions, rendered on transparent lawn or calico, and lit from various angles. On one side of the linen, Daguerre sketched a scene in lead. He used col-ors ground in oil, applied them with essence of turpentine, then concealed the brushstrokes with badger's skin. On the other side of the linen, he applied a wash of transparent blue and sketched the desired effects of light and shadow that would be seen through the first side. The viewer saw a seamless rendition of na-ture, a scene of perfect shade and hue.

The first diorama was based on the Valley of Sarnen in Switzerland, where dog-toothed mountains rimmed a valley floor. The audience watched as the scene migrated through early morning into noon before an afternoon storm threatened. Louis watched a woman reach for her parasol as protection from the oncoming deluge. Later, when he rendered Holyrood Chapel, old men doffed their hats and genuflected upon entry. This was exactly the effect he wanted—a realism that was felt in the body.

But something else was emerging in his work—an emptiness that was, in part, a result of such naturalism. It was a journalist for *The Times* who mentioned this new element in the very first diorama, noting, . . . *in the midst of all this crowd of animation, there is a stillness, which is the stillness of the grave. The idea produced is that of a region of a world desolated; of living nature at an end; of the last day past and over.* A quarter century later, Louis Daguerre would think of these words and wonder if he'd foreseen the apocalypse all those years before.

In the first year of its operation, the Diorama earned him two hundred thousand francs, though it was not until later that he fully realized his sudden wealth. Dioramas soon opened in London and throughout Europe, all under contract with Louis. He knew on some level that fame is not the story we tell; it is the story the world tells us. And the world was telling Louis it wanted to see itself reflected in the gouache and charcoal of painted calico; that the human eye longed to trust the illusion of likeness. Render perfectly a meadow at dusk, a horizon at dawn, and people will love you for it. For giving them something they didn't know they already had.

Louis continued to take his walks through the Paris streets in the autumn of 1823. He passed through the Arc de Triomphe, its massive shadow looming over the outdoor cafés in the late afternoon. There was money in his pockets, there were gold cuff links on his wrists. He walked with a cane and a folded newspaper under his arm. At his regular café, he sat and smoked a pipe and read of the world—the shipping news of the South, the stock reports of London, the crop yields of Provence. He found pleasure in commerce and weather. He was, in a sense, happy. He felt a part of things, not in the way he had amid the saffron fields around Orléans, but in a new way. He felt a sense of balance and order, a rush of benevolence at the curbstone.

He read the newspaper reviews of his dioramas and sometimes repeated to himself favorite adjectives and journalistic phrases. Fame was a ripple, a springhead. People selected words to describe your creations. He wondered about the empty perfection suggested by the journalist from *The Times*. Wasn't he trying to empty all artifice from a scene? Another journalist asked why no people appeared in the dioramas and called Louis Daguerre a misanthrope. *No,* he thought, *I am connected to everything that matters.* And when he set off on his evening walks, he smiled at the faces waltzing past on the promenade and felt part of a widespread fraternal emotion—the simple pleasure of being alive in a century whose great ideas were progress and per-fectability. *The reason I don't paint people is because they move. If I were to paint an old man into the Valley of Sarnen, we might see him age and die in the light cycles of an afternoon. Nobody would pay two and a half francs for that.*

The initial steps towards photography were accidental. For years he'd used the camera obscura, measured the opacity of Paris light, attempted to infuse reality into a stagnant piece of fabric. What came to him now, as if in a vision, was the idea that nature could sketch herself using nothing but sunlight; that, given the right cavelike aperture—just like his childhood bed-room window, just like the rotunda and light slats of the Dio-rama—and the right receptive material, light could emblazon a scene for all time. The secret of light was this: it carried images with it. Loosed from the helium roil of the sun, light streamed down and traced everything in its path—the brain-shaped sil-houettes of clouds, the Y of midflight birds, domed rooftops, spindle-trunked trees, a man's hand held aloft. It not only painted shadow but rendered—somewhere, if only we could see it—a crystalline blueprint of the material world. Find the right receptor and nature would do the drawing for you.

Louis set up a laboratory-cum-studio next to the Diorama. From its window he could look out and see people lined up for the dioramas, and this always fueled his work. One autumn af-ternoon he prepared a canvas for a diorama study. He mixed a small amount of iodine into his whitewash and brushed it onto his canvas. He wanted a darker undertone in the picture of Holyrood Chapel, and he hoped the iodine would create a heav-ier effect. Normally, he left his prepared canvases for an hour be-fore painting on them, but today he was called away by the crank man, who ran in yelling that the shaft had broken and three hundred people were waiting to see the next diorama roll into place. Louis, ever resourceful, went out into the street, hired a few sturdy and unemployed men on the spot, and supervised as the barebacked team heaved the next diorama along the circular rail of the viewing chamber. He didn't return to his studio for several hours.

When he entered, he found a startling effect: the silhouette of the window—quadrants, some latticework—had been etched onto the iodine-prepared canvas. Somewhere in the hazy geometry was also the outline of nearby rooftops. This effect sent Louis's mind ticking, and he began painting new canvases and mixing varying amounts of iodine into his whitewash. He left them for a day and returned to find the same effect. The iodine had trapped shadowy images using only sunlight. There began a three-day stupor in which he did not leave the studio. He surrounded himself with books on the history of optics and light manipulation. He discovered he was part of a quixotic lineage of light tinkerers. The search for the sun-sketched image was the conjugal child of chemistry and optics. Here were the chemists who blackened horn silver from the mines of Freiberg in 1556, who treated papers with caustic and chalk and silver nitrate and tried to write characters on the surface, who tried to harness ultraviolet light as if it were a species of alpine flower. Here was the dark chamber—Giambattista della Porta's black box with a hole. The genius of the camera, a pinprick of light through a swath of darkness. It must have been how God made the stars. Then there were the 1802 experiments of Wedgwood and Davy, two Englishmen who claimed to have found a method of copying paintings upon glass, using the agencies of light and nitrate of silver. They called the effect *sun drawing*. A Swede named Schecle had exposed silver chloride on bitumen and yielded a fleeting image from the sun. As Louis read, he sensed that momentum was

gathering in this slipshod realm; a major discovery was looming sidelong in the murk of minor triumphs. *I shall go further. I
shall capture these fugitive images.*

He sought out a shop run by the father and son opticians
Vincent and Charles Chevalier. The shop stood in a ferny alcove
on the Left Bank, its front window full of bifocals and optical
equipment. Inside, the walls were lined with more spectacles,
ground glass and crystal instruments, lenses and cylinders for
kaleidoscopes and microscopes. Myopic old ladies and tweed-
clad astronomers browsed the aisles.

Upon meeting Louis Daguerre, Vincent Chevalier said, "My
son makes these lenses by hand for the Paris Observatory.
Surely you are an astronomer." He governed the shop with a so-
licitous air, a proprietary style that suggested *patrons* more than
customers.

"No," said Louis. He did not want to share the nature of his
experiments. "I am the painter behind the dioramas. My interest
is in using lenses to paint nature with greater clarity."

"Yes, a delight, those dioramas. I took my wife last Sunday
afternoon" said Vincent. He was balding, mustachioed, with
murky pale eyes that suggested a fondness for self-pity.

"I'm glad you enjoyed them," said Louis.

"Charles," Vincent called, "fetch Monsieur Daguerre some
coffee."

Charles—a thin, young man in a leather apron—appeared
from the rear of the shop. Head down, he crossed to a small
stove where a coffeepot smoked.

"He makes the lenses and I sell them," Vincent confided.
"But one day," he said loudly, "this shop will be his and he'll be
forced to become a salesman."

"I see," said Louis. He scanned the walls of glass.

"What exactly are you looking for?" asked Vincent.

"A lens for a very small aperture."

"How interesting," said Vincent. Charles did a half-turn at the stove and angled an ear back towards the shop.

Vincent took out a tray lined with scarlet velvet and placed several lenses in it. He carried the box, Louis at his side, and laid it in the middle of a ramshackle table piled with screws and wires and splinters of fine glass. He gestured for Louis to sit, and something shifted in the optician's manner; he was now lost to a reverie of glass discs and framed lenses. Vincent arranged the offering on the velvet and slid it across the table to Louis.

"You must excuse this unsightliness," Vincent said.

"Reminds me of my studio," said Louis.

Both men chuckled at this, and Charles arrived with coffee. He set the cups amid the tin-wire squalor, the lens tray a velvet sanctuary in the middle. Charles looked at the two men, waiting to be dismissed. Vincent obliged and, without looking up from his rumination, said, "Charles, I believe Madame Fabriose will be returning for her reading glasses this afternoon. Could you attach the lenses to the wire rims for me?"

Charles nodded and left for the rear workshop.

"Normally," Vincent said, "we custom-fit the glass. So perhaps you could bring me the apparatus."

"Apparatus?" said Louis.

"I assume you are using a camera obscura or observation cylinder of some description."

"Oh, yes, of course."

"For your paintings." There was an elliptical tone, perhaps irony, in Vincent's words.

Louis took out each of the lenses and looked through them. He said, "I may purchase one or two different types and then return them if they don't work as I wish."

"That is a possibility," said Vincent.

Louis now understood that Monsieur Chevalier hand-selected his clients. This was clearly not commerce, but the shopfront of a family renaissance guild. Louis changed strategies. "You are the expert on light," he said. "What do you suggest if I want to sharpen the light before I paint something? I will probably use my camera obscura and sketch from the view. But I want the light to be very sharp indeed. I need brilliance."

"We all want brilliance," said Vincent, turning jovial. He blew across his coffee as if to excuse this brief lapse in taste. He handed Louis a convex lens and said, "This will do the job."

"Just the ticket," Louis said, picking it up and holding it to the light. "How much is it?"

"Consider it on loan," said Vincent. "I would not dream of charging you until you are perfectly satisfied with the achieved effect. Charles could also manufacture a lens to your specifications. It takes six weeks."

"So fast," said Louis.

"We work quickly," called Charles.

Vincent cast a glance to the rear of the shop. Charles bent over a pair of wire-rim spectacles.

Vincent took the lens from the tray and wrapped it in several layers of cloth. He led Louis to the front of the shop. He said, "There is no job too strange for the Chevalier family. If you dream up a chandelier made from granulated wine bottles, we will make it for you."

"I appreciate that a great deal," said Louis. He had the wrapped lens in his hands. "Goodbye, monsieurs."

"Do let us know how your experiment proceeds," said Vincent.

"Of course," replied Louis.

"Au revoir," called Charles from the workshop.

Louis raised a hearty wave. Vincent closed the shop door. Louis resisted the urge to run back to his studio. He walked briskly, and within minutes of arriving, he loaded the lens into

the camera obscura. He placed an iodized plate into the back of
the camera obscura and opened the diaphragm before a view
from his window. It was aimed down at the diorama crowd, and
he left it for several hours. When he returned to check it, he saw
that the new lens had yielded no new depth or clarity. He waited
for several hours, but soon the sketchy image had faded. Standing by his studio window, looking down into the street, Louis realized that the light was not the problem. It was the receptor.

Amid his early attempts to fix a fleeting image, Louis saw Isobel
again. One summer afternoon, as he paced his workshop, he
looked down at the line for the diorama and noticed a woman
with caramel hair. Then he saw a husband and teenage daughter
at her side. It stood to reason that it was Isobel—the dioramas
and Louis Daguerre had received national attention; surely this
was a daytrip from Lyons. He felt his pulse quicken. He closed
the curtains. He stood by the window, fob-watched, cuff-linked,
a man who knew weather and the increments of daylight and
where to find lapis lazuli in the Pyrénées, a man not yet famous
but on his way upstream, and in a second he was completely undone. The old hunger rose. The smell of camphor and rain on
her skin. He left the room and descended the stairs two at a time.

In the dimness the crowd was ushered inside. Louis made his
way to a small landing where he could observe the audience in
anonymity. A metallic voice called, "to your seats, straight
ahead." Louis curled up small and compact, his knees to his
chest, and felt like some earth-burrowing animal. There was a
hushed commotion. Shadows swam in the lantern light. Louis
watched the Lyons family take their seats. The girl was as tall as
Isobel. He calculated that she must have been fifteen, but he had
to count on his fingers up from 1807, allowing for a birth in
1808, because his mental acuity at the moment could not have

summed a dozen wine bottles without the use of his hands. The diorama glowed like an ember. It was a scene of jagged coastline, and as the white foam and agate rocks were lit, Louis saw the first real image of Isobel's face. The daughter sat between husband and wife, and Louis could see the faces of mother and daughter shot with half-light and striking in their counterbalance. Isobel was supple-skinned, with a slight but reverberant poutiness still in her face—her chin cantilevered with pride, her eyes steady and defiant. The daughter was altogether different: heavy-mouthed, full-lipped, hair tousled, a countenance that suggested sloth and slow rising; a girl you imagined taking breakfast in bed, sitting propped by pillows with hot buttered toast and a chapbook.

Louis watched Isobel smile at the shifting scenes of ocean and shore. Several times the daughter leaned close to the mother and whispered something, but Isobel seemed unable to break away from the tableau to respond. Louis wanted to stand and claim his creation. He wanted to kiss Isobel in full view of her daughter and husband. His cheeks burned hot with shame, but nobody could see him, and the shame soon turned to anger, then remorse. He could not yield. He knew his success was connected to this loss—after all, losing Isobel had triggered his desire to be loved through his paintings—but the situation also seemed part of some inscrutable misunderstanding or quarrel he had made with God. *Give me Isobel for one night, and I will offer up the dioramas, my money, my brushes . . .*

He left the gallery while the audience sat rapt and slack-jawed. He ran up to his studio and opened the curtains. He waited, and waited, timing the dioramas and knowing the chance of an audience member looking up at his window was fair, being as it was large and directly over the exit, and he imagined the portrait his figure might strike. He disgusted himself. He wanted to smash things. He wanted her to know that the perfectly rendered diorama was love abandoned, grief under glass. Then the audience spilled out, fanning into Rue Samson slightly dazed by the relative normality of a Paris afternoon. Surely the gas streetlamps were crude and the gutters coarse after his seaside sonata. The family filed out. The banker replaced his stovepipe hat. The daughter took her mother's arm, a little sleepy. There was no chatter, just a languorous walk to a nearby carriage. None of them looked up. Louis watched them load into the carriage, and the last image he saw was Isobel flanked by her family, their backs above the rim of the carriage seat; the daughter's messy hair, blond and with a stray organdy bow, was spilling into the wind and tangling with Isobel's. He flat-palmed his hands against the window, and if an audience member had looked up, he or she would have seen a dark figure, arms wide, mouth open, staring out with the severity of a man who either craves or hates God.

ELEVEN

ouis resisted the idea of taking a naked portrait of Isobel's daughter. So much floated about him: the haze of mercury, the memory of the girl and the mother's hair intertwined that day in the carriage, the recognition that Pigeon was the walnut-sized life that had curled inside Isobel's stomach that day on the Pont Neuf. He saw visions in the Paris daylight. From his balcony he saw a grove of plum trees growing from a high-walled courtyard. A white swan nested on a gabled roofline. He positioned his camera obscura on the balcony and tried to photograph these images, but nothing rendered. The flask of mercury rested on his kitchen table like a carafe of wine. At night he heard it shudder and lap, a river preparing to break its banks.

Louis cared for the injured dog, propping it with pillows, cleaning its wounds with soap and water. He didn't collect his tooth from the observatory, but each night, as he and the convalescing dog sat on his balcony, he pondered the history of stars and teeth, the secret journeys that result in form. The reddish-brown mutt was prone to long naps and hobbled about between sleeps, chomping uninterestedly on bones Louis fetched from the butcher. As the animal regained its strength, albeit with a hind leg that would forever resemble a gnarled tree branch, Louis grew attached to it. He awoke from his strange dreams in the empty hours of predawn and found the dog curled at the foot of his bed. He took it for walks before the sun was up. During these walks, Louis thought of Isobel and Pigeon and the infinite permutations of a man's life. Louis ruffled a hand through the spiked hair on the dog's back and connected the sight of Pigeon's lustrous hair at age fifteen, the heartbreaking organdy bow, with the idea of her as a prostitute many years later. Had Isobel's subsequent life been so cursed that she'd raised a whore? Inevitably, Louis was wrenched from these ruminations because the dog would dash under a bush or scramble for a ditch. The mutt was ungainly and seemed to have lived a feral existence. Louis scolded the animal but found himself carrying it in his arms to get home.

One afternoon, Louis was sitting on a park bench with the dog at his side when he saw Baudelaire bounding towards them. The poet's hair had grown in slightly, giving him the appearance of a man recently escaped from jail. His white teeth flashed as he called out and dodged several charabancs. His words were lost in a gust of wind. Louis sat adrift in his thoughts and did not stand to greet the poet.

"Damn you, Daguerre," Baudelaire said, panting.

"Oh, hello, Charles."

"Don't hello me." Baudelaire dropped onto the bench.

Louis adjusted his collar to shield the wind coming off the open boulevard. "What on earth?"

"I have been trying to reach you for weeks. I've left notes under your door. I've knocked at all hours."

Louis thought back on the past few weeks. There had been some noises and notes, that was true. "I am sorry," he said. "I have been hard at work on my portraits. Only a few items remain on the list now."

"Yes, well, that's why I wanted to talk to you. Incidentally, what a strange-looking beast."

Louis looked down, almost surprised by the sight of the scraggly mutt beside him. "I ran him over and have taken him in. He's partially lame."

Baudelaire cast another glance at the dog, its mouth hinged open, then looked at Louis. "Listen, Daguerre, Pigeon has been hounding me about her portrait. She wants to pose, and I think she'll be perfect for it. She's a little old, almost forty, but nonetheless a fine specimen. I've been tempted to pay for the privilege of her flesh, let me tell you."

Louis sat bolt upright. "You will do no such thing. I won't have it."

"She's a whore, Daguerre. That's what she does."

"No. You will not. She cannot continue in that trade."

"Well, perhaps if you paid her to pose nude, you would keep her fallow for a night or two. I don't know if you've noticed, but times are hard."

"I can't take her portrait."

Baudelaire took out his pipe and lit it, and the two men passed a moment of silence while the dark smoke streaked by in the wind.

Baudelaire sighed and said, "I'm inclined to believe the world *is* ending. Ever since that night of cannabis, everybody has been acting most peculiar."

"Take my word for it, that cannabis will be enough to turn the world into a whirligig," Louis said.

"On top of that, I've run out of money completely. A poet must die a martyr to become a great poet. We all know that. But I have money my mother won't give me. She's a sea wench."

"Don't say such things. God will punish you," Louis said.

"I mean it. She cut me off. I'm forced to write garbage for the papers to buy bread."

Louis looked at Baudelaire's outfit—nankeen trousers and a black woolen waistcoat. "But look at you, your clothes are fine."

"I spend my last sous on looking like a dandy. Salvation through style and all the rest of it. I'm deep in discontent, Louis. This time it's in earnest."

"But your criticism, surely it pays well," Louis said.

"When it pays. Last piece I did took six months to get a payment."

Louis ran a hand across the dog's back.

"I need that hundred francs, Daguerre. Take her portrait. Please."

Louis did not like the feeling of imposition in the air. "I can help you with food, for heaven's sake. Come and I will give you whatever is in my pantry. Brandy, wine, meat. How did you afford that decadence of several weeks past?"

Baudelaire studied his perfect shoes. "All of it was donated by rich lawyers and merchants and weepy-eyed ladies with a weakness for oil paintings and verse. Every now and again they get a sorry heart and want to throw lamb chops to the dogs."

"I see."

"Maybe you could take my portrait and pay me. You need a poet on your list. How about it?" Baudelaire pointed at his face with a finger on each hand. "Look carefully, Daguerre—if this is not a doomsday face, then I don't know what is."

Louis said, "Too bad for you I already took the portrait of the horses."

"That's not funny."

Louis again looked at Baudelaire, whose eyes were slightly jaundiced. Louis reached for his leather wallet and removed a small bundle of francs. He handed it to Baudelaire.

"Go see Pigeon and take her portrait. If nothing else, you

must share your wealth before the end of the world. You can't take it with you when your French brothers and sisters are in need. Something is rising in the garrets."

"Goodbye, Baudelaire."

"Long live France," said Baudelaire. He trotted off towards a nearby tavern where, no doubt, he would spend the money on wine and snuff and perhaps a scratch of food. Louis had no delusions those francs would garner much in the way of real sustenance.

He sat for a long time, watching the dog sleep the sleep of the wild. Finally, when he felt the streets had emptied a little, he walked back towards his apartment. But soon he was taking a detour via 72 Rue de l'École, standing in the street with his hobbled mutt, trying to understand Pigeon from the exterior of her ground-floor apartment. Her wood-framed building was wedged between a pawnbroker and a brothel whose wide veranda was full of recumbent whores. Her windows were covered in gauzy curtains, and the medicinal plants, lined along a sill, sprung their foliage in front of the gossamer cloth. Louis imagined the comings and goings of such a street, the young soldiers coming to hock family heirlooms and spend their dividends on a consort. He pictured Pigeon on the veranda, done up, her cheeks rouged like a Russian doll's. *The organdy bow.* He could not bear it. He tugged at the leash and the dog gimped at his side, head up, ears back. He would not come back to this address until he had a plan to rescue Isobel's daughter. Whatever else the final plan had in store, Pigeon could not die a whore.

TWELVE

aris in the years of cholera. The epidemic swept down from India and Russia like a mistral, blowing into London and Paris with a vengeance. At its worst, cholera killed five thousand Parisians a week. Passings in the night — men dry-lipped with thirst, their nails blue, heaving themselves out windows and into buckets, a torrential unleashing that hadn't been seen since the bubonic plague. It peaked in the summer and spring when the Seine warmed. People called it pestilence, a divine rebuke for their sins; whorehouses closed for lack of business, churches were full of widows and orphans. The doctors administered bloodletting, laudanum, saline solution — all of it powerless.

For years Louis had thought cholera was coming for him. After that day when he saw Isobel ride away in the carriage, he half wanted the blue-lipped fever to pull him under. He had made some contributions — the diorama, certain innovations to panoramic painting — and he could imagine a peaceful death. Cholera decreased ticket sales for his dioramas, and soon the lines were thin, then nonexistent. The expanses of transparent linen that took six months to paint stood unobserved in the gloomy gallery like entombed saints in a sealed crypt. He continued with his photography experiments, making various permutations with lenses and iodine-coated plates, but nothing significant yielded.

On a blustery day in the autumn of 1826, he made his pilgrimage to see Vincent and Charles Chevalier. For four years he'd been coming here and dodging their inquiries. He had made slipshod progress and returned every few months to try a new lens or filter, each time Vincent becoming more brazen until he was asking questions with the directness of a glassblower, of a man whose lungs doubled as bellows — *What's this for, then? Must be building a colossal spyglass, is that it, Monsieur Daguerre?* Vincent would allow Charles to witness the art of customer interrogation before dispensing his son to the workshop or to an amateur astronomer come for a stop-lens. Vincent would sit down at the ramshackle table, up to his elbows in refraction glasses and prisms, and in a hushed and conspiratorial manner tend to Louis's requirements with a theoretician's conjecture. Each requirement, Louis was led to believe, posed a great dilemma, a trade-off between the practicality and the divinity of light. "This is just the thing for you. Of course, you will lose some prismatic effect. This lens here, for example, will give you hue without glare, and what is hue without glare? Why, it's church without the hymns."

But today, something was different in the Chevalier shop. Louis walked in to find father and son standing before a framed picture whose composition Louis could not discern. Upon hearing the clamor of the tin bells on the door, Vincent immediately covered the frame with a flannel cloth and set it aside. Charles went to the workshop without the customary dismissal from his father. Louis came to the rear of the shop and sat at the worktable.

"Monsieur Daguerre, must be a new season if you have come for a new effect," said Vincent.

"What were you fellows just looking at?" Louis asked.

Vincent winced slightly, as if this were the highest indiscretion imaginable. "We are not at liberty to say."

"Vincent, come. You've become my opium merchant. How can I be denied?"

"I mustn't."

"And why, may I ask? People are dying in the streets. Let's out with it."

"Sworn to secrecy. We have this here just for safekeeping while Monsieur Niépce goes to London."

Louis squinted at a display of reading spectacles. "Niépce. I know that name."

"Perhaps."

"An inventor and natural philosopher of some kind."

Vincent nodded and looked sidelong at the cloth-covered frame.

"Vincent, you can trust me."

"It is not a question of trust but of my word. Our word."

"Solemn as a pact," called Charles.

"You gentlemen disappoint me greatly," Louis said. He could sense the magnitude of this thing, and there arose in him the same determination he reserved for replicating nature. "How much business have I brought you in the last four years?"

"A good deal, monsieur," said Vincent.

"Let's see, the old ladies from the diorama, my fellows artists who want new effects . . . I have even given you a plaque outside my building acknowledging your contributions to my double-effect diorama. I imagine that has brought you a tidy amount of commerce."

Vincent took a sip from his coffee. He held it in his mouth for a beat, letting it settle over him. "Monsieur Niépce has developed something called heliography."

Louis could feel a biting pain between his shoulder blades. He played dumb. "Really? What is that?"

"It's still very cursory, but he's found a way to use the sun to etch a picture."

"Ah." Louis's voice came out dry, uninflected.

Charles came from the rear, reveling in his father's violation. "Niépce is off to London to present some findings to the Royal Society. Thinks the English might enlist him. But he was afraid this might get stolen or damaged on the trip over the channel." Charles gestured towards the covered frame.

Louis felt the words in the back of his throat for a long time before he allowed them to come out. "May I see it?"

Charles looked to his father for guidance. Vincent took another swallow of coffee and gave his son a slight nod. The hair on Louis's neck bristled; the heliograph was as good as shown.

"You must not mention this to anyone," said Vincent. "We imagine others may be working towards this same end, and poor Niépce would die if his technology were stolen."

"I understand," said Louis. "You have my word that I will keep this to myself."

Charles reached down and picked up the picture. He leaned it against a ladder-backed chair and removed the cloth. It was a pewter-plate depiction of a view from a high window, perhaps a dormer, and the composition was of a barn, a pigeon house, and a pear tree. There were scratches and a brownish effect, as if someone had rubbed the entire picture with dirt, but the reality was undeniable—this was a still life painted by the sun. There were no brushstrokes, no errors of proportion. The artist's hand was invisible. Louis stood involuntarily and leaned close to it.

"Niépce says he had to let the image cure for an entire day," said Vincent.

"Is that so?" Louis held out his hand with a slight tremor and saw that there were two sets of shadows lengthening on either side of the barn, as if two suns of equal strength were swimming across the heavens. The image registered a day's worth of sunshine.

"How does Monsieur Niépce make such a picture?" he asked.

"That we do not know," said Vincent. "But I know he uses the very same camera obscura you use for your diorama pictures. Amazing how the same instrument can yield such different results."

"Yes, amazing," said Louis. He looked closely at the picture, tried to ascertain a smear or wrinkle that might give the origin of execution. He recognized that it was not the definitive thing he'd been seeking—it was transient. The image was still rather crude, and the long exposure gave it a surreal quality, an ethereal suspension. Nonetheless, it was closer than anything he had produced.

"Niépce is a funny old bird," said Vincent. "Retired he is, though from what, nobody can recall. Comes in here, and we make him camera obscuras and lenses, and then he does the rounds of the neighborhood. Goes across to the apothecary and the grocer and bundles home in a carriage to Chalons-sur-Saone and pays everybody with small franc notes and coins, like he's an old miser raiding his coin jar."

"That is strange," said Louis. An intuition rose up in him, a startled hunch. "Gentlemen, please excuse me. I must be on my way."

"No lenses for you today, then?" asked Charles hopefully.

"No, thank you, Charles." Louis was already out the door and heading into the neighborhood. He ran across the street to the apothecary and entered. It was a maze of ceiling-high shelves with small wooden boxes lined out, each of them labeled.

"Morning," said the puglike man behind the counter.

"Hello," said Louis. "I wonder if you can help me."

"Are you sick?" asked the man, resting his fleshy hands on the counter.

"No, no. I have a friend who comes in here quite often. Monsieur Niépce."

The apothecary gave a quintessentially French shrug.

"You don't know him?"

"Not from a wheel of cheese."

"He comes in here perhaps once a month, and he always has a lot of coins about his person."

Now the man nodded, chuckled. "And he keeps a purse around his neck on a lanyard?"

"Yes."

"What about him?"

"Well, he can't come to town just at the moment, and he has sent me for his usual supplies."

"I thought he was off to London."

"Delayed," said Louis.

"How much of it?" The man sniffed the air, relishing the simplicity of small commerce.

"Ah, let's see, what does he usually get?"

"A jug."

"Well," said Louis, all levity, "a jug it is." He could feel his hands mist the counter with sweat as the pugish fellow moved around. He returned and placed a heavy ceramic jug on the counter.

"Thirty francs, that is," said the apothecary.

Louis placed fifty francs on the counter. "What is the name of this stuff, anyway?"

"Can't you smell it? They say oil of lavender will raise poets from the dead."

"Of course." He lifted the cork and took a heady whiff. What came to him was not poetry but the lavender-scented water Isobel used to soak her poultices in when they had lived outside of Orléans. So this was Niépce's fixing agent—perfumed flower oil. It seemed too romantic to be true. He replaced the cork, picked up the jug.

The apothecary tapped at the counter. "Don't you also want the bitumen of Judea?" he asked.

Louis stood in place, nodding. "Yes. How silly of me. Niépce would be very cross."

The man placed a cloth bag of the powder on the counter. Louis took his change, a colossal smile on his face, and left the store. Outside, the wind had died and the light was dazzling.

The letters between Niecéphore Niépce and Louis Daguerre were perfectly cordial—full of phrases like *in conformity with your aspirations . . . our mutual gain . . . with the certitude of science and goodwill.* It was Louis Daguerre who wrote the first letter, galled after a series of failed attempts to duplicate the pewter-plate heliograph. He had confessed to the Chevaliers of his experiments and asked for Niépce's address. The brothers gave out the address and within a week had briefed Monsieur Niépce, recently returned from London, on Louis's work. It was no coincidence that Vincent and Charles Chevalier invented the Parisian spyglass that year.

The letters went back and forth in a kind of chess game. The writers hedged the Latinate names of minerals and salts, the techniques that issued tone and shade. Niépce divulged that he came from money and had trained for the priesthood before sacred orders were abolished under Napoleon. He was now a full-time inventor and was working on many projects, including a patent for his method of extraction of dye from the woad plant; he hoped this would prove profitable in the face of a continentwide indigo shortage. Niépce said his interest in heliography was primarily to improve lithography, his longtime passion. Louis cared little for the man's biography or motivation and wrote back more candidly; *Did the English show interest in your near-consummate technique? Alas,* Niépce wrote back, *they seemed uninterested. And I met another man in pursuit of a similar method of sun drawing by the name of William Henry Fox Talbot. He sensitizes paper and places it in a camera obscura, but to very little effect. Still, it shows promise.* This sentence made Louis feel ridiculous; he had imagined for a time that his manipulations with the camera were unique. Now there were at least two other men attempting to harness its powers. He returned to his studio in earnest, taking his meals there, and refused to tend any quotidian concerns for months on end. He went back to earlier methods and tried a broad range of chemicals for fixing. Progress was slow and erratic. The letters continued, both men trying to convey that they were more baffled than they actually were. At least three men in Europe now knew that the missing ingredient in photography was the primary fixing agent—the solution that would emblazon the latent image permanently to the plate. And they were all doing it with different motivations: Niépce was trying to improve lithography, Talbot was trying to make up for a deficiency in his drawing ability, and Louis was trying to trap nature. But he was also trying to punish the world, and Isobel, with his fame.

THIRTEEN

ouis Daguerre drove his carriage through the streets towards Pigeon's flat. It was autumn and the leaves had turned, all gold and wine, and the wind cast them through the alleys like dazed butterflies. Pedestrians—bundled and shawled— sloped into a headwind. The sky hung a high, pale blue. Everything felt cleansed, emptied, the windowpanes a little aqueous in the early morning. The omnibus rang throughout the city, empty and glassine. Paris was on the verge of something.

Louis now had a very clear portrait of Pigeon in mind. A full-plate daguerreotype depicting a nude with her back partially to the camera. There would be nothing sexual about her womanliness—a swath of flesh caught up in sunlight, shadows in the hollows of her back, perhaps the amorphous suggestion of an amber-tinted breast. Staring away from the camera, she would lend an ambiguity to the end of womanhood. *As long as she faces away from the camera she will remain anonymous, an artifact of the end.*

Louis turned in to Pigeon's street and noticed a cat in a bakery window passively taking in the world. He smiled at it; the rescued dog had given him a feeling of communion with animals. Paris was full of cats, he realized, who held that aloofness of looking down from a height. But mostly they were asleep in wine- and cheese-shop windows, Angoras curled and impervious to grief or happiness. They were silent witnesses, spies of the apocalypse. Louis suspected that cats, like the souls of the dead, could not be photographed.

At eight o'clock on a Sunday morning, Louis stopped his carriage beside the whorehouse with the wide veranda. He was the only moving figure in a street whose daylight hours were reserved for a long, slow ascension from excess. He tied his horses to a hitching post and unloaded his apparatus. Among the many objects were a zinc camera obscura, a wooden tripod, two silver-plated copper sheets, two small phials—one of olive oil and the other of nitric acid—a flask of mercury, a box of carded cotton, a pumice stone in a muslin bag, a wire frame, and a spirits-of-wine lamp. He placed these items on a small dolly he'd made from a wheelbarrow and approached Pigeon's ground-floor apartment. He knocked loudly on her door. There was no answer, so he moved to the front windows and rapped. He peered inside.

Pigeon dragged herself from bed, suspecting that a drunken soldier had mistaken her window for the brothel. Still in her cotton nightdress, she pulled back the curtains to reveal Louis Daguerre, flask of mercury in hand, hair tousled by a windy carriage ride, flat-nosed against the plate glass, peering through the gossamer curtains. Startled, Louis visibly jumped back a step and dropped the flask of mercury. The flask shattered, and beads of mercury rolled across the footpath. Louis struck the air with his fists, settled into a burst of violent coughing, cursed and head-bobbed as he attempted to collect the mercury with his hands. To Pigeon, on the other side of the glass, this was a dumb show of lunacy.

She grabbed her dressing gown and came out onto the front stoop, then down to where Louis was on his hands and knees.

"Monsieur Daguerre?" she called.

Louis stood but could not look at her. He held his hands in front of him. Splinters of glass and pinheads of blood shone from his hands. His eyes were unnaturally blue, the vivid blue of illness.

"My God, your hands," she said.

Louis looked down at them. A bead of mercury rolled back and forth in one cupped hand.

"Come inside, please. I'll bandage them," she said.

"You're not dressed," he said, addressing the street.

"It's still early, and I danced all night. I told you to come in the afternoon."

Louis nodded seriously at the word *dance*. Finally, he looked at Pigeon. Her hair was down, resting and curled against her collarbones.

"My barrow," he said. "I can't leave it out here."

"Wait a minute," said Pigeon, disappearing into the apartment. When she returned, she carried a towel and handed it to Louis. He wiped some of the blood from his hands and walked over to his equipment. With his right hand—the left was augered with glass shards—he delicately pulled the barrow towards Pigeon's front door. She held the door open for him and he wobbled it slowly inside. Her apartment was sparse: two rooms, a stove and wooden table in one corner; through a bedroom doorway, her unmade bed on wooden posts.

Louis stared down at his hands. He did not like the sight of his own blood. "I'm afraid your towel will be ruined."

"Let me get the glass out. Come over to the window, where the light is better."

Louis followed her to the window and held out his hand. She took him by the wrist and studied his palm. The small tributaries of palm lines and mercury-tinted blood made Louis think of deltas, of drained waterways. *Time is running out.* Pigeon wiped his hand with the towel. His hand was now relatively bloodless and Pigeon began to pick out the shards of glass. After placing several wedge-shaped pieces into her dressing-gown pocket, she laughed. Her head was down, but Louis could see her small white teeth under the rim of her mouth.

"You looked like a madman at my window," she said. "I thought you were a drunk midshipman."

"I must have looked a fright."

"There's a piece I can't get. Right here." She pointed to the heel of his hand, where the head of a glass shard shimmered. Louis reached inside his waistcoat and retrieved the paring knife he used to scratch powder from pumice stone. He handed it to Pigeon.

"I don't know that amputation is called for," she said.

Louis looked up from his hand. *Ah, yes, a joke.* He forced a smile to his lips. "Would you like me to do it? It needs some digging around the flesh."

Pigeon nodded at the window. "Look out at the street while I do it. Watch for sailors going home or widows hocking their gold."

Louis obeyed and stared outside. He was heartened by the sight of a few people emerging from doorways, dressed in their Sunday best. He had never been much for churchgoing, but he was comforted by those with devoutness, moved by the sound of vesper bells calling them inside a church. Louis felt the paring knife gouge his hand, but the pain came slowly, like an aftertaste.

"I need my hands," he said.

She held the bloody piece of glass between two fingers. "I think that's the last of it. Now, if you'll excuse me, I need to dress." She turned and walked towards her boudoir.

"I'll go check on my horses," he said.

"As you wish."

He went outside and rinsed his hand with a water bottle he kept in his carriage. He dried his hands on a horse blanket and adjusted the straps of his gig. Several minutes passed before he tapped gently on Pigeon's door. When she opened it, she was dressed in a crinoline dress that fluted out from her hips. Holding his left hand palm up like a beggar, he came inside and unloaded his apparatus, placing the various items on the kitchen table.

"Would you like some coffee?" she asked.

"As long as it doesn't have any hashish in it."

They both laughed at this and she moved towards the stove. She said, "I don't think I'd ever do that again. I had chills for a week after."

"I consider myself a scientist as much as an artist, and that was not science," Louis said, placing the phials beside each other.

"And this is science? Asking strangers to pose naked for you?"

"I'm a student of light," Louis said.

"And a poet."

"No, I leave that to Charles Baudelaire. My job is to capture things before they disappear."

"Am I going to disappear, Monsieur Daguerre?"

"No, I meant — capture things in their essence."

She threw pure coffee grounds into the pot. Louis was a little surprised that a whore could afford coffee without chicory. Without turning around, she said, "And what is my essence?"

He carefully lifted the spirits-of-wine lamp out of its case, taking his time to reply. "I don't know until I see it on the copper plate."

Pigeon brought him a cup of coffee. She had brushed her hair, but it was still down — perhaps she had photogenic ideas of her own. He tried not to stare at her; the past was trapped in her flesh. He dusted the two plates with the fine powder of pumice, then swabbed them with carded cotton and olive oil. Next he rubbed some nitric acid in a circular motion across both plates.

"Who makes the photo drawings—you or the sun?" Pigeon asked.

"You might say we are partners. Is the stove still alight?"

Pigeon nodded. He inserted each plate into a wire holder and took them over to the stove. He ran the plates, silver coating faceup, back and forth above the hot burners for several minutes. "This works even better than the spirit lamp," he said. He brought the plates back to the table and repeated the coating with pumice dust and acid. "Now, once we're ready, I'll set up the camera on a tripod and expose the plate to iodine." There was little fussing left to do. There came a silence.

"Your coffee is getting cold," she said.

"Yes, of course." He took up the china cup and drank. "A room that is too warm will adversely affect the image."

"Is it too warm in here?"

"Perhaps."

"Of course, I won't have any clothes on."

A slight bristling at the back of Louis's neck. "For the briefest of time. I'm hoping for a short exposure."

"How long?"

"A few minutes, at the most."

"That's an eternity for a naked woman."

He looked into his coffee cup; a murky brown eye stared back at him. "And you must remain very still," he said to the cup.

Now he looked down at the wide floorboards. Her apartment had no smell and there were few personal effects. She tapped at the edge of the wooden table. *The money,* he thought. He reached inside his coat, then stopped. Should he pay before or after? He didn't want to insult what dignity she might have remaining.

"Mademoiselle, I am most grateful for this opportunity. You will go down in the galleys of history." He winced from the sound of his own voice and placed a hundred francs on the table.

She pretended not to notice and took another sip of her coffee. "Are you ready?"

Louis bit at his mustache.

"Don't worry. I have posed for some drawing classes and I am quite comfortable with the procedure of removing my clothes."

The *procedure*? "I see."

"In my bedroom?"

He looked at the poison-blue bottle of iodine. "How is the light in that room?" He made it sound clinical, a doctor's inquiry—*How is the fever?*—even while blood jumped through his limbs.

"There's a window that overlooks the alley. At this time of the day, it's quite bright."

"Very well, then."

"I'll go and position myself."

"Yes, fine. With your back to the window."

She left the room and Louis wiped his brow with his kerchief. He fumbled with the cork of the iodine bottle. He poured a small amount into the camera chamber and fixed a plate inside to prepare it to receive light. *This is science; fasten your mind to that.*

"Very well, then," he said audibly.

"Pardon?" she called from the bedroom.

"I said nothing."

"I'm nearly ready. Crinoline is the curse of the Parisienne." The sound of her undressing; waves of crinoline. He felt a searing in his cheeks that made him wonder if he'd gotten some nitric acid on his face. He performed a mental inventory of equipment: gauze, camera, tripod, plates. She called from the bedroom. The words were unintelligible, a piping cheeriness. He picked up the tripod, the camera and the plates, and walked delicately towards the bedroom. In his peripheral vision, he could make out her outline on the bed.

He set the tripod down and attached the camera to it. In a minute, he would have to adjust the unpolished glass to set his focus. There was no way to avoid looking at her. He looked up at the ceiling: a cheap fleur-de-lis was embossed in the molding. He thought for a moment of afternoons in bed with Madame Tread-well.

"In a moment, mademoiselle, I will insert the plate and find my focus." He sounded to himself like a stage magician.

"What position should I assume?" she asked.

"You may cover yourself while I make some adjustments. If you'd be more comfortable."

"Would you be more comfortable?" she asked.

"It's of no consequence to me," he lied.

He tightened the small tourniquets that held the copper plate in place and sealed the camera. "You would be surprised to know, mademoiselle, the intricacies of light in making the daguerreotype. The exposure time varies by latitude, time of day, and season. Paris outside in June at two in the afternoon may require a minute or two. Whereas Rome in August at noon may require thirty seconds. Do you see the proposition?"

"Should I be on my stomach or back? Sitting, perhaps."

"Your back must be towards the camera, and you should look at something on the opposite wall."

He craned down to adjust the focus glass. In his line of sight sat Pigeon, backlit by the light from the alley window, a naked white shoulder rising from the bedsheet she used as a shawl.

"I need the light to come in from the side. Could you turn and face the other wall?"

She swiveled her body to accommodate. Louis moved the

camera and looked once again. The cut of her white shoulders; a net of hair on her neck.

"And what if you make a sun drawing at noon in the North Pole in December?" she asked.

"I would grow into an old man while holding the diaphragm open. There are some places that will never be photographed." The nervousness had largely disappeared. He was a technician now, coaxing a machine into compliance. He focused the glass by using the lines of her mouth and teeth as benchmarks of clarity. He was in service, dilating the pupil of God. "I believe us to be ready, mademoiselle."

She nodded and smiled.

"I should think if you recline on your feather pillows . . ."

When she leaned back against the pillows, the bedsheet slid down her side, exposing her thigh. Louis looked out into the alleyway. But he managed to notice a small blue bruise on her hip—a tiny sapphire star, as if someone had held a pen nib against her flesh.

"I think we'll expose for two minutes, since it is quite light in here. I will, of course, leave the room while the image is registering, but you must remain very still. Any sudden movements could ruin the entire thing. As for your expression, I ask only that you imagine looking back through time."

"I'll try to remember that."

"When you're ready, you may remove the sheet."

She cast a glance to the window and pulled the bedsheet off her reclined body. Louis stood for the briefest of moments to ensure the model's position before beginning the exposure. Her back was to the window at an angle, perpendicular to the light, and her head rested in one hand. Her feet were unexpectedly slender and arched. The serpentine line that extended from ankle to hip to shoulder to head was well lit and would register as milk-stone. The darkened areas—the recesses beneath her arms, the shadow of her hair—would register as rust, brown if the mercury was too hot. Louis opened the diaphragm and hoped for perfection, for a rosewood frailty.

He sat down at the kitchen table, packed his equipment, and took out his fob watch. He marked the two minutes. How could he bring up the subject of Isobel without arousing suspicion? Was it wrong to withhold his acquaintance with her mother? The minutes passed within such questions. He stood up from the table and walked slowly into the adjacent room, where Pigeon remained in position. He closed the diaphragm and went over to the windows and drew the curtains. Pigeon wrapped the sheet around her. There was an awkwardness between them now. *Has something been stolen?*

"I must fix the image within the hour, mademoiselle," said Louis. "It will be more effective if I take it to my studio."

"Everybody else calls me Pigeon." She moved her head, loosened her neck. Louis took his camera into the kitchen while she dressed. She emerged in her crinoline. "Will you stay for a quick meal? I'm not at all bad with food."

"I probably shouldn't," said Louis. Then, "Did your mother teach you how to cook?"

She cinched a ribbon on her dress. "Yes. She had a way with herbs."

Louis looked out towards the windows where the plants flourished. "You must be the only woman in Montmartre growing valerian."

"You know it?"

"Yes. I took it as a child for fevers."

"I use it in tea. I secretly believe it gives me protection from sickness. They call this section of Montmartre the cholera kingdom."

"A very nasty illness," said Louis. He tapped his shoes together. He had forty-five minutes to fix the image to the best effect. He would have to decant more mercury from his jug. "Pigeon, I hope you don't think me prying, but I wonder how such a woman as yourself has fallen to this profession."

"Fallen?"

"Baudelaire told me of your, what, your nighttime occupation."

"I dance," she said, not looking at him.

"Yes, you dance."

"And sometimes I work next door."

"As a whore."

"We don't use that word." Her eyes steadied in a beat of anger.

"What word do you use?" Louis tried to soften the sound of judgment.

"Companion, friend, soldier's accomplice, apprentice bride, marriage saver . . . If it weren't for us, Napoleon's army would have been defeated long before they fell at Waterloo. It was us who sustained the revolution. I feel no shame whatsoever in what I do, monsieur. So do not cast that patronizing stare at me. I do it for pay, to eat, to give me the freedom to dance." Her eyes bore down on his.

He said tentatively, "It must make your life very difficult. You are unmarried, for example."

"Yes, and so are you."

"That's true."

"I don't believe in love."

"But surely you are the product of a loving marriage?"

"My mother never loved my father."

A tremulous bite came about Louis's jaw. He was unable to speak for a moment. "I don't believe it."

"You do not know her. She was poisoned by something that took place before I was born, and never recovered."

"A wild plant, perhaps, a berry with toxic effect?"

"Yes, the wild berry of regret."

Louis had not quite planned on this turn. Instead of giving him hope that Isobel had loved him all these years, it dashed his spirit. He had also hoped she'd been happy and that this penance was something he alone carried. He looked again at his fob watch. Pigeon seemed close to tears.

"Mademoiselle, I am sorry for this imposition. I really should go and fix the image."

"Will you let me see it? Nobody has ever taken my picture before."

"I will certainly bring it by to show you." Louis sidled towards the front door. "I think the daguerreotype portrait will be lovely. Good day."

"Goodbye."

Louis wheeled the dolly of equipment outside with one hand and loaded his carriage. He heard the door close behind him. He climbed up into the carriage and pulled down the street. The camera sat beside him on the seat, the latent image of Pigeon trapped inside. If he could execute the picture in his mind, it would render the silver canvas at its most perfect—capture the intersection of two spheres, where the underworld appeared sun-kissed. A woman of the night, forlorn and light-spun. She might crown his doomsday list. These images, when stowed in the catacombs, would survive the cataclysm and stand as silent monuments of what men held in their hearts. The camera obscura was the eye of God, and these final portraits would be His keepsakes. Here a half-turned harlot. Here a flock of swallows. Here a king in the last days of his kingdom. Put your children under glass and go back to sleep for another million years.

FOURTEEN

ne December afternoon in 1838, Louis climbed the stairs to his laboratory. The room was a clutter of chemical flasks and decanters. The day before, he had exposed a plate of a street view and placed it inside a desk drawer. It was a dismal picture—the light was bleak and the cloud-capped sky was gauzy and pale; the buildings and lampposts were smears of charcoal. He had exposed and developed the plate in pursuit of the right chemical fixing agent. He'd tried a new mixture of petroleum and vinegar and left the unsatisfactory plate to cure overnight in the drawer of his workbench. Now, when he removed the image, he saw immediately that something had changed. The edges of the buildings had darkened; the clouds were absorbed into the silver skin of the plate. Instead of fading, as was usually the case, the image had etched deeper.

Louis began rifling through the drawer to see what could have affected the plate in this way. There were a dozen other items in there—phials of iodine, petri dishes of glycerin, mineral oils, spools of wire, theater ticket stubs, mixing inks, a defunct brass compass, and a damaged thermometer he used to measure

the temperature of chemicals. He spent the rest of the day conducting a process-of-elimination test. He exposed a plate, removed all the items bar one from the drawer, and then left the
plate to fix inside the drawer. The fifth item he left in the drawer
was the thermometer, which he now saw had a fracture in its
glass casing. Tiny globules of mercury had bled out of the glass
and gathered in the seams of the thermometer. Within an hour,
the new plate was fixed. He did another test, then another. He
smashed the glass tube and emptied the mercury into a petri
dish. Same effect, only faster. He gathered his chemistry and
alchemy books and rifled through the pages that mentioned mercury. Melts at −39 degrees. Boils at 357 degrees. Insoluble in
water. Here it is, he thought, the Trojan horse.

He told nobody about what he'd found. From under a loose
floorboard he produced a wad of francs and went out into the
street. There was a hatter factory behind the Left Bank, beside
an abattoir, where he knew they used enormous vats of mercury
to fasten hide into hats. He would buy himself a barrel.

A guard sent him into the factory in pursuit of the foreman,
a stout-chested man in overalls. Louis walked down a succession
of cooling and stretching aisles, where women in bonnets han-
dled strips of animal hide. The smell was ghastly—a combination
of offal and the high, sweet chemistry of tanning solutions. A
woman pointed him towards the mercury room where the hats
were taken for bolstering.

It was a low-ceilinged room with no windows or ventilation.
There was a sunken area where enormous copper urns bubbled
above wood fires and thick mercury steam rose towards the ceiling. Upon entering, Louis heaved a cough. The air was liquid,
hot, and burned on the way in. A motley collection of men,
women, and children dipped hats on wooden paddles in and out
of copper boilers, their faces drenched in sweat. There was a stupefied look on their faces. Later, Louis would recall this tableau

and imagine that the mercury had literally fixed their faces, etched their countenances pale, waxy, and hangdog. But for now he had discovered something wondrous, and no amount of squalor would dissuade him from his entitlement.

The foreman swiveled his torso slightly when Louis called out to him. It was an economy of movement that suggested orders barked from the side of the mouth. It reminded Louis of Marius, the head apprentice and prop boy from all those years ago.

"I have come to buy a barrel of mercury," said Louis. "How much is it?'

The man wiped the great shelf of his forehead with the back of his wrist. "You a hatter?"

"Not exactly," said Louis.

"What, then?"

"Does it matter? I am willing to pay whatever you ask."

"Is you now?" The man clicked his teeth together and yelled something incomprehensible to a boy in the corner. When he turned his head back to Louis, he inspected his shoes and hat.

"Don't sell the quicksilver. Hard to come by, it is."

"May I speak with the owner?"

The foreman did not like this tack. "If you catch a ship and go to Morocco, you might."

"I see."

"Yes, you see." The foreman walked off, wiping his hands on his thighs. Louis followed. He reached into his pockets and produced the wad of francs.

"There is five hundred francs here," said Louis. "I don't know what it costs you, but I wager it's not that. You may keep the difference." He held the faded francs in front of the man's chest.

The man involuntarily extended his eyebrows like archers' bows. "Quicksilver don't come in barrels. It's a keg you wants.

And heavy as lead it is." He snatched the money from Louis and used his chin to point to a row of metal kegs, each one painted with the symbol *Hg*. Louis turned to ask the foreman for some assistance carrying the keg, or to hold it until he could bring his wagon, but the man had disappeared.

Louis rolling a metal keg of mercury through the Paris streets. Passersby thought he was a drunkard with a keg of home-brewed beer. A policeman stopped him, suspecting it was a gunpowder keg, that revolution might be fuming in the garrets. Louis was all politeness and lies, masking the ridiculousness of his predicament. *Yes, Officer. No, monsieur, not gunpowder. Yes, I'm a hatter.* He hunched and pushed the keg, rolling it up and down gutters, the metal clinking on the macadam, his back aching, the ferment of boiled mercury still in the back of his throat. He arrived home and heaved the keg to his shoulder. He grunted up the stairs like a rag-and-bone merchant, complaining and panting with every step. The sound of the laboratory dead bolt sliding into place was supremely satisfying. Louis sat on the floor, his hands blistered and red. The keg rested on its end, and now he saw the dented tin and wondered how he ever got the monstrosity home. He laughed at the prospect of the keg rupturing on the way, a gushing river of quicksilver coming down on the cobblestone. They might have arrested him. He allowed himself another exhausted laugh, and soon he noticed his top hat was torn on one side, and this prompted another chuckle, this time at his own expense, at the fool in the ragged hat loping his way through the boulevards. He had never felt so ridiculous and lucky.

He worked all day and night, refining the process. He decanted mercury from the keg into metal trays. These became his mercury baths, heated on the wood-burning stove and taken into the confines of the darkroom. If he angled the exposed image above the hot mercury, passing it back and forth, he obtained the best result. He watched the mercury vapors draw line and edge onto his plates. The air thickened around him, a metallic brume that watered his eyes. It had an elusive smell, something acrid but fleeting, like iron railings in the rain. It caught in the back of his throat, and sometimes he felt faint. But the images themselves made this discomfort inconsequential—here was time stolen, wafered, and pressed onto silvered copper; here were nature's blueprints, transcripts of light, from the finial point of a flagpole to the tweed edge of a man's jacket, all of it replicated in nuance, shadow, and substance.

After several months he perfected the bathing technique and was already showing the first signs of mercury poisoning—stomach cramps, headaches, soreness in the mouth and jaw. But what ran parallel to this progression of symptoms was the infatuation he developed for quicksilver. The liquid metal adorned his workshop and apartment; it glossed from jars along the windowsill, it lay beaded in the washroom sink. He didn't want to be without it and carried a phial of mercury around his neck at all times. In the middle of the day he would think about its silver sheen, about the way it defied chemistry and, like glass, stood between liquid and solid, between substance and reflection. He was, in a sense, in love again.

Madness began as a seduction. There were portents and omens; everything reminded him of his beloved. The world was infused with quicksilver—the Paris winter fogs were a lambent metallic gray, fixing pedestrians' images onto glass shopfronts; jars of rainwater gave off vaporous fumes; the coins in his pocket were silvered with it. He walked the streets, jangling his coins. He knew the process would carry his name— D-A-G-U-E-R-R-E-O-T-Y-P-E—and there was something scientific and stately about it, like the regal sound of geological ages or the Latin names of plants. The impossible vanity of it, he thought, but then he was struck by a sense of entitlement, of being chosen. He wrote a letter to François Arago at the Academie des Sciences, declaring his process with such phrases as *your humble servant* and an endowment for *His Majesty*. What he didn't write, but wanted to, was the simple and brash truth: *I see things others don't; I always have.*

Now Louis made a quick ascent. Here was the extended hand of fame. On August 19, 1839, nine months after hauling the keg of mercury across Paris, Louis Daguerre stood with Niépce's son — the elder Niépce had recently died — and François Arago in the great chamber of the Academy. The announcements in the newspapers had brought heavy crowds. People bustled into the baroque meeting rooms three hours before the sitting was due to commence. Louis opted not to make his own presentation, being satisfied with what he had set out in a pamphlet. He let Arago discuss the history of optics, the methods of the process, the applications for astronomy, art, and geology. When Louis heard the process referred to as the *daguerreotype*, he felt a sting of embarrassment; all the geriatric men of the Academy — patent-holders with hooded eyes, aldermen with aquiline noses and snuff pouches — peered in his direction. The vanity, the gall. But by the time Arago had woven a tale with the exactitude of a man who could prove the existence of planets with numbers and Greek letters, there was a palpable wonder and silence in the vast gallery. The process, said Arago, though seemingly mystical, was quite simple: a plate of silver upon copper is sensitized, then iodized, until it assumes a tint of pale yellow; the plate is inserted into a camera obscura, the aperture opened for a varying length of time, and then the plate is removed and the image is fixed with mercury vapor before being exalted in daylight. It was an exact replica of the scene before the camera, sketched by the sun herself. Arago held several of Louis's plates high above the lectern and then passed them around the room. Monocles came out; the old vanguard, the owl-faced men in frockcoats and gold-buttoned waistcoats, exchanged their Tartarean frowns for expressions of stifled awe. People had come in from the countryside—cattle dealers and their wives, gentry from the coast—and these folks clucked and cheered with delight, puzzled audibly over the verisimilitude of human faces and cottages before them. A band of Louis's old theater buddies—understudies and scenic painters—started a chant of *Honor to Daguerre*. Louis, wedged between Arago and Niépce's son, looked out at the crowd from the front of the room, at the nobles and workingmen, all of them rapt at the possibility of their own images enveloped in skins of silver. A sea of doffed hats. A standing ovation rippled through the crowd. He felt Arago's congratulatory hand at his shoulder. He shook hands with Niépce's son, Louis's other hand on top, sealing the shake in the manner of diplomats and mayors. A profound levity overtook his whole body. Louis took a very slow bow.

Within an hour of the presentation, Paris was crazed with photomania. Hundreds set out into the high-summer streets, descending on the optician shops for the makings of Louis's mercury dream. Within a week of this event, the country and the world knew him by name. Within three months, Louis's pamphlet went through twenty-five editions and five languages. Within a year, his process was being used on five continents, in service of almost every field of human endeavor—to yield photogenic drawings of fossils, for phrenology portraits of captured Congo slaves, to study the geological strata of the American West, to catalog the medical pathology of the harelipped and the goitered and the leprosied, to chronicle eclipses and astronomical events, to render portraiture of politicians and kings and heads of state. In America the luminaries paid their respects: Samuel B. Morse at the annual supper of the National Academy of Design said the daguerreotypes *could not be called copies of Nature, but portions of Nature herself* and that *the name Louis Daguerre will stand beside Columbus and Galileo.* Edgar Allan Poe called the daguerreotypes *miraculous beauties* and *photogenic drawings of absolute truth,* and a few years later, Walt Whitman, then-editor of the *Brooklyn Daily Eagle,* said the new art form possessed great magnetism and *captured the soul of the human face.* If Louis's portraits captured the mezzotint of reality, then these articles and kind words, unfurled across the newspapers and journals, were telegrams of his passage to fame. He had arrived.

FIFTEEN

here were other portraits of Pigeon, each of them brasher than the previous—her face coming towards the camera, her smile widening, her hair lit so that it resembled nothing but strands of copper and bronze. Then, in the middle of the night, the idea of a rooftop portrait came to Louis. He slept little these days, and the dog shared his insomnia. They went out onto the balcony, the wind gusting up from the streets. Snowdrifts blew in front of tavern doors, forming great waves above the gutters. From this height, with the wind a-gale and the slow blink of kerosene lamps behind a curtain of high-spun snow, Louis felt himself sway. He was standing on a ship's prow, the night cloaked around him. He studied the snow, the way it wheeled and flurried about the eaves. He saw an image of Pigeon reclining on a rooftop, tuberoses in her hair, white on white, a thousand smears of snow against her flesh.

The next day Pigeon met him at Baudelaire's derelict mansion. She was only too delighted to receive another hundred francs. When she arrived, he led her up the gloomy staircases to the rooftop terrace of Poet's Corner. Baudelaire, hair grown back, sat bundled in a deck chair. He wore a ragged fur coat and read Poe's "The Raven" beside a frosted brandy balloon. He looked up as they approached. "You can't take her portrait out here, Louis. She'll die of exposure."

Louis said, "Imagine it: the alabaster nude in front of the snow-tinged battlements."

Baudelaire considered this and looked at Pigeon.

She shrugged. "Makes no difference to me."

Baudelaire said, "And what about my portrait? When will I be commissioned for the list?"

"Please leave us," said Louis, spreading the legs of his tripod.

"I wouldn't mind watching, to be honest."

Pigeon bit at her nails and gave the poet a stage scowl.

Louis said, "I need my model's undivided attention."

"Yes, I'm sure you do." He winked at Pigeon.

"Goodbye," said Louis, looking off at the Paris rooftops.

Baudelaire stood and slouched across the terrace. He looked at Pigeon and said, "My balls are frozen. One by Poe, the other by the fucking cold."

Pigeon slapped Baudelaire on the shoulder before he disappeared inside.

Louis pulled from a cloth sack a satchel of hothouse tuberoses. There was a Dutch woman who kept a glasshouse on the Left Bank and used a system of mirrors, lamps, and skylights to grow veronica, roses, and carnations all year long for aristocratic families. King Louis-Philippe had once commissioned her to grow orchids in February. Louis handed the tuberoses to Pigeon.

"Where did you get these?" she asked.

"You'd be surprised what people do in the winter to stay sane."

"I know what soldiers do to pass the time," she said.

"Yes," Louis said gravely.

She walked towards the stone wall. Louis stretched out a bolt of red satin on the snowy terra-cotta of the rooftop and placed a number of tuberoses on the ground. He handed Pigeon several of the flowers.

"Do you know how to make a crown?" he asked.

Pigeon took them and began to weave a chain of stem and socket. "Mother taught me."

"She had a way with plants, no?"

Pigeon nodded. "Our house was filled with plants."

"Herbs?"

"Everything. She'd send off to London for seeds that came from the West Indies. We had a rubber plant in our garden."

"In Lyons?"

"It died. Lots of her plants died. She didn't care. She'd grow anything once."

"I see."

Louis rubbed a plate with carded cotton and inserted it into the back of the camera. With the snow and the wintry sun, it would have to be a long exposure.

"This may take quite some time to expose. I'm sorry if it will be very cold. As a result, I have decided to pay you an extra fifty francs."

"No, you can't."

"It will be fifteen minutes."

"I don't mind."

"Just the same, I am paying you more. There is a guild, you know, for nude models. I intend to comply with all their stipulations. A nude portrait in snowy weather is an automatic fifty percent increase."

"Stop teasing me. What am I to do?" she asked.

"I was thinking you might recline on your side, with one hand holding your head. I will have the camera tilted up so that you are in the foreground and the skyline is in the background. The turrets and steeples will be behind your head."

"And my expression should be happy or sad? Indifferent, perhaps?"

"Let's say beckoning. Not seduction, exactly, but a welcoming look."

"Louis?"

"Yes."

"Do you find me beautiful?"

Louis fumbled with the tourniquet screws at the back of the camera. "Why do you ask?"

"I'm merely curious. You must be the only man in Paris who hasn't made eyes at me."

"Well, I'm sure that in your line of work, you are surrounded by men."

"I don't mean my customers. Just men on the street. They all look at me."

"I see."

"What *do* you see?" She dashed her arms out to her side in a dancer's final pose.

Louis looked down at his hands; there was an opiate tremor in his fingers. She was a blond-haired emissary in the winding down of humanity. "I see a child of God," he said.

Pigeon hesitated to take his comment seriously. Then she saw his eyes, the unflinching gas blue she imagined burned in all artists, and she knew that he was earnest.

"Would you mind taking your position, Chloe?" said Louis. He made her real name sound like a rare and exotic bird.

She removed her boots and walked barefoot across the dusting of snow. She stepped gingerly onto the red satin and removed her coat and dress.

"I will take these from the frame," said Louis, crossing to the pile of clothes without looking up. There was something doctor-and-patient about their portrait rituals. He did not look at her without the protection of the camera lens. She lay on her side and propped herself on one elbow. He stood behind the camera. The wind had subsided and the air glittered with snow.

Louis craned up at the pale yellow sun, looked at his fob watch, then took a reading from a thermometer. Three degrees Celsius. "I will set the exposure for fifteen minutes. I will go inside and warm some coffee for after."

"I don't mind if you stay."

"It will show in the portrait."

"How? You will be behind the camera."

"It will be there. Like the shadow of a hand on a marionette." Louis held up his hand as a signal. "Are you ready?"

"Yes. I think I'll smile as a grimace from the cold."

He waited a moment, then opened the diaphragm. He imagined the meager sunrays burning into the plate, the falling snow reduced to a million droplets of iodine and mercury, the image unpeeling against the copper plate, the simultaneous bleaching and tanning that composed an image. *Capturing beauty is more chemistry than art.* He went inside and warmed the coffee.

When they left Baudelaire's mansion, Pigeon was shivering. Louis could hear the slight click of her teeth as they rode along in the carriage. He wrapped a blanket around her shoulders and apologized six times.

She said, "I will jump from this carriage if you say *sorry* again."

"I think you mean that."

It had stopped snowing. Old ladies bundled out of doorways to make a dash for the bakeries.

"May I take you somewhere to eat?" asked Louis.

"You may. But I will buy my own dinner. With my artistic earnings, you understand?"

"I support the rights of *les citoyennes*. You may buy my dinner, too, if you wish."

"I just might."

"Very good. I will eat nine courses and take brandy."

They pulled along the Montmartre streets, searching for a restaurant. A stream of carbines and carriages slowed up ahead, and they were forced to wait. From around the corner came a funeral procession, a frayed line of black coats and top hats. The casket rode on a wheeled flatbed, pallbearers trudging beside it. Pigeon stood on the box seat to get a better view. "I so love a funeral."

"Is that so?"

"Come on, let's join them." She stepped down from the carriage into the slushy street.

"It's the most indecent thing I've ever heard of."

She looked up at him, riled by his indignation. "You don't think the dead want a few extra admirers?"

"I doubt they care."

"Trust me, they don't mind. I have always loved a good funeral. Ever since I was a girl. By the look on your face, you must be very appalled."

"What about our dinner?"

"A funeral parade is good for the appetite. We'll follow them to the cemetery, then go eat."

"The devil himself."

"Perhaps the devil is a woman."

"I don't doubt it."

She turned from him and said, "Bring your camera."

"Impossible."

"Bring it."

"Good God, lady. These people have lost a loved one."

She began walking in the direction of the procession. Louis could see the priest carrying a leather missal, a scarlet cloth around his neck. Only recently had the Catholics come back out of hiding after so many godless years under Napoleon. Louis tied his horses to a hitching post and covered his equipment with blankets. He stopped a few paces from the wagon, then returned and took out his small zinc camera obscura. It carried a prepared plate, and he sometimes used it as a study camera. He placed the camera under his coat and hurried to catch up to Pigeon.

He fell in beside her, his eyes averting the huddle of family members at the rear of the procession.

"What is it, precisely, that you like about a funeral march?" he asked in a low voice.

"I feel an enormous peace settle over me."

"You are a very strange child."

"And you are a rather odd old man, if you must know. No one has worn a hat like that for fifty years."

Louis touched the rim of his hat.

Pigeon said, "The trick is to look at the ground. That way they don't notice you."

Louis looked down and assumed a dramatic bereft gait. "How is this?"

Pigeon laughed. "Very good. You're a natural showman."

"I've never been an actor, but when I was a young man, I threw elaborate dinner parties. I was the consummate host. I told stories and danced."

"You must have been quite a fellow."

"Indeed. The ladies swooned." He felt windblown, light; the mercury was nowhere to be felt in his lungs.

The procession ambled up a small hill. An old lady at the front lost her footing, and for a brief moment, everyone stopped and waited for her to regain composure. Her black veil blew a little in the breeze as she surveyed the short distance to the ceme-

tery. Louis realized with a slight feeling of shame that she was
the widow. She stood in front of the priest now at the vortex of a
wide V and led the procession up the hill with a slow and careful
plod.

"Sometimes they have pastries afterward. Usually at the
home of the widow or widower. Catholics send their dead off
with butter cake."

"I see. You come for the cakes."

"Not entirely," Pigeon said.

"I imagine your father had a large funeral. A man of wide
connection, was he not?"

"My father went into a crypt with his grandfathers and un-
cles, all of them bankers. The family legend was that the crypt
was full of Spanish gold. They buried themselves like pharaohs."

They passed onto the elm-lined gravel road of the cemetery.
Louis looked around at the headstones and adjusted the zinc
camera beneath his vest. "Were your parents happy in the beginning?"

"I have always suspected that I was conceived by mistake.
Later, when we moved and my mother started selling herbs and
medicines, pregnant women would come to her in secret. They
would stay in the carriage house, and she would slip out and take
them dark green teas and broths. Sometimes, when Father was
gone, I heard screams. She told me she helped women give their
babies back to God. That's how she spoke of it. We were very
close, though. That was to our detriment in the end. She could
not bear to let me marry the man I loved. Told me I should become a woman of substance and forget romance. He was a mu-
sician and a poet."

The funeral crowd now gathered around an open pit. The
pallbearers lowered the coffin into the ground and the priest in-
toned Latin. Louis and Pigeon stood near the back, under an
oak, and allowed the lilt of the priest's words to rise without

comment. A benediction, a scattering of dirt—to Louis a single death seemed such a trivial errand compared to what was coming. He pictured rivers spilling their banks, hillsides gouged and singed, horses and cattle dead in the fields. For now everything was stilled and waiting. It seemed possible to capture anything in the lens of the camera obscura, as if the world itself were frozen with a kind of mercury poise. Was the earth spinning slower, allowing time to slacken? He took the zinc camera from his coat. Without a tripod, he didn't hold much hope for the clarity and brightness of the image, but he pressed the camera into his chest and steadied his arms. He braced with his elbows and quietly opened the diaphragm and let the funeral scene register for several minutes. The sky was cloudy, the light bleak. Everyone stood more or less motionless, hunched and cold around the grave pit. The widow wept into a damask cloth. A sturdy man, perhaps the brother of the dead, placed his greatcoat over her shoulders. Later, when Louis revealed this image, he would see the shimmer of these movements—the phantom traces of embraces and condolences—and, above the pit, a clear and luminous rectangle of space where nobody cried or otherwise moved and where, presumably, the dead man hovered to hear his own eulogy.

The funeralgoers departed, and the gravediggers appeared in their dungarees and ale-colored hoods. Louis recalled that during the Reign of Terror, the executioners always received bread at their doors, but it had appeared upturned. He wondered if these men, clad in grime, their faces shadowy, did not receive some recognition from the living, perhaps a bowl of beef broth but with a crucifix of sorrel afloat. Louis, intrigued by the prospect of using a camera without a tripod, took Pigeon by the arm and walked towards the men.

"You men want some wine?" Louis called. He prided himself on still being able to talk to stagehands and apprentices.

"If you be that way inclined, we'll take an entire barrel." The two of them continued, shoveling the sodden earth as they guffawed.

"I should be glad to bring you some wine and bread. But I have a small favor to ask."

They stopped and leaned against their shovels, waiting with glazed curiosity.

"I would like to take a daguerreotype of you two."

"A what?" said the heavier man.

Pigeon said, "He wants to make a picture of you."

"With paint, then?" said the thinner man.

"No. I have an invention that will make the picture for me."

Some leaning on shovels, some gap-toothed skepticism. Louis realized these men had probably never read a newspaper in their lives. He produced the zinc camera and held it in front of him. The men visibly winced.

"We won't be captured with one of them things. Seen them out in the streets with what's-all pride of rich folk so that they can look at dead people on their walls. Dead don't want no pictures, no need for the living, neither. Take us in that contraption and we'll be dead by morning. We be digging out our own graves."

Louis looked down at the men. *Here we are in the Congo of Paris.* In New York there were hundreds of portrait studios with his name embossed above the transom, yet here among some of his own countrymen, he was a heretic, his invention a thief of souls.

"Good day, gentlemen," said Louis.

"Graveyard closes at dusk, and it's a rule we intend to uphold. You and your daughter should on your way."

Pigeon smiled, took Louis by the arm, and led him towards the gravel road. "At least they didn't say *grandfather.*"

"They would have made quite a picture," said Louis. "Gravediggers in the pit at dusk."

"I think you see things in a rather peculiar way."

"That has been the case since I was a boy. I loved a woman then and it changed the way I saw nature."

Louis could hear his feet on the gravel and looked out over the headstones. *The dead shall know their number.*

Pigeon took his hand. "Come on, Grandfather, cemeteries do strange things to a man. Let's find you a plate of mutton." They walked back down to the snow and pewter bowl of Paris.

SIXTEEN

Dear Isobel,

The last time you saw me, I was a child, barely hatched from nature's wonderland in Orléans. That kiss in the mouth of Notre Dame has always stayed with me. I ran home in the rain, cursing your name and stubbing my feet. But that was not the last time I saw you. One time, many years ago, you came to see one of my dioramas, and I watched you and your family observe my spectacle. I could not bring myself to say hello. You appeared to have a daughter.

Forgive my nostalgia for the past. I find these days I am somewhat infected with it. I pass washerwomen using a certain kind of soap, their hands deep in metal tubs of cold water, and I am transported to the days of my youth, to the smell of starched laundry on the breeze. You have been dredged up countless times in this mania for what I have already lived and seen.

I remember a day on the estate. We sat among the brook weed, half exposed to sun and air, and we watched fishes swim staidly beneath the surface. There were shoals of golden and silver minnows and occasionally one broke the surface to observe the heavens. They seemed aware of their watery prison and longed for what we had, all that sun and air. Then one fish leapt so high and continuously that we figured him for dead. But the more we looked, the more it seemed to be a simple lust for what he could not have.

Let me to the point. At the core of my life these past forty years has been a puzzle I cannot cipher. Even now it is difficult to say the broadside of what I intend . . . I loved you from the first. We played under the fronds of that love. And I always thought, suspected, hoped that you loved me in return. That day on Pont Neuf, you with child, began the rise of my career. I have often thought it ironic that losing you was what led me to fame. The grief that you would marry another and raise a child harnessed my deepest creativity. I wanted to singe life into the fabric of my canvases. At first from sorrow, then later in anger; I have tried to deny the power you have exerted on me countless times, but I cannot yield and now things have slipped . . . the flowering of our age is upon us, Isobel, but it is taking an unexpected turn.

I have reason to believe that time is running out. Not because I am an old man with a cough and thinning hair, but because there is a great disaster coming. A mighty wind of change is preparing to blow across our pond and we must prepare. Few know of God's conspiracy. Go out into a field at night and listen to the braying of horses and the lowing of cattle and look at the jaundiced tint of the moon and the recession of stars, bleached to a very empty white. Make friends with your enemies. Make peace with regret. This is my counsel.

Before the end I would simply like the chance to spend an afternoon with you. Is it possible that for a spill of hours we could be friends? I cannot yet tell you how I found you. There are things to *unfold. Please know that I carry this mission with much humility and forgiveness. You were, it seems, my best friend; somehow I lost you to the revolution and life and regret. I hope you find it possible to receive me as a visitor.*

Very sincerely,
Louis-Jacques-Mandé Daguerre

SEVENTEEN

inter left for a week in early 1848, a grace period of sun and shirtsleeves. Louis and Pigeon rode out into the countryside to take more portraits, not just of Pigeon but also of Louis's remaining list items. There were horses and birds still to render. They rode through small, indolent towns where the houses sagged, out along country roads with the farms all run out, wintered to brown and sod. These were towns of young girls and garrisons, of men lost to the revolution.

There were now two documents on Louis's person: the doomsday list and the letter, both fondled to the crepe of old maps. Sometimes, when not taking portraits and still lifes, he put them out on a café table and looked at the words. The loom and arch of his ink-work was infinitely fascinating to him; it seemed to be the hand of a man he was still yet to meet. Neither document was perfect, but both would serve. The letter would force him to make his reconnaissance with Pigeon more pointed. He needed, in short, the address of her mother. *The End* was upon them, all around, like the breath of a dog. And yet he did not want to reveal his place in her mother's life, both for some fear of involving the daughter in the sorrows of the past, and to avoid the awkwardness of the revelation.

Paris fell away. They passed pine houses flanked by meadow, a district of privacy, of stone walls and shuttered windows. There were woodlots where farmers presided with axes; there were provincial squares and public houses with low doorways. Sometimes, as they rode through these satellite towns, Louis saw a daguerreotype hanging within a parlor or a lobby. He couldn't help judging each rendition—summing up the concentration of mercury, the thickness of the silver coating—and pronouncing to Pigeon where the artist had made error.

"That one there misses the point entirely," he said, pointing to a grocer's window. A portrait of an old man behind the counter, presumably the owner, hung in the window next to canned meats and hand brooms. It seemed to be an advertisement of ownership, an incentive for street trade—*herein lies the owner, as portrayed in the window.*

"What's the matter with it? The old man looks sweet," Pigeon said.

"The artist has skimped on the silver coating. I look at that portrait and think cheapskate. I would never shop there. He probably hollows out the bread."

"You are sometimes convinced the world is pursuing you with some special vengeance."

"That sounds suspiciously like Baudelaire. Have you been in his company?"

"Maybe I have," she said, looking to the side of the road.

Louis felt the reins tighten in his hands; the horses began to trot. "I have warned you about Baudelaire. The bohemians say a woman is ambergris and wine, when they really mean pork and potatoes."

"He wrote me a poem."

"May I see it?"

"Certainly not. He said my hair holds an entire dream, filled with sails and rigging."

"Good Lord."

"He says he's dying of loneliness."

"Poets die of loneliness; the rest of us die of cholera and old age."

Pigeon looked away and studied the bend ahead. The little town, a village, really, gave way to low hills, a solitary windmill churning above an empty field. Louis scouted for more horses for his list. He had captured summertime mares and foals but wanted something darker, a wintering nag surrounded by patches of snow. It was not just beauty he wanted to capture, but decrepitude, nature gone to rot. There were no horses, but he saw a stand of bare elms where a lone crow hopped between the branches. He stopped the carriage. "I should like to take a portrait here."

Pigeon looked out into the barren field. "Of what?"

"The tree crowns and the crow."

"But up ahead there is a windmill. We could climb it. Imagine the view from up there, Louis. These fields extend in all directions from up there."

"A friend of mine climbed Notre Dame and took a picture up there of a man suspended in a hammock between the gargoyles. You know what it looks like?"

"What?"

"A man taking a nap."

"What is your point?"

"I open the eye of the camera to something I sense is there but cannot fully name or see."

"But surely there is a difference between a daguerreotype of horse dung and a picture of a naked woman."

He laughed. "Yes, the naked woman is more expensive to photograph."

"You delight in baffling me."

"That is the privilege of the old and dottery."

"All the same, I don't see what there is to capture out there except dead-looking trees and a mangy old crow."

"When you look at a funeral, you see cakes and a sweet kind of grief, isn't that so? It is a beautiful thing to you, but try to explain that to a baker's son, and he'll call you the devil. I have spent my life trying to understand light and this I know . . ."

"What?"

"I am being dramatic. The pause is dramatic."

"Stop." Her face flushed.

"There are two requirements for a powerful image: good light—by which I mean dynamic, strong in some regard, however fleeting—and composition, which lends itself to the light. If there were a beautiful mansion standing in that light, I would keep driving. It is the crow, the blue-black of its plumage, the ribbons of shadow and snow at the base of the trees, the way the clouds have gathered behind the hills in the distance. Look out into that field, Chloe. Do you see the way the shadows are weak?"

"Yes. Because it's late in the afternoon in winter."

"Correct. But look at the blueness in the snow; the shadows are fuzzy because they are essentially resting on top of water. I cannot fully capture that in the daguerreotype, but the facsimile will evoke the effect. There will be a slight brilliance in the coat of the crow."

She folded her arms. "Unless it flies away, which it might, if you keep yammering."

"It has a nest there. Crows can possess an entire field if they want."

"Oh, of course, you are also a bird expert."

He carried some equipment over into the field and began setting up. The sun moved in and out of cloud cover. Pigeon took a blanket and brought it out to him. "You should set your things on the blanket."

"Thank you," he said.

Louis adjusted the tripod. The sun was in the southwest quadrant and would shine almost perpendicular to the crow and the hem of trees. From this distance of about twenty feet, he would include the hills and the uppermost branches in the frame. The snow patches would be daubed across the hilly background. He polished a plate and inserted it into the back of the camera. They sat on the blanket, watching the clouds funnel around the pale sun.

"What are we waiting for?" asked Pigeon.

"The mercury moment."

"Which is?"

"When the image says, *Steal me now.*"

"But the sun is only growing weaker," she said.

"When the light and composition are mutually in balance, I will take the image. We also call that the kiss."

"The *kiss*?"

"When light kisses the object in a way suggested by its nature."

"So much philosophy!"

Louis lost a strand of patience. "Dear girl, are you so inclined to think that sunlight and love are not inexorably connected? That kisses do not happen in nature? That light upon a pond at dawn is not the sweetest form of lovemaking?"

She looked out at the windmill, the slow whorl against the snow. "Have you ever been in love?"

"Yes."

"Who was she?"

"She was a friend I fell in love with. There was a material discrepancy in our ages, and she, I think, disregarded her love for me on that basis."

"Then we have both lost the love of our lives. We are good pals on that front." She placed a hand on Louis's shoulder and began a series of concentric circles with her finger. Louis felt his breaths shorten. He could imagine kissing her and was appalled by that—it seemed like a desire to lie facedown in an icy stream, to burrow inside the very marrow of her youth and beauty and somehow indemnify himself against Armageddon. He looked down at his shaking hands, at the cordage of vein and tendon, at the sun splotches and freckles, at his own material surrender to the sun's chemical blackening. He felt impossibly old. He stood up, thereby interrupting the finger reverie at his shoulder, and went to tend his camera.

"The light is changing," he said.

"Is it?"

"Dusk is a kiss between night and day."

"You have an eye for romance, but perhaps no heart for it. Otherwise you would have married."

He ignored this comment. He tightened the tourniquet screws and sat back down on the blanket. "I'm an old man with a mission," he said. He looked down at the camera.

"I am a young woman with no mission at all."

He stepped back from the camera and looked at her. "You imagine you have some fondness for me," he said.

"I wasn't aware placing my hand on a man's shoulder indicated fondness."

"What, then?"

"Pity."

"*Pity?*" There was gall in the word when he said it.

"Yes. Sometimes I think I would kiss you out of a sense of pity. I want to rescue you, Monsieur Daguerre, and I cannot say from what. From the way you sometimes suddenly look in the street, like the cold hand of death is at your back. I would take you into my bed and give you a passing hour of joy just to make you forget whatever burden you think you carry on our behalf."

"*Our?*" He was near speechless. *Pity?* No one had ever pitied him, least of all a whore. He had a medal of honor from the king.

She continued, "Us. The living. Those feeling pleasure and making errors of judgment. I would sleep with Baudelaire, and do you know why?"

"Do I want to know?"

"Because when he had finished, I would have a moment when he would be mine, and he would say something I would not otherwise have heard. I would grant him permission to feel whatever he wanted. I do it for the money, but these men do it out of need or lust or weariness. When I grant them permission, it ceases to touch me. I could make love to the devil and be unscathed as long as I could look him in the eyes afterward. I do not love them individually. But sometimes I think I love them as a whole. Sometimes I imagine there are soldiers going into battle and getting killed with my name on their lips. We do not pretend it is love. But it is honest, Louis, and I will not be ashamed for what I do."

"Do I shame you?"

"In a manner, yes. By your money, by your silly knighthood, by your old-world manners that seem to pretend I hatched out of a salmon egg. I am the product of a marriage of convenience. I am a whore. I have chosen this life. I don't know myself to be capable of loving one man anymore."

Louis looked out into the fields, at the apparition of veined cloud and the transom of sunbeams west to east. He knew the mercury moment was coalescing, and he felt an urgency in his chest. He put his finger to his lips and Pigeon fell silent, drawn in by the quietude of the scene and the intensity of his expression. They sat motionless as it unfolded, as the cloudscape grew backlit and the trees gave off the shimmer of ice granules trapped in bark. The snow shadows gained definition in a sunburst, blued and deepened by a rise in contrast. Louis stood and moved slowly to the camera. He made a few adjustments to the angle and looked out at the radiant sky. Here was the way the vault of heaven would crack open on the final day, with those dazzled and portentous clouds, with shunts of granulated light. It resembled nothing so much as a sea of glass. He imagined saints driven through with sabers, chariots of righteous angels, a red dragon rising through coal smoke.

He became aware of standing in a field at dusk, of his life uncoiled. He felt the wind on his ankles. The light seemed to recede.

"Did you take the picture?" Pigeon asked.

He was suddenly light-headed, run through with grief. The era did not deserve this penalty. Men plucked theorems from the night sky, discovered new planets, proved the rotation of the earth. This was a spiteful God. He sat on the cold earth, his head between his knees.

Pigeon came and knelt beside him. "Are you all right?"

"The image got away," he said. He could feel the cold in his teeth.

"There'll be others."

"I need to sit for a spell."

"As long as you like."

She placed her coat around his shoulders and he was too weak to protest. In silence, they watched the crow guarding its nest and the dog-tooth line of stone fences. Then the darkness fell very rapidly. The sunset blackened to night, as if someone had lowered an awning over the day.

EIGHTEEN

ouis walked the city adrift, lost against the small munitions of the sensory world. His emotions were erratic. He felt a wave of fraternity when he saw a man being measured for a suit within a tailor's shop, fabrics laid out like so many striped walkways. The smell of verbena and green coffee made him maudlin; the colors of hempen sacks of winter vegetables made him hopeful, then dashed.

Signs were everywhere now. Men read poetry in the squares before bands of moved and cheering peasants. Funeral processions marched along the riverbanks with open coffins. People woke with cold fevers and came out onto the curbstone to look up at the stars. Crows flew into chimneys and windows. The fishmongers sold nothing but eel and herring. A woman leaped to her death from a town hall window. Somewhere in Paris a man was shooting dogs.

There were mercury chills, agues that scalded his eyelids. Louis lay in bed in his rooftop belvedere, surrounded by the brandied twilight of his portraits. He got drunk inside the husk of the fever. Faces brindled, boulevards receded, the room shimmered. *I may rise. The mind has mountains.* He could feel himself on the verge of great knowledge. The photographic record, the catalog of creation. Nothing was denied him. Then sleep, long hours in the pale afternoons.

Civil unrest was in the papers. The anti-royalists were organizing an outdoor banquet to protest the government's policies. Louis read about the dinner plans and thought of bunting, of paper lanterns strung between chestnut boughs. The workers' struggle—strikes, marches for higher wages—were an abstraction, a dinner story to tell grandchildren. It wasn't until he read about the fiscal crisis that he took it personally; his life's savings were in the National Bank.

The next day at noon, he went to close his bank account. He had no delusions that he could take his money into the afterlife, and neither did he want to spend it before the final day. He simply wanted to hold his accumulated funds in his hands. Here was fame made manifest, watermarked and bundled, secret codes lurking in the treasury inkwork. The bank gallery was a procession of bespectacled tellers behind mahogany and brass counters. Louis waited on the marble floor. Men in suits sidled as they filled out their withdrawal requests—*is there a run on the bank?* He filled out a withdrawal form for fifty thousand francs and presented it to a pink-faced teller. As Louis waited, he looked down at his own feet and noticed he was wearing a pair of mismatched shoes—on the left, a black English brogue; on the right, a brown Italian slipper. He stood looking down, baffled.

"Going on a trip, are we?" the man asked.

Louis paused, looked up. "Yes, a trip." The man's solicitousness and his skin, ruddy as a winter apple, bothered Louis.

"I will, of course, need the manager's signature," the man said. He gave Louis another look and went to the manager's office in the back. Louis looked around the bank. The vault door— a lead portal with lock-wheels at the end of the marbled

gallery—stood serene. It emitted a power over the bank customers, Louis thought, like the tomb of a virgin saint. People
kept their distance, regarded it sidelong. The teller returned,
pinker, more officious, and informed Louis that this amount of
cash was not kept in the drawers and that the manager was organizing to have the vault opened. Louis took a step back from
the counter and unleashed a torrential cough. The teller winced,
then the two of them looked on as the manager, a balding man
with a monocle, and two guards marched to the vault. A curtain
was drawn while the manager administered the combinations
and key locks. Louis heard the vault open. The smell of money—
something clothbound, like hymnals in an old church—wafted
into the bank gallery. After a moment the guards emerged with
a metal box and they carried it to the pink-faced teller. The teller
counted the money, and Louis presented him with a carpetbag.
He watched the stacks mount.

"What is your name?" Louis asked. It suddenly seemed important.

The teller puzzled this for a moment—perhaps no customer
had ever asked—then said, "My name is Antoine Cousier."

"Godspeed, Antoine Cousier," said Louis. "May you die in
peace." He carried his bag outside and strode home in his mismatched shoes.

Apocalypse came on February 22, 1848, the same day that the
government canceled the reformists' outdoor banquet. The
sound of bronze convent bells rallied in the streets. A wintry twilight settled over the river and pushed up against the tavern
windows, giving the glass an obsidian polish. Quietude as well as
a particular Parisian rot consumed the air—the offal of the abat-
toirs spilled across patches of snow; perfume factories funneled
expired ambergris and musk into the gutters. Louis knew it was

happening when the calm was ripped apart by cannon fire. The high-caustic smell of gunpowder rose from the garrets. He awoke from an afternoon nap in his bedroom, where he slept beneath the accusing burnt-almond eyes of his daguerreotype portraits. He dressed with some measure of calmness, putting on a silk cravat, a woolen suit and waistcoat, a top hat. In front of the silver-backed mirror, he resembled—for the first and last time—his father. His parents had passed away some years before, his father leaving Louis a gold-tipped pen, a watch and a compass, and half a century's worth of ledgers that balanced, month to month, down to the last hobnail. That this fatherly resemblance bloomed on the final day seemed both ironic and appropriate. *This is the day we become our fathers.*

Louis ran a bone-handled comb through his pomaded hair and then through the dog's bushy coat. He applied some mustache wax to the animal's chin and whiskers. "We must all be dressed for the occasion." Another sonic boom of cannon fire. Louis and the dog walked out to stand on the balcony. There was smoke and a light dusting of snow but no proscenium of cloud yet, no naphtha flash or magnesium flare from above. It would come slowly. At the end of the street a band of men were erecting battlements with all manner of household items: ladder-backed chairs, divans, kitchen tables, an old pianoforte that emitted an off-kilter arpeggio as it rattled across the cobblestone. They were going to try to fight it, Louis realized with simultaneous delight and horror. Only a nineteenth-century Frenchman would attempt to bring down the angel assassins with a musket or a flintlock. A blockade of carriages formed at the other end of the street, and Louis was galvanized into action, for it was clear they intended not to let anyone in or out of the faubourg. He needed to escape with his portraits, stash them in the catacombs beneath the Paris Observatory, find Pigeon, and have her lead him to Isobel. The immediacy of the world's decline would allow

Louis to take Pigeon to her mother without argument or resistance. Everything would be revealed.

He came in from the balcony and, in a gesture of finality, closed the heavy curtains that hung from the doorway. In the relative dimness, he gathered his supplies and took down the framed daguerreotypes. He had completed all but two of the portraits on his list — Isobel and the king — and this would have to suffice as a final testimony. He wrapped the pictures in hessian and secured a length of twine around each mummified portrait. But then he found a dozen more daguerreotypes he believed worthy of leaving to history, and it took him nearly ten trips to load them into his carriage. Each time he reentered the gloomy staircase, he felt his pulse throb in his neck. He stopped and leaned against the banister railing, his legs cramped, the brine of daytime sleep still in his mouth.

He loaded the carriage with a few other incidentals — his brushes and inks, his accumulated funds stacked inside the carpetbag. He felt a little silly bringing money into the apocalypse, but here it was, enough to buy a Paris apartment. He looked up and down the street. The barricades had become a leaning metropolis of housewares and furniture. A makeshift flag — a man's shirt dipped in red paint — hung from a broomstick at one end of his street, and at the other end a convoy of unhitched charabancs and buggies spanned from curb to curb. Perhaps an hour had passed, and a sulfurous storm had gathered in the distance. God's fury would begin with the mineral balm of rain before the gutters flowed with blood. Louis set the dog on the seat, climbed into the carriage, and gave the reins a snap. The horses took off at a trot in the direction of the wagon blockade. When the men at the blockade saw him approach, they converged upon their weapons — rifles, hoes, machetes, a bedpost with a metal spike attached. The leader, a bearded peasant in a brown hood, took a few steps ahead of the rest and raised his hand to the trotting carriage. Louis could see there was no opening in the line, so he had no choice but to stop.

The man in the hood yelled loud enough so that all his fellows could hear. "Slow down, old man. Not so fast. We're not letting anyone in or out."

"We both know what day this is, and I cannot be denied my final errand."

"Will you fight with us, citizen Daguerre?" a familiar voice called. It was the neighborhood stable boy.

Louis answered the crowd of militants. "It is futile to fight, but fight we must. Each in his own way. I have a battle to run on the other side, and time is running out. You see the storm approaching."

There was a brief conference during which Louis heard himself accused of being part of the ancien régime. The hooded man ordered several of the men to move their carriages, and soon a gap formed through which Louis could drive.

"See you on the other side, gentlemen," Louis called.

The men raised their weapons as he passed them by.

Louis could not gallop his horses on account of the glass-fronted plates, but he continued to trot through Montmartre and out towards the Paris Observatory. He wended past the old mansions of the Right Bank where scenes of terror and discord played out—bonfires of antique furniture and heirlooms burned in stone courtyards; favored pets, Abyssinian cats and green parrots, were being released by servants. He moved up a hill and heard the distinct and lonely sound of piano scales coming from an open Gothic window. He passed a looted department store, its windows smashed and all the mannequins broken apart in a scatter of white clay limbs. He saw a hospital with all its doors and windows flung open. Some of the gowned patients—men with the blue-white pallor of malaria and typhoid—wandered out into the street. Peasants hauled off wheels of cheese and pairs of leather boots. Bankers and merchants paced on their mansion rooftops with pistols. Bands of gypsies wandered out of ransacked churches with candles and incense. A priest's white robe was slung over the back of a mule. Through all this Louis passed unhindered. He rode through the sinuous streets with the same authority that Pope Pius and Napoleon had possessed on coronation day forty-three years earlier. Out of certain door-ways, Louis saw hunched women and old men. Those too scared or too old to fight God's judgment gave him a solemn salute or the sign of the cross. For a moment he imagined himself a saint of the people.

The Paris Observatory stood in the gloom like a galley ship, its stone wings flanked by shadow. The looting had not come this far, and Louis was able to tie his horses and unload his portraits onto the stoop of the main entrance. The main door was closed and he knocked with the heavy brass ring. He feared for a moment that the observatory had been abandoned along with the grocer shops and wine cellars. Then he could see in his mind the image of Arago on the rooftop, watching the celestial scene unfold, and he was not at all surprised when France's eminent astronomer came to the door himself.

"Daguerre."

"I've come to stash my portraits. As we discussed."

"What on earth has happened to you?" Arago looked him up and down.

Louis looked down at his clothing. "I've just ridden across the city. There is mud in the streets."

"Quickly, come in, before the Municipal Guard sees us. There is an immediate curfew."

"I suppose you know, then?" said Louis, entering.

"I think all of France knows by now."

"We will all be dust soon enough." Louis came close and pressed a hand against his waistcoat. "The key to the catacombs, François. Take me there."

Arago reeled from Louis's acrid breath before complying. They brought in the portraits from the stoop and bolted the door.

"Wait here and I will get the key from my study." Arago climbed the spiral staircase to the landing above and returned in a moment with a silver key on a chain. "If we are caught, I know nothing of this. You stole the key, do you understand me?"

"Of course. I am eternally grateful," Louis said absently.

"I must leave with my family in less than an hour. I will show you where it is, but you must take the portraits there by yourself."

"Lead on."

Arago turned on his heels and walked to a small iron door beneath the spiral staircase. He took the key and slid it into the barrel. The opening of the iron door unleashed a pestilential stench from the catacombs, a fetid smell that Louis imagined as the dead getting ready to rise. Arago lit a torch and handed it to Louis.

"At the bottom of the stairs is a small chamber and an informal crypt for our illustrious colleague. That would be a good place to store your pictures."

"Thank you for this kindness, Arago."

"I worry about you, Louis. I think perhaps you're out of your head."

Louis dusted off his coat sleeve and glanced up. "No matter."

Arago kissed Louis's cheek and they embraced.

"Long live the freedom of France," said Arago. He turned and headed for the main entrance.

❊   ❊   ❊

Louis made his first trip into the bowels of the catacombs, passing down a long, winding staircase. He carried two portraits and a torch and took the steps two at a time. The air was thick with the chalky smell of lime powder. At the bottom of the stairs, he reached a kind of anteroom. There were entrances to stone tunnels in five directions, each with a Roman numeral inscribed above the portal. Between two of the entrances stood a small shrine to Cassini. Far from being an informal tribute, it was a gilded coffin with an observation window, so Louis could see that the dead man was wearing a shroud worthy of a medieval prophet. The body and the face had evidently been lacquered or varnished, because in places where more than bone was visible, the skin appeared chipped. Behind the coffin was another small alcove, and it was here that Louis leaned his portraits up against the relatively dry walls.

He made a dozen trips up and down the stairs until all his portraits were in the alcove. He stood before them. The edge of a plate poked out from a frayed corner of hessian. It was his rooftop portrait of Pigeon, and as he attempted to reseal it, he was overcome with a desire to keep it. He unwrapped it entirely and looked at it under the reddish light of the torch. The snow was a coppery vanilla, her pale shoulders and breasts the color and texture of bone shank. He wrapped the portrait and put it under his arm, certain that he would die holding it as a battle shield. He climbed the last flight of stairs and emerged breathless and heaving into the gun-smoke clamor of the street. Night was everywhere.

The section of Montmartre where Pigeon lived and worked had been spared the worst of the rioting. Louis brought his carriage into the head of her street and was surprised by the relative tranquility. The bells of Notre Dame rang incessantly like a storm warning, but the storm itself had come no closer. A branch of lightning appeared in the south. Louis pulled up in front of Pigeon's apartment. He knocked on her door, but there was no answer. He looked over at the veranda of the brothel, where all manner of dandies and whores smoked in the first hour of darkness. Yellow paper lanterns swayed in the breeze, and every now and then a waft of cannon smoke blew up from the garrets. Louis called out to a man who was wearing nothing but a stocking cap. "Has anyone seen Pigeon?"

The man looked over blearily and shrugged. Louis was forced to take the stairs, and as soon as he reached the top, three ladies took his arms.

"Everything's half price," one of them whispered into his ear.

"Good God," said Louis. "This is how Paris dies? At the feet of a whore?"

"No," said another, "not the feet."

"I'm looking for Pigeon. Have you seen her?"

One of the women pointed inside, and Louis walked through the double doors. He was in a sitting room of soft lighting, with sultry accordion music coming from an unknown source. Half a dozen men sat upright and stiff on a divan. Louis walked past them without eye contact and down a hallway of crimson velvet wallpaper. There was an unbroken line of closed doors on both sides of the hallway. He had not permitted his entry into Pigeon's house of employment before, so he would tell himself various conceits and lies about what she did — she was a mere companion, someone to draw a bath for a weary man. Now, as he walked past each door and heard female panting, the delirious name calling, the catcalls and whistles, the shuddering wrought-iron beds, the grit-toothed noises of men on the verge, there was little room for doubt about what she really did to pay her rent. A blond woman in a brassiere emerged from a room at the end of the hall and saw Louis standing, hands across his chest, stupefied by the sexual cacophony.

"Have to see the madam first," she said, ushering him back to the sitting room. "Go wait with the rest of them."

"No, you don't understand. I am here to see Pigeon."

"You and half the men in Paris. Now, see the madam."

"No. I am her friend. I am Louis Daguerre," he said, sputtering slightly.

"I don't care if you're Louis the Fifteenth back from the fucking dead. Everyone's got to see the lady of the house and wait in the sitting room."

At that moment a voice called out from farther down the hallway: "It's all right. He can talk to me."

The woman in the brassiere huffed past Louis and into the sitting room to collect her next client. Louis turned around to see Pigeon peeking from a half-open doorway.

He took a few steps down the hallway. "Pigeon, we must leave at once. The day is here, and we have something of magnitude to perform. There isn't much time."

She continued to speak through the crack in the door. "What's the point? I intend to cash in on the revolution this time. I'll service both sides, the army and the rebels, and together they will buy me a little house in the country. I want a garden, Louis."

"Stupid child, this is not a revolution. Have you not seen the warnings?"

"Call it what you will, but there is money to be made."

Louis walked slowly towards the door. He stood a few feet away and could see part of a man's figure lying on the bed. A sheet was draped in front of his lap, and he reclined against pillows.

"Who is it, for God's sake?" called the man.

"Keep quiet," Pigeon told him. She turned back to Louis. "I will be finished in a short time, and then we can talk."

Louis pinched his eyes shut. "No, you don't understand. We must leave now."

The man's voice came more strongly. "Come on, my little raspberry. I'm withering in here." The word *raspberry*. Louis felt his back tighten and his hands curl into fists. He could see the whites of Pigeon's eyes. She instinctively closed and locked the door, leaving Louis in the dim hallway by himself.

"I am sorry, Louis," she called. "This is my business."

"Please step away from the door," Louis shouted.

"Jesus and Mary, is that Daguerre?" came Baudelaire's voice.

"Don't be rash," called Pigeon.

Louis scanned the hallway for weapons. Nearby was a side table piled with postcards from America and Greece, the well wishes from wealthy clients abroad. Louis swept the postcards to the floor. He dragged the table in front of Pigeon's door. He took a few steps back, reared the table, and made a fumbling assault. The table slid out of his hands and fell to the floor. Several of the men from the sitting room, roused from their prefornication vigil on the divan, gathered at the end of the hallway.

"What do you intend with that, brother?" called one of them.

Louis looked to his side but couldn't make out any of their faces. "That is my daughter on the other side of this door. Will you boys help me?"

A rabble began down the hallway, three of them pounding walls with their fists. The idea of a man's daughter in this place galvanized them into an evangelical thunder. A big man in a dun-colored coat took the side table from a shaking Louis and set it on its end. He then positioned himself in front of the door and shouldered it with one sudden movement. The door snapped open to reveal a half-dressed Baudelaire and a fully dressed Pigeon. Baudelaire looked at Louis and knew in an instant that his apocalypse had arrived. Baudelaire smiled faintly. "Louis, what a surprise."

"If Pigeon stays here, I will instruct these men to help me murder you," Louis said. He could feel his hands shake.

"For the love of God, calm yourself, Daguerre."

"Louis, stop it," said Pigeon.

"My carriage is outside. We have somewhere to go, Chloe," said Louis.

The mention of Pigeon's real name changed the atmosphere in the room. The men found this further proof of the familial relationship between father and daughter and assessed Baudelaire as a man in leg irons.

Louis said, "Baudelaire, I suggest you leave and go fight for your life with the devil."

"Louis," the poet said imploringly.

But Louis had already turned away.

"Please leave," said Pigeon to Baudelaire.

"Very well. Good day, gentlemen." Baudelaire, shirtless, a dragon-green cravat over his shoulder, stepped gingerly through the rabble of men. Louis heard the sound of Baudelaire's brogues in the hallway and folded his arms. The three men took this as their cue to exit. Louis regained composure and turned to face Pigeon.

"Don't worry about packing a bag," he said. "We must leave at once."

"I told you, I'm not going anywhere."

"Your mother will be dead by morning." He said it without any hint of melodrama. "I assume you would like to make peace with her before it is too late."

Pigeon waited for further explanation. Her forehead gathered toward a single knot. Louis turned for the door and said, "I will wait for you outside." As he passed through the sitting room, he noticed that the men who had helped him had quit the brothel, their lust no doubt killed by a display of righteousness.

When Pigeon plunked down into the carriage, she said only

one word: "Orléans." It made perfect sense—Isobel had returned to the countryside of her youth. Louis rode along the
back roads south of Paris. The way was littered with small
proofs that this was, in fact, the first day of another French revolution rather than the last day of man's tenure on earth. If he'd
had the eyes to see it, Louis might have noticed that the storm
had evaporated into the cobalt night; that men were shooting at
one another and not at the clouds; that the king's soldiers were
deserting not in celestial fear but in solidarity with their peasant
brothers. They rode out past burning churches and boarded-up
shopfronts. Every now and then the night came alive with the
phosphor of pistol fire. Burning projectiles—lit rags in wine bottles—were hurled from windows. A dead quiet settled over the
hamlets and villages. Candles glowed from basement windows;
root cellars were nailed shut. Pigeon and Louis traveled along in
silence, the carriage horses barreling them towards the Loire
Valley.

About two hours from Paris, there was evidence of skir-
mishes between the National Guard and the peasants. The
charred remains of carriage blockades smoked through the darkness, piles of wheels and ravaged timbers. Peasants were forti-
fying the squares, black-clad and nimble—an army of dairy
hands and blacksmiths, petty clerks and town criers. Louis assumed these men were battening down for the apocalypse, shel-
tering from the storm, even as they yelled revolutionary
warnings at his passing carriage.

Pigeon finally broke the silence. "You had better tell me what
you know of my mother." She looked straight ahead at the road,
into the narrow cone of illumination from the carriage lantern.

Louis, in finery besmirched with ash and dirt, regripped the
reins. The horses were slowing; they would need to water before
long. He turned back to check on the dog; somehow it dozed
happily beneath a blanket on the flatbed. He didn't know how to

answer Pigeon's question. "I knew your mother from before you were born."

"I see," she said. "You've lied to me this whole time. Digging for information about her."

"Partly," said Louis. "The other part was that I really did need a nude model."

Pigeon angled her chin and then her eyes at him. "What were you to her?" she said flatly.

"A friend."

"And what else?"

"She was my maid when I lived on an estate outside of Orléans." Three shots rang out across a meadow. They both turned to look in that direction. "I was in love with her. But she married your father instead."

Pigeon nodded. "Why?"

"Why what?"

"Why didn't she love you back?"

"Because I was fourteen and she was seventeen."

The simplicity of it stung him. Of course she had been unable to love him back. Had he spent his life puzzled by such a straightforward matter? But even when she was twenty-two and he nineteen, and the age gap had become more respectable, it was still no use. The finality of Pigeon's existence had separated them for life.

"It's possible I have loved your mother for forty years," Louis said, squinting at the dark road.

"She is not who you think she is," Pigeon said.

"I knew her before she changed."

"The woman you'll meet tonight is a stranger to love. Prepare yourself for that."

"I simply wish to spend these final hours with her."

"Don't be so melodramatic. The revolution will come and go, the king will be overthrown. We'll get some socialist bandits at the helm for a while. The cost of bread will go down for a few months."

Louis knew that he had to tell her of the dark angels. Who knew what was going on right now? Judgment Day surely had an administrative side, the weighing of evidence, the examination of sins and good deeds. Somewhere angels were performing inquisitions, scanning the clamor of Paris for the light rim of a good and noble soul. Just as Louis lost himself to this line of speculation, they passed a small band of peasants who stood hollering by the roadside, weapons held aloft.

"You'd better stop," said Pigeon.

"They'll kill us. Things are desperate now."

A loud voice called from behind. "The road's closed!"

Louis kept their course. Several men mounted their horses and came in pursuit. Pigeon turned and yelled, "We are socialists on our way to see my dying mother." But her words were broken off, lost to the chill night.

"I will not be detained," said Louis. "Not by some shit-pants peasant with a riding crop." He bellowed a cattleman's yell and the beleaguered horses rushed on.

Pigeon turned to see one of the horsemen galloping nearer, his white horse snorting smoke in the cold air. The man, bald and bearded, swiveled his torso to the side and reached beside his saddle. He was no more than twenty feet behind them.

"Stop in the name of the revolution!" he cried.

Louis hunched forward, eyes down. The night cracked open around him. He looked out at the dark furrows packed with snow, the transepts of the pasture fences, the unlit pine-board houses, the road ditches stippled with dead weeds. He thought of the old country, the France of his father; had it been a sylvan province beyond God's scorn? He was faint, dry-mouthed. Pigeon's voice beside him —*errant girl*— a dog barking from a dell. *Grant me the rectitude of the great.* The lather and fetor of horse sweat, the whitened eyes. The tremor started, as always, in his hands. He felt it mount. He thought, oddly, of cats sleeping behind cheese-shop windows. He thought of animal eyes—the haunting irises of his horses like twin bronze discs, the glazen contempt in the stare of a wolfhound. The animals had known all along, he thought, the little bastard spies of the apocalypse. Something sharp from behind; a tenterhook in his shoulders. Now the teeth, the taste of bone in his mouth.

The musket shot ripped him open.

The horses whinnied and the carriage swaggered towards a ditch. Louis slumped forward with the deadweight of stone, his hands reaching behind his back where the lead shot had flayed his back open. Pigeon grabbed the reins and steered the horses. The horsemen fell back. She heard the leather straps strain as the horses unleashed themselves, their teeth clacking at their bits. She cinched the reins around her hands; Louis slumped at her feet.

By an old barn she pulled off the road. He was still breathing, his hands quivering by his side. He lay there looking up at her, openmouthed, incredulous, as if another man's fate had befallen him. "Not here," he said.

Pigeon laid him flat on his stomach and examined the wound. His woolen jacket was shredded, soaked through with blood. She rummaged in the back of the carriage for a makeshift bandage and came upon the dog, sleepy-eyed but startled. She had seen the strange animal at Louis's studio before, but in this moment it looked menacing—eyes down, teeth bared, its fur raised. The dog circled a crate and lay back down. She found a piece of torn muslin, came back to the front of the carriage, and wrapped it around Louis's wound.

"I'll be furious if you die," she said.

Louis's eyes opened, then closed. She got back on the box seat and yanked at the reins. The horses—froth-mouthed, near-broken—barely noticed. She took hold of the riding whip and snapped it out in front of her. It gave a sudden crack and the horses mustered up a trot. She forced herself to sing to Louis as they continued towards Orléans, old songs her mother had taught her about shepherds and monks all protected on their hilltops.

NINETEEN

sobel Le Fournier had always lived like a maid in her own houses. Her profession as a young woman became her disposition in later life, so she never fully settled into the role of banker's wife and lady of the house. She bickered with the cook like a surly underling, insisted on clearing her own plate, rose at first crow to leave for her solitary walks via the kitchen. On her honeymoon—a steamer cruise through the Greek islands—she had criticized the tautness of the bedsheets and the flower arrangements in the dining cabin. These were not comments of aesthetic disapproval so much as scathing criticisms of the indolence behind such failures. Although there was a part of Isobel that despised the rigors and small humiliations of servitude, she also secretly believed this was her lot in life and resented those who served ineffectually. Her skill in healing, the fact that she had a reputation in the valley as a master apothecary and herbalist, did not stop her from half believing she was a maid engaged in a hobby, a dalliance with leaves and seeds.

Her widow's cottage stood on a hectare of marsh and field. She had chosen it for the purpose of growing old in a region where she knew the plants by name. The house had large south-facing windows and a wide veranda where she sat in the afternoons in a wicker chair. Inside there were two sparse bedrooms, a kitchen, a sitting room, a glassed-in room for her plants. There was an unfinished air to the interior, a reluctance to settle. After five years, unpacked wooden crates had become furniture. The curtains were hung with pinned hems. The main exception to this unfinished theme was in the rear of the house, where Isobel kept her herbarium. It had all the order and Latinate charm of a royal botanical garden. She'd had a walnut counter made with transparent drawers in which she stored dormant seeds and the alcohol for her tinctures. Her exotic and medicinal plants were labeled with common and botanical name and arranged in neat rows, the tallest of them farthest from the sun. This ensured an economy of sunlight, a system whereby those that prospered were moved to the back. When townspeople came to buy herbs or potions from her, they went to the back of the cottage and rapped on the glass and iron door. If she liked the customer, she would recommend additional herbs to supplement his or her health: horehound in honey for coughs; rosemary infusions for shiny hair; valerian for insomnia; milk thistle for a healthy liver.

There were runs on certain herbs. A miracle cure for earache would result in mothers of all stripes tapping at her back door, and for a period of time almost every child in Orléans was free of ear infection. She cleared an entire hamlet's constipation with flaxseed after they ingested excess calcium from their limestone well. Recently, the owner of a restaurant had come to commission a new strand of sorrel and mint for his culinary use. Under Isobel's hand, these herbs gained a medicinal potency—customers returned to the restaurant just for glasses of minted springwater and river fish infused with sorrel. They claimed the mint cured their bad dreams and the sorrel banished their vertigo. But when the restaurant owner returned to commission ad-

ditional hothouse plants, Isobel denied him. "This is not a factory," she said, handing him the last seeds of the wonder mint.
She was known for this kind of action, for renunciation at the
first sign of prosperity. Isobel's biggest fear was continuing anything past its prime.

Amid this lifestyle of reluctant healing and ramshackle
decor, Isobel had discovered solitude for the first time in her
life. In her simple stone house, the low-ceilinged rooms smelling
of sagebrush, she spent most of every day alone, drinking nettle
teas for her cold-prone lungs, reading seventeenth-century novels, and pruning her plants with a pair of nail scissors. She
wrote no letters, received only visits of purchase or begging.
She kept a stable hand—a boy who slept in the barn rafters and
performed chores—but he was too young to be of any use as
company. There had been a few vain attempts from widowers
and aging bachelors in the area to court her. One man, a Vitien
Spargo, became a hypochondriac, complaining of everything
from ingrown toenails to premature balding as excuses to return
to her back door. Isobel had sent him away, declaring his symptoms were the early stages of syphilis. She woke alone each
morning, a little lonely but relieved that she had finally escaped
the world of men.

Isobel was home and tending the fire this winter night in February 1848. She didn't know that the country had risen up again.
She placed a piece of oak onto the flames and sat down with her
needlework. Embroidery occupied her hands and stilled her
mind. Although her days were slow and sometimes dull, her mind
rattled with lists—seeds to germinate, repairs and errands. After
some time, she set aside the needlework and returned to her
novel, a saga about maritime warfare. The hero had just been
shipwrecked on an island off the coast of Africa and built himself

a shanty out of driftwood. It rained a deluge and the man was sodden through; but as she read, she couldn't help but think of the wife and child he had in Brittany. Shipwrecks and driftwood shanties seemed like extravagances of men. The wife worked in a soap factory. While her man keelhauled Madagascan pirates, slept with bare-chested sub-Saharans, and ferreted for gold, she worked her hands to the bone.

When Isobel heard the carriage pull towards the house, her first thought was that a customer had come for some emergency herbs. She put her feet back in her slippers, wrapped a woolen shawl about her, and brought a lantern to the back door. The loud banging, when it came, was from the front door. She took the lantern to the front of the house and lifted the crossbar that secured the door. In the doorway stood a ragged woman, muddy in the face, her hair wild with the wind.

"What in the Christian world!" Isobel said.

The woman looked down at her bloody, chafed hands. She shook all over.

"Are you hurt?" asked Isobel, softer.

"Mama, it's me," Pigeon said, looking up from her hands. Her eyes were rimmed red, widened back. "I have a man with me and he's been shot."

Isobel's hand rose to her throat, as if to stifle a cough. "Chloe," she said. The plainness of her daughter on the stoop, bloody-handed. Involuntarily, she took a step back and tightened her shawl. Again, "Chloe."

"He's bleeding quite badly. I've bandaged it a little."

Isobel came out into the cold night, wrested from her shock. They walked towards the carriage, where a man lay flat on his stomach, draped with blankets. The stable hand was already unhitching the ragged horses.

"What happened?" Isobel asked. She pulled back the blankets to reveal the back wound.

"Some peasants shot at us. There's going to be another revolution," Pigeon said.

Isobel ran her hand along the wound's edge. "He's lost a lot of blood. I'll fetch a bedsheet and we'll use it to carry him inside."

She rushed into the house and returned with a sheet. The two of them rolled the unconscious man onto the sheet and attempted to hoist him from the carriage flatbed. They cleared the railing but immediately had to set him on the ground. They made a dozen small lifts and landings to get him inside and lying on Isobel's bed.

"If he dies in my bed, it will be the end of my herb practice. The house will be cursed," Isobel said. She lit a carbide lamp at the bedside and pressed the bedsheet into the man's wound. He was, at this moment, anonymous—a list of repairs. She retrieved some warmed water left over from her tea, some cloth, her nail scissors, her sewing kit, and a pair of pincers she used on her seedlings. She came back into the room and set these things on the night table. Pigeon sat down on the bed. "By the time we've fetched the incompetent old doctor from town this man will have bled to death. I'm going to try to remove the bullet fragments. Get me the brandy from the kitchen table." Pigeon was lost in the weave of the bedspread. "Chloe, I need your help. Get me the brandy now." Pigeon stood, retrieved the brandy, and set it down. Isobel heated her nail scissors over the lamp. After a minute or so, she swabbed the scissors with a brandy-dipped cloth. She wiped the wound and began prying down with the scissors, looking for metal glints in the lamplight. Half a dozen fragments shimmered. "Lead shot is everywhere," Isobel said.

Pigeon watched her mother dig through the constellation of lead-blue stars. She considered briefly revealing his identity, but with each cut and retrieval, Louis Daguerre receded, becoming little more than this augered rent of flesh. Isobel's hands worked nimbly for an hour—cutting, probing, dabbing—until a neat row of shrapnel lined out her nightstand. She cleaned the wound with soap and water, then stitched it with the thick-gauge cotton she used for brocade work. The close stitches seamed the divided skin, creating small red nubs between the threads of cotton. She covered the wound with a bandage.

"Who is this poor wretch?" she asked.

"An artist from Paris," said Pigeon.

Isobel set Chloe up in the spare bedroom with warm water and fresh clothes. She put some soup on the stovetop, staring down through the metal hatch at the coals. The world did not contain the words of magnitude to redress five years' silence. What was she meant to do? Inquire with civility, offer bread. She stared into the embers. It came to her that Chloe had been born on a Friday in August, at midnight.

Isobel fetched her daughter a bowl of soup and they sat by the fire. Pigeon fell asleep near the end of the soup. Her spoon pinged against the stone floor. Her head slumped against her chest. Isobel watched her for some time. Chloe had aged, and there was the suggestion of excess in her face—day freckles, worry lines, ashen half-moons beneath her eyes. Paris had not treated her well. Sometime after midnight, Isobel got up from the fire and draped a blanket over Chloe. She leaned down and smelled her daughter's hair. She wanted to kiss her forehead but didn't. She went to check on the shot man in her bedroom. He slept soundly, his face half submerged in her pillow. She pulled the blanket up to his collar and whispered, "May you wake without pain."

Pigeon woke in the empty and cold hours of the morning, her body stiff from the chair. She checked on the sleeping Louis, then went to find her mother. Isobel stood in the herbarium, leaning over a plant with her nail scissors.

"Do you operate on them as well?" asked Pigeon.

Isobel looked up, smiled briefly, cocked one eye at a frayed leaf edge. "Good morning, Chloe. How did you sleep?"

There was something formal and stiff in the greeting. Pigeon reminded herself that she was Chloe again. "Not very well. I had frightful dreams."

"A fog's come up overnight. They say fog is bad for your dreams."

"Who says that?"

"People who have bad dreams when it's foggy." Isobel placed her nail scissors on the bench. "Would you like to take a walk before breakfast?"

Chloe nodded. They went to the front of the house and bundled into the coats and hats that hung by the door. Isobel unlatched the door and they stepped outside. They walked without speaking for a while, back behind the house and the woodpile, where the acreage gave onto a marsh and a thicket of leafless oaks and sycamores. Fog ribboned across the marsh and they both watched it, waiting for the other to speak.

"Where have you been, Chloe?" Isobel said. "I finally gave up making inquiries. Somewhere in Paris, that's all I could find out."

Chloe put her hands into her coat pockets. "I've been trying to survive. That's not easy to do in Paris."

"You could have asked me for money."

"No. I didn't want your support. Not after what happened with Richard."

"I admit I didn't want you to marry that man. He had no way of supporting you."

"When Father offered him money to stay in England, you never spoke up for me."

"He didn't have to take your father's money. But he did, and you never forgave him for not coming back."

"No, I never forgave you and Father."

They came to a stand of oaks and walked the edge of the marsh. Neither of them looked up from their feet.

Chloe said, "I was already old when I met Richard, Mother. He may have been my last chance."

Isobel could hear their footsteps on the ice-laden grass.

Chloe said, "After Father died, you wanted me to be a spinster. You wanted someone to get old and lonely with."

"That's unfair," Isobel said.

"Is it?"

They stopped walking. Their breath smoked in front of them.

"You failed at love, and you wanted me to fail," Chloe said.

"Don't be ridiculous." Isobel took off her woolen gloves.

"Well, you'll be happy to know that I gave up on love many years ago."

"You have your whole life ahead of you. There are plenty of good men in society."

Chloe looked back at the fog. It was everywhere; the world was edgeless. "I am almost forty, Mother. What kind of man would want me now?"

A long silence. Birds in a tree.

"Who is that man inside my house?" asked Isobel.

"Don't worry. He would not have me. He's in love with something only he sees in his photographs."

"He's a photographer?" asked Isobel.

"Yes."

"And there's nothing between you? Because he's old enough to be your father."

"He could have *been* my father."

The fog buried sound, tamped their voices.

"What?"

"I said he could have been my father."

"What do you mean by that?"

Chloe waited for the force of the revelation to make its way from her stomach to her throat. She knew she was about to shatter her mother's life in some way. She felt it the instant she'd walked inside the stone cottage and seen the crates arranged like furniture. She'd recognized it in the herbarium, with the world's plants arranged and labeled like so many museum specimens — the pharmacopoeia of loss. It was not the result of idle hands but the passion of an idle heart.

"The man sleeping in your bed is Louis Daguerre. He says he has loved you his whole life. If it weren't for him I never would have come."

Isobel looked down at the ground several times, then out into the thicket. She felt herself go white. She looked back at the house. It rose bleak and amorphous as a sloop through the fog, the veranda aslant, the windows darkened. The past had rapped on her door, white-knuckled. "I did not ask for this," she said.

"He told me he might be the reason you stopped believing in love."

"The man is clearly insane."

"Is he?"

"I stopped believing in love when your father died."

"You're saying you loved him with all your heart?"

Isobel's lips grew thin and tight. In an instant she aged bitterly; there was the pull of an unspoken rant about her mouth. She said, "I didn't have my whole heart to give."

"Why?" asked Chloe. She stood her ground. Her mother's eyes scattered and drifted. "Why, Mother?"

"Let's go inside and eat breakfast. I'll tell you about Louis Daguerre as best I can."

They walked back towards the acreage. On the front stoop of the cottage lay the dog, dead and dusted with snow. It lay there, its eyes open and glaring, frozen with the menace of a griffin guarding a tomb.

The story unraveled over endless tea and brandy, broken here and there by the stoking of the fire or the braids of silence that wove themselves into a story that had eight beginnings and no real end. It was a lifetime ago. The time of the glade. Louis was a delicate but wild animal brought into Isobel's care. She loved him fiercely. It was the rawboned love a mother has for her child. But sometimes it wasn't, and she would lie on her bed in the servant quarters and picture herself receiving his breathy kisses. She laughed at the thought of Louis in buckskins and a topaz cravat, so earnest and hungry for passion of every kind. They lived at the quiet edge of the world; outside Orléans, life was waiting to sweep them along. The revolution meant nothing to them. Then it all changed in a day. A new era began with the burning of the old mansion. The time after the estate consisted of lonely nights in the desolate vineyard, Isobel's hands calloused at the wine press. She was awakened to pick grapes at midnight during harvest. She fell asleep standing. "When I met your father, I was very tired. He was kind to me. He'd lost his first wife and was deeply wounded by it. He was very sweet and kind. But then we grew to see we had nothing together. We were mostly friends."

"And then I came along?" Chloe said.

"I took you as a sign that I was meant to marry your father."

"But you never loved him."

"I loved him as best I could."

"Because you loved Daguerre?"

"It was more complicated than that. I couldn't love Louis because he wasn't real."

"He is real, and he's asleep in the next room, Mother."

Isobel looked towards the windows. "I have read about him all these years, wondering . . . When I saw his name in the papers, I felt a rush of pride—quite ridiculous. I felt somehow responsible for his success, wanted to tell people I'd been his maid when he was a boy. I felt sure he hated me after our falling-out."

"He never married. You obsessed his life."

"Impossible."

"If he ever wakes up, you can ask him yourself."

They spoke into the afternoon. The house was warm and quiet. They retired before dinner, Isobel to her plants and Chloe to a nap. In the dead quiet of a winter afternoon, Isobel left her tending and went into the room where Louis Daguerre slept. The day outside the bedroom window brightened a little before dusk. The fog had lifted and the sun hung a low, pale orange. Isobel stood beside Louis's prone figure. He seemed to have battled with his covers in the course of the day. She fixed his bedding and stood staring at his face. He had a civic aspect; his silvered hair and the strong line of his jaw suggested more a member of the judiciary than an artist. Certain features were familiar—the unlined forehead, the full, feminine lips. The veracity of him lying there, sick and helpless, stunned her. The boy in buckskins had become an old man.

TWENTY

sobel and Chloe restored Louis Daguerre one sense at a time. They filled the room with aromatic herbs, linden blossoms, gingerroot. Isobel rested poultices of arnica and rainwater on the wound. They washed him, shaved his face with a straight razor and a paste of soap and aloe. During his convalescing sleep, the mercury damp lessened in his lungs. They massaged his body with rose oil, not the entire body but the arms, legs, and torso, to keep them supple. Isobel recognized his flat hairless chest, his thin arms and looped shoulders. But despite this corporeal ease, neither she nor Chloe could bring themselves to clean his genitals. They cleared the bedpans without looking. Then, at the end of the third day, they sent for the town doctor. He arrived, gouty with the weather and bundled in a fur hat. He criticized Isobel's stitches as "cross-stitching where loose thread would suffice" and left a phial of smelling salts by the bed. "Use these in case he doesn't wake up by tomorrow," he said, latching his leather bag.

"There is one thing more," said Isobel. She looked over at her daughter, who was looking down at the floorboards.

"What is it?" the doctor said.

"He needs his manly parts cleaned, and neither of us will do it."

The doctor scowled, his day ruined. He instructed the women to provide him with cold water and a cloth and leave the room.

"Cold?" asked Isobel.

"The man will not die from being bathed with brisk water. It may even help invigorate him."

"Very well," said Isobel. She fetched a pan of well water and some torn cloth. After handing it to the doctor, she left the room and closed the door behind her. She and Chloe stood in the hallway, waiting.

The doctor emerged a short time later and said, "Rest assured, ladies, your man is clean." He left his invoice on a lamp table in the hallway and walked out into the blustery day.

Under Isobel and Chloe's aromatic care, Louis Daguerre slept the sleep of the dead. The world had not ended, but it was full of turmoil. In Paris fifteen hundred battlements had sprung up overnight. The air smelled of tar smoke and gunpowder. Peasants read petitions atop bronze statues. The National Guard had defected. King Louis-Philippe had been ousted. Revolution spread through Europe like apple blight—Vienna, Venice, Berlin, Prague, Rome. Monuments toppled and the foundries gave over to the manufacture of guns. Louis Daguerre slept, oblivious to what had started.

When he woke on the fourth day, he smelled lavender-scented water and thought for several moments that this was the fragrance of heaven. He lay in a feather bed, beneath a down quilt, his face perspiring. He could hear the sound of women's voices outside the window. Sitting up in bed, he pushed his covers down and immediately became aware of a gripping pain in his back. He put his right hand to it and felt a corrugated welt. With one hand at the bedpost, he set his feet onto the floor and stood. He ambled towards the window and saw, out in a sodden field, a woman chopping wood while another woman placed the cut logs into a basket. He watched the older woman raise the full-length ax over her head and arc it towards a piece of gnarled oak. The younger woman stood by with her hands on her hips. Something about the way the younger woman moved, some physical certitude, made Louis recall Pigeon's rooftop portrait, then her name, and finally that the woman standing with the ax was the very person who had ruled his mind for half a century.

"Isobel," he said, one hand against the windowpane.

After another moment he tapped on the glass, and both women looked up at him. He couldn't make out what they were saying, but Isobel dropped the ax and they both rushed towards the house. He saw them move, through the warped perspective of the mottled glass, as if underwater. Isobel stopped short of the house and looked up at him. Something moved between them in that short distance of chilled air and glass. Their eyes locked for a fraction of a second, in the interval it takes to haul another human being out of the broth of memory.

The women ran into the room while Louis continued looking out the window.

He heard them come up behind him, and before seeing Isobel up close, he could smell the camphor liniment, the herbage of her skin. He turned slowly and looked into her jade-colored eyes. Her face had aged, but there was something unchanged about her countenance; it had retained the sulky insolence of youth. She was not sullied by time so much as etched deeper into a more resolute version of herself. He would have recognized her instantly in the street. Now he realized those recent sightings in Paris were encounters with phantoms, shards of someone else's life. He was staring and making her self-conscious. He looked down at his shoes and then at the floorboards.

Isobel came forward and embraced him. Her hands touched the back of his shoulders. He closed his eyes; her smell was all around him.

After a moment he said, "Are we all dead?"

She released him and stepped back to take him in.

He saw a flurry of images from the night of the shooting, the magnesium flare of musket fire.

Isobel said, "You were shot."

"Angels," Louis said.

"He's delirious," Isobel murmured to Chloe.

"A peasant on horseback," Chloe offered.

Louis crossed to the window and looked for signs of the post-apocalyptic order. A plume of smoke rose from a distant house, but nothing suggested carnage. "Are we spared?"

"They're going to get rid of the king forever. That much looks certain," said Isobel.

"A reprieve, perhaps," said Louis.

"Have some water." Isobel poured him a glass from the jug. He drank it and asked for another. The water tasted soft and artesian, as if from a mineral well.

"I'm very thirsty," he said.

There were still glasses of water to be drunk.

"How long have I been asleep?" Louis asked.

"This is the fourth day," said Chloe.

"We were about to resort to the smelling salts," said Isobel, a note of humor in her voice.

Louis looked down at his hands, at their blunt existence. *What happened to the righteous fury?* Something hooked in his chest and he heaved a mercurial cough. He saw flashes of silver in his peripheral vision. He doubled over and held on to the windowsill.

"Oh, dear," said Isobel, putting a hand on his shoulder. He waved her away and regretted it before his hand had left his side. He'd waited a lifetime for the touch of that hand.

To take away some of the sting, he said, "I'm an old man. I've had this cough for years."

Isobel stood with her hands in front of her. Louis could see in her eyes that he was a patient, not a man.

"You're not that old," said Chloe. "I'll fetch some food. You must be starving." She left the room, leaving her mother just a few feet from the love of her youth. Louis rested his eyes on Isobel's. He felt another undulation of pain. He reached a hand around to the wound.

"I appear to be alive," he said.

"You will take some time to heal. You should lie back down while we get your food ready."

Louis edged back towards the bed and sat. Isobel smoothed her skirt, then turned for the door.

Louis, suddenly very weary, reclined against the feather pillows. They smelled of illness, of night sweats. The pain throbbed in his knuckles and shins, bright and pure. There was a hollow feeling in his stomach, a bronzed taste in his mouth. Outside, a horse whinnied; the wind blew under the eaves. The thought tapped, relentless and inexplicable: *The world has not ended.*

TWENTY-ONE

he next morning at dawn, Louis lay in bed, scalded by his false prophecy. So much for portents of the apocalypse. He wondered if the startled solemnity he'd seen in his portrait subjects—alarmed men presiding over mantel and wife, omniscient-looking dukes on their deathbeds, their eyes grave and lucent—was actually physical discomfort. The early portraits had required the subjects to sit motionless for an hour. The look of foreboding, an omen of *The End*, might have been simply men waiting to scratch themselves.

He felt betrayed, part of some larger misunderstanding. *Does God exist?* He lay there, stunned, and felt the rawness of his back wound. Perhaps *he* was dying, and not the world. Had he walked the streets of Paris a marked man? Was this an apocalypse for one? Perhaps God was indifferent to human endeavor and bored by cataclysm; He preferred to let men dwindle a good while before cutting them down one by one. He granted a man his passions, allowed him to make images as delicate as nets of smoke, allowed him to capture the rill of a lunar valley on a copper plate, then snuffed him like a tallow candle.

Louis took the room in. First he became aware of objects—the joints in the rafters, the windowsills, the wooden jewel boxes on Isobel's dresser—then he thought of the human labor embedded in each thing, how the hours of men's lives were tallied all around him. What was the point of all this? Was the world just an assemblage of blunt objects? Was a man no different than a hobnail on the Day of Judgment? He got out of bed and went to the window. It was an ordinary winter morning, midway through the nineteenth century. Snow was on the ground. Everything seemed exactly like itself. A catalog of mundane and exquisite beauty stood on the other side of the glass. He did not want to die.

Isobel entered the room with his breakfast. He returned to the bed and got under the covers.

"How are you feeling?" she asked.

"A little disoriented."

"That's to be expected."

Louis looked at her. She looked away. She looked back. It was not flirtation so much as a visual verification of the person with the memory, the old man with the boy in the topaz cravat, the sullen-faced widow with the girl in the tuberose crown.

"You make a fine widow," Louis said after an interminable silence.

"I don't know that I should thank you for that remark," she said.

"I mean to say that you have aged with grace."

"Like an old hen."

Louis nodded. "And you've still got your humor."

Isobel looked out the window. "Widowhood suits me."

"How so?"

"I have the means to cultivate my plants, and nobody bothers me."

"Life still raps at the window now and then, surely."

"Don't think me unhappy."

"I know loneliness, and I smell it in this house. It's everywhere, choking up the chimneys, fuming in the kitchen." He lifted his head from the pillow, like a final exclamation point.

"You're impossible—that hasn't changed. I am quite happy, thank you. Loneliness is an indulgence of the artistic and the privileged."

The return of the silence. She was still beautiful. It was as plain as the fact of the ceiling above him. But there was something unapproachable about Isobel in her sixties. She possessed a devoutness, a matronly vigor in her gestures. Louis wondered if she believed in God. As a girl, she'd believed in nothing but nature harnessed—the palliative effect of certain herbs, the fortitude of rainwater, the soundness of walks before bedtime.

"Your dog has died," she said. "We found it on the doorstep the morning after you arrived. I think perhaps it froze to death."

"I see," he said. There was something inscrutable now about the idea of death; he could not grasp it. The wind rattled at the windows. "I ran over that dog in Paris. I took it in because I thought I should do the world a good deed."

"The stableboy buried it out behind the barn."

"Yes, good." He thought of the dog in the cold earth—an object now—and wanted to feel a hint of sadness.

Isobel pulled her sleeves up her arm. She set a small tin bell at his bedside. "If you get hungry before lunchtime, ring this bell."

"I am capable of calling out your name," Louis said.

"Well, I may not hear. I will be in the back of the house."

She turned and disappeared down the hallway.

That evening, Louis got out of bed and dressed in the clothes that had been laid out on the dresser. He wondered if they had belonged to the dead husband or if they were borrowed from a neighbor. He went out into the living room and found Isobel reading by a candle.

"That light is terrible for reading," he said, taking a seat by the fire.

Isobel was reading her buccaneering novel and instinctively covered it with her hand.

"May I ask what you're reading?" he asked.

Isobel crossed her legs. "What a woman reads is private."

"Ah," said Louis.

Isobel attempted to wedge the novel between the seat cushions, but it fell to the floor and splayed open, revealing its cover. In the same instant, they both looked down at the title — *The Seaward Heart.*

He raised an eyebrow. "Sounds riveting."

"Silly book," she said. But then she felt an urge to defend it. "It takes place in Madagascar. I've always been interested in Africa."

"Really?"

"The plants and so on."

"Of course," he said. He felt an urge to scratch his ankle but resisted. He looked around the room and thought about the letter he had written her. The doomsday list and the letter were in his pocket, like artifacts of another age. He wanted to cut to the heart of things but did not know how to proceed.

"Isobel," he said.

"Yes," she said, picking up her book.

He gave in and scratched his ankle through his sock. "Is the weather still good in these parts?"

She smiled, folded her hands. "Windy and cold in the winter, mild in the spring. It hasn't changed since we lived on the estate."

"Ah." He hated everything about himself: the sound of his

voice, the drift of his thoughts. "Please excuse my sudden appearance. I thought something terrible was going to happen, and I had to find you."

"I'm glad you did. Forty years is too long."

"Did you ever think about me?"

"Never," she said, her mouth holding back a smile. She looked at the fire. "Of course I did. I read about you in the papers. Once there was even a photograph. But you look different in person."

"I have not been well. Some nervous complaint the doctors cannot cure."

"Perhaps herbs can do a better job than leeches."

"Perhaps."

Isobel shifted in her seat. "And you never married?"

Louis leaned forward. "We're having a conversation that moves from leeches to marriage. That's what I've missed about you. The fact that everything is linked to everything else—love to insects, dirt to heaven."

Isobel laughed. "Are you avoiding the question?"

"Yes," he said, spreading his hands. "And in a moment I may have a coughing spell to extinguish the question altogether."

She folded her arms. "Come now, out with it."

"No, I never married."

"That seems surprising, given your wealth and fame. I would have thought that women were standing in line to marry you."

"At best, I dabbled in women."

"Is that like dabbling in wine and gambling?" she asked.

"Largely. Although the odds with horse races are much better."

She nodded seriously, picked up her needlepoint, set it down, then said, "What happened to your ideals about love and the ever after?"

"My ideals about love went into my paintings." Louis looked off at the windows.

Something changed in the room; they could both sense it. Isobel picked up her needlepoint again. The sound of Chloe singing in the kitchen came into the room.

"You have a lovely daughter," Louis said.

Isobel pulled some thread through her fingers. "I can't take much credit for that."

Louis looked at the needlepoint design. It was a bird with brocade plumage. It reminded him of a thought he'd had forty years earlier, the night he'd seen Isobel at the opera—that she was like a bird with an injured wing—and he marveled that his mind could fish such items from the sea of memory. *Do memories have a life of their own? Do they float like clouds through the ether of the mind?*

He looked at the floorboards and said, "Besides, I gave up on love after that night at—" He stopped himself, folded his arms, then added, "I don't think you realize what happened to me after I learned you were pregnant."

Isobel had wanted to keep things light. She had no desire to rake through the past. "Does it still matter?"

A beat of silence.

"If the course of a man's life matters, then perhaps it is important."

"Such melodrama," she said, though she instantly regretted the hollowness of such a comment.

Louis stiffened and shot up from his seat. A bolt of anger took hold of him, and at first he thought it was a seizure. There was a bitter taste in his mouth. Now that he was standing, he could not remember what he had intended to do. Should he leave the house and go out into the night? He stood there a moment, his eyes down. Finally, he rifled through his pockets for the letter and crossed to the fire. He placed the envelope in the flames and managed to scald his fingertips. He shook his hand loose, as if he had just punched a man. They both watched the letter ignite.

"What is that?" Isobel asked.

"A letter seeking your friendship."

It was satisfying to watch it burn. He returned to his seat slowly, his footsteps measuring the pause before her response.

"It's quite likely that I am not worthy of your friendship."

He felt his throat go dry. "Self-pity is not becoming in a woman."

"I know my own character and what I deserve from life." She set her needlepoint aside once more.

"You don't know the first thing about yourself."

She straightened her skirt. "Why did you come?"

"You've haunted my life." His hands were gripping the chair arms.

"And you want to put the ghost to rest? Is that it?" She resented the shrillness in her voice but continued. "Well, yes, it is a curse, and like some kind of bewitching, it makes very little sense."

Looking at a spot above the mantel, he said, "I think I may still love you." He had not intended to say those words, not yet, and felt an urge to actually cover his mouth with his hand. He could not look at her.

"A kiss in a wine cave when you're fourteen does not amount to love, Louis." She said it as gently as she could.

He allowed those words to hang in the air for some time. He was afraid of what he might say if he remained in that chair a moment longer. He stood slowly and said, "I dressed and came out here because I was thinking of taking the dog for a walk. Have you seen him?"

Isobel waited a moment before answering. "I imagine he won't be needing walks anymore."

Louis strained his eyes through the darkening room, trying to gauge her meaning. "Is he lost?"

Isobel looked baffled. "I told you this morning that your dog had died."

Louis grappled for the details but had no recollection. His memory was unraveling in patches and runs, like the hem of an old gown. Some days he could not remember what he'd eaten for breakfast but could remember an afternoon, in all its detail, from his childhood.

"Of course," he said. "I was making a joke. Good night, Isobel."

"Louis," she said.

"Yes," he said, turning.

"I continue to feel a great fondness for you and what we have shared. Please know that."

He straightened his back, felt the uneasiness of his wound, and walked into the bedroom. The room was on the verge of darkness, and he felt a dozen objects looming towards him.

Isobel sat there for a long time. She felt on guard and slightly numb, then resented that Louis Daguerre's arrival had unmoored her. She would go check on the horses and help Chloe prepare dinner. She stood, fetched a lantern, and went outside to the barn. Louis's carriage stood by the horse stalls, still unpacked. As she passed it, she noticed part of an exposed picture frame from beneath a wrapping of hessian. She was curious to see Louis Daguerre's work, to see what had become of his talent. She unwrapped the frame and held her lantern to the plate. At first the image was vague—a cornice, some snow, a rooftop terrace in winter—but then she saw the naked figure. Chloe's face looked into the camera with a bemused smile; her body reclined, so utterly naked. There were tuberoses about her feet. Suspended before her, Isobel imagined, were five years distilled to a single moment. She angled the plate in several directions and each time garnered new evidence of her daughter's decline in Paris—the brandy balloon to one side, her hair a tangled curtain about her face, the skyline behind her suggesting the brasseries and tenements of Montmartre. Her daughter sat in the cold snow with the flowers of nostalgia in her hair, mementos from the glade. There was something depraved about the portrait—a still life of a lonely man's fantasy. Isobel threw the hessian back on the portrait and walked towards the house. She saw Louis standing in the yellow light of her bedroom, looking out into the wash of night. She was suddenly appalled that this man was sleeping in her bed.

TWENTY-TWO

ach morning for a week Isobel left a breakfast tray by Louis's bed. There was a briskness in her manner that he did not like. Had he imagined the look on her face when he first rose from the bed? Couldn't they find solace in the vintage of their affection—all those small moments on the glade? But whenever he brought up the past, impatience washed over her face and she found some chore or ailed plant to tend. One morning he deliberately closed his curtains to provoke the distant memory of their curtain-closing game when he was sick in his rooftop bedroom. He watched her come into the dim room with her tray. She set the breakfast things down and pulled back the curtains in one swift movement, oblivious to the past. She even opened the window a crack. The smell of fog and marsh salt come into the room.

"A sick man can't heal without sunlight and fresh air," she said briskly.

"I thought the sick needed to block out the light."

"Only the feverish," she said. "The rest need daylight. Your fever has already broken."

He looked and waited for the slightest sign of tenderness. She tended him like a sick calf, her movements steady and bucolic, a pat here, a pat there, the distant and managed concern of animal husbandry. It occurred to him for the first time that he had made an enormous mistake, that he'd spent his life in love with a ghost.

One night Louis got out of bed to join Isobel and Chloe for dinner. When he came into the living room, he found Chloe standing by the fire in a velvet dress. She was holding a glass of wine and staring into the flames.

"What's the occasion?" Louis asked.

She turned and smiled. "Louis, how are you feeling?"

"Fine, I suppose. Are you having a party?"

"I told Mother we should celebrate the revolution, and she's making a special dinner."

He looked down at his plain clothes. "I wasn't aware."

"We've been talking about it for days, but no matter, I'm sure you can trade your farmer's clothes for one of my father's suits. Mother must have some of his clothes around the house. Let me go see." She walked towards the kitchen.

"No, please," he called out.

Chloe stood in the kitchen doorway, conferring with her mother. Louis could not see Isobel but could tell from the tone of the conversation that she was not pleased. Finally, Chloe returned, wiped her hands down her dress, and said, "Sir, will you follow me."

"But—" Louis began.

"Come on, Grandfather, we can't celebrate with you in those plowman's clothes."

She led him down the hallway to the small room where she slept. It was full of boxes and picture frames covered with drop-cloths. Chloe stood in front of an armoire and opened its doors to reveal a few dozen suits, immaculately hung, each with a silk cravat flowering from a breast pocket.

"My father had a suit for every day of the month. At the bank, they knew how business was doing by the color of his cravat."

Louis looked at the suits. He remembered the image of Gerard at the opera all those years before, but these suits belonged to a much larger man. "I'm not entirely comfortable wearing the clothes of a dead man."

"He won't mind. He'd be glad that they were being put to some use."

"And what did your mother say?"

Chloe ran a hand inside the lapel of a worsted blazer. "She said you have fifteen minutes before dinner is ready. And you don't want to keep Mother waiting."

Louis sighed. "Very well."

Chloe kissed him on the cheek. "Excellent, I knew you'd be a sport. Now hurry and dress." She walked out into the hallway and closed the door behind her.

Louis ran his hands over the shoulders of each suit and pulled out a charcoal-gray one. It smelled of verbena and old newspapers. He put on the jacket, and just as he had suspected, it was too long in the sleeves and too wide in the chest. Had the man been barrel-chested or simply fat? He tied the cravat—a stately blue—and stood before a mirror. He looked like a man in borrowed clothes, a sick uncle come to live with his moneyed kin. Something protruded from the pocket of the jacket. He put his hand against the cool satin lining and retrieved a half-smoked cigar and a piece of paper with numbers scrawled across it. The chewed cigar and the spidery numbers reinforced his image of Gerard—the tycoon calculating his wealth in a haze of cigar smoke—but then Louis saw a few lines of verse on the other side of the paper. It read: *Blind with thine hair the eyes of Day, / Kiss her until she be wearied out.* It was from a Shelley poem, though Louis could not remember which one. He read it several times, shocked at this display of romanticism in the banker; was he a man who also brought home roses and recited verse at the dinner table? What if he had been worthy of loving? What then? Or was this a message from the grave, from a man who'd never possessed Isobel's heart and mind? Perhaps Gerard was telling him to pursue Isobel until she surrendered.

"Are you coming, old man?" Chloe hollered from the hallway.

"Yes," he called back. He put the cigar and paper back in the pocket and went out into the living room.

Isobel was still in the kitchen. Chloe handed him a glass of wine, trying not to laugh at the suit. "It's a little big," she said.

"I'm swimming in it," Louis said. "I feel ridiculous."

Chloe looked over her wineglass at him. "You look dashing."

Isobel came into the room to announce that dinner was ready. She looked at Louis in her dead husband's suit and wondered if this was not disrespectful to his memory.

"Mother, doesn't Louis look dashing, even if the suit is much too big?"

Isobel shrugged. "Dinner is ready. We'll be eating in the kitchen." She brought her hands to her sides.

Louis looked at Isobel. She had dressed somewhat formally in a navy dress, her hair pinned up in a chignon. She could have passed for a diplomat's wife, he thought, if not for the hands. They were maid's hands—calloused, suntanned, nails bitten to the quick.

They went into the kitchen and sat at the table. Isobel served them plates of beef and herbed carrots. Chloe refilled their wineglasses and said, "Louis, would you make a toast?"

"If your mother doesn't mind."

"As you wish," Isobel said.

Louis stood and raised his glass. He felt the cigar in his pocket—had the banker been a man of wedding toasts and brandied tales? "Ladies, there is so much that I am grateful for. This last week you have cared for me and saved my life. The world is different now . . . I can feel that there is a whole new beginning upon us . . . I see it in doorways and windows—" He lost the thread of his remarks and discovered he was looking down at his carrots. "I am not good at speeches, forgive me. Mostly I'd like to say thank you for your hospitality. And here's to the future—ours and the nation's."

Isobel and Chloe raised their glasses and drank. Louis sat down. An awkward silence fell over the table.

Chloe said, "This is delicious, Mother." She leaned close to Louis and put a napkin in his lap.

"Indeed," said Louis, embarrassed by the napkin on his pant leg. He scanned the table to see if there was anything else he had forgotten to do—where was the salt?

Isobel nodded but said nothing.

A moment later, Louis looked at Isobel as she was looking off at the stove. Her eyes were unnaturally fierce. He rifled through his mind for diverting conversation, ran a perimeter check on appropriate topics, but before he could speak, Isobel brought the silence to a point.

"Will you return to Paris, Monsieur Daguerre?" she asked. Her voice was flat and measured, an inquiry of weather.

Louis put down his glass and looked at her. The wine was the first alcohol he'd had since the shooting, and it loosened his chest and palate. "*Monsieur?*" he said. "Why so formal?"

"I wasn't aware that calling a gentleman by that title was an offense."

"No," he said, sipping his wine. "But what is an offense is your amnesia."

Isobel looked at her daughter and smiled, trifling Louis's words. She faced him. "What am I supposed to remember?" She touched her wineglass. "That you were a gifted child in buckskins, a boy who went to the city and became famous? That we played out in the woods and one day we got drunk and kissed? That you wasted your affection on a woman who never asked for it?" Her face was burning.

Louis could not speak. He could hear a clock ticking from the hallway.

Isobel drew breath and spoke slowly. "You insist on reliving my days as a chambermaid as if it were a great beginning. I have left all that behind, Monsieur Daguerre."

Louis looked down at his plate. He had wasted his life on this woman.

"He doesn't mean any harm," Chloe said.

"I wasn't aware that this was your concern," Isobel said.

"Pigeon, it's all right," said Louis.

Isobel flashed her eyes from her daughter to Louis. "That is not the first time I have heard you call my daughter by that abhorrent name. While you are in my house, you will call her Chloe just like the rest of the civilized world. *Pigeon*—it makes her sound like something you feed with breadcrumbs."

"That's what people called me in Paris," said Chloe.

"Well, I can only imagine what circumstances gave rise to such a name. I imagine that posing as a nude model leads to all kinds of intimacies."

Chloe looked at Louis; he could see the whites of her eyes.

"I think there has been some misunderstanding," said Louis. He had rarely called her Pigeon but something about the wine and the domestic setting had made him feel more familiar.

"What's to misunderstand? I found a naked portrait of my daughter with your signature on it. There were tuberoses scattered in that ridiculous picture, as if you were engaged in some epic fantasy. The whole thing is disgusting. If you have been as intimate with my daughter as that portrait suggests, then you're a worthless old wretch. I should be glad when you go back to

Paris and leave us alone." The threat of tears hung in the back of her words.

"I worked for Louis, Mother. He never even watched me pose. He was nothing but a gentleman, believe me. It was I who begged to do it. And he paid me well."

"I'm sure he did. Fame can afford a man his trifles."

"This is not warranted," said Louis, but he could feel the indignation in his face. Had he indulged the lust and vanity of an old man?

Chloe drank a long sip of wine and turned to her mother. "I worked as a whore in Paris. Louis was trying to save me from it by paying me to pose. But I kept doing it. I don't know why I kept doing it. The money was the least of it. Until I walked into this house, I never felt ashamed."

Isobel found it impossible to react. A self-loathing rose in her stomach, but nothing made it to her face. She sat stone-faced, her head tilted. The girl at the banister; the girl who fell asleep at the dinner table—stolen. *I have raised a harlot.* She said, "I may take a walk." Now she felt the wine and humiliation in her face, flush on flush.

"No, you should sit here so we can talk about this," Chloe said. Her voice was brittle, broken off.

Mid-swing, Isobel saw her hand in the air and felt her shoulders tense. Chloe's head snapped to the right, her face abstracted by motion. The harshness of the blow left a crimson handprint. Isobel felt her hands shake. Chloe touched her face very slowly. A single tear appeared on her cheek. Isobel remembered her husband on his deathbed; when he was gone, a single tear had appeared from one eye. It had been the only time she'd ever seen him cry—in death—and this economy of sentiment had made its way to her daughter. Chloe stood and rushed outside.

Louis sat for a moment. "I will return to Paris as soon as the roads are open," he said, head down. He wished she had slapped him instead. He looked up and saw a deep bitterness in her face—the desire to be hated, to steep and wallow. She was a selfish, indulgent woman, always had been. Standing, he set his napkin on the table and went out into the night in search of Chloe.

Isobel sat there and felt the room slip away. The thought burned her insides, scoured her through. Of course it was her fault. In her widowed vengeance, in the bleakness of her regret at not having married for love, she'd ruined her daughter's chances, sent her out into the world penniless. Her daughter had paid the price for her own safety.

TWENTY-THREE

he widow's house stood in silence for two weeks. The fog rose off the marsh. It surrounded the house at dawn and dusk. Spring advanced. Bands of militant peasants drifted along the roadways, a ragged formation returning from Paris—boys with bandaged heads, old men with blankets draped around their shoulders. It grew warmer. Plowmen rode the fields in preparation to seed. But Isobel kept her house shuttered and the fire stoked. Condensation gathered in the herbarium. It was the perspiration of overtended milkweed, the breath of rampant lilac and chamomile. Chloe found the air stifling and slept by an open window each night. Louis, no longer an invalid, took to sleeping in the barn, huddled beside the stableboy.

Isobel and Chloe passed each other, eyes down, passengers on the decks of some lost ocean liner. Isobel was adrift in self-loathing. Moving about the house, she dredged the image pool of Chloe's childhood: the girl in her first dress, the birthday princess presiding over her gifts. Where was the moment of undoing? She saw Chloe at the threshold of womanhood—standing at the top of the stairs, lavender-frocked and shoeblacked, a basket of gathered flowers in one hand. She'd blushed when boys looked her way. At sixteen, she'd spoken of boys the way a skeptic speaks of God—such strangeness, such fuss in all their difference, their spindle-legged energy and defiance. Then Isobel saw a depiction of her daughter beneath a seaman, some ham-fisted merchant, a man grabbing at her neck and hair. The images came unbidden, appalling in their detail—a scuffed wallet on the nightstand, the bicep tattoo of a serpent.

Chloe felt pent-up. She imagined the respiratory fumes from the herbarium to be blue and vaporous, the plants exhaling her mother's angry out-breaths. In their beds at night they were being poisoned by a cloud of remorse. She wanted to scream, to tear down the pinned curtains. She would return to Paris with Louis, pick up the thread of a new life. It was distraction she desperately wanted, but she couldn't sustain a simple task; her attempts to read and chop wood ended abruptly with book throwing and cleaving the ax into a rotten stump. She spent hours on her back beside the marsh watching clouds, looking up through the proscenium of branch work. She looked out at a dusk-shot field of turnips and waited for the mercury moment, the sun kiss.

She went to the barn in search of Louis, but he was off with his camera and tripod. She saw the portrait and unwrapped it. Her body was foreign to her—her shoulders sloped, her thighs dimpled—but these imperfections seemed to blend with the Paris twilight, the chimney cowls aslant, the tar smoke pluming across the skyline. She saw her mother's body in the picture, the foreboding of age. *I will die childless, ruined.* If only she could undo time, set things right, reclaim her body before it had become the empty flat where men lodged their desires. She remembered their names, the ones who gave them—George, Pascal, René, Manuel, Esteban, Charles, Phillip, Andrew, Bernard . . . British,

Portuguese, Spanish, so many Frenchmen she could have formed an army. The international language of the unpeeled bed. She remembered their faces; the averted eyes or the cajoling stares, the ones who asked for permission to touch her; the ones who pressed bruises into her wrists. Some wanted to know her real name and where she was born; they wanted another strand, the veracity of her life. "Marie from Marseille" was what she'd told most of them. This alter ego had taken on proportions of the living over the years; Chloe knew where Marie went to school, how her parents died of typhoid when she was very young. Chloe felt a sisterly affection for this invented personage; she could see her building the pine house in the South she'd always wanted, long-haired daughters running in the yard, the simple and kind grocer husband who believed she'd worked as a nurse in Paris. *At some point kindness is better than love.* The truth was she had no idea why she did it. *Punishing my mother, declaring love a hoax, the emptiness of losing Richard—none of these explain it. Because I could do it; because I had something they needed; because one man had a bandaged eye; because one called me the girl among the roses; because one made me frightened; because one bought me coffee—there are as many reasons as there were names.*

Louis took to the country lanes. He walked briskly, tripod over his shoulder, flushing birds and rabbits from the downs. At first he was stultified by the thought of what to capture. His doomsday list now seemed false, an exercise in self-indulgence. He wanted to capture ordinary objects: an orange against wood grain; a cup of coffee gathering a dying afternoon in its brown bowl; a brindled cat asleep in the barn; a piece of chocolate on waxed paper; a smoking pipe on a yellowed edition of *Le Gazette de France;* the skeletal frame of beech trees against snow. He would search for the minuscule and the uncelebrated, the unlikely structures of elemental form—the helix inside honeycomb, the symmetry of a thyme leaf, the arciform of a daylily. Perhaps the whorl of the cosmic mind was contained in a nutshell.

He set up a workshop in the barn. He had a few dozen remaining copper plates, ten pounds of mercury in a flask, plenty of iodine and carded cotton. The spirit lamp had survived the maelstrom ride from Paris. One night he held the exposed plate of a hawk feather over the mercury bath. It was his first exposure to mercury in a month, and the metallic cloud stung on its way into his lungs. He felt its acrid breath on his windpipe, the gossamer veil it placed over his thoughts.

When the image was fixed, he set it on a bed of straw. The picture showed a bone-white quill cut through crosshairs of brown. He went outside into the cold of night. The cottage was yellow-lit and seemed to float through the dark. He could see Isobel and Chloe eating in the kitchen. Isobel left his meals on the veranda with the stable hand's. Pathetically, he looked for signs of hope in the soup and the fish—a sprig of rosemary set upright, a heart carved from a fillet of sole. He saw himself as an old man standing outside a widow's house, afraid of having squandered his love, unmoored by the continued rotation of the earth.

The fresh exposure to mercury had made his head ache, and he returned to the barn to lie down. He climbed the ladder to the barn loft and felt the pressure in his head get worse; his pulse throbbed behind his eyes and in his teeth. Panting, he sunk down on his straw bed. The stableboy, sitting beneath a hanging kerosene lamp, was cleaning a rifle with an oil cloth. Louis stared at him. He was a blunt-faced lad, smelled of saddle soap and leather, spoke few words but was known to have a soprano voice and a penchant for singing to horses. His hands were rough and blistered, but his fingers were precise. He polished the barrel and then held a bullet between two fingers—Louis saw it in profile, something as perfect as a basilica dome — before kissing it and pressing the bullet gently into the chamber. Was the boy going out to join the revolution? As Louis watched, his peripheral vision dimmed; suddenly, it was like looking through a keyhole. Everything seemed to move away, blink, recede. An empty feeling rose from the pit of his stomach and settled behind his shoulder blades.

The boy looked up from the rifle. "Are you all right, sir?"

"If Degotti sees you with that rifle in the dormitory, he'll make you sweep the floor for a year," Louis replied. "Do you understand me? We are painters, not soldiers."

Smiling, the boy looked back down at his rifle, set it aside, and blew out the kerosene lamp. In the darkness, Louis heard him say, "We'll never win the revolution if the Parisians are always drunk!"

Isobel and Chloe brooded over a meal in the kitchen. Chloe sat idling her potatoes. Isobel looked at their twin reflections, ghostly and warped, in the kitchen window. She hated the insufferable silence but felt pinned by it. The past had ransacked her house.

Chloe watched her mother cut her potatoes with a surgical precision. When Chloe's voice filled the house, she realized neither of them had spoken since breakfast.

"When the roads clear, I will return to Paris also," Chloe said.

"I see," said Isobel.

Some silence. A gust at the windowpane.

The thought returned to Isobel, the image of sixteen-year-old Chloe descending the stairs. She said, "When you were in Paris, did he really try to save you?"

"Yes, like I told you. He paid me to model so that I would

quit working in the brothel. He would have done anything to make me stop." Her mother's face startled her—the tight, with-held mouth, the hostility in the eyes. *This is the face I will someday inherit.*

Isobel nodded almost imperceptibly and looked around the room. "And he never touched you?"

"Never."

"Surely a man who wants to look at naked women cannot have honorable intentions."

Chloe set down her silverware and moved her plate to the center of the table. "Mother, you've been asleep since 1800. The world is different now. Artists command the cafés and the brasseries in Paris. Painting a nude model is a form of philosophy, a religion, almost. They pay twice as much as a man who wants to sleep with a whore—so why would he bother if it weren't legitimately about art?"

The logic of it caught in Isobel's throat. How she wanted to bellow, to shatter the windows with a single held note.

"Do not use the word *whore* in this house," she said. A moment later, she added, "Ever." Her voice was sharp, even to her.

Chloe said, "You hate me. I can see it when you look at me."

"Don't be so dramatic."

"And you hate yourself—that much seems certain. You are terrified of being loved."

Isobel perched her fork halfway between plate and mouth.

Chloe said, "You're the most indulgent woman I've ever known. What is this cross you bear? I knew women in Paris who sold their children to eat. How dare you. Your biggest burden is that a man has loved you his whole life."

Isobel set her cutlery on her plate. "No, my biggest burden is that my daughter has ruined her life. And as for that lunatic of a man, I never asked for his love."

"No, and frankly, you don't deserve it," Chloe said. "I would give anything to have a man love me like that again, just once." She stood and left the table.

Isobel watched her daughter move through the lamplight of the hallway. She had a brief sensation of time slowing, of the silent intervals between Chloe's footsteps. The bedroom door opened wildly, as if it might swing off its hinges. Then it closed with a stiff wooden shudder. In its aftermath, she sat, looking down at her empty plate, gripped by the enormity of the silence.

Later, they were both awakened by a loud crack from the rear of the house. They rose and hurried down the hallway, Isobel holding a candle in front of her. In the herbarium, the night lamps cast a paraffin pall on the miniature trees and the potted herbs. Behind a bamboo plant culled for stakes and stirrers, a windowpane had cracked—a splintered vein that ran the course of the whole panel.

Isobel ran her fingers carefully along the crack, tracing it down to the bottom of the frame. She saw that a bamboo shoot had grown into the glass, pressed into the liquefacient surface like a specimen in a microscope plate. "Even the plants want to escape this house," she said.

They both stood there for a moment.

"I'm going to stay up for a while," said Isobel. "I wasn't sleeping anyway."

"I'll go back to bed," Chloe said.

"Good night, then."

Isobel picked up her pruning scissors and scanned the foliage for the errant tendril or leaf. She trimmed the stalk of a miniature myrrh tree, its resin coating the bark in amber tears. She used it as a cure for digestive complaints, but she recalled that the Egyptians had used it to embalm the dead. If only she could believe in something beyond the rectitude of plants—the goodness of men, the benevolence of God, the efficacy of science. There was time, her plants, the spool of the seasons. She pricked her finger on the sharp end of a myrrh branch. A speck of blood appeared under her fingernail. Thwarted, she wrapped a cloth around it and retired to bed.

She tossed and turned, the cut pulsing like a beacon. *You are terrified of being loved.* The thought gathered around her. As a child, she'd avoided the boys for whom she had real affection; Gerard had been a widower unable to love. The closest he had come was unbridled kindness, a tenderness that flared sometimes on a birthday or anniversary, and she had been safe, satisfied with knowing all she had to give was wifely camaraderie, a kind of connubial friendship. She opened her mouth to yawn only to find herself in tears. Her hand went to her mouth to stifle the sob—the slapping hand, knuckled with age, with a wedding ring from a dead man she had never loved. She took off the ring and placed it on the night table. Somehow, its removal allowed her to weep freely.

Her sobs floated through the house, passing through the timber walls. Chloe woke to the sound. She had not heard her mother cry in many years. Even at her father's funeral, her mother had been stern-lipped, already assuming the icy pose of the dutifully stricken widow. Chloe stood in her darkened room and, without lighting any lamps, went to her mother. She fumbled towards the iron bed frame and felt the contour of Isobel's body. Her mother lay curled, pillows clutched to her stomach and face. Chloe said nothing. She sat down next to her and took hold of her hand. She could feel her mother's pulse throb between her fingertips. Isobel, her voice cut with fatigue, said, "I can't live like this anymore." Chloe made no reply. She lay down beside her mother. They passed in and out of sleep, their hands intertwined.

In the morning Chloe got up and made a pot of coffee with

chicory, the way her mother liked it. She brought two cups into the bedroom. Isobel sat up in bed and took an earthenware mug. They sat on the bed, drinking coffee, letting the morning take hold of them. Chloe opened the bedroom window a little. They looked out at the slow stain of morning. The smell of acacia and lime came into the room. The present began to reveal itself.

TWENTY-FOUR

Dear Louis,

These last weeks have brought me an impossible sadness. I confess I felt a real betrayal and violation at seeing the naked portrait of my daughter. But it seems there is nothing to be gained from dwelling on the mistakes of the past. I acted horribly and never should have struck my daughter. I regret you witnessed such appalling behavior. So much has passed between us and I don't think myself capable of offering anything but well-intentioned friendship. Chloe and I would be glad to receive a visit from you, if you are so inclined. Please come out of the barn and join us.

Sincerely,
Isobel Le Fournier

TWENTY-FIVE

ouis paced on the back stoop. He waited a long time before knocking. Isobel appeared within seconds of his rapping so that he wondered whether she'd seen him poised on the steps.

"Louis," she said. She appeared sallow and worn.

"The Paris road has opened. I'll be leaving in the morning." He looked at her hands, at her bandaged finger.

"I see," she said, looking out at the marsh.

"Thank you for your note," he said.

"Of course." She dabbed her nose with a kerchief.

"Are you unwell?" he asked.

"My lungs play up in the early spring." Looking at her kerchief, she said, "Would you share a meal with us before you leave?"

"Today I plan to visit the old estate, and I'll leave from there in the morning. A silly errand, I know. I can't seem to shrug nostalgia. It's dogged me my whole life."

"There's nothing wrong with a fondness for the past," she said.

"Perhaps an acceptance of the present is better." He touched his chest—the threat of a cough.

She held on to the rim of the doorway.

"I'd like to say goodbye to Chloe as well, if that's all right."

"Of course. She's gone for a walk, but I'll send her over when she gets back."

"Thank you."

"Louis?"

"Yes."

"We'll make you some food for your trip."

"Don't go to any trouble."

"It's the least we can do. I'll send it over with Chloe."

"Goodbye, Isobel."

She looked at his mouth. "Yes. Goodbye, then." She closed the door hurriedly.

He turned and descended the stairs.

She walked slowly into the living room and watched the fire. She noticed that the fireplace bricks were stained black. She sat down in a chair. A cold, bereft feeling came over her. She saw her days stretched before her, the afternoons lined up like soldiers. She got up from the chair and moved to the window. His carriage stood in front of the barn. He was nowhere in sight.

From the front of the house came the sound of the door. Chloe came in with flowers. She was breathy, flushed in the cheeks. "It's such a beautiful day out there."

"He's leaving today. He's going to the old estate, then on to Paris."

Chloe came and stood beside her at the window.

Isobel said, "I told him we'd make him some food for the trip."

"We can't let him leave, Mother. Not after all this mess."

"He's set to leave."

"I can't know your heart, Mother. I don't think you even

know your heart anymore. But it's not right to watch your oldest friend disappear. You will never see him again."

"I know. I can feel it in my bones." Isobel put her hand against the chill of the glass.

"You can't let him leave without a proper mending of ways. I'll go talk to him."

"No, you mustn't."

Chloe moved towards the door, flowers still in hand.

"Chloe, I'm begging. Don't. This is for the best."

"Well," Chloe said, "these flowers are for him, and I intend to deliver them."

She went outside. Isobel watched her daughter move across the farmyard. Louis appeared from inside the barn. Chloe held the flowers in front of her and Louis stood uncomprehending, hands at his sides. Slowly, his hands came out to receive them and his face washed with a smile. He bent his head to smell them. Isobel moved from the window and went into the herbarium. She stood looking at her plants. A short time later, Chloe rushed into the house and Isobel reached for her scissors and began pruning.

"It's all settled, then," Chloe said from the doorway.

"What have you done?"

"We're going to have a picnic with him at your old estate. That'll give you two a chance to patch things up. He'll drop us back and leave for Paris first thing in the morning." Chloe ducked down the hallway. Isobel stood, waiting for something to compel her to move. The thought of returning to the glade made her stomach turn. A breeze passed through the broken window of the herbarium. It felt like an exhalation.

They dressed for the picnic, the women in frocks. Louis wore a waistcoat and a wool suit that had belonged to Gerard. He

parked the carriage in front of a neighbor's field and waited beside it, hat in hand. As the ladies came from the house, Isobel
was struck by the image he made—a man dressed for the opera,
haloed by a field of saffron. Louis helped them up into the carriage; he'd made seats for them with blankets and cushions in the
back. He sat on the box seat and clicked at the horses. They rode
along the river, through groves of horse chestnut, meadows of
sedge pool and hawthorn. The clatter of the wagon made it too
loud for them to converse. Louis found this a point of relief.

They waved at men fishing from punts on the Loire. Louis
saw washerwomen haul laundry up from the bank, their backs
bowed under the weight of their baskets. He thought of the revolution, of the endless battle for liberty. A young woman looked
up as they passed, her face ravaged with blisters. Here was brute
unpleasantness, he thought. Perhaps it was possible to kill nostalgia, to lift the gauze that softened life's edges, to live unflinching at the frayed edge of the world.

They headed north, skirting the Paris road, and passed into
the district of châteaux. The ruins of the estate were surrounded
by sodden, fallow fields. Louis looked off from the road: the
brook ran clear and blue down to the Loire; the glade was over-
grown with honeysuckle and clover. Beside the razed mansion
were burned-out hulls of carriages, charred bed frames, a
residue of metal and cinders.

Isobel said, "Haunted as a churchyard cemetery."

They rode past the front entrance, a single griffin atop a half-
wall of stone. Louis saw the last forty years etched into the pas-
tures and yards. The forest to the east had been converted into
woodlots where villagers no doubt came to cut and cord their
wintering fuel. The stone fences were overrun with moss and
wild grapes. Beyond the mansion was Louis Daguerre's childhood house, mostly intact. He was surprised by its humble appearance—essentially a stone cube with a raised roofline, a box

topped with dormer and crest. It resembled a countinghouse on some mundane trade route, a way station of small commerce.

They stopped in front of the mansion and got down.

Chloe said, "I want to know everything you did here."

"It looks like a scene from Waterloo," Louis said.

They walked over the ashen ground, over a glass-studded mixture of dirt and crumbled sandstone.

"There were fifty rooms," said Isobel. "Each of them with a window. There was a great hallway full of armor and wooden clocks and paintings of gouty old Frenchmen with ruffled collars." She looked at an intact corner of stone and mortar. "This was the gallery, which doubled as a small ballroom on special occasions. The other maids and I would sneak in here and dance the new waltzes from Vienna."

"I can picture you," said Chloe. "How did you have your hair?"

"It was a mess most of the time. I kept it up, but it was always falling down in my face. Madame Boulier, the head maid, was always at my throat because of it."

"Maybe that's why they volunteered you for tending the head clerk's son," said Louis.

Isobel smiled. "They all knew I was good with herbs and poultices. Plus I wanted out of that house."

"Where did you live?" Chloe asked Louis.

"That humble-looking outbuilding over there." He pointed across the sea of honeysuckle and clover.

"Let's go see it," said Chloe.

Chloe walked between them. For a fleeting moment Louis imagined her as their child, as the unlikely dividend of his youth. He imagined living at the helm of this family, breakfasting together, trips to the South, struck with the wild luck of domestic bliss. Somehow the confusion of another man's destiny blown across his own, a banker's lineage small but indelible beside him.

They stepped through a series of hummocks where badgers and field mice burrowed and nested. Sparrows and finches flitted and wheeled from the dormers of his boyhood house.

His childhood rushed in with the liquidity of a dream. He saw his covens and cubbies, his dens where he'd observed the dynasties and spectacles, both large and small, of nature. Here the old tree under whose boughs he'd studied armies of ants and the kaleidoscope of light through shifting foliage. Here the stretch of rose quartz and granite where he'd observed high noon splintered and reflected. He felt his whole body go loose. The air smelled of distant rain.

They entered the cottage through the front door. It was a grim replica of his childhood house—the walls, windows, and doors were intact but covered with four decades of bucolic rot and mold. It felt more like a grotto than a house. The place where his father had sat on Sunday mornings with his merchant's daybooks, ordering his accounts, resembled a pigsty. Everywhere the walls were run through with cracks and split plaster. The floors were bloated with moisture. Horizontals of light came in under the architraves and through the derelict shutters. Nobody spoke. The scurry of vermin sounded in the rafters.

They continued through the house, and neither of the women flinched as Louis headed for the narrow stairwell that led up to his old bedroom. He wanted to see what had become of it. This was where life had taken its first important turn.

He asked the women to stay at the top of the stairs while he investigated the room. He opened the door and stepped inside. It was so dark that he could barely see his way to the window. He pulled back the curtains and took down a piece of board covering the broken glass. He turned back to the room, inspected the corners, and then called Isobel and Chloe inside. His old bed—a narrow wrought-iron cot with pyramid coils—was at the opposite end of the room from where he remembered. How many desolate poets, country wayfarers, deserting soldiers had slept in his old bed?

"This was your room?" asked Chloe.

Louis nodded. He looked all around him. There was nothing left. His childhood room had been denuded of all that was familiar. "This is where I lived as a boy," he said. "Through those very curtains I saw an apparition of a walnut tree. Later, in Paris, that memory convinced me that nature held the means to draw her own image." He stood by the bed, looking out the window. A spider had webbed in an entire section of broken pane, forming a lacy trap for flying insects. How many generations of spiders and ants had called his bedroom their dingy universe?

Isobel clutched herself, chilled by the dankness and the wall rot. She felt impossibly old. She saw the image of herself at the bedside, her maid's tunic so clean and stiff. She could remember the feel of the starched linen against her back and neck and remembered how she started to wash her tunic with rose hips to soften it. But the white cloth had turned pink, and this unsightliness had lost her a week's wages. Was that really the bed where she had witnessed Louis as the edgeling of a man? There lay a boy so supple-bodied and high-minded that he was like a prince of the hallowed wilds. His fevers were brought on by turns in the weather, by witnessing the woodmen cut down an apricot tree without due cause. He was sensitive to the point of frailty. Yet somehow he'd harnessed his own nature, and she realized now, in the tomb of his childhood, that it was this boyhood sensitivity that had stopped her from ever collapsing into her love for him. At one time she had possessed visions of them together, and there was Louis in that future with head presses and his magnifying glasses and India inks. She'd feared a dandy of ostentatious hats and engraved hip flasks. She had believed that he would remain a dabbler lost to distraction, that he would never become a man of means and substance. And how wrong she had been; all along he had possessed the disposition for artistic success. The very traits she feared would create a man of sloth—sentimentalism, distraction, an obsession with beauty—had fanned the embers of his fame like a bellows. She felt a great wave of sadness come over her. *My whole life, I have judged so unfairly.*

"I must get out of here before I start a sneezing fit," Isobel said, turning for the stairs.

"I will be down in a moment," said Louis. "Mind your step on the way out."

Chloe turned and followed her mother out of the house.

Louis stood in the middle of his room. He turned to the metal cot and spoke aloud. "You don't know anything of how the world works yet. You think those feelings pulsing through you with such veracity are felt by everyone, but they're not. God or a curse has put inside of you a tremulous love of everything that is great and beautiful. You will live to be an old bachelor, in the shadow of an unrequited love. You like to suffer. You will make a career out of it. Do everything you're going to do. But know what awaits you. There is no grand house with Isobel in your future. But you will capture man's frailty in your portraits. And that, I suppose, is something."

He turned and walked out to the stairwell, closing his bedroom door behind him.

Outside, he could see Isobel and Chloe by the brook. He looked up at the sky and saw nacreous clouds advancing from the north. As he drew closer, unseen, he heard Isobel talking about the day that he had proposed marriage from the rock parapet in the middle of the brook. He felt a surge of humiliation, then heard her voice, her words, softened by a discernible fondness. He listened from the shadow side of an old willow.

". . . he had the entire brook and the sandy bank arranged

with flowers . . ." She laughed. "There was even a turtle, and I swear I think he'd polished its shell to gleam just a little brighter in the sunlight."

Chloe smiled. She stood barefoot on the sandy shore.

"And he began listing his character traits and strengths. He said he was a good swimmer. It was impossibly sweet. He was fourteen, you understand."

"Oh, Mother," Chloe said. "He was smitten. It's beautiful."

"Yes," said Isobel. "It *was* beautiful."

Louis came out from behind the willow and walked down to the bank. "Ladies, I think a storm is threatening. We may have to delay our picnic."

"That's a pity," said Isobel. "I was just telling Chloe about the way you proposed to me."

"Yes, I was romantic to the point of absurdity."

"No, not absurd," said Isobel. "But always so earnest and dramatic. We were never suited for each other."

"Love, madame," said Louis, "is not like choosing a partner for whist. It has a life of its own. Our duty is merely to follow its call. I will meet you back at the carriage." He turned and headed back across the cloven glade.

Chloe and Isobel waited for several moments on the sandy bank. There was a bite to the air.

"I think he's right, Mother," Chloe said. "I don't think we choose love. It chooses us."

"Don't tell me you wouldn't be daunted if he loved you. Have you seen those eyes? There's something unworldly about the way that man loves. He's mad with it."

They walked to the carriage. The clouds had turned leaden. Louis helped them up into the carriage and they rode off at a pace. From the road, Louis looked back at the ruined mansion, now darkened by the approaching storm.

The deluge hit on the open road. The Atlantic winds gusted

from the west, driving the rain horizontal. The women huddled beneath blankets on the bed of the carriage. Louis stopped at an old bridge keep and they took shelter inside. The wind batted at the small mullioned window. The room was ten feet square.

"So much for our picnic," said Chloe.

Isobel stomped her feet to keep warm. Louis put his coat over her shoulders and handed Chloe his suede riding gloves.

"Thank you," said Isobel.

Louis said, "The storm will pass and we'll get you home to the fire. I think we're only twenty minutes away."

They stood with their backs to the wall, their shoulders touching, Louis in the middle.

"I can't believe what's become of the estate. My father would turn in his grave," Louis said.

"What did you expect?" Isobel asked.

"I don't know. A sign of life."

"I thought it was charming," Chloe said. "I could picture you two getting into mischief." She smiled and looked out at the rain.

The windows turned opaque from their breathing. Louis blew into his hands. He looked out at the storm, his eyes harried and quick. Isobel looked at his face in the gloaming of the storm. For the first time in many years, she remembered their first kiss inside the wine cave. She remembered her delight and abandonment as she'd held the boy by the collar. It had been a dare, a wild declaration. But kisses, like births and deaths, set things in motion. They could set a man on a collision course with his own fate. Louis had bundled that kiss through revolution and fame and now, shivering beside her, appeared deeply weary at having carried it this far.

They waited for the better part of an hour. The rain stopped as abruptly as it had started. When they emerged, the world had changed: the Loire was a river of mud; the road was rutted and brown. Louis wiped the horses down with a blanket. Chloe and Isobel climbed up onto the carriage bed. The women were pale to the point of luminescence. Louis climbed up and rode as fast as the conditions would allow.

Back at the house, they got out of their wet clothes. Louis and Chloe made a fire in the hearth while Isobel prepared some dinner. Over a meal of pike and potatoes, they sat and stared at the fire, stultified by exhaustion. They ate each bite deliberately; safety and warmth seemed extravagances. They sipped wine and took brandy when the meal was done.

Louis looked at the fire, then at Isobel. In the bridge keep there had been something new in her face, a softness and vulnerability he hadn't seen in decades. Now there was the indifference of her mouth and the high forehead that seemed almost belligerent. He felt the old ache. She sniffled, interrupting his reflection. They looked at each other for an awkward interval; a flicker of startled recognition.

When the fire burned low, they finished their brandy and retired. Louis accepted a place on the divan in front of the hearth. Chloe got him a twill blanket and a pillow.

"You're much too big to be tucked in," she said. "But when I was standing in your old bedroom today, I could see you as a boy. I could see you in buckskins, pouting and sullen. It was sweet." She leaned down and kissed him on the forehead.

"I was a strange lad," he said. "Good night, Chloe." She walked down the hallway to her bedroom. Louis slumped back on the divan and closed his eyes. The day swelled behind his eyelids. There was a presence in the room, a slight shifting of air. He opened his eyes to see Isobel standing over him, a hand clasping the neckline of her nightdress. She held a shawl in her other hand, a look of consternation in her face.

"I'm a bit short on extra blankets, but I thought you could use one of my shawls if you get cold in the night." She ran her hand over the weave of the shawl.

"Thank you. I think I'll be fine. You or Chloe should use it."

"No, we're fine." She placed the shawl over him. "Good night."

"Good night, Isobel," he said.

He lay back down on the divan and stared up at the ceiling. The fire was all but dead, and he had a sense of the darkness pouring in through the windows. Although the storm had passed, it was still cold and blustery outside. He kept still and, above the wheezy draw of his lungs, listened to the sounds of the house—the coals giving off an occasional hiss and sputter, the wind blowing across the veranda, the small and precise movements of Isobel readying for bed. *A human life is a series of preparations.* Then there was another sound, of the house simply at rest, of the walls moving imperceptibly away from the foundation piers. *A house is a feeble stand against weather and time.* He listened to the wooden floor joists contract in the cold like the ribs of a ship. Suddenly, he could not sleep. Something was pressing down on him—a shunt of pain in his back, a burning dampness in his lungs. The air felt heavy and he suspected that he could be crushed by it; darkness, like water, had volume and weight.

TWENTY-SIX

sobel did not come to breakfast. She lay in bed, asleep, chilled to the marrow. Chloe and Louis came to check on her. Chloe placed her hand on her mother's shoulder.

"Mother, are you all right?" she said.

Isobel stirred and looked up at them, startled. "It's so cold," she said. She turned on her side. "Heavens, what time is it? I've slept half the day away."

"Stay in bed," said Louis. "You're not well."

"I just have a little cold. I'll take some nettle tea first thing."

"I've just boiled the water. I'll bring you some," said Chloe. She left the room and went to the kitchen.

"You don't look well," said Louis. Her hair was plastered down with night sweat.

"Never tell a lady that," she said, forcing a smile.

"Will you let me fetch the doctor?"

"He's a horse physician at best. Diploma from a barnyard. I have all the medicines we need right here. I may need you or Chloe to prepare them."

"Of course," said Louis. "I'll delay my return until the afternoon." He sat on the edge of the bed.

"Oh, I forgot you were leaving."

"I'm in no hurry," he said. "And the horses could use the rest."

"Thank you," she said. There was something exposed in her voice. "How did you sleep?"

"Not badly, I suppose," he said, clearing his throat.

Chloe came back in with the tea. "Here, Mother, sit up."

Isobel propped herself on the pillows, gave out a slight but asthmatic sigh, and received the mug of tea between both hands. She closed her eyes and let the nettle tea steam up into her face. "That's just the thing," she said. "I'll stay in bed till lunchtime. Don't let me oversleep, you two. Now go do something useful instead of ogling me."

"Call if you need anything," said Chloe.

"Would you like to use the little tin bell?" Louis asked.

"That won't be necessary. Now go."

Louis and Chloe left the room and closed the door behind them. Isobel immediately retrieved a clean bedpan from the floor and, upon coughing as silently as she could, spat into the copper bowl. It left her shivering and feverish. She opened the window by her bed for a brief moment, but it immediately filled her bones with ice. She got back under her blankets and pulled an extra pillow across her chest.

Isobel did not rise at noon. She slept a long, feverish sleep, waking here and there to cough into the bedpan. The cough made her stomach convulse and her eyes water. In the aftermath, she lay back on her dampened pillow and stared up at the ceiling. She looked at a clock in the afternoon and discovered to her horror that it was almost four o'clock. She got out of bed and sat before her mirror and began brushing her hair. Her face had the pallor of oats. Her eyes were yellowed and bloodshot. She walked out into the hallway, wrapped in a shawl, and found Louis in front of the fire.

He turned and stood. "How are you feeling?"

"Terrible, actually. Where's Chloe?"

"Went for a walk."

"I'm going to show you how to prepare me some herbs."

"Of course," Louis said.

"Come with me, then," Isobel said.

They walked to the back of the house and she opened the door to the herbarium. A thick and humid air came over them as they stepped inside. "It's almost time to open the windows," she said.

Isobel brightened slightly at the touch of her plants. She took out her pruning scissors. "I'm going to cut up some nettles and eucalyptus leaves, perhaps a few others as they come to me. We're going to prepare a thick paste using menthol leaves and mix it with Jamaica ginger and Batavia nutmeg."

"Sounds like we're making a dessert," Louis said, trying to elicit a smile.

"I'm going to put the paste across my chest," Isobel said. "It should help alleviate the cough." She cut a variety of leaves and placed them on a tin tray. "I'll need you to grind them with a mortar and pestle. Can you do that?"

"Of course."

She handed him the tray and showed him to the stone mortar and pestle. She took out some crystals of Jamaica ginger from one of the drawers and threw them, along with the leaves, into the grinding bowl.

Suddenly, she felt exhausted. "I'm going to get back into bed," she said. "Thank you for staying—that was very thoughtful of you." She placed her hand on his shoulder for a moment and left the room.

Louis ground the leaves. The eucalyptus oil made his eyes sting. He took great care to ensure an even pulp, picking out pieces of stem. The ginger and the nutmeg consumed the room and he felt himself on the verge of memory, of walking one of his serpentine routes in the Paris of 1804 and smelling the dusk come alive with roasted walnuts, supper fires from the garrets. When the leaves and spices were ground as finely as he knew how, he brought them to Isobel. She sat up and dipped her finger into the mixture.

"Perfect," she said. "We'll make an apothecary of you yet. Now, if you'll excuse me, I'm going to spread this across my thorny old lady's chest."

"Stop," said Louis.

"Stop what?" she asked.

"Don't disparage your body. You have only increased in loveliness and grace all these years. But your pride is enough to poison us all." He left and closed the bedroom door behind him.

Several hours later, he went to check on her. It was nearly evening and the light was fading fast. Her room smelled like a spice market, and in the gloom, he felt he was stepping towards some exotic sleeping goddess. He stood by the window. He watched her until everything was drawn into the rind of dusk. The sun was gone very suddenly. The furniture, the bedspread, the tint of her skin, all of it surrendered its color. This was the transom into night, when the world became muslin-toned and amorphous, when it matched closely the vaporous quality of his daguerreotypes. He imagined he could see her breath passing in and out of her lips. The veins in her eyelids resembled bolts of delicate lightning. He hated himself for wanting to kiss them. He stood there, watching her. The amber world faded to black. He lit the carbide lamp.

TWENTY-SEVEN

sobel spread her chest with the pungent green paste and slept beneath a cloud of eucalyptus and ginger. Louis waited another day to return to Paris. He watched her give herself over to long hours of sleep.

When she was alone, Isobel took inventory of her life. She could feel the frailty of her own existence; she was aware of her staccato lungs, the pulse of her blood. In the top of her armoire was a vintage leather suitcase that contained the artifacts of her youth. She took it down, locked her door, and sat back in bed. For four decades she had resisted nostalgia, hemmed in the past like a paddock, but now she felt the allure. Just as she had pondered the fatal turn in her daughter's life, she now pondered her own. Several of Louis Daguerre's portraits of her on the glade lay between sheets of fabric, brittled and yellowed with age. In one sketch she appeared as a Nubian queen—recumbent on a limestone ledge, crowned with a holly wreath, looking out towards a vanishing point of field and sky. In his drawings he had always tried to find her noblest aspect, but this continued in real life; she had always suspected that what he loved most about her was an illusion. He loved mystery, the withheld aspect in people and places. What he loved was love, she thought, the feeling of being pulled under, not this assemblage of pride and bones and dampness. And rather than his high-minded love making her want to be that mysterious person, it had made her want to correct his mistake. There was something damnable about being the love object, the capstone in some epic delusion. Still, she could not deny the comfort she felt when he was around. Life was more mysterious with Louis Daguerre in a room. When he looked at something closely—an arabesque in the rug, a polished beam of oak—she found herself following his gaze, expecting to be awed.

There were theater ticket stubs from the night the mansion had burned down. There were poems that Chloe had written as a young girl, her late husband's will, and some handwritten recipes she'd gotten from her mother's kitchen. On the back of a recipe for potato and veal stew, her mother had written the date—*January 20, 1815.* The year countless men died at Waterloo, her mother—one of nine cooks for the duke of Orléans—painstakingly wrote down a lifetime's worth of recipes. This was her opus, the fortitude of winter stews, the inherited ratios of meat and spice. Had her mother's life amounted to three dozen recipes? Isobel put away the things and replaced the suitcase in the top of the armoire. She unlocked her door and climbed back in bed, riveted by the past.

She slept through the afternoon, disturbed by dreams just beyond her recollection. She woke with cold feet and hands. Louis and Chloe came to her bedside. They looked at her with such tenderness that she knew she was getting worse.

"Is the boy feeding the horses?" she asked.

"Of course, Mother," said Chloe.

"You've barely eaten," said Louis. "We've brought you some rabbit stew."

Isobel put her hand to her throat. "Some broth," she said. "I could take some broth."

"I'll go get some," Chloe said. She went out to the kitchen.

"How long have I been asleep?" asked Isobel.

"All day. We've sent for a new doctor from Orléans."

"That will cost a fortune."

"I am paying for it. Money is pointless if it cannot serve our needs."

She nodded, absolved from argument.

"He should be here before the end of the day."

She nodded again and turned her face from him.

"What is it?"

"Nothing."

"What?"

Her breaths were short and fitful. "What do I have when you and Chloe go back to Paris? Some herbs and a cure for earache."

He looked at her. There was something bruised and defeated in her eyes. He recalled his own convalescence, looking down at his exiled toes in the wave of a fever. Everything came to the surface. He pulled up her quilt and tucked it under her chin.

The doctor arrived before dinner. He was a slovenly man from Orléans. A cockscomb of white hair stuck up on his head. A pair of spectacles hung around his neck, and every time he inspected Isobel at close range, he squinted through two smudged ovals of glass. He was prone to incessant talking, perhaps as a mild sedative. Sitting on the edge of Isobel's bed, taking her pulse, he began a litany of his last month's house calls.

"It's been a regular factory of laments," he said. "I've been running about on three hours of sleep thanks to this latest political mash. Bilious colic, quinsy, flux, summer complaint—turn on your side, madame—not to mention jail fever, hip gout, and lumbago. It's been a veritable jumble sale of maladies." He put his listening device to Isobel's back. He moved it into several different positions and gave a gravelly *humph* each time.

"What is it?" asked Louis.

"Lung fever, serious at that," said the doctor. He wrote down something in a black leather book.

"What is to be done?" asked Chloe.

"Absolute bed rest, and I will leave a phial of laudanum with you. It should ease the fever and the cough. Send for me if it gets worse. And please desist with that horrid paste spread across her chest."

"This paste has saved countless lives," said Isobel.

The man folded his spectacles and shrugged. "Yes, well, it might not save your life, dear lady. Please take a dose of laudanum in the morning and at night. Good day and good luck." The doctor stood and Louis showed him out to his carriage. He paid the man his fee without speaking and went back to Isobel's bedroom.

"He was an ass, just like every other doctor I've ever encountered," said Isobel.

"He may be right. Perhaps it is too late for the herbs," said Chloe.

"So now he wants me to take opium in alcohol solution. That sounds just the ticket."

"Please take it," said Louis. "I have taken it myself and found it to be quite helpful." This was not true, though he knew Baudelaire swore by the palliative effects of laudanum.

"Leave it beside the bed," Isobel said curtly. They complied and left the phial on her bedside table.

❊   ❊   ❊

Isobel lay in bed, aware of her limbs. *So, here it is, the ridiculousness of illness, the thing I cure but also do not believe in.* She could feel her body weaken, the thin line of nausea that extended from stomach to mouth. Convalescence required faith, a resoluteness she did not have. She feared the infections of nostalgia. *No. There is only this room. That man outside my door.* A man smitten with her but also with the countenance of a ripened pear, the ashen light of a dusky boulevard. She was nothing but an effigy, something raised above his solitude. In all likelihood he was quite mad — she saw something strange in the Antwerp blue of his eyes. But the question did not flinch, it only grew: *Do I love him? Have I always?* Several times she had looked at his stern jaw and imagined his mouth pressed to hers. There had always been an excitement about his dazed belief; it was like standing at the confluence of whitened rivers. *I would allow him to kiss me,* she thought, *if he dared.* And if the kiss lacked feeling, if it was worn and scuffed like her vintage suitcase of mementos, then that would be the end of it.

Later that night Louis came back to her bedside. She was sitting up and doing needlework in the light of the carbide lamp.

"Is it time for my opium?" she asked.

"You sound in better spirits."

She looked down at the brocaded fabric. "This is the first productive thing I have done in days. It's giving me hope that I won't be bedridden the rest of my life."

"Do you want me or Chloe to give you the laudanum?"

"You may administer the opium, sir," she said.

Louis took the phial from the bedside table and removed the cork. It gave off an acrid smell. "Just a small nip," he said. "This stuff can be very strong. In Paris you see drunken, deranged poets sitting with bottles of absinthe and laudanum." He handed the phial to her. She took a swallow. Her mouth bittered.

"It tastes like rancid almonds," she said.

She handed it back to him. They passed a moment of silence.

"Well, I'll come back in a while to check on you," he said. He turned to leave.

Something about his shoes on her floorboards, the walk of a man who had known an hour of fame, compelled her. She couldn't abide the waiting.

"Could you switch off my lamp and light a candle?" she said.

Louis did so and stood stiffly by the bedside table, awaiting her next instruction.

"Do you want to kiss me?" she asked in the half-light.

"What?" He was all breath.

"You heard me. If you want to kiss me on the mouth, then go ahead. But close the door first." She said it flatly and pointed blithely to the door.

"Isobel, you're feverish and you've just taken laudanum," Louis said quietly.

"I may never ask again," she said. "Later, I'll deny it or blame it on the opium."

Louis crossed to the door and closed it. He walked back lightly and nervous, raised on the balls of his feet. He sat on the edge of her bed, not knowing what to do with his hands.

"I apologize if I smell like an Indian bazaar," she said.

"Don't speak just now," he said.

He leaned over her and placed his lips gently against hers. He opened his eyes at close range only to find the stunned jade of her eyes looking back at him. He closed his again and was surprised to find that beneath the bitter-almond taste of the laudanum, she was familiar. For her part, Isobel tasted something woody and myrrh-like in Louis's mouth, but far from finding this disturbing, she was reassured by it; she had feared all this time that he would taste mealy and decrepit, or worse, like a butter-mouthed shopboy. This mutual consent of taste and smell entered the kiss. He felt her body rise towards him, her mouth open slightly. He placed his hand at the back of her head, lightly, fingers intertwined with her hair. The kiss that had waited half a century lasted five seconds, and when it ended, because Isobel needed to draw an uninhibited breath, they looked at each other. Her cheeks had been left scalded by the kiss.

"That was impossibly sweet," she said.

Louis began, "My whole life . . ." He looked off at the window, eyes on the verge.

"You must treat me like a fledgling. I cannot hear your proclamations yet, Louis. They have scared me to death my whole life. Let me pretend you hold me in fond regard, but I am not ready to hear about love."

"As you wish," said Louis, collecting himself. "Anyway, I meant to say that I don't think you half bad."

She smiled and coughed but managed to curb a full-blown spell. He took her hand and kissed the back of it. He pressed its soapstone cool to his cheek.

"Don't tell Chloe about that kiss. I suspect she has feelings for you," Isobel said.

"Don't be absurd," said Louis.

"I see it. A mother knows her daughter, no matter what's passed between them." There was a pause. She kissed him on the cheek. "Good night, Louis Daguerre."

Louis quietly left the room. For a long time Isobel lay there, staring at the ceiling and the walls, waiting for the tide of laudanum to wash over her. She watched the yew branches projected on the opposite wall. She did not know what the future held. Summer was coming, the wallflowers were coming into bloom, the days were lengthening; soon she would collect hyssop on the meadow. *Nature doesn't seem to care if we give ourselves over to love.* As for Louis Daguerre, she held but one hope: that the fury of his love would not overwhelm her before she had a chance to develop a lasting affection. She could picture him in the bed beside her each morning, could imagine leaning into the embrace of this vintaged regard.

The grace note of Louis Daguerre's courtship was a field mushroom, rare and spotted. He had set out early for a walk with his camera and tripod when he came upon a field of daylilies. He cut a bouquet and brought the flowers to Isobel's bedside. When Isobel awoke, she found gold and white lilies beside the phial of laudanum that she now regarded with some fondness. She gathered them up to smell and noticed the spotted beige head of a mushroom between the flower stems. She had seen this particular type only once, back on the estate, when she had witnessed a midwife curing a woman's bleeding with just a speck of the fungus made into a tea. The *Trois Lions* was a distant cousin of the *champignon de Paris*, which was first gathered from the graveyards of the capital in the eighteenth century. It was said they got their vitality from the bones of the dead. The one she held in her hand had enough medicinal potency to create a thousand tinctures. She rolled it around on her palm and held it up to reveal the brown velvet gills beneath the cap. She called out to Louis, who rushed in, fearing the worst.

"What is it?" he said. His hands were wet and he was running them down his trousers.

"Where did you find this?" she said, holding it up.

"Out on the field behind the marsh. Down towards Bartot's farm. Why?"

"This is very rare, Louis. It was in among your flowers."

"Yes. Of course I meant to pick it. I searched over dell and meadow for that rascal. A devil it was."

"Kiss me," she said.

Louis came to her and leaned down. He allowed her to pilot the kiss, her hand against his jaw. He straightened when the kiss was over. He placed his hands behind his back, then in front, then finally stuffed them into the pockets of his woolen trousers.

To fill the silence, he said, "They say Napoleon's nephew might be staging a coup."

"Let them have their revolutions. I would like to get dressed today. I would like a sit outside and then perhaps have a real dinner tonight. Would you take me to see where you found the mushroom?"

"I don't think that's wise."

"It's not like you to be prudent."

"On the contrary, I am very prudent. I safeguard myself against the future."

"How is it you do that?"

"I try for nothing that I can't afford to lose. That way I am guaranteed success."

"And do you think you will win me?"

"I have never doubted it," Louis said, giving his waistcoat an insistent tug.

The three of them set off in a wagon, pulled by the widow's old bay horse, in search of a hallowed mushroom field. Louis showed them where the lilies were and the place he suspected he may have picked the rare mushroom. But there was nothing else to be found. Isobel sat bundled in the wagon, directing Chloe and Louis to search certain likely spots—at the base of an oak, beside a patch of briar, in the shadow of a willow. On a hunch,

Isobel told Louis to dig two feet at the base of the old gnarled oak. Something about the tree suggested an abundance of mold and rot at its roots, and sure enough, Louis found a perfectly formed truffle, about the size of a fist. He held it above his head, his hands blackened with dirt. Then he wrapped it in his kerchief and they rode back to the house. Isobel said, "Tonight we shall cook a very fine dinner with this truffle."

"That would be wonderful," said Louis. He looked at her and saw the fatigue etched into her mouth and eyes. The lung fever had turned her face a pale, indelible blue, so faint it was like a watermark in the cloth of her skin.

They cooked all afternoon, the three of them gathered in the stone-floored kitchen. Isobel sat reclined in a wicker chair, instructing in the manner of a benevolent governess before her charges. Louis made a hot fire of cypress and oak. Chloe prepared the assemblage of spices and herbs in the herbarium as her mother called out their locations. Isobel watched her daughter grind juniper berries, sage, and mustard seeds. Chloe added narrow strips of truffle and butter to the herbs and spices and mixed until it became a marbled yellow-brown paste. Louis had bought a leg of lamb from a neighbor and now sliced it open so Chloe could stuff it with the paste. She inserted cloves of garlic into the fleshier parts and sprinkled the entire thing with Asian white pepper, white wine, and rosemary. It went into the oven. They prepared the vegetables, sitting around the kitchen with greens and roots in their laps. Chloe topped the asparagus and carrots; Louis peeled the potatoes and placed them in a pot of rainwater; Isobel cut the Swiss chard on a wooden board.

Isobel dressed for dinner. She emerged from her bedroom in a magenta gown gathered at the sleeves and the waist. Her hair was down and an amber necklace hung around her neck. Louis looked at her over the pots of simmering vegetables.

"You look lovely," he said.

"Thank you," she said. Dressing for dinner had given her confidence, a suggestiveness in her smile.

"Mother, you look wonderful," said Chloe.

"The last time I wore this dress was in Paris," she said.

They served the meal with a bottle of 1839 burgundy that had been given to Isobel as payment for an herbal remedy. They set a table by the fire. Louis played man of the house and carved the roast lamb. Isobel served the vegetables from a large clay pot. The meal was full of delightful contrasts — the dark, woody taste of the truffle, the subtlety of the herbed carrots. The wine was dry, with a citrus afterbite. They ate and drank, falling into bouts of reverent chewing between conversations about remembered meals and epic parties. Isobel reached for Louis's hand under the table. He looked up from his plate, fork in hand, stunned by the veracity of the meal and the candlelight and the hand he now held. The women were talking about the department stores of Paris, about barege and silk ball gowns, about extravagant outfits that existed mainly in the mind. Louis listened to the women as if through a long corridor. He nodded. He smiled. Night pressed in at the windows. There was nothing else he wanted. For the first time in his life, he thought, *So this is happiness.*

After several glasses of brandy, they retired, leaving the kitchen a scatter of pots and pans. Chloe said good night. Louis helped Isobel up from the table. They were both a little drunk and they moved down the hallway a little unsteadily, their hands gliding out to touch the walls now and then. Isobel opened her bedroom door. She had always instinctively closed a door behind her, ever since she was a child.

"Are you going to bed?" he asked.

"Yes." She entered the room, still holding his hand. They fumbled in the dark for a moment before Louis lit the lamp.

"I need to get into my nightclothes," she said.

"I'll leave the room," said Louis.

"Just turn your back until I say," said Isobel.

"Very well." He turned to face the wall farthest from the bed. He could see his own shadow sway in the carbide glow. A moment later, he saw the shadow of Isobel undressing. He watched her arms rise above her head like twin serpents, the dress coming off, the undergarments being unlatched, her body gradually coming into silhouette. Louis felt his heart thrum in his ears.

"You may turn around now," she said.

He did so. She lay on the bed. She was wearing a black slip open at the neck and shoulders. He stared at her collarbones, the delicate hollows at the base of her neck.

"Come and lie down," she said.

"I'm still dressed for a party," he replied.

"Take a few things off," she said. "I won't look."

He came and sat on the bed. He took off his shoes methodically, folding his socks neatly inside. Then he removed his coat and waistcoat and lay on his back. Isobel settled next to him. Their heads were on adjacent pillows, and a net of Isobel's hair spilled onto Louis's shoulder. He wanted to hold it to his face and smell it, but he felt timid. She reached for his hand, then rested her head on his chest. She could hear his heart thud. She had expected it to be steady and regular as a waterwheel, but it beat sporadically, fading in and out like a tired waltz from a previous century.

"I'm sorry I ever doubted your intentions with my daughter," she said.

"It's nothing. Any good mother would be suspicious."

"She was such a wonderful child, you know. She used to bring me daisies and leave poems on my pillow."

"I can picture it."

In the island of lamplight they both felt a deep calm. From outside came the distant call of a screech owl.

"Are we to be lovers?" Isobel asked.

"It seems that way."

"Well, we should approach this matter like adults. I have not made love with a man in ten years, Louis. I have no intention of doing so beneath the weight of this difficult breathing."

"I understand."

"Ridiculous."

"What?"

"Lovers at our age."

"We've been brought together."

"You tracked me down like a bloodhound."

"I was guided here. I think perhaps I have always been guided." He thought of a boy being led into a forest.

"You sound like a man of faith," she said.

"Yes, but in what?"

"I lack faith."

"You always have," said Louis.

"Yes."

A silence.

"Louis?"

"Yes."

"I think I could grow to love you."

Louis leaned on his side. He touched her face so tenderly that he resembled a man roused from prayer. He kissed her forehead, then her closed eyes, her cheeks, and her neck. Isobel let out a low sigh. She took his face between her hands and brought her lips to his. As they kissed, she felt them mingling in a broth of brandy and solace. These were the kisses of the old, she thought, born of a mutual empathy for the frailty of time. Their bodies were neither allies nor enemies at this way station of sentiment; they were like neutral nations being called upon in a moment of war. The kisses would stay on the roof of her mouth, burned in. She would allow herself to be infected with Louis's love; it had dogged her into the far reaches of widowhood. Love was, finally, a decision. They lay beside each other, half clothed. They took sips of water in the small hours. Every time one of them moved, the other reached out, maintaining the bas-relief of their union. They stayed like this until morning, until the blue light of dawn bled into the room and changed everything.

TWENTY-EIGHT

ouis and Isobel slept in the same bed each night. They refused to acknowledge the growing illness, the bloody sputum that swam in the bedpan every morning. It became a conspiracy, a pantomime of life. Chloe brought her mother breakfast each morning, but by then Isobel had emptied her bedpan onto the rosebushes outside her window. Between the hours of eight and noon Isobel could summon her brightest face, but by midafternoon she was fatigued and slept under a tide of laudanum and damp-lunged dreams.

Nonetheless, Louis was buoyed by hope. He took no photographs and the absence of mercury granted him bouts of lucidity. Then, because the mercury was now blended in his blood and bones, he would do something inexplicable — stop speaking in the middle of a sentence, gripped by an ineffable thought, or dress without socks, or give off a shudder in the middle of the night. Isobel was not alarmed by these moments; she accepted that his mind was worn in places. She wondered, in fact, if any man could love the way he did and be mentally sound. Each day he showered her with wildflowers, with strange and half-finished poems.

They woke sometimes together, in the middle hours of the night, and lay awake talking through a reconstruction of the past. There were so many gaps to fill. They smiled at the surprise of a person unfolded, of secrets and lies offered up to the yew-latticed ceiling. Life had brought them together in this final chapter, and their task, they both felt, was to discover what had happened to the other in the middle of the book.

"I will of course want to know all about your lovers before we ever make love," announced Isobel one night.

"What is it you require?"

"Names, for a start."

"Let's see. The first was Matilde, then Claire, Rose, and Audrey. Then came Madame Treadwell, an English widow with a penchant for theater boys."

"How many were there?" she asked.

"More than five and less than ten."

"Oh."

"Are you horrified?"

"I'm afraid you'll find me dull and unpracticed. I have made love to only one man my whole life, and that was like tending the compost—a few scraps on the pile. Poor man, may he rest in peace."

"Those women meant nothing to me. They were auditions of the heart."

They held hands and waited for the next phrase to arrive. They watched the ocean of night at the window.

"What are we to do with Chloe?" asked Isobel. "She is so lonely."

"We will find her a good man."

"In these parts they're all drunks and farmers hard of hearing."

"One has to trust life."

After a long pause, he turned to face her. She had fallen asleep. He stared at the sibylline calm on her face.

The next morning Isobel sat in front of the silver-backed mirror. Louis stood behind her, a bone-handled brush in his hand. She sat in her negligee, staring at her own figure. It came to her as if from a very long distance. *This* was her body. Her eyes were sunken, her skin waxy. The youthful quality she'd had in the early stages of the lung fever had vanished, and in its place there was a dryness, a withered look to her neck and mouth. She visibly shivered as she looked at herself. Louis pretended not to notice and began brushing her hair.

"Oh, God, Louis," she said. "Look at me."

Louis looked at her reflection in the mirror. There was no denying. She carried it now—the chromatic suggestion of death. Their eyes met in the hologram of the mirror. They both looked away.

"Fetch me a shawl, Louis."

He went to her armoire and took down a cashmere shawl. He wrapped it around her shoulders and knotted it in front of her neck. They couldn't look each other in the eyes.

In the afternoon Louis sent for the doctor. He arrived smelling of ambergris and snuff, apparently prospering from the revolution. He sat beside Isobel in her darkened room, the curtains drawn at her insistence. Having this man see her wither seemed like an insufferable affront; would he ridicule her herbal ways again? Here, science, another footnote in the argument against folk remedies. But, to her surprise, the doctor became moved in her presence. She glowed, a jaundiced blue. Louis watched at the foot of the bed as the doctor unwrapped Isobel's nightgown and examined her chest.

"My dear woman," he said. "You should have been dead weeks ago. This is the worst lung fever I have ever seen." His voice was gentle, almost reverent.

Isobel smiled weakly, somehow flattered. She had not given up. The brine in her lungs was proof of her struggle to love Louis Daguerre.

"What can we do?" asked Louis.

The doctor said, "If you are religious, pray."

A sudden sob came from behind them. Chloe stood in the doorway, her hands folded across her front. "I don't understand," she said.

"From the way this has flared up, I'm guessing she's had the fever for years," said the doctor. He turned to Isobel. "You have a remarkable grace in illness, dear lady."

Isobel looked at him solemnly. "I have given myself over to love, Doctor. I recommend you prescribe it to go with laudanum."

The doctor squeezed her hand and closed her nightgown with great tenderness. "When the pain and the breathing become intolerable you may increase the dosage. I don't want you to suffer anymore."

"Thank you," Isobel said.

Louis ushered the doctor outside to his carriage.

"She is a remarkable woman. May she find peace." The doctor gathered the reins and rode out into the road. Louis stood there and watched the doctor disappear into the chalky-white distance. An enormous weight gathered in his chest, but he could not bring himself to cry. He had wept like a stage actress at the sight of a well-made shoe just months before, and now he was losing the lamp of his life and he stood there stoic, tearless, unbelieving. Death seemed dismissive, an arrogance of a distant God. Why bother with this ritual of transfiguration? Then a horrifying thought came to him: that he might live to be ninety without Isobel and the world would continue to spin, unfettered by angels, forever. He stood there stricken by the thought of infinity. Finally, he went back inside and found Chloe and Isobel embracing on the bed. He closed the door and went to light the fire for evening.

He felt her slipping beside him each night. Her lungs hooked on the out-breath. Her skin grew cold to the touch and her camphored fragrance turned to night sweat. It seemed to Louis that they were beginning their old age together, holding hands in the carbide quietude of Isobel's bedroom. They allowed all the nuances of age to filter through the days. In half a week they lived out half a century. They talked of houses they might have owned in Marseille, of Louis's studio in Paris where they might have stayed when they went to the opera.

"I abhor the opera," said Isobel.

"It's not possible."

"Bores me to the eyelids."

"Well, then, we'd better call the whole thing off."

"Is this really our fate?" she asked, almost in a whisper.

He could not bring himself to answer.

"Louis, we haven't squandered our lives by not being together."

"Nothing is squandered," he said.

"Because I was never before ready. And this"—she paused for breath—"is perfection in its own way. I have given myself wholly to you these last few days."

"I know."

"We haven't made love. Will you forgive me for that?"

Louis leaned up in bed and took her face in his hands. "In my mind I have made love to you a thousand times."

"Better in the mind, then. Because it would kill me."

Louis looked away.

"Allow me my gallows humor, even now."

"What is going to happen to us?" he asked.

"This might be all there is. This bed. This room."

He looked at her. Somehow they had skipped the trials of nuptial life to arrive here. They had skipped the excitement of newlyweds, the tedium of middleweds, the rancor of old married couples with their ritual resentments kept aglow like rubbed bronze. What existed now was a love based not just on life but on the certainty of one's end, the winnowing of all emotion down to the care of another.

They slept, gripped by dreams. Isobel woke in the middle of the night to find Louis standing at the end of her bed. He appeared fully dressed—trousers, shirt, waistcoat—with a glazed look in his eyes.

"What is it?" she asked.

Louis made no reply. He looked slightly stunned. His eyes were on the luminous windows, the rectangles of wan moonlight. She realized he was sleepwalking. He began navigating the room, a hand touching the walls. "My shoes. Has anyone seen my shoes?"

"Louis," she called.

He walked barefoot over to the closed door and stood there, waiting. "I need my shoes," he said. "It's very cold down in the mixing room."

Isobel got up slowly from the bed and crossed to him. His face was unblinking, the startled look of a dog roused from sleep.

"Louis," she said, "you're having a dream. Come back to bed."

He did not respond. For a moment she was chilled by his countenance, by his dead-white stare. She took his hand and led him back to the bed. Without resistance, he lay down. She

curled beside him and felt a terrible loneliness; she held his cold
hand and cried. She understood these tears were for herself, not
for Louis nor Chloe, but a kind of self-grief for the woman she
had not become. She reached for the laudanum and took several
swallows. The opium softened her remorse; it calmed her glands
and swam up her spine. She doubted the existence of God, even
now. Perhaps there was benevolence, sometimes an invisible
kindness that intervened. She kissed Louis on the cheek. *He saw
who I could become. He loved what I wanted to love in myself—a woman
of the earth, a healer, someone who carried passion, who yearned for grace
but found pride instead. Pride is a house locked from within.*

The next morning Louis sat up in bed, baffled by his waistcoat and trousers. Isobel told him of his nightwalk.

"You stood at the door, asking for your shoes."

"I see," said Louis.

"We had quite a conversation."

"Did we?"

"No."

"What a relief."

"I have a favor to ask," she said.

"What is it?"

"I'd like you to take a portrait of the two of us."

"Today?"

"Yes."

"As strange as this might sound, I have never appeared in a
photograph. It's an old superstition, something about the con-
jurer looking back into the mirror."

"It's time you changed your superstition. Is noon a good time
for the light?"

"Yes, of course," said Louis. "Are you sure you are well
enough?"

"Quite certain." But Isobel could feel her lungs sag like
dampened cheesecloth. It hurt to breathe.

❋ ❋ ❋

At noon they dressed as if for a ball. Isobel wore her finest barege gown, her pearls and antique broach. Louis wore a top hat and a wool suit. Chloe had gone into town, but still they locked the door; this seemed like a private indulgence. Louis set up a timer on the camera obscura and took inventory in the dusty light of the room. He set the exposure for one minute because the yew branches outside the window filtered out much of the sun's glare. They decided to recline on the bed, propped by pillows. This was partly because Isobel felt unable to stand, but partly for the strange appeal of a couple dressed to the hilt, recumbent on a bed in a country room.

Isobel sat on the bed, her hands in her lap. Louis made a few final adjustments to the camera obscura and released the timer. He had five seconds to make it to the bed.

"My hat on or off?" he asked, sitting beside her.

"Off," she said. "Let the camera see your face."

"We must stay very still for one minute," he said. "Don't move until I say."

They held their positions, hands intertwined. The metallic click of the timer measured the seconds. She wanted to move her face, to hold Louis to her chest. How would she appear in the photograph—upright and proud, or slumped and broken? She would be brave, she told herself. Wear it as an undergarment to pride. She had never given herself to excess; she had strived to help others. Wasn't that admirable? A hollowness moved through her body. She continued staring into the camera, time unraveling. Death was everywhere now, in the tips of her hair, in her toenails. Horehound in honey for coughs, milk thistle for the liver, rosemary for shiny hair, the names of plants, the first kiss in the wine cave, the loveless marriage, the thwarted daughter looking for redemption, her wedding ring in the white envelope, the fragrance of gardenias from the window, the stupid surprise of death, all of it came to her during the exposure. An eternity of sitting still. Finally, she could bear the stillness no longer. She said to the camera, "I think I may have always loved you, Louis." His hand tightened against hers, but he remained looking into the camera, into the future.

The timer closed the eye of the camera. He turned to her.

"I have loved you through kings and emperors . . . since before Paris had gas lamps."

He kissed her on the mouth. They took off their ballroom clothes and lay beneath the covers in their underwear, trembling, pressed together.

Isobel woke to the crush of her own breathing. From outside came the minuscule screams of frogs in the marsh. *Spring is here, full-blown,* she thought. She sat up in bed and looked out the window at the crimson dawn. She wanted to die with grace, to be one of those matriarchs who gave counsel on their deathbeds — whom to marry, how to stave off loneliness, the virtue of prayer. But the truth was, she had no advice to give the living, and she could hear from the withheld rattle of her lungs that there would be an unsightly struggle at the very end. The blunt graspings of the body. She was too weary now for goodbyes and would die, as she had lived, with the door closed.

She placed her head on Louis's chest.

"What is it? Are you all right?" he asked.

"I think I need some tea. Would you fetch me some?"

"Of course." He sat up. "You know what I was dreaming?"

"What?"

"That you and I were riding in a hot-air balloon. It was a fête or something. We floated over the valley."

"That's a wonderful image," she said. "Louis?"

"Yes?"

"I want you to promise me that you'll look after Chloe."

"You know I will."

"Because my estate will not be much. Gerard was in debt near the end."

"Don't think on it now. I'll fetch your tea."

"Do you believe in God?" she asked, grabbing his hand.

He sat back down. He thought of his false apocalypse, of the way God had tricked him into his prophecy. His image of God had changed from one of benevolence to one of calculation and reckoning. During those doomsday months, God had been a hooded falconer, his arm held aloft. Now God slept in the wheel-house of some colossal, ghostly ship. "I believe that the world is strung together by something. I believe that beauty is the stain of the cosmic mind. I believe that you and I will always be together." He kissed her eyelids.

"I want to believe that," she said.

"Belief is mostly a matter of the will."

"I love you, Louis. I can't tell you how wonderful it is to say that."

"I've waited fifty years to hear those words, and I won't tire of them easily."

He kissed her again and stood to fetch her tea. She watched him move across the floor, head down, a slight shuffle in his walk. She understood that his own death was not far off. He carried an illness—it was in his eyes, the mismatched shoes, the portent he found in a teacup.

"Louis?"

"Yes?"

"Would you mind closing the door?"

"Why?" he asked, turning.

"There's a terrible draft from the hallway," she said.

"I see." He looked at her from the doorway, framed against the darkness in the hallway. She saw the beryl blue of his eyes, the look of knowing. He nodded and attempted to smile through a scrim of tears.

"Kiss me again," she said very suddenly.

He came to the bedside and kissed her on the mouth. He heard the containment of her lungs. She took her thumb and collected a tear from his cheek. She brought it delicately to her lips. "There's an old remedy that calls for the tear of a man in love."

"What does it cure?" he asked.

"Nervous complaint in young girls."

"I see," he said. "It opens them up to love and life."

"Fathers give it when they can't marry their daughters off."

He smiled.

She looked away and said, "Now, brew the nettles until they're tender."

He collected himself and stood. "Use the bell if you need to."

"I think I'm capable of calling out your name, Louis Daguerre."

He nodded again and left the room without looking back. She lay staring at the white rectangle of the door for several moments. She would not cry. She gave it permission to come now, to seal her lungs and clench her throat. *Leave me my doubts.* She did not want a godly conversion. There was a recession of morning stars at the window. There was a bell at her side. There was a man—the man she should have married—making tea in her kitchen. There was the faint smell of lucerne, of the sun warming the paddocks. These things were somehow enough. She closed her eyes and tried to make Louis's ballooning dream her own— the two of them passing through the ether, rising in an apparition of silk and fire.

Louis waited to return with her tea. He knew she would be loosed from her body, but he'd made the tea anyway. He stood with the steaming mug, shaking by her bedside. Her head rested on the pillow, her eyes open, looking up. He would wait for Chloe before closing them. Outside there was activity, normalcy. A row of cypress bent along the hillside. A farmer was turning his fields. A nightjar perched in a tree. He thought of springtime brooks, of Isobel collecting wood-ear mushrooms. He sat on the bed, her dead foot resting lightly against his leg. He looked around the room. A carafe of water—half empty from their late-night talks—stood beside the bed. The phial of laudanum sat beneath the lamp. Objects seemed frail. The windows hung like portraits of a tin-white sky. *The world has ended after all.*

TWENTY NINE

pring had arrived, fully fledged. The doors and windows of the stone cottage were flung open. Spiders claimed the eaves and the sills. Dandelion spores floated through the hallway. The horses whinnied from the barn, neglected and unshod. Chloe and Louis buried Isobel beneath her herbarium plants, back behind the marsh, according to her wishes. She lay beneath rosemary and milkweed, beneath herbs for the blood.

Louis stayed on to help settle Isobel's small estate. She'd left him a phial of lavender-scented water that he could not bring himself to open. Chloe inherited the house, the old bay horse, a few of her father's maritime stocks. Louis did not develop the copper plate of him and Isobel reclined on the bed. The camera stood on the tripod with the exposed plate inside, sealed as a mortuary house. In preparation to leave, he used his other cameras to catalog her acreage—a goldfinch on the camber of an oak branch, a wallflower aflame on the barn wall, the bone-gray spines of the rosemary on her grave. It was impossible to cure nostalgia, he thought. Briefly, with the audacity of being still alive, he had tried to find nature's hidden mechanics, her subtle architecture woven into leaf and stem, seed and taproot. But every time he chose an object to photograph, he captured its luster, not its form.

He slept in Isobel's bed each night. The sheets had not been washed since her passing, and they retained a hint of her smell. This was the closest he came to being maudlin. He seemed unable to cry, and this unsettled him. His emotions felt trapped in a single memory—the quiet formality of the afternoon portrait, the timer gears clicking, a minute wound tight inside the camera, their images burning into the copper plate, then her words, "I think I may have always loved you," and the sound of deflation, of a small surrender.

There was this memory and there was the world, spread beyond its edges. Nature was corpulent and overripe, as if to accentuate his loss. Wild grapes draped the trellises; the marsh danced with battalions of mating dragonflies. There was a smell in the air as of salted meat. The windowpanes swelled inside their sills, bloated by so much spectacle.

The world felt poised. He walked through the house and felt a quiet allegiance with glasses of water, fluttering curtains, things waiting to be called upon to act their little part. Outside, the sky and hills rocked past. The sun flared. Planets made apogee turns in their orbits. He had the sense that he was merely pacing inside a curved chamber, scenery scrolling past, the star dome spinning slowly, while somewhere a man in overalls bent over the day's crankshaft.

Chloe took refuge in sleep. In Paris she had been famous for her noon risings. Here, she had briefly opened herself to mornings, to her mother's schedule. Now she lay in bed past lunchtime, hemmed in by pillows. She ate oranges in bed, dropping the peels on the floor. She heard Louis move about the house, his walk of shuffling distraction. They were fugitives; she knew that. Neither could comfort the other. She wanted to be held, to have her hair stroked. Meanwhile, Louis blundered about in gingham-patched trousers, muttering to sparrows and door hinges.

The day Louis was due to return to Paris, a knock came at Chloe's door. He appeared in the doorway, hat in hand. She suddenly felt guilty that she had not prepared him some food for his trip. Her mother would have done that. The thought of cooking made her ill.

"I want to buy this house," he said.

She sat up, rubbed her face. "What?"

"You said you'd sell it and move on, and I can't bear the thought of somebody else living here." He blinked rapidly, looking down at his feet.

"You would live here?"

"No. I'm still leaving for Paris."

"Oh," she said.

"Where will you go, Chloe?"

"I don't know."

"The South is pretty. And slow, of course."

"I could go to the South," she said.

"Yes. You could go to the South," he said distantly. He raised his eyebrows and blew some air through his lips. "I will give you twenty thousand francs for it and not a sou more."

She stared at him, waiting for a grin. "Don't be ridiculous, Louis. It's worth nowhere near that."

"The money's already arranged," he said, addressing the windows.

"What do you mean?"

"Come out here."

She followed him into the living room. Francs bundled with ribbon stood in neat inch-high stacks by the hearth.

"My God," she said quietly.

"You'll need to sign a deed. I'll send it when I'm settled."

"Louis, why are you doing this? I can't accept."

He touched the rim of his hat. "Doing what? It's quite simple. You now own a piece of property I wish to acquire. There is no place for sentiment in business."

"I don't know what to say."

"How about 'Thank you and good luck.' I earned this money by capturing light and selling it to people. It's a scandal, really."

She turned and brimmed, suddenly, with tears. "Could you hold me, Louis?"

He swallowed, eyes down. "I could do that."

She inched towards him and put her head on his shoulder. He stood, stiff as a plank, while she wrapped her arms around him tightly.

"Do you remember when you said I was a child of God?"

"Yes," he said.

"I could tell from your eyes that you really meant it. That was the moment I knew I could have another life."

"I'm glad for that," he said. "And I'm glad we rediscovered Isobel together."

The word *Isobel.* He was not expecting to be unhinged by her name. A sob bolted through his chest. He pressed his face to her shoulder and brought his arms around her. They stood there, locked together, unable to let go.

THIRTY

ack in Paris, Louis tried to return to the fold of his life. The city pulsed with violence and protests. Forty thousand people marched from the Champ-de-Mars to the Hotel de Ville. The May elections returned a conservative chamber and now there was more rioting. Troops from the provinces came in by train and they marched along the streets with bayonets — Burgundy farm boys, fishmongers from the South, the sunburnt Provençal.

Louis kept his door locked and his curtains drawn. Revolution was no longer an abstraction to him. One afternoon, as he ate his lunch, a brick hurtled through his window. He looked at it with a certain admiration and proceeded to make a daguerreotype of his street through the star of shattered glass. He did not go to collect his doomsday portraits, but he often thought of them entombed in the catacombs, resting beside the man who had mapped the moon. He lay in bed, tethered to mercurial dreams and fevers, and listened to the sounds of distant looting. He pictured Isobel's cottage in the woods, shuttered and sealed, losing itself to dusk. Within a few years he would lie next to her grave of rosemary and hyssop. The thought gave him comfort. He imagined their bodies in the ground, a woman returned to the earth and a man removed from the light, their twin fates finally resolved.

He rarely saw anybody. Sometimes he was invited to take portraits of generals and memorial images of the wealthy dead. He invented excuses and declined politely. He took his supper at a nearby tavern and ventured no farther than the wineshop at his corner. The mail, when it came, carried his pension checks and, now and then, letters from Chloe. The envelopes carried chatty letters and dried cornflowers. They bore the hopeful blue postal stamp of Marseille.

One day near the end of August 1848, Louis received an invitation from a bishop, asking him to make a daguerreotype from the roof of Notre Dame. He wrote back to say that such images had already been made and with little success. The bishop wrote again and told him that this would be a birthday present for the pope. Louis thought of Degotti and his papal portraits inside the Vatican and agreed to go.

A week later, at noon, Louis found himself climbing the tower steps of Notre Dame. Two assistants, assigned by the bishop, hauled his equipment to the rooftop. His lungs ignited with the climb and several times he had to stop on a landing to cough and recover. They reached the top and the assistants set his equipment down. They stood for a moment, flanked by gargoyles, and took in the city. Louis attached the camera to the tripod and prepared a plate.

The jigsaw of Paris sprawled in all directions. He had never seen the city from this height and he noted, in outline and detail, the routes and warrens of his life. The blue-gray Seine cut the city neatly in two. He saw the patchwork of shanties and the mud-daubed poverty behind the Left Bank; this was where he had taken his walks as an apprentice and named colors as an antidote to love. He saw the old Right Bank mansions, tired and ravaged with ivy, their stone courtyards still protecting family shrines and cherubic fountains. In just such a house he had made love with a woman for the first time. To the north were the Montmartre tenements stacked and buttressed by common walls, laundry lines flapping ragtail flags of breeches and work shirts. Near the Tuileries, along the boulevards, were the mansard rooflines of the grand town houses, the dormers shuttered against the sun and the revolution. There was the wide, open boulevard where Louis Daguerre had taken his very first portrait and where the first man to be photographed had stood with one foot up on a shoe-shine crate. He saw the old theater where Degotti had taught him how to use a camelhair brush and to paint from both memory and sight. He could see his studio and the site where the Diorama building had stood. He could see the monuments—the Arc de Triomphe, the Obelisk—diminished in scale. They were paltry, towers in a child's city of blocks. Below him, unseen, was the Gothic mouth of the cathedral where he had kissed Isobel on the night of his first opera. In Paris, he realized, everything important had happened within the same square mile.

He loaded the plate and tightened the tourniquets on the back of the camera. The light was good, despite the clouds. There were clearings of blue sky that resembled alpine lakes. To the west, if he waited long enough, verticals of sunlight might throw the Palais Royal into silhouette. The three men stood in silence, awed by the sight of Paris at noon. Louis turned the camera to face the west. He leaned down to the eyepiece, his life spread beneath him, and waited for the perfect sunburst.

"Gentlemen, if we're prepared to wait a little, the pope will have a river of light for his birthday," Louis said.

The assistants chuckled at this and returned to silence. After an eternity of staring into the brightening west, one of them asked, "Monsieur Daguerre, how long do you think that will take?"

Without looking up, Louis said, "I can't be sure. But I am prepared to wait a long time."

ACKNOWLEDGMENTS

I am deeply grateful to the James A. Michener Center for Writers at the University of Texas at Austin, the Texas Institute of Letters, and the Dobie Paisano Fellowship for financial support during the writing of this novel.

I am also indebted to James Magnuson and Elizabeth Harris for their expert guidance and for offering their time to me on countless occasions; Wendy Weil, my agent, for her hard work and insight; Suzanne O'Neill, my editor, for her vision and enthusiasm; Darin Ciccotelli, Lee Middleton, and Vivé Griffith for their friendship and for being such demanding, generous, and attentive readers; Jeff Tietz for being the writing friend I can call with random complaints and ideas; Laura Smith for her belief, tireless enthusiasm, and support of my writing over the last fifteen years; Thom Knoles for eight years of friendship and guidance; the late Glenn Leggett for being so passionate about literature and life; Evelyn Foltyn and Jacqueline Rolfe, my high school English teachers, for inspiring me with their love of language; John Dalton and Emily Barton for being the first in a series of great and dedicated writing teachers; photography professor, Lawrence McFarland, for sparking my interest in

Daguerre. This book benefited greatly from the daguerreotype collection at the Harry Ransom Center.

A special thank-you goes to my parents and my three sisters for their love and encouragement.

A final and immense thank-you to Emily Zartman for her love, humor, and support while I tried to find the time to finish this book.

THE MERCURY VISIONS OF LOUIS DAGUERRE

DOMINIC SMITH

Reading Group Guide

INTRODUCTION

Paris, 1847. Louis Daguerre has achieved the height of fame for his invention of the daguerreotype, but his legacy has come at a great cost. He is falling deeper and deeper into delusions caused by repeated exposure to mercury, the key ingredient in capturing photographic images. Daguerre believes the world will end within a year and creates a "Doomsday List," ten things he must photograph before the final day—including a portrait of Isobel Le Fournier, the woman he loved and lost nearly a half century ago. With the aid of colorful poet Charles Baudelaire and a beautiful prostitute named Pigeon, Daguerre sets out to locate his subjects and fulfill his quest.

The Mercury Visions of Louis Daguerre weaves together the strands of Daguerre's life: his youth in rural France, the ruined love that gave rise to artistic achievement, and the eventual unraveling of a prodigious mind. As Daguerre counts down the days to his apocalypse, he is caught between memory and reality. Ultimately, he must confront his haunting past if he is to finally win the heart of the only woman he has ever loved.

QUESTIONS AND
TOPICS FOR DISCUSSION

1. Item number 10 on Louis Daguerre's "Doomsday List" of images to photograph is Isobel Le Fournier. Why is it so important to Louis that he find Isobel before (as he believes will happen) the world expires? Why does Louis confide in the poet Charles Baudelaire about his doomsday prophecy? What about the other items on the list? What do they reveal about Daguerre?

2. As a *rapin* at the theater, Louis is subjected to an "initiation" by his fellow apprentices, who attempt to frighten him by taking him to a morgue and having him sketch a portrait of a dead woman. Louis, however, stays inside the morgue for hours, long after he is free to leave. Why does Louis put so much time and effort into his drawing of the corpse? What does this incident reveal about Louis? What does Degotti mean when he later tells Louis, "You drew what you wanted to see" (78)?

3. Under Degotti's tutelage, Louis serves as the master paint mixer and brush washer at the theater for more than a year. What makes him finally stand up to Degotti and

demand that he be allowed to paint a set? Is it a coincidence that Louis takes a stand on the same day he has his first sexual encounter with Madame Treadwell? Why or why not?

4. In what ways do the instances of civil unrest in France mirror Louis's states of mind, including the burning of the mansion in Orléans, the rioting taking place in Paris the first time he has a vision, and the uprising on the day his "apocalypse" arrives?

5. Why does Louis develop such an intense fascination with quicksilver, to the point where he "carried a phial of mercury around his neck at all times. . . . He was, in a sense, in love again"? What does the quicksilver represent to him?

6. On the night Louis and Isobel kiss on the Pont Neuf in the shadow of Notre Dame, Isobel says to him, "Life is more complicated than you know." Louis replies, "Life is more mysterious than you know" (99). What do these statements reveal about Louis and Isobel's respective attitudes about life in general, as well as about their relationship?

7. On that same evening in Paris, Isobel tells Louis that someday he will be famous. "Louis knew this to be true; he saw it sometimes in the shop-windows when his reflection passed, the glimmer of who he was becoming" (100). Why is Louis so certain that he will achieve renown? Particularly when his discovery of the daguerreotype, as even he admits, is primarily accidental?

8. Describe the way Louis looks at the world both before and after the onset of his mercury-induced visions. What similarities, if any, are there? How did Louis's experiences

as a boy, particularly his fascination with light and his youthful love for Isobel, shape his artistic viewpoint?

9. In a letter to Isobel (which he never gives her), Louis writes, "That day on Pont Neuf, you with child, began the rise of my career. I have often thought it ironic that losing you was what led me to fame" (184). What validity is there in Louis's belief that his losing Isobel is what led him to become famous? In what ways are his shifting feelings for Isobel reflected in his art and the arc of his career?

10. Why is Louis compelled to help Pigeon and save her from a life of prostitution? Is it merely because she is Isobel's daughter? Why does he not tell Pigeon about his connection to her mother? Does Pigeon even want to be "rescued" by Louis, or is she content with the life she has chosen?

11. Louis stores his portraits in the catacombs beneath the Paris Observatory before fleeing the city, but he decides to take one with him: the portrait of Pigeon on the rooftop of Baudelaire's mansion. Why does Louis choose to keep this particular image? What does it represent to him?

12. On the morning he awakens in Isobel's cottage, Louis realizes that "he did not want to die" (229). Why does he have a change of heart, particularly when he had been preparing for the apocalypse with determination and even a sense of detachment?

13. What is your overall opinion of Isobel? Why do you suppose she turned down Louis's marriage proposal? One evening at her cottage, Isobel asks Louis to kiss her. After nearly half a century, why does Isobel finally acknowledge her feelings for Louis?

14. When Isobel knows that she is about to take her last breath, she asks Louis to leave the room and make her a cup of tea. Why does Isobel send him away? And why does Louis, knowing what she is doing, agree to her request?

15. Discuss the impact of Louis's invention of the daguerreotype on France and on the world. Why were some people quick to embrace this new medium while others denounced it? Is it possible for us to fully understand the impact that such an invention would have had at the time? Why or why not?

A CONVERSATION
WITH DOMINIC SMITH

Q: You mention in the Acknowledgments section of the book that a photography professor sparked your interest in Louis Daguerre. How did you go from that instance to using Daguerre as the central character in your novel?

A: During that professor's class we talked about early photographic processes, including the daguerreotype. It was speculated that Daguerre may have had some level of mercury poisoning due to his constant use of mercury vapor as the fixing agent for his images. I wondered whether Daguerre had suffered delusions on his road to fame. While I was spending lots of time in the darkroom and out in the Texas Hill Country taking pictures, I began research on Daguerre's life and methods. As it turns out, the University of Texas at Austin has an important archive of early photography and I spent hours at the Harry Ransom Center looking at images from the nineteenth century, including some made by Daguerre and other early Paris photographers. There was something immediately ghostly and intriguing about the pictures—the way portrait subjects looked somberly into the lens, the way the image of a daguerreotype appeared like a hologram if viewed from different angles. They were otherworldly. As I dug into Daguerre's story I found that there was really only one biography about him and it left me with a lot of unanswered questions. The novel began by trying to fill in the gaps in his creative and personal life and with the notion that he was going mad from mercury poisoning. Just as I had seen an ethereal world in nineteenth century daguerreotypes, perhaps Daguerre—his mind slipping—had seen something ominous in his own metal-plate portraits.

Q: How true did you stay to details of Daguerre's life, such as the fact that he received a Legion of Honor medal? Did you find the process of blending fact and fiction a difficult one?

A: The main thrust of Daguerre's creative life in the novel is taken from historical accounts of Daguerre's rise to fame. For example, he did apprentice as a scenic painter, invent the Diorama, and receive the Legion of Honor for his daguerreotype invention. The love story and the degree to which Louis Daguerre had mercury poisoning are the main fictional elements in the book. Blending fact and fiction is tricky; the writer faces a moral issue of how much to play around with a real person's life for the sake of a narrative. In the end, I hope that I posed new questions and insights about Daguerre's legacy.

Q: Is there historical evidence that Daguerre was romantically linked with a woman such as Isobel Le Fournier, or is she entirely a literary invention?

A: No. Isobel is pure fiction.

Q: The poet Charles Baudelaire, known as "the Prince of Clouds," appears in *The Mercury Visions of Louis Daguerre* as a character. Is there evidence that Baudelaire and Daguerre were acquainted?

A: Charles Baudelaire was certainly familiar with Daguerre and his work. The poet also wrote a lot of criticism, some of which expressed disdain for photography and other forms of realism. He was part of the rebellion against the new invention. Although I can't be sure that the men interacted to any degree, I thought it would be interesting to combine their worlds in the novel. The two men had spent a lot of time in the bohemian, artistic world of Paris but ended up on different sides of the Seine, so to speak—Daguerre a Legion of Honor and an internationally known artist and inventor, and Baudelaire a controversial and impoverished poet who was against anything that reeked of the establishment.

Q: Your descriptions of Paris are wonderfully vivid, from Daguerre's meanderings through the city streets to the catacombs beneath the Paris Observatory to the view from the top of Notre Dame. How important is Paris as a backdrop to the story?

A: Paris as a backdrop is essential. I started with Daguerre's madness and the Paris streets in the novel and wanted the two to mutually inform one another. We sometimes see the city through Daguerre's mercury-addled consciousness and sometimes we see it through a seemingly objective reality. Both ways of seeing Paris give it a sense of place and provide Daguerre's madness with a context. And without the political turmoil and bohemian culture of Montmarte, Daguerre's journey has less urgency.

Q: There are several mentions of Edgar Allan Poe throughout the novel, including his reaction to the daguerreotypes, which he called "miraculous beauties" and "photogenic drawings of absolute truth." In another instance Baudelaire is reading Poe's poem "The Raven." Are you an admirer of Edgar Allan Poe? Did his literary explorations in any way mirror the artistic territory that Daguerre was charting?

A: Edgar Allan Poe exerted significant influence on nineteenth century French writers in general and in particular on Charles Baudelaire. Baudelaire translated a number of Poe's short stories and poems from English to French, including "The Raven." Making reference to Poe's work in the novel is a nod to the writerly relationship between the two men.

Poe was also a figure of some renown for the general public; as the world received the news of the daguerreotype invention they looked to important cultural icons for interpretation. Walt Whitman, Edgar Allan Poe, and Samuel Morse were among the first to praise the form.

I certainly admire Poe's work, but I think his mission is much more like Baudelaire's than Daguerre's. Poe and Baudelaire seem to be interested in the enduring nature of both beauty and evil. The historical Daguerre, it seems to me, was mainly interested in a kind of ultra-realism. He wanted to capture nature in its essence. I don't think he had much interest in exploring the nature of evil through his work. In the novel, my Daguerre character is actually somewhat blind to squalor and ugliness in his delusions;

this was inspired by the way that the historical Daguerre had such an eye for beautiful detail and wanted to render nature in all its perfection.

Q: If you were to create your own Doomsday List, what would be some of the things you'd photograph?

A: I'd probably prefer to think of it as a list of images I'd love to look at . . . since a Doomsday List implies either me going mad or the end of the world approaching.

Anyway, I would capture: a coastal scene (I grew up from the age of ten by the beach in Australia); mountains and hills (I spent my early years in an area called the Blue Mountains outside of Sydney); a field of wildflowers (Texas has some spectacular wildflowers in the spring); and clouds (I've always had a fascination with them); pictures of my family and friends.

Q: Have you spent a lot of time in Paris? If so, what was your favorite experience?

A: I lived for a year in Europe and made numerous trips to Paris. My favorite memory was trying to have a quintessentially French gourmet meal in Montmartre. I consulted guide books and asked locals for recommendations. I heard about a restaurant that was tucked away in an alley and which was so small and informal that you had to knock on the kitchen door to be let in.

I searched for hours. I imagined delicate sauces being ladled out by an old couple from Provence. I pictured a cheese cellar and wine that made your heart jump. After scouring the streets in search of this culinary experience, I finally gave up and bought a chocolate-filled crepe and a cup of espresso at a roadside eatery. I took out a book—I was reading a lot of Hemingway at the time—and enjoyed a great Parisian moment. I never did find the mythical restaurant but that coffee and crepe have lingered on in my mind.

ENHANCE YOUR BOOK CLUB

Enliven your get-together—and your taste buds—by meeting at a local café or bistro. Or serve up your own French-inspired fare with recipes from www.epicurious.com. There are more than 800 delectable choices in the French Cuisine section. Bon appétit!

Learn more about Louis Daguerre, the daguerreian process, and how it was received in America by visiting www.daguerre.org, the official website of the Daguerreian Society.

In a nod to Louis Daguerre's famous invention, appoint one or two members as "official photographers" for the evening. Then have each member select one or two photographs and compile them into an album to commemorate your group's discussion of *The Mercury Visions of Louis Daguerre*.